DURHAM PUBLIC LIBRARY

11/18

P9-DNA-387

NIGHT AND SILENCE

DAW Books presents the finest in urban fantasy from Seanan McGuire:

The October Daye Novels:
ROSEMARY AND RUE

A LOCAL HABITATION

AN ARTIFICIAL NIGHT

LATE ECLIPSES

ONE SALT SEA

ASHES OF HONOR

CHIMES AT MIDNIGHT

THE WINTER LONG

A RED-ROSE CHAIN

ONCE BROKEN FAITH

THE BRIGHTEST FELL

NIGHT AND SILENCE

The InCryptid Novels:
DISCOUNT ARMAGEDDON

MIDNIGHT BLUE-LIGHT SPECIAL

HALF-OFF RAGNAROK

POCKET APOCALYPSE

CHAOS CHOREOGRAPHY

MAGIC FOR NOTHING

TRICKS FOR FREE

THAT AIN'T WITCHCRAFT*

The Ghost Roads:
SPARROW HILL ROAD

THE GIRL IN THE GREEN SILK GOWN

*Coming soon from DAW Books

SEANAN McGUIRE

NIGHT AND SILENCE

AN OCTOBER DAYE NOVEL

DAW BOOKS, INC.

DONALD A. WOLLHEIM, FOUNDER

375 Hudson Street, New York, NY 10014

ELIZABETH R. WOLLHEIM
SHEILA E. GILBERT
PUBLISHERS

www.dawbooks.com

Copyright © 2018 by Seanan McGuire.

All Rights Reserved.

Jacket art by Chris McGrath.

Jacket design by G-Force Design.

Interior dingbat created by Tara O'Shea.

Map by Priscilla Spencer.

DAW Book Collectors No. 1797.

Published by DAW Books, Inc.
375 Hudson Street, New York, NY 10014

All characters and events in this book are fictitious.
Any resemblance to persons living or dead is strictly coincidental.

The scanning, uploading, and distribution of this book via the Internet or via any other means without the permission of the publisher is illegal, and punishable by law. Please purchase only authorized electronic editions, and do not participate in or encourage the electronic piracy of copyrighted materials. Your support of the author's rights is appreciated.

Nearly all the designs and trade names in this book are registered trademarks. All that are still in commercial use are protected by United States and international trademark law.

First Printing, September 2018
1 2 3 4 5 6 7 8 9

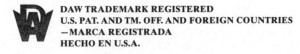

DAW TRADEMARK REGISTERED
U.S. PAT. AND TM. OFF. AND FOREIGN COUNTRIES
—MARCA REGISTRADA
HECHO EN U.S.A.

PRINTED IN THE U.S.A.

For Pamela Dean,
without whom I would never have found my way to this story.

ACKNOWLEDGMENTS:

Toby's adventures continue, and with them, my gratitude only grows, because there's no possible way I could have done this alone. Thank you to everyone who has followed me this far, trusting me to tell a story that's taking years to finish, but which I have loved every step of the way. Your love for it helps to keep me striving to be the best I possibly can. Toby is my imaginary friend, but you're the ones who truly allow me to bring her to life.

Writing a book is little bit like fishing: it's a solitary activity that works better when it's done with a support structure of some kind. Because of that, my thanks must be extended to all the people who've supported me through the writing of *Night and Silence*, including the Machete Squad, whose tireless efforts make my books better than I would ever have believed that they could be, the entire team at DAW Books, where they tolerate my strangeness with cheerful, if slightly befuddled grace, and the convention team from Penguin-Random House, who have allowed me to hide a startling amount of Diet Dr Pepper behind their booths. Also, huge thanks to all the people who have hosted me all over the world during the writing of this particular chapter of October's story.

Thank you to my Vixy, who is the star I set my sails by; to my dearest Amy, who is the only siren I would trust to lead me home; the entire Sailor Gods RPG group, whose antics have allowed me to remember what fun it is to tell people a story; the cast of Desperate and Poor, for similar reasons (including the world's pinkest bard); Brooke, for coming to visit when I needed her most; Shawn, for dinosaur noises; Jay and Tea, for Emma Frost reaction pics; and as always, to the Crowells, for everything. Thanks to Margaret and Mary, for their own sides of the story, to Whitney, for mathematical wonderlands, and to Priscilla, who is simply a delight.

I could never do this without Sheila Gilbert, whose tolerance and kindness define what an editor should be, and Joshua Starr, who answers the phone when I call (even if he doesn't want to). Diana Fox puts up with more than anyone will ever know, while Chris McGrath brings Toby gloriously to life book after book. I've added a new cat to the clowder since our last outing, and Elsie is basically a tortoiseshell hive of wasps that pretends to be a cat. She is perfect. Finally, thank you to my pit crew: Christopher Mangum, Tara O'Shea, and Kate Secor.

My soundtrack while writing *Night and Silence* consisted mostly of *Hadestown*, by Anais Mitchell (still), *Standing Stones*, by Marian Call, *The Hazards of Love*, by the Decemberists, endless live concert recordings of the Counting Crows, and all the Ludo a girl could hope to have (eternally waiting for a new album). Any errors in this book are entirely my own. The errors that aren't here are the ones that all these people helped me fix.

Let me show you what's waiting a little deeper in the woods. I think you're going to enjoy it.

OCTOBER DAYE PRONUNCIATION GUIDE
THROUGH *NIGHT AND SILENCE*

All pronunciations are given strictly phonetically. This only covers races explicitly named in the first twelve books, omitting Undersea races not appearing or mentioned in book twelve.

Aes Sidhe: *eys shee*. Plural is "Aes Sidhe."
Afanc: *ah-fank*. Plural is "Afanc."
Annwn: *ah-noon*. No plural exists.
Bannick: *ban-nick*. Plural is "Bannicks."
Barghest: *bar-guy-st*. Plural is "Barghests."
Blodynbryd: *blow-din-brid*. Plural is "Blodynbryds."
Cait Sidhe: *kay-th shee*. Plural is "Cait Sidhe."
Candela: *can-dee-la*. Plural is "Candela."
Coblynau: *cob-lee-now*. Plural is "Coblynau."
Cu Sidhe: *coo shee*. Plural is "Cu Sidhe."
Daoine Sidhe: *doon-ya shee*. Plural is "Daoine Sidhe," diminutive is "Daoine."
Djinn: *jin*. Plural is "Djinn."
Dóchas Sidhe: *doe-sh-as shee*. Plural is "Dóchas Sidhe."
Ellyllon: *el-lee-lawn*. Plural is "Ellyllons."
Folletti: *foe-let-tea*. Plural is "Folletti."
Gean-Cannah: *gee-ann can-na*. Plural is "Gean-Cannah."
Glastig: *glass-tig*. Plural is "Glastigs."
Gwragen: *guh-war-a-gen*. Plural is "Gwragen."
Hamadryad: *ha-ma-dry-add*. Plural is "Hamadryads."

Hippocampus: *hip-po-cam-pus*. Plural is "Hippocampi."
Kelpie: *kel-pee*. Plural is "Kelpies."
Kitsune: *kit-soo-nay*. Plural is "Kitsune."
Lamia: *lay-me-a*. Plural is "Lamia."
The Luidaeg: *the lou-sha-k*. No plural exists.
Manticore: *man-tee-core*. Plural is "Manticores."
Naiad: *nigh-add*. Plural is "Naiads."
Nixie: *nix-ee*. Plural is "Nixen."
Peri: *pear-ee*. Plural is "Peri."
Piskie: *piss-key*. Plural is "Piskies.'
Puca: *puh-ca*. Plural is "Pucas."
Roane: *row-n*. Plural is "Roane."
Satyr: *say-tur*. Plural is "Satyrs."
Selkie: *sell-key*. Plural is "Selkies."
Shyi Shuai: *shh-yee shh-why*. Plural is "Shyi Shuai."
Silene: *sigh-lean*. Plural is "Silene."
Tuatha de Dannan: *tootha day danan*. Plural is "Tuatha de Dannan," diminutive is "Tuatha."
Tylwyth Teg: *till-with teeg*. Plural is "Tylwyth Teg," diminutive is "Tylwyth."
Urisk: *you-risk*. Plural is "Urisk."

KINGDOMS OF THE WESTLANDS

Kingdom of Frozen Winds

Kingdom of Warm Skies

Kingdom of Evergreen

Kingdom of Leucothea

Kingdom of Silences

Kingdom of Starfall

Battle of Silences

Kingdom of the Mists

Kingdom of Painted Skies

Kingdom on the Golden Shore

Kingdom of Angels

Kingdom of Copper

Priscilla Spencer

ONE

December 22nd, 2013

Night and silence—who is here?
    —William Shakespeare, *A Midsummer Night's Dream.*

YOU CAN SAY WHAT you like about San Francisco, but one thing is eternally clear: it's a city that could only have been built by human hands.

The fae, faced with a landscape made almost entirely of hills and dells, with very little flat, arable land between natural obstacles, would have shrugged their shoulders, waved their hands, and either turned the entire thing into a range of beautiful crystalline spires, accessible only by twisting spiral stairways, or flattened it into a perfect pastoral meadow, ready to be planted with whatever their homesteader's hearts desired. In other words, extremes. The fae like to traffic in absolutes, not this mucky, glorious middle ground.

San Francisco is a city of hills and valleys, impossible slopes and ridiculous workarounds, with residential streets so narrow that trying to park becomes an eternal game of slow-motion chicken interspersed with wide tourist boulevards designed to present everything in the best possible light. It doesn't help that so much of San Francisco burned down in 1906, allowing city planners to design half of the metro area according to a reasonable, sensible grid system, while the remaining slices of old San Francisco . . . weren't. And still aren't, and never will be, since the odds of the city burning down again are, thankfully, pretty slim.

This does make San Francisco a challenging place to do my job, since the terrain is frequently working against me. My name is October Daye. I'm a knight errant in service to the Court of Shadowed Hills and, by extension, in service to the Kingdom in the Mists. Worse, I'm a named and recognized hero of the realm. All this is a fancy way of saying that when fae problems impinge on the mortal world, it's on me to take care of them before they accidentally reveal the existence of Faerie to the mortal world. We've been in hiding for a long time. "A flying hedgehog slammed into my front window" is not how we want to be discovered.

Hence my evening. Quentin, Danny, and I had been running around a residential neighborhood for more than two hours, moving as quietly as we could in an effort not to wake the neighbors. They weren't *our* neighbors, thankfully. If one of us did make too much noise and wake them up, we could make an excuse about a lost dog or something and run, secure in the knowledge that we'd never see them again.

Humans are good at sleeping through ordinary night noises. Blame it on centuries of diurnal living. They tend to write off things that go bump in the night as overenthusiastic raccoons rummaging in their trash. The noises we were apt to make weren't quite as ordinary, and humans are substantially less inclined to ignore pointy-eared strangers running around outside their kitchen windows. Especially when those strangers are waving butterfly nets over their heads like a bunch of weirdoes.

To be fair, we *are* a bunch of weirdoes. It's just that we were a bunch of weirdoes on a mission, and I didn't want that mission to involve yet another run-in with the local police. I think they're getting tired of my face. I know I've long since gotten tired of theirs. And, really, waking the neighbors was less of a concern than what would happen if we were still outside when the sun came up and burned away all our illusions. That would be when we declared ourselves officially screwed.

As if we weren't screwed already. Because so much of San Francisco is built on impractically steep hills, many residential streets are connected by narrow alleys which serve as conduits for the stairways lain along the line of the hills. Some of the stairs are stone, some of the stairs are wood; all of the stairs are maintained by the local residents, and that means most of the stairs are death traps. No two steps are the same height, making them a constant tripping hazard, and half the wood stairways have at least one stair that's been rotted through for a decade without anyone getting around to fixing it.

In case that wasn't bad enough, a damp wind had blown in from the Bay, and *all* the stairs were slippery. The night had been an adventure, and I was not in an adventurous mood.

Danny—our designated driver for the evening, and one of my staunchest, most indestructible allies—propped his butterfly net against his shoulder and frowned. "I'm just sayin', maybe you'd feel better if you actually learned to open up about your feelings," he said, voice deep and gravelly enough to have come from a concrete mixer instead of from a man.

The impression wasn't far off. Despite the illusion which made him look like a reasonably nonthreatening human man, Danny is and has always been very far from human. Like most Bridge Trolls, he stands easily seven feet tall, with skin the color and consistency of granite. He's as difficult to injure as your average mountain, which is one of the many things that makes him such desirable backup when I'm called upon to do knight errantry in the local cities.

I heal fast, but it's easier on my wardrobe if I have something—or someone—I can duck behind to keep myself from being hurt in the first place. That's a very healthy attitude on my part, especially considering how often my friends and allies accuse me of having a self-destructive streak.

Unfortunately, those same friends and allies seemed to be too busy focusing on my latest set of problems to see how proactive and mature I was being. I glowered at him.

"I don't want to talk about this right now."

"You didn't want to talk about it in the car, either."

"Quentin was in the car."

Danny scowled down his nose at me. "He's not a kid anymore. You know that better than anybody."

"Tell me about it," I grumbled. My squire, Quentin Sollys, had been a dandelion-haired bundle of limbs, manners, and annoying points of etiquette when he'd initially forced his way into my life—and I do mean *forced*. I hadn't been looking for a squire. I hadn't been looking for someone to take care of. I certainly hadn't been looking for a teenage boy to eat all my groceries and complain when I was out of ice cream. I'd somehow managed to acquire all three of those things in one body, and it had turned out to be surprisingly wonderful and exactly what I'd needed.

Until I'd learned he was the Crown Prince of the Westlands, aka, "all of North America." That had been less wonderful, since suddenly it wasn't just my squire I was shoving merrily into danger as a learning experience, it was the future of my entire continent. Not that the knowledge had stopped me for long. What's a squire for, if not testing for traps?

And he'd continued growing up the whole time, going from a kid whose biggest romance had been the hand-holding and kissing kind with a human girl from a local high school to full-on dating one of the local Counts. Trying to have the sex talk with my squire was not an experience I wanted to repeat. That meant never taking another squire, and honestly, I was fine with that if it meant sparing myself the squirming indignity.

"So how about you actually *talk* for a change, and not go looking for excuses?"

I pinched the bridge of my nose. "You really think this is the time?"

"I ain't seeing a better one." Danny shrugged like a landslide. "I also ain't seeing any magical flying piggies, so I guess we can take a few minutes to talk about the elephant in the room."

"There are too many nonexistent animals in that sentence, Danny." I dropped my hand. "We're not looking for pigs, we're looking for hedgehogs. Totally different."

Specifically, we were hunting for arkan sonney, a fae creature originally found in Avalon. They aren't supposed to exist in the mortal world. They certainly aren't supposed to infest upscale San Francisco neighborhoods. Unfortunately, a changeling named Chelsea Ames lost control of her powers about two years ago, and "supposed to" no longer reliably applies. Chelsea's father, Etienne, is Tuatha de Dannan, and she inherited his teleporting magic without inheriting his control, or the natural limitations that would have kept her from opening doors Oberon wanted closed.

Chelsea's lack of limitations might have been okay, had she not come to the attention of a local Duchess with an interest in expansion. Duchess Riordan had decided to use Chelsea to rip open doors to deeper Faerie, which Oberon had sealed for a thrice-damned *reason*.

It wasn't pretty, but in the end, Chelsea survived, Riordan got her just desserts, and we wound up with a minor monster problem. Because, see, open portals go both ways, and Chelsea hadn't exactly been watching to make sure none of the local wildlife followed her through. Being fae creatures, some of our unwanted guests had proven incredibly adept at concealing themselves, and we only found out they were in the mortal world when they popped out and scared the locals.

Danny snorted. "Pigs, hedgehogs, whatever. They have wings, they shouldn't be here, and they're *not* here, which means we have time to talk."

"Danny, this isn't—"

"If he blames you, he needs to stop. And if he won't stop, then maybe you need to think about whether he's good for you. Or whether you're good for him."

I froze. For a terrible moment, I wasn't looking at Danny, my friend and ally. I was looking at Tybalt, my former enemy, current lover, and best friend, as he stepped into the shadows at the corner of my bedroom and disappeared, leaving me alone. The one thing he'd promised I was never going to be again. The scent of pennyroyal and musk hung in the air, taunting me with my inability to follow him.

I blinked. The moment passed. Danny reappeared, looking concerned, and I hated him, oh, how I hated him. Not for long. More than long enough.

"No," I said.

"I'm sorry, but yeah," said Danny.

Being a hero of the realm means I'm constantly putting myself in the path of danger, like I want nothing more than to have my bones broken and the skin stripped from my body. Being a person means I'm never doing it alone. I have friends. I have allies. Not just Quentin and Danny, but others, like my Fetch-turned-sister, May, and her girlfriend, Jazz.

Like Tybalt, the King of Dreaming Cats. The man who'd hated me, helped me, fallen in love with me, and saved my life more times than I cared to count. The man who was supposed to marry me.

The man who could barely even look at me anymore.

Who hadn't been able to look at me since my mother, Amandine the Liar, had decided to lock him in a cage and trap him in feline form until she was done with him. Tybalt didn't blame me for my mother's actions—I blamed me more than he did—but when he looked at me, he saw her, and it was breaking us both.

"I don't want to talk about this," I said softly.

"I know. But maybe you should."

"I don't think that's for you to decide."

Danny sighed. "Toby, this isn't healthy. You need—"

Whatever he thought I needed was cut off by the sound of Quentin's sudden, high-pitched yelp. I whipped around, scanning the shadows until I spotted the outline of my squire, half a block away and struggling to keep hold of his butterfly net. He'd managed to snare something the size of a small raccoon, and whatever it was, it looked like it was winning.

"Later," I snapped, casting a quick look back to Danny before I raised my own net and ran toward Quentin, ready to join the fray.

The trouble with hunting creatures no one has seen in hundreds of years is that when figuring out how to capture or subdue them, we have to rely on the accounts of people who have long since forgotten what the beasts were actually *like* and have, instead, started remembering them through pleasantly rose-tinted nostalgia. According to the records in the Library of Stars, arkan sonney are sweet, playful creatures, like hedgehogs with wings longer than their bodies, capable of bestowing great fortune on people and places that please them. Supposedly, they're also about as intelligent as the average sheep, and regularly had to be fished out of wells or freed from hunters' traps back when they coexisted with the rest of Faerie.

The thing Quentin had snared in his net bore about as much resemblance to something sweet and innocent and bumbling as I did to a eucalyptus tree. For one thing, it was far too large, and the records hadn't mentioned anything about arkan sonney being chalk white with blazing red eyes and enormous tusks. It looked less like an ordinary hedgehog than it did the result of some unholy hybridization of a porcupine and a wild pig, with the wings of a falcon stapled on for good measure.

It thrashed. It squealed. It gnashed its terrible teeth at Quentin, who quailed but stood fast, refusing to let go of the net and allow the creature to escape. Brave boy. That was on him, although if I'd asked, he would have said it was all because of what he'd learned from me. Quentin had always been brave. He'd just needed someone to let him show it.

The sound of my approach caught his attention. He shot me a grateful glance, still struggling to keep hold of the net. Our location meant we couldn't shout the way we normally would have, and Tybalt's absence meant we didn't have a major part of our backup. We'd grown shamefully accustomed to having someone who could step through the shadows in the field with us.

I am nothing if not a skilled improvisor. I glanced frantically around. A trash can rested on a nearby curb, set out for the garbage collectors. Saying a silent apology to the sleeping homeowners, I grabbed it, dumped its contents out, and hoisted it over my head as I ran toward Quentin. Realizing my intent, he let go of the net right before I slammed the trash can down over the shrieking pig-thing.

Silence reigned. I looked up, meeting Quentin's wide, startled eyes.

"That's one," I said.

His shoulders sagged. "Her Majesty said there were at least three."

"Her name is Arden," I said. "She's not here. You don't have to use her title."

Quentin actually smirked at that, although the expression wasn't enough to drive the weariness and worry from his eyes. "Can I be there when you tell her that?" he asked. "Better yet, can I be there when you tell my *father* that?"

I grimaced. Arden is the daughter of the last legitimate King in the Mists, Gilad Windermere, and as such, has been a princess all her life. The throne was always going to be waiting for her, no matter what else she chose to do . . . or what else was done to her. Thanks to the machinations of Evening Winterrose—once my supposed friend and ally, always secretly my enemy, Firstborn daughter of Oberon and Titania, and stone-cold bitch—Arden had been in hiding for most of her life and had only recently been able to claim her father's throne. We were all still getting used to the idea that we had a queen who wasn't regularly going to try to have me arrested or banished from the Mists.

There are nights when I feel like my life should come with some sort of flowchart, and then there are the nights when I feel like even that would be too confusing to understand.

The arkan sonney in the trash can made a sad whining noise, somewhere between a pig's squeal and a songbird's hum. "I'm not calling your father anything that implies overt familiarity," I said. "The last thing I need right now is for him to make another stab at taking you away from me."

Quentin cast a quick, uneasy look at Danny, who was scanning the nearby bushes for signs of another arkan sonney. My squire's status as Crown Prince is supposed to be a secret, and while more people know about it than is probably ideal—his fosterage was meant to be completely blind, keeping the rest of us from knowing his family—we're still not advertising it. Fortunately, Danny didn't seem to have noticed. That, or Danny was politely pretending he had no idea he was standing only feet away from a fairy tale cliché. Either one was fine by me.

"Hey, Quentin, tell your knight she needs to talk to her boyfriend," said Danny.

I groaned. Audibly groaned, drowning out the sorrowful whine of the arkan sonney. "I said I didn't want to talk about this."

"See, if there's one thing I've learned *for sure* since you called my cab and pulled me into your weird world of monsters an' shit, it's that you never want to talk about anything that seems like it might be hard." Danny sounded perfectly matter-of-fact, like this was something I should already have realized for myself.

"You're a *Troll*, Danny," I said flatly. "You've always lived in a weird world of monsters and shit."

"Yeah, but before you, they were always paying customers."

Danny drives a taxi. I'm pretty sure he has a medallion, since he spends about half his time ferrying mortal customers around the city, and San Francisco has strong opinions about independent contractors taking money away from people who've actually paid for the privilege of letting strangers into their cars. At some point a very long time ago I did a favor for his sister. As a consequence, he's sworn to help me with whatever I need, forever. I try not to take advantage. It's bad form to abuse the kindness of your friends. But wow, are there times I wish I paid to ride in his taxi, just so he couldn't say that kind of thing.

Lacking the moral high ground, I scowled at him.

Then Quentin spoke. "I think Danny's right," he said, voice small and worried. "Not about this being a good time to talk about this sort of thing—I think that part is sort of stupid and maybe we shouldn't be doing this—but talking at all needs to happen, and it's not. Happening, I mean." He paused before he added reluctantly, "Raj is really worried, and so am I."

Raj is Tybalt's nephew, and one of Quentin's best friends. Raj is also the Prince of Dreaming Cats. With Tybalt not fully capable of performing his duties, Raj was being called upon to spend more and more time in the Court, covering for the fact that his uncle wasn't taking care of everything he was supposed to handle.

It was a mess. It was a big, convoluted, complicated mess, and I didn't know how to deal with it, and I wanted it all to go away. I wanted everything to be back the way it was supposed to be. I wanted to get out of bed one afternoon and find Tybalt in the kitchen, eating toast and arguing with May about the right way to poach an egg. I wanted my *life* back.

I had no idea how to make that happen.

Because, see, once upon a time there was a girl named October, and her mother was a princess out of a fairy tale. Only that turned out to be a little more literal than I could ever have dreamed: my mother, Amandine, is the youngest daughter of Oberon, which makes her Firstborn among the fae, terrible and powerful in ways the rest of us can never fully understand. She raised me to believe I was Daoine Sidhe, like Quentin, when the truth is, I'm Dóchas Sidhe, the second one ever born, and no one, not even her, can say exactly what my magic is capable of. That's the first big problem.

The second big problem came when she forced her way into my house and took Tybalt and Jazz—May's live-in girlfriend—as hostages against my good behavior. She had wanted me to find her first daughter, my older sister, August. She had informed me, in no uncertain terms, that unless I could bring August home, I'd never see my loved ones again.

"Home." That's a funny word, especially given the way Amandine had invaded mine and what she was trying to do. The children of Faerie take many forms. There are the ones like me or May, who can almost pass for human in the right light; for us, fitting into the mortal world is a comparatively simple thing, especially when compared to what someone like Danny has to go through. No matter how many illusions he spins to change the color of his skin and the composition of his features, he'll always weigh more than the average car, and no matter how short he makes himself appear to human eyes, low ceilings will always be his bane.

Then there are the people like Tybalt, and Raj, and Jazz. Shape-shifters, skin-changers, equally at home in fur, or feathers, and skin. When Tybalt is in his humanoid form, he looks a lot like a Daoine Sidhe, if you're willing to overlook his vertical cat-slit pupils and the black stripes in his brown hair. When Jazz sheds her cloak of feathers, she looks like any beautiful human woman, assuming you overlook her bird-bright eyes. Neither shape is their "natural" one: they're meant to switch back and forth at will, transforming to suit their whims.

That's how it used to be. That's how it was *supposed* to be. But Mom forced them both into their animal forms and locked them there, denying them the freedom to choose. Shapeshifters locked too long in one shape can start to lose themselves, forgetting who and what they're really meant to be. I'd located August as quickly as I could, fear and anger driving me to do in a matter of days what Mom and all her power had failed to do for more than a century . . . and it hadn't been enough. By the time I regained what she had taken, both Tybalt and Jazz had gotten stuck in their animal forms.

Freeing Jazz had been difficult but doable. Freeing Tybalt had been . . . harder. His magic was stronger than hers, and when faced with what it viewed as another attack, it had resisted.

I'd been able to do it—it turns out one of the strengths of the Dóchas Sidhe is a certain understanding of how magic can be unraveled—but it had come with consequences. Tybalt is one of the strongest, canniest men I've ever known. I would trust him with my life. I *have* trusted him with my life, over and over again, until falling in love with him had seemed like the most sensible thing in the world, until agreeing to marry him had been the only right and reasonable thing to do. And since I'd recovered him from my mother, he had been sinking deeper and deeper into his own fear, unable to break himself free, unwilling to let me help. That stung. It would have stung more if he'd been willing to reach out to anyone else, but he hadn't been willing thus far to even admit there was a problem.

Tybalt was drowning, and every time one of us tried to throw him a rope, he batted it away like we intended to strangle him with it. So far as I was aware, he hadn't changed forms once since I'd brought him home. He was a shapeshifter living in a single skin, and it was slowly but surely destroying him.

Quentin and Danny were right to be worried. I was worried,

too. I was terrified. But I couldn't see a way to fix it. Not when Tybalt left every time I tried to start the conversation, until we had reached the point where he wasn't coming to see me at all. How do you tell your fiancé "I think you're killing yourself" when they're not willing to slow down long enough to listen?

Given how often he'd accused me of having a death wish, it was hard not to see the irony there.

The arkan sonney whined again, louder. An answering whine echoed from a nearby bush. I straightened, pointing with one hand while gesturing to Danny with the other. He nodded, creeping toward the sound with all the stealth of a man big enough to punch through walls. I leaned forward and shook the trash can, making our captive's cries even louder.

The second arkan sonney burst into the open, wings spread in fury, ready to fight for the safety of its companion. Danny dropped his net, leaned down, and grabbed it with both hands, pinning its wings to its sides in the process. The arkan sonney squealed, kicking at him with its hooves and slapping him with its tail. Quills broke against his stony skin, unable to puncture it. Danny grinned.

"Aw, they're adorable," he said. "Think I can keep 'em?"

"The Barghests may not like that, but as far as I'm concerned, sure," I said, scanning the bushes. There was a third one around here somewhere. My head felt strangely light, as if a weight had been lifted when we'd been forced to let the subject of Tybalt drop.

I shouldn't feel that way about the man I'm going to marry. I knew that, and it hurt just knowing that it was even possible for me to be grateful for the subject change. If he would only let me *help* . . .

"Danny, shake the pig," I said.

"Thought you said they weren't pigs."

"Danny, shake the thing that isn't a damn pig. I want to get out of here."

Danny heaved a long-suffering sigh and shook the arkan sonney. It squealed fury and indignation, and the third member of their little herd—pack? What the hell was I supposed to call a group of winged hedgehog-pig-monsters from the depths of Faerie?—charged into the open. This one was bigger than the others, with quills as red as its eyes. Crimson streaks blazed across the brown feathers of its wings. It didn't take a genius to guess that this was the male, and that we had captured both of its mates.

It looked around, eyes blazing, and squealed a furious challenge before charging straight at Quentin. He stood his ground. Once the arkan sonney was close enough to pose a serious danger, I shouted, "*Now!*"

Quentin lifted the edge of the trash can, revealing the cowering arkan sonney inside. The male rushed in, still squealing. Quentin dropped the trash can back over both of them. I threw myself against the other side, holding it down.

"Danny, a little help here?" I demanded.

Danny rolled his eyes. "See, when *I* want to have a serious conversation about feelings, you say it's not the time, but when *you* want me to wrestle pig-monsters—"

"*Please?*"

With a huff, Danny carried his captive arkan sonney over to me. I let go of the trash can and grabbed the discarded lid. He gave me a nod. As if we had practiced it, Quentin lifted the can again, Danny flung the third arkan sonney at the other two, and I swept the lid into place, sealing the three intruders safely inside.

They whined and squealed, kicking at the metal. Their hooves left dents. All right, maybe not *safely* inside, but at least we had them all—

"Um, Toby?"

I turned toward the sound of Quentin's voice, and groaned at the sight of six puffball monster piglets creeping out from under a hedge, their flightless wings drooping and their snouts to the ground.

Danny laughed. "Oh, man, that's great!"

"We're going to need a bigger carrier," I said dolefully. The people who lived in this house were never going to know where their trash can had gone. Maybe that was for the best. There are some things that should never be explained.

Fairy pigs in hand, we faded back into the San Francisco night, and left the uncomfortable conversations, however temporarily, behind.

TWO

DANNY DROVE ALONG the winding road leading into Muir Woods like it had somehow personally offended him, his foot smashed down on the gas and his face set in a thin-lipped scowl. I sighed.

"You can't be mad at me forever," I said.

"I'm pretty sure I can," he replied. "Let's find out."

Quentin cleared his throat. He was sitting in the backseat with a cat carrier full of baby flying hedgehog-things in his lap. The trash can containing the adult arkan sonney took up the rest of the seat, occasionally rattling ominously as they slammed against the metal. Quentin was sitting as far away from them as he could—which was surprisingly far, thanks to Danny's extensive investment in expansion charms. Those don't come cheap, but without them, he would never have been able to fit behind the wheel.

Done properly, magic is difficult for humans to notice or focus on, and Danny's mechanic knew her stuff. His human passengers probably came away from trips with him thinking they'd never been in a cab that spacious but wouldn't necessarily realize that the car was bigger on the inside than it was on the outside. Danny's *fae* passengers included Centaurs, Merrow, and even his fellow Trolls, and all of them could get their seatbelts on.

"I'm still here," said Quentin. "In case you forgot."

"I never forget you," I said.

"You forget to answer my questions all the time."

I groaned, letting my head slam back against the seat. It was padded, making the gesture less effective than it could have been. "Seriously, is this 'gang up on Toby' night? Can you let me know when you schedule these, so I can arrange to be somewhere else? Like, I don't know, another Kingdom?"

"Most other Kingdoms won't let you in," said Danny, almost reasonably. "You keep deposin' their monarchs."

"I've never deposed anyone who didn't deserve it," I said. "And I've only done it twice."

"Uh-huh. Y'know, ordinary people don't commit treason *once*, much less twice."

"Oh, root and branch." I groaned again, with more feeling this time. "Can we not?"

He wasn't wrong—I knew that. It was still frustrating. Sure, I'd been instrumental in bringing about two regime changes, but neither of them had been intentional, and neither of them had been undeserved.

When King Windermere died in the 1906 San Francisco earthquake, he left behind no legitimate heirs. Arden and her brother, Nolan, had been born and raised in secrecy, never publicly claimed by the king. It made sense: his own parents had died under mysterious circumstances, and he'd been trying to give his children a better life by giving them half a chance at survival. Good for them, not so good for the rest of us. In the absence of a clear line of succession, Evening Winterrose had been able to endorse a stranger, putting her own puppet on the throne. The nameless Queen of the Mists, mixed-blood and mad, had strangled the Kingdom like kelp for decades, becoming less yielding and more cruel with every passing year.

She might still be on her stolen throne if she had *listened* when I came to her and told her goblin fruit was becoming a serious problem. The stuff gives purebloods sweet dreams, lets them forget the troubles of the mortal world for a little while—no big deal. But for anyone with a drop of human blood in their veins, it's instantly addictive and invariably fatal. Changelings were dying. My people were dying. So I had gone to the Queen and asked her to save them. All I'd wanted was for her to do her duty and, silly me, I'd thought she might. She'd always hated me for reasons I've never quite been able to understand, but I hadn't believed she would allow her hatred to blind her to the necessity of taking care of her people.

I hadn't believed a lot of things. Or maybe I'd believed the wrong ones. I'd believed she had a right to her throne; I'd believed the High King would never have confirmed her if she wasn't really Gilad's daughter. But she didn't, and she wasn't, and when she'd ordered me banished for daring to speak up about the goblin fruit, the only solution I'd been able to find had involved putting Arden—the rightful Queen in the Mists—on the throne. Elevating her had resulted in new restrictions on goblin fruit, a fairer, more considerate regime, and me being named a hero of the realm, which proves that no good deed goes unpunished.

My second act of monarchal treason involved King Rhys of Silences, who had been granted his throne by—surprise, surprise—the false Queen of the Mists, after her army had overthrown the rightful ruling family in a short, brutal war. But again, it hadn't been his Kingdom to begin with, and by returning the crown to Queen Siwan, I'd helped to right a great injustice and stabilize the region.

This did not change the fact that Danny was right, and most of our local monarchs *really* don't want me coming for a visit. Ever. Developing a reputation as a king-breaker has definitely been keeping me out of the best parties. Given how much I dislike parties, it's difficult to see this as a bad thing.

"The High King invited Toby to get married in Toronto," said Quentin.

Danny snorted. "The High King is smart enough to want to keep her where he can see her. Arden doesn't kick her out of the Kingdom because the only kings she doesn't overthrow are the ones she likes. If I had a Kingdom, I'd be signin' her up for every cookie of the month club I could find."

"There are some ice cream of the month clubs, too," I said mildly. "Mix it up on the dessert front. Really bribe me if you're going to bribe me."

Quentin laughed. The sound woke one of the piglets, which whined, kicking off another chorus of squeals and thumps from the trash can. His laugh faded, becoming a scowl. "How long are we going to be cleaning this up?" he asked. "Every time I think we've found all the monsters, something else pops out of the bushes and starts threatening to bite the humans."

"I don't know," I said. "We could ask the Luidaeg, but . . . "

"But she'd have to charge us for the answer," sighed Quentin. "Right."

"I need to finish paying down my debts before I go incurring anything further."

The Luidaeg is the eldest daughter of Oberon and Maeve, which makes her my aunt, a fact that I find bizarre, sort of disturbing, and kind of comforting, in a weird way. She's also the sea witch and bound to truthfully answer any question she's asked. The geas forcing her to do so wasn't very well constructed. She's allowed to charge whatever she wants for her services, so she sets the prices as high as she can, hoping to dissuade the unwise and unwary from winding up in over their heads.

Me, I've been in over my head since the first time we met. She's been in my debt a time or two, but at the end of the day I owe her enough that I may never finish repaying it all—and that's a good thing, because the Luidaeg never lies. She can't. And she's said, more than once, that she'll kill me someday. Hopefully, as long as I'm the one in debt to her, she won't feel motivated to get it done.

"I sort of like the monster huntin'," said Danny, easing his cab around the last curve between us and the parking lot. A chain hung across the entrance, supposedly barring us from going any further. He kept driving. The car passed through the chain like it was made of mist. One more convenient charm, courtesy of our increasingly stable local government.

As a state park, Muir Woods is supposed to be closed after sundown. As the royal seat of the Kingdom in the Mists, that's never going to happen. But we're pretty careful not to be seen, since no one wants to start trouble. Danny parked in front of the bathrooms, next to the large sign informing us the park would open for business at eight o'clock tomorrow morning.

"We got about two hours before the rangers start showing up," he said, shoving the door open with his foot. "Get it done."

"Can you get the trash can?" I asked, getting out with a little more decorum. It would have been hard to get out with less. "Quentin has the piglets."

"Why do *I* have the piglets?" Quentin shifted the carrier gingerly in his arms as he slid out of the car. "They're squirming around all over the place."

"Because you're the squire and I'm the knight, which means it's my duty to make you do unpleasant things in the name of your ongoing education." I waved a hand airily. "Tonight, you're learning that you don't like flying pigs."

Quentin glared without any heat. He knew the real reason I was making him carry the piglets: I'm still part human. Fae are nocturnal, with the eyesight to match. I can see in the dark almost as well as I can see in the daylight, but "almost" doesn't always cut it when walking through a place as tangled and treacherous as Muir Woods. My reflexes aren't up to the pureblood standard, either. Since I didn't want to slip on wet wood and wind up tumbling into one of the multiple streams, creeks, or rivers crisscrossing the valley, it was better to let him deal with the livestock while I focused on staying upright.

Danny slung the trash can over his shoulder, protesting pigs and all, and cast a quick don't-look-here spell over his car to hide it from any rangers or police who happened to come by on patrol. Then we turned, the three of us moving together, and made our way into the wood.

Even if it weren't the royal seat of the Kingdom in the Mists, Muir Woods would still be the kind of place that makes even the most stubborn humans think magic could be real, if only for a moment. The redwoods reach for the sky like beanstalks out of a fairy tale, their branches straining upward until they pierce the clouds. Thick underbrush covers the ground, ferns and bushes and native flowers providing a home for so many creatures, both fae and mortal. At night, everything is shrouded in fog, thick and soft and silencing.

The wood is even more incredible through fae eyes. Sparks fill the fog, dancing lights that tempt and tease. Bogeys and bat-winged frogs peer out of the underbrush, attracted by the steadily increasing ambient magic and sheltered by Arden's protecting charms. She's something the Mists haven't had in a hundred years: a true Queen. Looking at the changes wrought during her short reign, it's impossible not to wonder what the Mists will be like in another decade.

I think they're going to be amazing.

Not that they're not already amazing enough. Brilliantly colored lights darted through the trees as the local pixie flock came to investigate us. The chiming of their wings took on a delighted, welcoming note when they recognized me. They swirled around me in a multicolored cloud, ringing louder than ever. I smiled.

"Hello to you, too," I said.

Several pixies settled in my hair like overdramatic ornaments, casting a soft glow that made it easier for me to see the winding trail that led to the door to Arden's knowe. The rest flew off, presumably to tell the other members of their flock that we were in the wood. I waved after them and walked on with more certainty.

Faerie has remained hidden despite its proximity to the human world through a variety of tricks, some more sophisticated than others. Things like the pixies and the arkan sonney, for example, hide themselves automatically, using a form of instinctual illusion magic that keeps humans from noticing them unless they force the issue. In the case of the pixies, they're intelligent enough not to cause trouble with people who know how to hold a flyswatter. In the case of the arkan sonney and other so-called "monsters," there's more risk of someone getting gored. Humans tend to notice being stabbed, even when the knives are invisible. That's why people like me wind up involved. Sometimes we have to police ourselves to prevent a crisis.

A human looking into the wood might see three silhouettes moving slowly toward the hillside trail. But they wouldn't see the lights, and they wouldn't notice the way the fog moved against the wind, keeping us out of sight, keeping us safe.

We wear human disguises and we cast keep-away spells and we hide, and we hide, and we hide. I'd say we can't hide forever, but we've been hiding for centuries, and it's worked out pretty well so far. Who am I to say that things need to change?

The scent of running water and redwood bark filled the air. From behind me, I smelled the frayed edges of Quentin and Danny's illusions as they released them, briefly overwhelming the natural scent of the wood with their unique magical signatures. Magic is a function of the blood, and everyone's magic is different, saying something about the caster and their specific heritage. Dóchas Sidhe are walking encyclopedias of magical scents. I can identify a magical trace even if I've only encountered it once before, and I can narrow it down from "roses" to "this specific kind of rose, over here, grown in this specific sort of soil." It's a mostly useless talent that has occasionally proven to be incredibly useful.

I released my own illusions, surrounding myself with the smell of freshly cut grass and coppery blood. It used to be more copper than blood. I used to be more human than I am now. Finding equilibrium has never been exactly easy for me.

Several more pixies returned, a rainbow escort lighting our way.

The pixies in my hair chimed softly as we topped the last rise, and the ancient redwood housing the door to Arden's knowe appeared. Knowes—better known as hollow hills—are points of connection between the human world and the Summerlands, the shallowest and last accessible realm of Faerie. They have doors in both worlds, although they're usually constructed entirely in the Summerlands, where real estate is at less of a premium. Seen from the fae side, Arden's knowe was a dizzying concoction of towers and spires, connected by stairways and paths that wound through the air with distressingly little consideration for gravity. Seen from where we were standing, it was just an inexplicable double door set into a tree that had no business being abused that way. Guards stood to either side, dressed in the livery of the Mists, with Arden's arms stitched above their hearts.

One of the guards grinned at the sight of us, a female Glastig whose armor had been cut to account for the fact that she had goat's legs from the thigh down, like someone had gotten bored in the process of sketching a Satyr. She had no tail, but she made up for it with a pair of goat's ears that stuck almost straight out from the sides of her head, covered in silky, strawberry-blonde fur that matched the fur on her legs.

"Toby! And Danny and Quentin as well," she said. "May I assume from the fact that you're toting someone's trash bin that your mission was a success?"

"Hi, Lowri, and yes, you can assume," I said. "Since we're assuming things, may I please assume there's some sort of cage ready for us to put these things in? We have some pretty pissed-off piggies."

"They're not pigs," said Lowri.

I could almost hear Quentin's eyeroll. "They have tusks and hooves and they know how to use them," he said. "That's piggy enough for me."

"Oberon would be ashamed of you, having so little concern for the proper names of things," Lowri chided. Then she winked to make it clear that she was kidding. "Her Highness directed some of the household staff to prepare the stables in hopes of a successful return. When last I spoke with her, she said the task was finished and the stables were secure. I'll take you there."

"We have stables?" I asked.

"Wonders never cease, do they?" Lowri nodded to the other

guard. He nodded back but stayed in position as Lowri led us into the knowe. Our pixie escort accompanied us, ringing gleefully.

The world spun lazily around me as we transitioned from the mortal world to the Summerlands. The ease of the transition was another sign of how much less human I am now than I used to be. There's a certain pushback against mortals crossing that kind of border. When I was more human, entering a knowe could knock me to my knees and leave me vomiting on the floor. These days, it's something I can overlook if I'm distracted enough, or in enough of a hurry.

"So how did it go?" asked Lowri. Her hooves clattered on the floor of the entry hall, echoing softly up into the chambered ceiling.

"Not too bad," I replied, trying to steal glances at the redwood carvings lining the walls. They change sometimes, adding major events and personages from the Kingdom. It can be embarrassing to see myself represented there, but it isn't embarrassing enough to keep me from scanning for recent developments.

Nothing seemed to have changed since our last visit. That was a good thing. It meant the Kingdom was relatively peaceful for a change. I could use a little peace. Especially while I was trying to help Tybalt with his current problems, I could use a *lot* of peace.

Assuming he was ever going to start letting me help him. Assuming he ever spoke to me again. I finally understood how my friends felt when I refused to reach out, and I didn't like it.

"You seem to have stolen someone's trash can."

"We can put it back," protested Danny. One of the arkan sonney hit the side of the can hard enough to make another dent. He amended, "Or not."

"Or not," agreed Lowri. She led us through an unmarked door, bypassing the throne room in favor of a long, mostly empty hallway. Smaller carvings lined these walls, showing scenes that were less heroic but equally necessary to the functionality of the Kingdom in general and the knowe in specific. Many of the people they portrayed were friends of mine, from Arden's seneschal, Madden, to her recently-hired chatelaine, Cassandra Brown.

Cassandra is the eldest daughter of my childhood friend, Stacy, and my adopted niece. I'll admit, I never expected her to wind up employed by a royal knowe, but she seemed to be doing well for herself, and Arden adored her. There are worse places to stand in our world than at the left hand of the Queen. I should know, having stood in many of them.

The hall wound around the edge of the knowe in a gentle spiral before ending at a narrow stairway. Lowri started down. We followed. Geography doesn't translate exactly between the Summerlands and the mortal world, but the longer the two areas are tied together, the more closely the bones are likely to conform: we were clearly following the slope of the hill into the valley. For all that Arden's palace doesn't exist in the human version of Muir Woods, and for all that the Faerie side of things has a lot more of the truly giant trees still standing, the basics are there on both sides.

Speaking of which . . .

"Where's Arden?" I asked.

Lowri's ear twitched in a mix of annoyance and amusement. "Her Majesty is occupied with the business of the realm. You didn't precisely call ahead to let us know you were coming."

"She's the one who sent us monster hunting," I protested.

"Regardless, she can't sit around waiting to hear whether you've succeeded."

"And she has queen shit to do, right."

Quentin audibly groaned. "As Sir Daye's squire, I must apologize, *again*, for her having the manners of a kelpie."

"Don't be silly, Quentin," said Danny. "Kelpies are politer."

"Kelpies are aquatic murder horses that want to rip you apart and eat everything but your liver," I protested.

Danny smirked. "As I was sayin'."

The stairs widened as we approached the bottom, until we emerged into an open-walled sunroom with a latticed ceiling dripping with fruit-heavy grapevines. The grapes were pale pink and glowed from within. The pixies in my hair gave a pealing chime of delight and launched themselves into the air, racing to fill their arms with as much fruit as they could hold before darting away. Lowri chuckled.

"When did Arden plant grapes?" I asked.

"They were planted by the previous chatelaine, who hailed from a Kingdom in France before she came to the Mists," said Lowri. "We found them here when we opened the lower levels. They've responded marvelously to care, haven't they? We should have enough fruit to begin pressing our first wines in a season or two, once the Hobs figure out where the wine cellar is, and we'll have drinkable vintages a decade or so after that."

"You haven't found the wine cellar yet?" Quentin sounded scandalized.

Lowri shrugged. "It hasn't been a priority. This way."

She led us across the sunroom to another set of stairs, this one made of redwood planks set into the side of the hill. More grapevines laden with glowing grapes twined around the trees around the steps, providing a soft light that led us down the last twenty yards or so into the valley, where a series of rough farm buildings had been constructed. There was something I recognized as a stable, a chicken coop, and several smaller, boxy structures that I assumed were for goats or sheep or the like.

There was also a dark-haired man in vaguely old-fashioned clothes, using a pitchfork to shovel hay into one of those smaller structures. It looked like a cross between a toolshed and an aviary, with wire mesh covering three of the four sides, and a door set into the fourth. He looked up at the sound of footsteps, smiling brightly at the sight of Lowri.

"Milady Glastig," he said, bowing around his pitchfork. His accent was as outdated as the rest of him, like he hadn't spoken to another person since sometime in the 1920s. Which, well, wasn't far wrong. "I had wondered if you would grace me with your beauty on this night."

"Sire," said Lowri, bobbing her head in greeting. Her cheeks colored under the force of his attention. "I believe your sister asked me to remind you that it is no longer the custom to greet those of no family name with the name of their species."

Nolan Windermere, Prince in the Mists, dismissively waved the hand not clasping the pitchfork. "So much has changed. How can I be expected to keep up?"

"Your sister bids you try." Lowri stepped to the side, indicating our motley band with a half-sweep of one hand. "Sir October Daye, squire, and companion, to see you, sire."

"Hi," I said.

The change in Nolan's demeanor was immediate. He straightened, returning his hand to the pitchfork, and offered a stiff nod. "Sir Daye. Squire Daoine. Master Troll."

I could see the utility of calling people by the name of their descendant line when they didn't have a family name—or, as in

Quentin's case, had chosen not to give it. Danny has a family name, McReady, but so far as I was aware, he hadn't met Nolan before, and I wasn't sure Arden could have told him Danny's surname if she'd tried. There are a lot of fae in the Kingdom in the Mists. Arden was doing her best to meet as many of them as she could, but there was no way she was ever going to learn all their names. The numbers were against her.

"Quentin," I said, pointing appropriately. "Danny." Then I pointed to the trash can. "Arkan sonney, as requested, no longer running wild in San Francisco. Am I correct in assuming you've been preparing a, um, sty for them?"

"They're not *pigs*," Nolan said, sounding faintly affronted. It was a nice change from the stiff, awkward tone that had characterized most of our interactions thus far.

At least we could have interactions these days. When I first met Nolan, it was extremely one-sided, on account of his having been elf-shot and put into an enchanted sleep by the false Queen. It was all part of her campaign to keep Arden from seeking the throne, and it had worked for a very long time. Arden had been too busy worrying about what would happen to her brother if she got killed or captured to even think about politics.

Then the false Queen had been dethroned. Then Arden had regained her place and been officially recognized as Queen in the Mists. Then—as if all that hadn't been enough—our friend Walther Davies had finally unlocked one of the doors alchemists throughout Faerie had been throwing themselves against for centuries and discovered the cure for elf-shot.

Nolan had been the first person Arden woke when the cure was approved by the High King. No one blamed her for prioritizing her brother, especially not me. I sometimes suspected Nolan might blame her a little, but if he did, he was smart enough to know it hadn't been her fault. Her trying to take her throne sooner wouldn't have woken him up or created the conditions that led us to the elf-shot cure. It might have ended with her dead and him waking up alone, in a world that had marched a hundred years into the future without him.

Elf-shot was created as an alternative to murder. Sometimes I wonder how anyone can possibly know that and still say the fae are kind.

"Pigs or not pigs, we have a bunch of them, and some of us need to drive back to San Francisco before bedtime," I said. "Is that where they go?"

Nolan started to answer, only to pause and smile as warmly as I'd ever seen him do, eyes fixed on a point behind my shoulder.

"You don't *have* to go back to San Francisco," said the voice of Arden Windermere, Queen in the Mists. "We have plenty of guest rooms."

"Last time we stayed in them, Quentin wound up elf-shot," I said, turning to face her. "Plus, I need to feed the cats. May gets pissed when I assume she'll take care of it."

Arden smiled wryly. "Oh, Maeve forbid your cats should go unfed. They might wither away to nothing."

I swallowed my first response. She hadn't been talking about Tybalt. I *knew* she hadn't been talking about Tybalt. That didn't stop my temper from flaring. "According to them, it's a constant risk." I indicated the trash can. "We got your beasties. Can we put them in the pen?"

"That's what it's for." Arden walked past me to stand next to her brother, not seeming to notice that her gown—dark blue velvet the color of the Pacific shore at midnight, with drifts of "foam" made from seed pearls and tiny opals stitched around the hem and neckline—was dragging in the dust. Then again, she never seemed to care much about that sort of thing. For her, queenship was a way to protect her family and her father's legacy, like a jumped-up form of customer service. She was doing a good job so far. She was never going to be one of the great elegant monarchs from the history books, and she didn't seem to have a problem with that.

Standing next to her brother, it was impossible not to see the resemblance. They both had hair the color of blackberries, so dark it managed to cross over into verging on purple, and mismatched eyes, one pyrite, one mercury. The order of the colors was reversed, his pyrite to her mercury, but apart from that, it would have been understandable to assume they were twins. I knew they were a few years apart, with Arden the elder, but little things like that don't tend to matter in Faerie, not once the parties involved are past childhood.

Tybalt has centuries on me. I have decades on Quentin. Someday we're all going to be adults together, and I'm just human enough to find that unsettling.

"Were any of them hurt?" asked Nolan anxiously.

"We nearly were," I said, guiding Danny into the open pen and helping him ease the trash can to the ground. Which was when we hit a snag. We didn't have a way to get the arkan sonney *out*, not without dumping them and hoping for the best. "Quentin, bring the not-piglets over here."

"There are *babies*?" Nolan actually clapped his hands as Quentin handed me the carrier. The prince looked as overjoyed as a kid being told they'd be getting a puppy for Christmas.

I groaned. "Look, Danny, I found you a new best friend. Introduce him to your Barghests. I'm sure they'll get along swimmingly."

"There's no reason to make fun of my babies just because you don't like them," Danny said reproachfully.

"Your babies are venomous, poisonous, and aggressive."

"But they love their daddy."

I let the matter drop, turning to face Arden and Nolan as I asked, "Any idea how we're supposed to release these things?"

"Come out of the pen and close the door," she said.

Dutifully, we did as we were told. There are times when it's good to argue with a queen. I do it all the time. At the moment, I just wanted to get this over with, so I could go home and crawl into my own bed before the sun came up.

As soon as the door was latched, Arden and Nolan exchanged a look, nodded, and sketched two virtually identical portals in the air with matching sweeps of their left hands. Hers smelled of redwood bark and blackberry flowers; his smelled of crushed blackberries and sap. They stepped through, still in unison, and appeared inside the pen.

Lowri grimaced. "I wish she'd stop putting herself in harm's way like this," she muttered. "She's the queen. She doesn't *have* to."

"I think she wants to," I said, watching as Arden knelt to open the carrier door, while Nolan gingerly tipped the trash can onto its side. He removed the lid, and the three adult arkan sonney spilled out, wings flared, eyes blazing, looking around for danger. They calmed when they saw the piglets, luring them out with soft grunting noises before surrounding them in a protective ring. Arden grabbed the empty carrier, Nolan grabbed the empty trash can, and they both stepped back through their portals, which closed behind them, leaving the arkan sonney in their new enclosure.

The winged pigs snuffled at each other and the ground, the boar flaring his wings and snarling like it would keep us from coming back in. Then the whole group moved to the corner and began grooming one another, seeming to calm down.

"That felt sort of anticlimactic," said Quentin.

"Word of advice, kid: take it," I replied. "Any monster hunt that ends with the monsters safely contained and us not gored is a good one."

"They're not monsters at all," said Arden. "They're adorable. And very lucky. They'll bring good fortune to the knowe. Are you sure you won't stay?"

"We're sure," I said, before Quentin or Danny could contradict me. Arden looked disappointed but didn't try to argue. I was grateful for that. I can be a smartass when I want to be, but there's disagreeing with a queen, and then there's fighting with one. I try to avoid the latter unless it really, really has to be done. "Can you tell Cassandra I said hello, and I'll try to grab lunch with her the next time I'm in Berkeley?"

"I can," said Arden. "You'll come back soon?"

"I will," I promised. "Quentin, Danny, come on."

We waved and made our escape, heading for the stairs while Lowri and the Windermeres were clustering around the pen, making cooing noises at the arkan sonney inside.

"Keep walking, don't look back," I said softly. "We might get away."

"Why can't we stay and look at the piggies?" asked Danny. "They're cute."

"They're cute, but I want to go to bed," I said.

"I'm supposed to call Dean before dawn," said Quentin. "The reception here is terrible."

"Aw," said Danny. Then, with a pointed look at me, he added, "At least some people remember how to talk to their boyfriends."

I didn't respond. I could argue as much as I wanted without convincing him that I wasn't the one who didn't want to talk. To be fair, in the past, all too often I *had* been the reason communication wasn't happening. Now . . . I would have gladly talked forever, if only Tybalt would let me. I was tired. We'd been running around for hours. It was time to stop.

Danny seemed to realize my silence meant he'd pushed things a bit too far. He didn't say anything else as we made our way out of the knowe, and I was grateful. The pixies rejoined us for the walk across Muir Woods, wings chiming as they flew. I slouched, letting the lights guide me. Some people need to worry about pixies tricking them into bogs and streams, but the pixies who know me like me, for a lot of reasons, and they wouldn't do that sort of thing. I hoped.

Maybe I needed to pay more attention to where I was going.

Danny dropped the don't-look-here as we approached the cab. I climbed into the passenger seat and Quentin got into the back, leaning his head against the window and closing his eyes. I looked at Danny. Danny looked at me.

"Mind if I put the radio on?" he asked awkwardly.

I managed a smile. "Not at all," I said.

He turned the dial. Rock and roll blasted out of the speakers, earning a small grumble from Quentin. I sank into my seat, turning to look out the window, and trusted Danny to get us where we needed to go. He hadn't let me down so far. I trusted him not to start letting me down now.

It was hard, going home and knowing that—unless there'd been some sort of miracle while I wasn't looking—Tybalt wasn't going to be there. He'd been there less and less as the weeks went by. Mom was off playing happy houses with August. As far as I was aware, she hadn't spared me a second thought since I'd fixed all her problems for her. And it didn't matter, because he wasn't getting better. He was getting worse, and I had no idea how to fix it.

San Francisco appeared ahead of us like its own kind of fairy palace, the lights in the high buildings glittering against the predawn sky. Danny drove like he'd never met a traffic law he didn't feel like breaking, weaving around the few other cars on the road without slowing down. There were so many charms in and on his cab that the odds were good none of those drivers even realized they were sharing the road, much less took note of the specific car that was so nimbly cutting them off. That was a good thing. He would never have been able to pay all the traffic tickets he'd be accruing if there had been a chance of the police getting involved.

Quentin was asleep in the back seat by the time Danny pulled into our driveway, stopping behind my parked car. Both of us twisted to look at my squire, smiling in fond unison.

"He's adorable like that," said Danny.

"I know. He doesn't. Don't tell him."

"Wouldn't dream of it."

Quentin had his cheek squashed against the glass, coppery hair falling to hide his eyes. He was drooling out of the side of his mouth, and he *still* managed to look perfect, elegant and composed and like every fairy tale prince Grimm ever decided to write about. That's the gift of the Daoine Sidhe. No matter what, they manage to look irritatingly amazing.

Really, that should have been my first clue that my heritage wasn't what my mother claimed it was. I have never looked elegant or composed a night in my life. In fact, it's a rare night when I'm not covered in my own blood.

Danny looked at me, regret and apology in his eyes. "I'm sorry I've been needlin' you all night. I know it's hard."

"I understand why you're doing it, honestly. But I can't . . . this isn't something I can fix with a wave of my hand." I leaned into the backseat to shake Quentin's shoulder. He responded with a grumbling noise. "Poor kid's wiped out."

"It was a big night," said Danny, and sighed. "I do know it's not goin' to be that easy to fix. I just want you to be happy. It's been so good watchin' you work your way toward happy, I don't want to let your mom get in the way."

"We'll figure it out." I looked over my shoulder, flashing what I hoped would be an encouraging smile in his direction. Really, I would have settled for a smile that didn't make me look sick to my stomach. "We always do."

"Yeah," said Danny.

I returned my attention to Quentin, shaking him again. When that didn't get the response I was looking for, I cleared my throat and said loudly, "Sure, Dianda, come on in. I'm sure Quentin will be thrilled to see you."

Quentin sat bolt upright, one hand already shoving his hair out of wide, very open eyes. Seeing me and Danny looking at him— Danny barely holding back his laughter—those eyes narrowed.

"Jerk," he accused.

"Absolutely," I agreed. "Get up, get inside, and call your boyfriend before you go to bed. We have about an hour before dawn."

Quentin rolled his eyes. "Later, Danny," he said, and slouched out of the car, heading up the driveway toward the back door. The kitchen lights were on. May was probably in there, baking something or having a last cup of tea before bed. No wards, not when people were home; he'd be able to let himself in.

I took a breath and reached for the door handle, only to pause as Danny's hand engulfed my shoulder. All the illusions in the world couldn't change the sheer size of him, especially when I wasn't looking at him. My eyes couldn't lie to me when they weren't involved.

"You're not alone anymore," he said softly.

"I know," I said, and opened the door. "Open roads and kind fires, Danny."

"Open roads," he replied.

I closed the door and waved before following Quentin toward the house. The kitchen door was shut to keep the cats from getting out. I let myself in, stepping out of the cool night air and into warmth and light and the smell of sugar cookies. Quentin was already gone. My Fetch, sitting at the kitchen table with a plate of cookies and a mug of cocoa, lifted her head and offered me a wan smile.

"Do you know what time it is, young lady?" she asked.

"About twenty years past curfew, and thank Titania for that," I said.

She laughed.

Fetches are rare, terrifying things, omens of impending death that flicker into the world and fade out of it again almost as quickly, leaving nothing behind to mark their passing.

And then there's May.

She came into existence when the universe decided that all signs pointed toward my inevitable demise, conjured by magic older than anything else I can name, made from my blood and from a night-haunt named Mai, who remembered me being her hero. It was a complicated mixture, and it made a complicated, confusing, wonderful person, my sister in every way that mattered. Ask me to choose between August—sister by blood and birth—and May— sister by magic and adoption—and there wouldn't be any contest. May would win. May would always win.

She wore the face I'd had when she was summoned, more human than the one I have now, round where I've grown pointy, soft where I've grown hard. Looking at her was like looking at a mirror that had somehow been permanently trained on my own past. Her hair, still more mousy brown than golden-blonde, was cropped short and streaked with purple and green, like some sort of fabulous bird. The weariness in her fog-colored eyes was familiar enough to be uncomfortable. I wasn't the only one whose life Amandine had turned upside-down.

"How's Jazz?" I asked.

"Asleep." She shrugged, the gesture barely more than a shiver. "She'll be up in a few hours."

Most fae are nocturnal. As a Raven-maid, Jazz is one of the few exceptions. Her relationship with May had been based on compromises from the beginning, the two of them stealing hours where they could be awake and together. But she'd been sleeping more and flying less since the incident, and sometimes it felt like she was avoiding the rest of us. Even May.

"Do you want to join her?" I asked. "I can put myself to bed. I promise, I remember the way."

"Quentin said you caught the arkan sonney?"

"We did. They're at Muir Woods now. Arden and Nolan prepared a cage for them."

"We're building quite the local bestiary," said May. She stood. "Soon, we'll have people from all over the Summerlands coming to look at creatures they'd almost forgotten existed."

"And they can all buy tickets and we'll be able to renovate the upstairs bathroom." I made a small shooing gesture. "Go. Sleep with your girlfriend."

May's lips drew down. "She won't even know I'm there."

"She will. Even if she can't show it, she will."

"Okay." She picked up her tea. "Sleep well when you get there." Then she was gone, and I was finally, blessedly, alone.

I sat down in the chair she had so recently vacated, looking at the cookies for a moment. I didn't reach for them. I knew they would only taste of ashes. Finally, I put my head in my hands and my elbows on the table and cried. When did things get so damn complicated? And why, for the love of Oberon, couldn't I make them go back to the way they were?

THREE

UNFORTUNATELY, IT'S IMPOSSIBLE to cry forever, no matter how appealing the idea seems sometimes—not that it stays appealing once the dehydration headache sets in. My tears eventually ran out, and I made it to bed with almost five minutes to spare before dawn slammed down on the world and all the magic burned away. The air filled with the phantom scent of ashes, chalky and tasteless on my tongue. I couldn't stop myself from breathing it in and coughed as I rolled over and closed my eyes, drifting into a fitful sleep.

As was almost always the case these days, I dreamt of Tybalt, smirking and flirting and arrogant and mine. He was wearing the brown leather pants he always wore when he wanted to get under my skin, and when he offered me his hands, I took them, and we waltzed together across a giant chessboard, the sky glittering bright with stars above us. We were alone, and everything was the way it was supposed to be. No curses, no quests, no Firstborn ruining our chances to be happy. Just him and me and the whole world keeping its distance until we wanted to let it back in.

Until the scene changed.

Until it was him and me in my bedroom, a week after I'd faced my mother's wrath in order to bring him home, and he was standing as far away as he could without actually leaving, his hair disheveled, his shirt untucked. He looked at me across the suddenly vast expanse of my bed—*our* bed—and the gulf of my mother's cruelty, and the only reason my heart didn't break on the spot was because there was still love in his eyes. It was veiled in fear and misery, but it was still there.

It wasn't enough.

"Please," I begged. "Talk to me. I just need you to talk to me. We can—"

"There's nothing to discuss," he snapped. "I'm fine."

"You're not fine, Tybalt. None of this is fine. Raj—"

"*Raj is not King*!" He didn't shout. He roared, hands curling as claws emerged from his fingertips, pupils narrowing to slits.

I'm virtually impossible to injure for more than a few minutes. Nothing Tybalt could do to me would stick. In the moment, that didn't matter. I flinched, taking a step backward, and saw the moment when the anger in his expression flickered out, replaced by shame and horror.

"Raj is not King, but I am, and I have a duty to my people," he said, voice gone dull. "A King must be strong. A King must be capable of protecting what is his. A King has *responsibilities*. I do not fulfill my responsibilities by standing here with you, talking about my feelings. What I feel does not matter."

"It matters to me."

"Then perhaps *you* don't matter."

I swallowed, forcing myself not to take another step back. If I did that, if I rejected him, it would be over. I knew him well enough to know that. "We both know that's not true. I matter to you." My fear of abandonment was screaming, telling me this had been inevitable, that he'd been preparing to leave me since our first kiss. He was older than me, King of a Court I could never belong to or fully understand; he was pure fae, while I clung stubbornly to the scraps of my human heritage. Of course, he was going to leave me. How could he do anything else?

His voice dropped to a whisper. "Maybe you shouldn't."

I looked at him, my lover, my friend, and said the only thing I could think of, the only rope I had to throw.

"I love you."

He didn't say anything. He just stepped into the shadows and was gone, leaving me alone.

I woke with tears on my cheeks, blinking blearily at my ceiling. Light slanted around the edges of my blackout curtains, confirming that it was daytime, but it didn't feel like afternoon. My head pounded from a toxic combination of grief and the shock of waking too early. I glanced at the bedside clock. Nine am. Why the hell was I awake before noon?

As if in answer to the question, the sound of someone hammering on my front door drifted up the stairs. It wasn't gentle knocking. It was the kind of pounding that comes from panic or urgency, and it traveled straight up my spine, leaving me on my feet before I had fully committed to the idea of getting out of bed.

My current nightgown was an oversized T-shirt with the logo from a recent production of *The Tempest* on the front. Decent enough. I grabbed a pair of yoga pants from the laundry hamper and yanked them on, pulling my silver knife from under the pillow and tucking it into the waistband where my shirt would hide it. I'd have to be careful not to stab myself, but finding the sheath would take too long and would involve putting on more complicated clothing. This would do for right now, until I knew what was going on.

What was going on was the person at my door still hammering away. They'd wake Quentin and May soon, if they hadn't already. Jazz was probably already gone, off to work in the antique store where she spent most of the time that wasn't in the house. I sent a silent thanks for that as I made for the stairs. She wasn't as fragile as Tybalt, but she wasn't in a place where having someone invade her home was going to do her any good at all.

I wove a rough human disguise from lingering shadows as I took the stairs two and three at a time, hitting the bottom with a thump and practically running down the hall. There was a pause in the knocking. I wrenched the door open just as the man on the porch raised his hand to start again. For a moment, it looked like he was getting ready to punch me. I tensed. The blow never came.

"Cliff?" I asked blankly.

My ex-fiancé—the father of my only biological child, no matter how many stray teenagers I brought home—lowered his hand. His face was pale and drawn. Given his Italian complexion, the pallor made him look sick, verging on collapse. The thick, dark hair I used to love so much was thinning. That was natural, given his age. Less natural was the fact that it didn't appear to have been combed. His shirt was unbuttoned, and one of his shoes was unlaced.

The woman behind him didn't look much better. Her buttercup-blonde hair was pulled into a thick braid, frizzy breakaway strands radiating in all directions. She was wearing a green sweater that needed to have its cuffs darned, and jeans with a hole just below the knee. Somehow, that hole was the most distressing part of the whole thing. I'd never seen my replacement—Cliff's first wife, Gillian's stepmother—looking anything other than perfectly groomed. To be fair, I hadn't seen Miranda more than a few times: our mutual dislike was one of the only things we had in common. But something about this was just *wrong*.

"Is she here?" rasped Cliff.

The world snapped into terrible, crystalline focus. I grabbed the doorway with one hand to keep from falling over. "Gillian's missing?" I managed to squeak. There was no air. Where had all the air gone? "When? What happened?"

"Don't," snarled Miranda. She pushed past me into the house. I didn't stop her. I couldn't stop her. All the good, logical reasons I needed to get in her way—Quentin and May were sleeping, none of us habitually wear human disguises when we're in our own home, there were probably swords on the coffee table and strange tea canisters on the counters—were gone, replaced by the sudden, heart-stopping realization that my little girl was missing. My little girl was *missing*, again, and this wasn't supposed to happen anymore. This was supposed to be over.

Once upon a time, I tried to live a human existence, to be part of the human world. Cliff was a part of that, the innocent mortal man who took a fairy bride without realizing it. Gillian, though . . . Gillian was the *best* part of that. She was my little girl, my beautiful daughter, and I would have done anything for her, anything at all.

Unfortunately, what I did for her was leave. I'd followed the wrong trail into the wrong place, and wound up spending fourteen years enchanted and transformed, unable to return to my family or tell them anything about what had happened to me. By the time I'd freed myself and tried to go home, they had given up on me. I couldn't entirely blame them for that anymore—human lives are so short, and fourteen years is such a long time—but having my daughter grow up calling another woman "Mom" was the sort of pain I'd never expected to experience. I'd thought I'd known what suffering was.

Then Rayseline Torquill, daughter of my liege lord, had decided to kidnap Gillian to get to me, and had nearly killed her in the process. The only way to save my child had been to change her, to pull the fae blood from her veins and let the Luidaeg edit her memory to take all the impossible things away. That kind of magic is fragile. The best way to keep Gillian from being consumed by memories of the impossible was for me to stay away from her completely.

I hadn't seen my daughter for more than two years, all for the sake of her well-being. And now she was *missing*.

"Her college called us last night," said Cliff. He seemed to realize his wife was already inside, because he straightened and followed her past me into the hall.

This time, I had the presence of mind to stop him, if I wanted to. It would have been so easy. He looked like he had no strength left in him, like it had all been drained away by the situation. I didn't move. Miranda had already breached my defenses, such as they were, and Gillian was missing. I wasn't going to keep him away from his wife, not now.

"What . . . ?" I managed. I turned to face them, only remembering at the last second that I should probably shut the door. I didn't even know where Gilly was going to college. That suddenly seemed like a grave oversight on my part. How could I not know where my own daughter was going to school?

"Her resident adviser said there was a break-in. Someone smashed every window in her residence building just after midnight, and when they took a headcount of the students, Gilly was missing. At first, they thought she might have been behind the vandalism. They were calling us to find out if she'd run home when the prank went wrong." There was no life in Cliff's voice. He was reciting facts because he had to, not because he felt any real connection to them. "We said we hadn't seen her. We said she wouldn't do that. And then . . ." He faltered, looking to Miranda for help.

Miranda turned from her narrow-eyed study of my hallway and said, "They found her car. All the windows smashed, blood on the seat, no Gillian. She's gone. Someone's taken her. Was it you? Is this how you get back at us, by kidnapping our daughter?"

There had never been any love lost between me and Miranda, but it still stung for her to jump straight to assuming I'd hurt my own child. I narrowed my eyes, reaching for every ounce of authority I possessed, and said, "Maybe it's time for you to leave."

"Maybe it's time for you to tell us where Gillian is," snapped Miranda. She wasn't making any effort to keep her voice down.

I scowled. "People are sleeping. Please, be quiet, and get out."

"Who?" Miranda demanded. "Who's sleeping? You don't have any family. Gillian?" She whirled, starting toward the stairs.

I moved without thinking, grabbing her arm and pulling her to a halt. She shot me a startled look, eyes gone wide. Apparently, the thought that I'd defend my home had never occurred to her.

"She isn't here, and my housemates are none of your business," I said, voice low. "You shouldn't be here, either."

"Toby, we're not here to fight," said Cliff. "We just want Gillian back. Please. If you don't have her, can you help us? Can you find her?"

For a moment, the world seemed to spin as an overwhelming sense of déjà vu settled over me. This, too, had happened before, when Rayseline had Gillian, when Faerie had reached out and tried take my child, who should have been safe, who had been isolated from me for so long that she should never have become a target. I closed my eyes and took a deep breath, chasing the vertigo away.

"Yes, I'll find her," I said, opening my eyes and leveling my best glare on Cliff as I let go of Miranda's arm. "She's my daughter, too. I didn't take her, and you didn't need to come here and accuse me like this, but there's no way I am ever going to leave her in danger. You should have known that. How could you have been with me for as long as you were and not have known that?"

Cliff had the decency to look ashamed. I turned toward Miranda.

"You, on the other hand, you don't know me at all. You've never liked me, and I guess that's okay, because I've never really given you a reason to. But you are never, *never* to do anything like this again. This is my home. You are not welcome here. You were not invited to be here." I paused. "How did you even know to come here? I never gave you this address."

Miranda looked to the side, expression turning shifty, like she was afraid to look at me. Cliff sighed.

"I paid someone to find it, after you moved out of that terrible apartment," he admitted. I stared at him, open-mouthed. "I'm sorry. It was low and shitty, and I shouldn't have done it, but Gilly wasn't sleeping after what had happened to her. She was crying all the time, and I needed to know where you were. For my own peace of mind, I needed to be sure you weren't going to come and try to take our baby away. And then you went and moved into this *house*, like you were getting ready to need more room, and . . ." He rubbed the back of his neck with one hand. "I thought you were going to challenge me for custody. I've been waiting for years for you to come after her. To say I was a bad parent for letting her be taken in the first place."

"Cliff . . ." I stopped, the protests dying on my lips. I didn't know how to finish that sentence. It felt like I didn't know anything anymore, like everything I'd fought so hard to learn had fallen away, tumbling into the abyss of my-daughter-is-missing.

Miranda returned to his side, looking down her nose at me. There was a condemnation as deep and wide as the Pacific Ocean in her eyes.

"Can you blame us for being afraid of you?" she demanded. "Can you blame *me*?"

Yes, I wanted to scream. *Yes.* Their fear sounded like an excuse. It sounded like the reason my little girl had become a woman in a house where I wasn't welcome. Other people split up. Other children grew up with parents in multiple places. It would have taken a lot of time and effort to rebuild those bridges, to find a way to reconcile the angry teenager with the loving toddler I had left behind, but I'd been willing to put the time in. The only reason I hadn't was because Gillian hadn't wanted me to, and I'd loved her too much to force her into something she didn't want.

Only now I was finding out that maybe *Gillian* hadn't been the one who'd wanted me to stay away. *Gillian* hadn't been the one afraid of custody challenges and missing mothers swooping in to snatch her from the home she'd always known.

I was tired. I was so, so tired. And Gillian was still missing. No matter how tired I was, I needed to go and bring my daughter home.

"All you ever had to do was tell me to stay away, and I would have stayed away," I said softly. "You never had to spy on me."

"We knew you weren't going to come to the house again," said Miranda. "If I'd thought there was any chance you were going to show up on our doorstep, I would have convinced Cliff we needed to move somewhere else a long time ago."

"Even as the noncustodial parent, I would have been able to fight that right up until Gillian turned eighteen," I snapped, before I could think better of it.

Miranda smiled, slow and broad. "And I would have *welcomed* a court case. After all, nothing like taking all your inadequacies as a parent in front of a judge to clear the way for my adopting my own daughter."

In that moment, I felt it would have been completely forgivable for me to smash her head against the wall until I was satisfied that I'd knocked all thoughts of adoption clean out of her skull. I didn't do it. I didn't move. I just stood where I was and glared at her, wishing all those old stories of the fae cursing people with a glance had any basis in truth.

Miranda's smile turned brittle before curling up and fading altogether. "I'm sorry," she said. "That was mean of me. I get petty when I'm under stress."

"I never would have guessed," I said. My teeth were clenched so tightly that it felt like they would shatter and dissolve into dust in my mouth.

"Gillian is *missing*," said Miranda, like I had somehow forgotten. "There was blood. Please. Can't we put all this behind us? Can't we agree to settle our differences long enough to find our daughter?"

The way she kept saying "our" was like claws against my skin, ripping and tearing at me, stealing the air from my lungs. I forced the feeling away and said, "I already promised to help. Where is she going to school? I'll head over there right away."

"Berkeley," said Cliff.

I managed to conceal my relief. Any local school would have been good, as long as it was inside the Kingdom in the Mists. I'd cause a diplomatic incident for my daughter's sake if I had to, but it was better if it wasn't necessary. Berkeley was the best-case scenario.

Thanks to an old land agreement, the city was unclaimed territory: Arden was the only noble with any direct authority there, and even she was mostly ignored by the inhabitants. Walther and Bridget were both on the faculty; they could get me the kind of access that would have been exceedingly difficult otherwise. Even better, Cassandra was a grad student there, which meant Arden wouldn't need to assign someone to keep an eye on me. If she got concerned, she could just ask her chatelaine. All my attention and energy could go to finding my daughter and getting her back where she belonged. That was good. Getting started would be better. My

initial shock was starting to thaw, replaced by the horrified conviction that I had very little time in which to find her and bring her
safely home.

"I need to get dressed," I said briskly. "I'll call you if I find anything."

"If you try to keep things from us—"

I leveled a flat gaze on Cliff. "You mean like you kept my daughter from me after I was abducted? Fuck you." The mortal profan-
ity felt good, like honey on my tongue. "Turnabout may be fair
play, but some of us have standards. Now I need to get moving, and
that's going to be easier if you're not standing here waiting for me
to pull a miracle out of my ass."

"October—" Cliff began.

"Get out your phone," I said.

He stopped talking, a look on his face that made me feel like I'd
just punched him in the gut—and it wasn't a *bad* feeling, much as
I might have wanted it to be; hitting him would have been real
satisfying right about then—and pulled a phone out of his pocket.

"Good," I said. "Go to contacts."

"Done," he said.

"Punch this in," I said, and rattled off my number, pausing when
I was done to ask, "Got it?"

"I do," he said. "Toby, please—"

"Good," I said, cutting him off again. "Text me, so I'll have your
number. Now get out, both of you. We're wasting time."

They walked toward the door, Miranda looping her arm through
Cliff's and giving me a poisonous look. I looked blandly back. I
didn't want the man she was clinging to so fiercely, hadn't wanted
him in a very long time—not since I'd fought my way home despite
impossible odds and been told I was no longer welcome, that home
was no longer mine to claim. Anyone who could reject someone
they had claimed to love so conclusively wasn't for me.

I didn't want the man, but I'd always wanted the child. I'd always
loved the child. And Miranda had been part of keeping that child
away from me. I was grateful to her for making sure Gilly grew up
with a mother, even if it hadn't been me. That was where my gratitude ended.

That was where my hatred began.

Cliff looked back when they reached the door. "I'll text you with her residence hall information," he said. "Please, bring her home. I know I haven't been fair to you, I know there's nothing I can do to make that better, but please . . . bring her home."

"I will," I said.

Sunlight lanced into the hall when he opened the door. I stepped back involuntarily, away from the burning brightness. Only dawn has the power to destroy illusions, but the one I was wearing hadn't been made to stand up to any real scrutiny. It would look wrong in direct sunlight. It would look like the lie it was.

Cliff looked at me in confusion as Miranda's eyes narrowed in something that felt like contempt. Then they were gone, stepping out into that terrible daylight.

It took everything I had not to slam the door behind them. I sagged, pressing my forehead to the wood and closing my eyes as I released my ragged illusions. They dissolved into the smell of cut grass and copper, and I sobbed, struggling not to let myself collapse. I couldn't. There wasn't time. I could have this, this stolen moment of tears and terror, but soon enough, I'd need to get moving. Gillian was out there somewhere, lost and scared, and while I couldn't say for sure that it was because of me, because of who and what I was, I couldn't discount it, either. Not yet.

I pushed away from the door and started for the stairs, wiping my eyes as I went, trying to look less like I was on the verge of collapsing. It wasn't easy. Dimly, distantly, I realized that I wanted Tybalt more than anything else. He was supposed to be here, giving me something stable to hold onto when the world was dropping out from under my feet. I couldn't be angry with him for being hurt by what my mother had done, but I could miss his solidity.

When had he gone from being an adversary to becoming my surest port in the storm? And how was I going to hold on now that he was slipping away, buried under his own terror and the weight of what it meant to love me? My mother would always be a part of who I was, just like I'd always be a part of who Gillian was. No matter how far we run, we never get away from family.

I plodded up the stairs, relaxing slightly when I reached the cool, shadowy upstairs hallway. May's door was closed. That was normal. Jazz was usually the first one up, thanks to her diurnal nature and desire to maintain a real job, and she closed May's door when she left, to keep the cats out. Cagney and Lacey mostly preferred to stay in my room these days, resting their tired bones in the piles of pillows and on the laundry that always wound up strewn on the floor, but when Tybalt came to visit—rare as that felt right now—he always kicked them out, saying that while a cat might look at a king, there were some things he'd prefer his subjects not observe.

I didn't want to do this. I wanted to leave a note and let her sleep. She could wake up in the afternoon with the problem already solved and Gillian safely back in Cliff and Miranda's arms . . . and I know that wasn't going to work. She would never forgive me. She would be right not to.

Carefully, I eased the door open, revealing a pirate's trove of casual treasure. Putting my magpie Fetch in a room with a woman who had a literal raven's eye for shiny things had resulted in a bedroom that looked like it was halfway through the process of transforming into a thrift store. There were two separate dressing tables, one on either side of the room, both covered in jewelry boxes and wire stands glittering with necklaces. Glass, precious stones, it didn't matter: what mattered was that they were beautiful. Silk sheets covered the ceiling, playing peek-a-boo with strands of twinkling white lights, so that it felt like they were trying to recreate the foggy heights of Muir Woods in their bedroom.

May was a curled comma in the middle of the bed, her arms wrapped around what I assumed was Jazz's pillow. I paused for a moment, looking at her without illusions or disguises. Her face was mine, blunted by a façade of mortal blood she had never truly possessed: whatever else she might be, my Fetch was a pureblood through and through. But she remembered being me, and more, she remembered being a girl named Darice—Dare—who'd died when she was young enough to be my daughter, who had considered me her hero.

Dare was the reason May existed. Without those memories to urge her on, the night-haunt she had been would never have been willing to activate Oberon's ancient binding and have herself called as a Fetch. It should have been the end of her. Instead, it had become a new beginning. I was grateful. I would always be grateful, just like I'd always be sorry that I hadn't been able to save her.

I sat on the edge of the bed, leaning over to gingerly shake May's shoulder. She made a soft mumbling noise and burrowed deeper into the covers.

"May," I said. "It's me. I need you to wake up. Come on. We don't have time."

May opened her eyes. Rolling onto her side, she pushed herself up onto one elbow and squinted at me. "Toby? What *time* is it?"

"Way too damn early," I said. I stood. "Get up and get dressed. You just missed Cliff and Miranda. There was an incident at Gillian's school last night. The campus police found blood in her car. I need to wake Quentin, and we need to get moving. I thought you might want to come with us."

May's eyes widened for a moment. Then they narrowed, a look of steely determination sliding into place. "There's no *might* about it. I'm coming with you. How dare you even imply I wouldn't."

I blinked. "I didn't think—"

"No, you usually don't. And I'm usually pretty forgiving of that, since I know how your head works. I know how easy it is for you to get swallowed up in that swamp you call 'logic.' But no. I am *not* sitting this one out." She rolled out of the bed and onto her feet, eyes wild, teeth all but bared. "She's my daughter, too. I'm helping you bring her home."

"Okay." I raised my hands, palms outward, trying to defuse the situation before it could get out of hand. "That's fine: that's why I woke you. We'll leave a note for Jazz, and . . . that's fine. I'm going to go get Quentin. All right?"

"Go," she said.

I went.

Quentin's door was slightly ajar. He didn't mind the cats, and when they weren't with me, they could usually be found with him, hogging the covers and somehow managing to force my adult-sized squire onto a strip of mattress about six inches wide.

There was no response when I knocked. I pushed the door open, choosing a small invasion of privacy over trying to wake him by making enough noise to rouse the dead. Assuming I even *could* wake him that way. If Cliff hammering on the front door for as long as he had hadn't been sufficient to wake Quentin up, I wasn't sure any amount of noise would get him out of bed. I sort of envied that. Sleeping deeply is a gift.

Enough light slipped around the edges of his curtains to illuminate the room, showing the hockey pennants and posters on the walls and the scattering of laundry on the floor. I didn't judge. Quentin has been keeping his room cleaner than mine since the day he moved in, which is pretty impressive for a kid who grew up in a literal palace, with servants to cater to his every whim. Most people would take "it's okay to be a slob" away from that. Quentin took "somebody has to clean up the mess, and it might as well be me." It's things like that that make me convinced he's better than I ever deserved to have in my keeping.

There was a tank atop the dresser just inside the room, filled with tiny hippocampi, brightly-colored fae creatures with the lower bodies of impossible fish and the upper bodies of horses. The stallion circled his mares, eyeing me suspiciously. The reason for his caution became clear when I looked closer: there were several foals at the middle of the herd, their equine bodies no larger than my thumb. Almost everything that lives is willing to die in the defense of its young.

I turned away from the tank and started for the bed. The cat draped atop the blankets over Quentin's hip raised its head and looked at me. I blinked.

My cats, Cagney and Lacey, are Siamese. This cat wasn't mine. The shadows were deep enough to turn most colors to gray, and for a moment, my eyes sketched stripes where no stripes existed, telling me the cat on Quentin's hip was a burly tabby, telling me things were getting back to normal.

The cat blinked enormous yellow eyes and yawned, showing me all its fine, sharp teeth. All *his* fine, sharp teeth. I sighed.

"Hi, Raj," I said in a low voice. "Didn't know you were sleeping over."

Raj licked a paw before looking down the length of his nose at me, his entire body forming a question of what the hell I thought I was doing there. I shook my head.

"It's a long story," I said. "Can you hop off, please? I need to wake Quentin."

Raj stretched with as much insolence as a cat could show and slid off of Quentin, landing on the mattress and continuing to watch me through wary eyes.

I tried not to think about what it meant for Raj to be coming here to sleep. It wasn't unusual to find him in the house—he'd basically moved in when Quentin became my squire, claiming that if one of them got to live with me, they should both be allowed to live with me—but normally, he told me when he was going to spend the night. That he hadn't done so smacked of trying to hide something . . . or trying to hide from me. To keep me from asking him questions he didn't want to answer. The fact that he was staying in his feline form made me suspect there was a lot he didn't want to talk about.

"Yeah," I said mildly. "Me, too."

I stepped over Quentin's discarded backpack, which I only ever saw him use when he was going to spend the night at Goldengreen with Dean, and shook his shoulder. He grumbled.

"I'm going on errantry, and I will leave you here," I said calmly.

He opened his eyes so quickly that if it hadn't been for the change in his breathing, I wouldn't have believed he'd been asleep at all. "You wouldn't dare," he said, voice heavy with exhaustion. He sat up, barely seeming to notice when Raj slunk out of the way, and ground the heel of one hand against his left eye. "Toby? What are you doing in my room? What *time* is it?"

"We need to go," I said. I took a step back so that I could address both boys at the same time. "My daughter has been taken. We don't know whether it was humans or the fae—I'm hoping humans, sweet Titania, I'm hoping humans—but we need to move if we're going to get there before the trail goes cold."

Raj meowed, the sound small and lost in the dark room. I looked at him and nodded.

"I know you can't help, and I know Tybalt probably can't help right now either, and I'm not going to ask how he's doing, because this isn't the time and it isn't fair to you. But, yeah, you can tell him. You should tell him. And tell him I'm going to call Arden and ask if I can borrow Madden." Madden is a Cu Sidhe, a fairy dog in the same way that Tybalt is a fairy cat. Which meant that his nose could be the difference between finding my daughter and not.

Quentin had finished rubbing his eye and was openly staring at me. "Gillian? But isn't she . . . ?"

"Yeah, she's human," I said. "I'm going to get ready; you need to do the same. May is coming with us. Cliff and his new wife were just here, since clearly if my estranged, adult daughter is missing, it must be because I kidnapped her."

The urgency that had flooded my veins when they told me about Gillian's disappearance was getting stronger, starting to burn. My daughter was *missing*. I needed to find her. Even if she wouldn't thank me for it, even if she would just . . . just turn away from me again, I needed to find her. I needed to bring her home.

I'd been forced to build a life without my child, one where I would always love and worry about her, but where she was no longer in the forefront of my daily thoughts. I had surrendered her to her father in a cave that shouldn't have existed when I pulled the immortality from her veins and allowed the Luidaeg to wipe the impossible from her memory. Cliff had never done any of those things, had never made any of the choices that would put our daughter out of his reach. He didn't know how to live without her. He'd never needed to know.

It was tempting to envy him for being that secure in his position as friend and father to our little girl. But there wasn't time for envy, either. We had work to do.

"All right," said Quentin, and slid out of the bed.

I nodded. "Good. Meet you in the hall in five minutes. Raj, open roads, and if Tybalt wants to find me, I'll be in Berkeley." I turned on my heel and left the room, heading down the hall to my own door.

We had so much to do and so little time. All I could hope for was that we'd be fast enough to bring my daughter safely home. Anything more than that would be greedy, and so I didn't even dare to think about it. Just let me bring her home.

Cagney and Lacey were curled up against my pillow, bodies compacted into the warm spot my body had formed during the short time I'd been allowed to spend sleeping. Spike was a few feet away, stretched out in the narrow sunbeam that had managed to slip through my blackout curtains, its thorny belly exposed to the ceiling. I couldn't stop myself from smiling, just a little, at the sight. Rose goblins are basically cat-shaped, impossibly mobile rose bushes. When Spike and I had met, it had been the size of a rabbit, or maybe a small cat. Now, after years of fertilizer, water, and all the sunlight it could want, it was nearly the size of a corgi. I didn't know how big it could wind up getting, but I was looking forward to finding out.

"Gillian's missing," I informed it, as I stripped off my sleep clothes and started digging in the laundry on the floor, looking for something that was suitable for dealing with the police. Sure, I could use illusions to make myself fit into the scene, but illusions always work better when they have something to work *with*. My magic isn't strong enough for me to discount that.

Spike rolled onto its side, thorns rattling in what sounded like a question. I shook my head. "I don't want to take you with me. May and Quentin are coming, and I don't want Jazz coming home to an empty house." Cagney and Lacey would be there, of course, but they were just ordinary cats. Spike . . . I'd never been sure how intelligent rose goblins were, but it was at least smart enough to keep Jazz company.

Spike rattled again. I leaned over, risking a pat to the top of its head before I returned to getting ready.

Dark jeans; black T-shirt; leather jacket; silver knife. Not much as armor goes, but all I've ever needed, and enough to have seen me through a lot of bad situations. Wearing black is a financial decision as well as a stealth one: I have a tendency to bleed on my clothes, made worse by the fact that most of my magic is blood-based, and anything pale doesn't usually survive being worn more than once or twice. Fortunately, dark colors often read as more formal in the mortal world, and that would make it easier for me to pass myself off as someone in authority.

I took a moment to run a brush through my hair, leaving it down to tangle around my shoulders. Not great if I wound up in a fight, but another layer of camouflage. Apart from my ears—pointed, although not as visibly as say, Quentin's—the surest betrayal of my heritage is in my bone structure, which is too sharp to be human, and too hard to look away from. Keeping my hair loose would make that less evident even if my illusions happened to slip—and might give me time to get out of sight.

My shoes were by the door. I grabbed them and stepped into the hall, to be greeted by Quentin, fully clothed and looking anxious. Raj was nowhere to be seen. I raised an eyebrow.

"He went back to the Court of Cats," said Quentin.

It was interesting that he didn't say Raj had gone home. I decided to leave it alone, saying instead, "Good. He can make sure Tybalt knows what's going on."

"Yeah," said Quentin softly. He glanced toward the stairs. "May already went downstairs. Is she . . . is she okay?"

"Wait here. I'll call you when it's safe to follow me," I said, and patted him once on the shoulder before I started down.

May was in the middle of the hall, arms wrapped around herself, staring blankly at the door. She was dressed and had donned a human disguise that made her look distressingly like my human twin. It was like standing outside myself, watching my own distress over my missing child. It ached. I stopped several feet away, trying not to startle her.

"May?"

"How did this happen?" She turned, looking bleakly at me. "I remember when she was born. I know the memory isn't mine, but I have it, and I'm not giving it back. I remember her being so *small*, and she had this one black curl," she mimed tugging on the air at the center of her forehead, "that was so long, right after she was born. It was like silk. I'd never touched anything so soft. I said I'd do anything to protect her. Remember?" She was almost pleading.

"I do," I said softly. I knew what she was asking: she was asking me to reassure her that she was Gillian's mother, too, because she remembered it, and those memories burned. "I wanted to keep her safe. All I wanted to do was keep her safe."

"You took the fae blood out of her to keep her safe. To keep her away from our world."

"I did." There was no point in arguing: she wasn't accusing me of anything. All she was doing was telling me the truth.

"Why didn't it work?" she asked, tears beginning to roll down her cheeks. "Why wasn't that enough to keep her safe? It should have been enough. It *should*."

I sighed and went to my Fetch and held her as tightly as I could, letting her press her face into my shoulder and cry. After a few minutes, Quentin came padding cautiously down and joined our silent embrace, and my family was so damn broken, and we were still holding on just as tightly as we could.

We were still holding on.

FOUR

THE DRIVE TO BERKELEY was quick. It would have been quicker, but Arden had insisted on speaking to me directly after May called and woke her, and since I was the one driving, we'd been forced to pull off to the side of the road. Quentin's don't-look-here spell would keep the human police from noticing and potentially ticketing me, but I didn't trust myself to carry on a conversation and steer the car at the same time.

At least the delay had been profitable. We pulled into the on-campus parking lot to find Madden waiting for us, his lanky frame propped casually against a pay station. He was wearing the glittering outline of a human disguise that simultaneously bleached and darkened his normally red-and-white hair to an even shade of blond. It had also dialed his canine-golden eyes down to a more human-normal brown, but there was no mistaking his broad shoulders, or the way he occasionally sniffed the air, checking for signs of our arrival.

Despite everything that was happening, it was hard not to smile at the sight of him. Madden had the kind of energy that could make things seem less hopeless, even when they shouldn't have been.

Quentin's spellwork was good enough that Madden couldn't see the car, but he saw us when we emerged and came bounding over to present me with a parking slip. "Here," he said. "Prepaid for the whole day. Arden didn't want you to worry."

"That's very kind of you," I said, trying to ignore the way my heart sank.

When I'd asked for the loan of Arden's seneschal, I hadn't been thinking in terms of debts incurred or fealties observed. I'd just been looking for a bloodhound. Trouble was, Madden worked for the Queen, and things weren't that simple. Arden hadn't been on the throne long enough to have fully internalized the rules of royalty, but she was catching on fast, and something as small as accepting a parking pass could have repercussions for me later. Like, say, the next time she wanted to talk about shifting my fealty from Duke Sylvester Torquill of Shadowed Hills directly to her.

"Why didn't you call your liege when you needed help?" was a reasonable question, but the answer was big and complicated and frustrating. The last time I'd asked Sylvester for help, he'd released his elf-shot brother, Simon, into my custody so I could find my missing sister, who happened to be Simon's daughter. It had been a gesture of infinite trust, since Sylvester had good reasons—quite a few of them—to want Simon asleep and suffering for as long as possible. And I'd turned right around and screwed it up by allowing Simon to escape, with his memories twisted by the loss of all the gains he'd made in the days since he'd given up villainy in favor of redemption.

Sylvester loved me as a daughter. He always had. He trusted my skills as a knight; had been, in fact, the first person to put that sort of faith in me. And I had rewarded his faith, over and over again. It was just that sometimes it . . . well, it took a while. I didn't feel like I could ask him for another favor until I'd managed to put my life back together to the point where I could go after Simon, return what had been taken from him, and fix things. Sweet Oberon, there had to be a way for me to fix things. I wasn't going to let down the man who'd never given up on me.

At the same time, I couldn't blame Arden for wanting to recruit me. She was building a household intended to control a kingdom, and she needed the best people she could get. I just needed her to accept that I was never going to be among them.

Madden watched as I placed the parking slip on the dashboard, watched as May and Quentin got out of the car, both of them sparkling with the soft haze of their own human disguises. May had tweaked hers to make her look less like my twin sister and more like a distant relative, or maybe just a person with one of those faces, frequently mistaken for someone else. Quentin fit right into the collegiate setting: the right age, the right level of awkward formality, even the right footwear. If we needed someone to talk to students without being flagged as an investigator, the job would be his. Which left . . .

"All right, Madden, you're here to help us follow Gillian's trail," I said. "Can you do that in your current shape, or do you need to be on four legs?"

"Four legs work best for something like this, and I can get in anywhere I need to be, but I don't know what your daughter smells like," he said. He paused before adding uncomfortably, "Before Ardy asked me to come here, I didn't realize you *had* a daughter."

"She's human."

He frowned, opening his mouth like he was going to ask a question. Then he caught himself and shook his head. "It's none of my business. Do you have anything of hers?"

"Not yet, but we can get something when we visit her dorm," I said. "I'd still like you to be able to pick up on any trails that might be around there."

Madden looked at me carefully. "Do you think one of *us* did this? You said she was human."

How to explain my family, my relationship with my daughter, without wasting time I no longer felt we had to spare? There wasn't an easy way to do it. I shook my head.

"She wasn't always entirely human, and when she was very young, people knew she was mine," I said. "She's been taken before by people who wanted to hurt me. It could happen again." Last time, it had been Rayseline Torquill.

I went cold.

Raysel was asleep; she hadn't done this. But before she had kidnapped my daughter, she'd been working with Oleander de Merelands as part of a complicated plan to kill her parents and convince me that I was the one responsible. Oleander—who was dead now, and the world would forgive me if I wasn't losing any sleep over that—had been cruel, and ruthless, and willing to do whatever it took to achieve her goals.

She had also been Simon Torquill's lover.

Simon, who knew I had a child. Simon, whose own fall from grace had begun with the loss of his daughter, who he believed was still missing. Losing his way home had stripped all knowledge of August's return from his mind, since knowing she was safe would have given him too much to hold onto. Simon, who knew that the best way to hurt a parent was through their children.

But even when he'd been so deeply embroiled in his villainy that he'd been willing to attack his own family, he'd done his best to make sure none of those attacks would be fatal ones. Even when he'd transformed me into a fish, he'd done it to save me from the far worse fate that his mistress had intended for me. I believed he would lie, and cheat, and kill to get what he wanted. I also believed that he still loved my mother. He wouldn't hurt her grandchild.

Unfortunately, Simon wasn't the only one who knew Gillian existed. Anyone who'd been in or around the false Queen's Court before my disappearance could easily have met her.

"Too many people know about her," I concluded, shaking the chill away and focusing on Madden. "Can you shift before we go in? Having a dog with us from the start will be less unusual than suddenly acquiring one."

"Especially if you're willing to wear a vest," said May.

"Sure," said Madden, and stepped away, moving into the shadow of the car. It was close enough to the wall that no one could have easily seen him, even if his outline hadn't blurred and melted as soon as he was behind cover. When he emerged, it was on four legs, with a plumed tail waving wildly behind him. The illusions he'd been using to look human were still intact, as transformed as the rest of him: instead of projecting a genial, ordinary man, they projected a genial, ordinary dog, a Golden Retriever that was maybe a little large for the breed, but nothing to attract any real attention.

"May?" I asked.

"On it." She removed a pair of hair ties from her wrist and pulled a scarf out of her pocket, walking over to kneel in front of Madden. With her free hand, she scooped a few pine needles and some shards of bark off the pavement, only hesitating for a second before she grabbed a broken chunk of a green glass bottle.

"Was a farmer had a dog, and Bingo was his name-o," she chanted, beginning to weave the pine needles into a chain connected to the hair ties at either end. "B-I-N-G-O, and Bingo was his name-o." She wrapped the scarf around the glass and chain, tapped it twice, and shook the whole thing free. It crackled and stretched as it moved, until she was holding a long leather leash attached to a collar from which the appropriate tags jingled. That explained the glass: nothing better for faking metal.

The scarf had become a black vest with "working dog" stitched on the sides, and a helpful pictogram advising people not to pet. Madden stood patiently while May put the vest on him, although he flattened his ears in displeasure when she fastened the collar around his neck.

"It's still braided pine needles and bark," she said, holding the leash as she straightened. "If you pull too hard, it'll break. Keep that in mind and try not to pull unless you're trying to get away."

Madden made a noise of acknowledgment. I rocked onto my heels, vibrating with the tension of wanting to get this over with, wanting to get this *done*.

"Come on," I said. "This way."

Knowing Walther and Cassandra—and growing up in the Bay Area—means I've spent enough time on the UC Berkeley campus to be familiar with its general layout, if not with all the little details I would have learned if I'd been a student or a full-time resident of one of its charming captive creeks. There *are* fae who live on campus, the wilder kind who swear fealty to no liege lord and mostly want to be left alone. I made a mental note to seek some of them out and ask whether they'd seen anything. It was unlikely. "Unlikely" has never been a good enough excuse to leave an avenue unexplored.

We walked from the parking lot lengthwise across the main school, passing groups of students, tables asking us to sign petitions or join clubs, and other people who looked like they were just passing through, taking advantage of the clean, safe, car-free passageway provided by the campus. It was strange seeing all this by the light of day. Most of the time, if I was in Berkeley, it was dark, and there were few people around.

Some of the students—not all, not even most, but enough to be noticeable—walked ringed in the glitter of their own human disguises. They nodded at us as we passed, but they didn't do anything to draw attention from mortal eyes. UC Berkeley, like Golden Gate Park, is neutral territory, claimed by none of the two-penny nobles or ravenous monarchs who divide and subdivide the Bay Area. Education is for everyone, royal or radical or in-between.

Quentin looked around with open curiosity as we walked,

drinking everything in. I nudged him with my elbow. He jumped, glancing guiltily at me.

"You could enroll, you know," I said. "I'm sure April would be happy to fake whatever paperwork you needed." April O'Leary is a friend of ours, a cyber-Dryad whose command of computer systems means she can make almost anything real, at least on paper. When it comes to false IDs or digital paper trails, she's the girl to see.

Besides, she owes me. Her mother, January, had been dead, and now she wasn't, thanks to my willingness to help them out. If Quentin asked for something as simple as a high school transcript and a valid mortal ID, April wouldn't hesitate to help.

"Maybe," he said uncomfortably. "I have a lot to do. I don't know if it would be a good idea for me to take that kind of time."

"Think about it." As Crown Prince of the Westlands, Quentin was expected to learn as much as possible about the continent he's eventually going to rule. Going to college would certainly be an educational experience. His parents might not like what it taught him, but hey, his parents probably didn't like most of what he was learning from me, and they hadn't taken him back to Toronto.

We reached the edge of the campus, where it spilled into the tree-lined avenues of the city itself. Small neighborhood stores warred for space among the satellite campus buildings and the dorms. We kept walking.

According to Cliff's text, Gillian was in off-campus housing, not a dorm but not one of the sororities either. A residence building rented by a coalition of students, probably from an alumnus or one of the satellite schools. It gave them a place to live without forcing them to share space with as many people as they would have encountered in a proper dormitory.

The trade-off was worse security and more isolation—good when it came to privacy, bad when it came to anyone seeing what happened when, say, the whole place was vandalized. Madden whined, scenting trouble a beat before we came around a bend in the sidewalk and saw the stately old Victorian house with the caution tape around the outside of the yard and the police cars parked along the sidewalk. Their lights were off, and their sirens were no longer screaming, but that didn't matter. The sight of them was enough to knock the breath out of my body and leave my skin feeling suddenly too tight. May put a hand on my arm, supposedly to steady me, but really to steady us both.

This was a crime scene. A crime had been committed here. A crime that had involved my daughter, my *child*, who was now missing.

I hit the base of the driveway and kept walking, faster all the time, until it felt like I was barely on the slow side of breaking into a run. A man on the porch saw us coming and moved, presumably to tell me I couldn't be here.

Like hell I couldn't. I grabbed a 7-11 receipt from my pocket and held it up, chanting, "The owl and the pussycat went to sea in a beautiful pea-green boat."

The scent of cut grass and copper lanced through the air, sharp and bloody, accompanied by a bolt of pain behind my temples. It passed quickly, but I took it for the warning it was. I hadn't slept, I hadn't eaten, and flower magic isn't my strong suit. There's nothing of Titania in my bloodline, and illusions come through her. I can do blood magic until I run out of blood, but flower magic wears on me fast and heavy.

The man's eyes became unfocused as my spell slammed into him. He looked at the receipt, not seeing it yet, waiting for me to tell him what it was.

"October Daye, private investigator," I said, not bothering to name the people with me. The spell would cover them as well, but it was better if I didn't try to define more than I had to. Magic works best when it's allowed to be a little fluid, to fit into the cracks in the world. "I'm here about the disappearance of Gillian Marks."

The vagueness fled the man's face, replaced by a vague distaste. "Ah," he said. "Our little runaway. Her father called you?"

In a manner of speaking. "Yes."

"Her room is on the second floor."

He was being more accommodating than I had any right to expect. Either my spell had hit him substantially harder than anticipated, or Cliff had already managed to piss off the entire investigative team. After the scene he'd made back at the house, I honestly wasn't sure which seemed more likely. Maybe both.

"Appreciated," I said, and stepped around him, the rest of the group following at my heels. Madden kept his nose pressed to the ground, sniffing his way through the house. Even without context for the scents, he'd be able to find and follow them later.

Speaking of scents . . . halfway up the stairs, out of sight of the men downstairs and whoever might be waiting upstairs, I stopped, closed my eyes, and breathed in deeply, looking for traces of magic. Then I coughed, catching myself against the wall with one hand before I could topple over.

When I opened my eyes, all three of my friends were looking at me with open concern. Quentin spoke first.

"What the hell?" he asked.

I shook my head. "I should have realized—we're on a *college campus.*"

May and Madden frowned, confused. Once again Quentin, bless him, figured it out right away. His eyes widened.

"Oh," he said. "The fairy brides."

I nodded.

Going to school—high school, college, even elementary school, although that's more likely to be as a librarian or preschool teacher than as a student—is one of the classic ways for purebloods to figure out what's changed in the human world while they were spending a century in quiet contemplation as a linden tree. It's an environment where people are supposed to be a little culturally "off," a little outside of the norm. People go to college to reinvent themselves. For the fae, that can sometimes be literal. The term for that kind of exposure to the mortal world is "playing fairy bride," regardless of the genders of the people involved. I'd been a fairy bride when I was with Cliff. Quentin had been a fairy bride when he was attending a mortal high school.

Based on the layers upon layers of old and faded magic lingering in this stairwell, Berkeley had enough fairy brides to buy out a David's Bridal and still need a good source of silver slippers. Every imaginable scent seemed to have been dropped here at one point or another—and since this was a women's residence hall, those scents were mixed with a healthy quantity of mortal perfume, body spray, and deodorant. It was like being assaulted by a farmer's market and a Macy's makeup counter at the same time.

"Do you smell oranges?" asked May tightly.

I knew what she meant immediately. Simon Torquill—our most likely suspect—smelled of smoke and rotten oranges. At least he did now. When he'd been a better man, acting for himself and the good of his family rather than at the command of Evening Winterrose, his magic had smelled like smoke and mulled apple cider. It was a much more pleasant combination. I breathed in again, more shallowly this time, before shaking my head.

"Yes and no," I said. "Someone around here likes orange blossom essential oil, but there's no magic in it, and it doesn't match Simon. He wasn't here."

That didn't mean he wasn't responsible, only that he had another way in, or had hired someone to do his dirty work for him. If he had come under cover of darkness, using a charm he hadn't crafted to hide himself, he could have been in and out without leaving a single trace of his magic behind.

I hated to be so paranoid. I didn't see where I had another choice.

"For magic, I've got . . . pine pitch, maple syrup, parsley, some kind of apple blossom, cardamom, and cinnamon. A *lot* of cinnamon. Nothing clear enough to point to a specific person." I started walking again, swallowing the urge to sneeze.

Some of the scents were almost familiar, although none were complete enough for me to identify. I had probably encountered their owners in social situations, at Shadowed Hills or in Arden's court or even back in the halls of Home. Not all of Devin's kids had been magically weak, and it wasn't unthinkable that some of them could throw a spell far enough to leave a trail behind. But they were tangled and layered on top of each other, and in the absence of anything that I could tie to Simon, I didn't have a trail to follow. It was better, for the moment, to keep moving.

Almost all the doors at the top of the stairs were closed. The one second from the end stood open, revealing an unmade bed with a girl in a UC Berkeley sweatshirt sitting atop it, head in her hands. There were no police in sight. I spared a moment to wonder where they had all gone before stepping forward and rapping lightly on the doorframe, trying not to sound too aggressive. The last thing I wanted to do was startle the poor kid.

"Excuse me," I said. "Is this Gillian's room?"

The girl gasped, jerking her head out of her hands and sitting bolt upright. Her hair was purple, clearly dyed if the brown roots were anything to go by, and her skin was pale, save for the hectic blotches of sunburn across her nose and cheeks. Either she was very fond of using glitter gel to accent her eye makeup, or she was wearing fairy ointment. The latter was confirmed when her eyes flicked to Madden and she gasped again, scrambling to her feet.

"Are you—I mean, is this—are you *her*?" she squeaked.

I lifted an eyebrow. "Right pronoun, at least for me, but I need more than that to answer one way or the other. Is this Gillian Marks' room?"

"Yes," said the girl. She was still staring at me like she thought there was a good chance I might decide to eat her. Not my companions, although she kept giving Madden little sidelong glances: just me. "You're really her. You're Gillian's mother."

Oh. "Yes," I said. "Are you her roommate?"

To my shock and dismay, the girl dropped to one knee like she was getting ready to swear fealty in some medieval court. May, who had to share at least some percentage of that dismay, gaped at her. Quentin, who was more accustomed to people bowing to him, snickered.

The girl raised her head. "My name is Jocelyn Lewis, and I am yours to command," she said solemnly.

"Uh," I said. "Or not. I don't really need any vassals today. What I need is for you to stand up and tell me what happened here."

"When she said her birth mother's name was October, I thought she had to be pulling my leg, but then she said she'd dodged a bullet by taking her father's last name, and I realized she meant *you*, she was *your* daughter, the only child of a hero of the realm, and she somehow chose human, you let her choose human, you hid her away so she could live her life even though she didn't want to be immortal." Jocelyn continued staring at me, starry-eyed. "I never knew a hero could be so *good*."

"You have fans," said Quentin, a note of malicious glee in his tone. "You have fans who keep track of what you're doing, and some of them share a room with your daughter."

"Shut up," I said. "This isn't the time."

He sobered immediately, regret sweeping the glee away. "I'm sorry."

"It's all right. I . . . it's fine." We were all running on not enough sleep and way too much adrenaline. Jokes and prodding at each other was how we stayed sane. Usually. Right now, in this strange place with this strange woman—this strange girl, and sweet Oberon, I had never been that young—kneeling in front of me, I just wanted to get things done. "Please, can you get up? I need answers, and this isn't helping."

"I am so sorry." Jocelyn finally got to her feet and sat back on

the bed, eyes huge within their surrounding rings of fairy ointment. "I just never expected to see you in person. You're a legend."

This was getting more uncomfortable by the second, and it wasn't
helping me find my daughter. "Were you here last night? Do you
know what happened? Anything that maybe you couldn't tell the
human police?"

May let go of Madden's leash. He began sniffing his way around
the edges of the room, focusing on the bed Jocelyn hadn't been
sitting on. It wasn't hard to guess why: the process of elimination
told me the second bed had to belong to Gillian. It was unmade,
sheets and blankets twisted in a lover's knot by her nighttime
thrashing. A corkboard hung on the wall above it, dozens of snap-
shots tacked up with brightly colored pins. There were pictures of
Cliff, either by himself or with Gillian and Miranda. There were
pictures of Miranda, staged the same way. One, of Miranda with
her cheek resting against the top of Gillian's head while Gilly
laughed and hugged her, seemed specifically designed to be an
arrow through my heart. I looked at it, and it *ached*. That should
have been me in the picture. That should have been me with my
arms around my child.

"I, um. My mother was . . . is . . . a changeling. A Gwragen."
Jocelyn stumbled over the word like it wasn't something she said
very often. Thin-blooded, then, probably weak enough never to
have been offered the Changeling's Choice. Her own children
would be merlins at best, if not entirely mortal. "I sleep at night,
like a *human*." The self-loathing in her voice made my stomach
clench.

"There's nothing wrong with being human," I said, fighting to
keep my voice gentle. I needed her help. I needed her to talk to me.
Snapping at her for being distracted while my daughter was missing wasn't going to help anything. "Gillian is human, and she's
amazing. You know that."

Jocelyn nodded, sniffling gratefully.

I pushed back another jet of irritation. "If you sleep at night,
does that mean you slept through the whole thing? Was she here
when you went to bed?"

"No. She was going to be out late, studying with friends. I don't
think she likes me much." Jocelyn wrinkled her nose. "I don't understand why she never wants to talk about you. I mean, I know

she doesn't know anything about Faerie, but I never said anything that would have broken secrecy. I just wanted to hear about you. What kind of person you are, what it's like to be your family."

The clenching in my gut got worse. This wide-eyed girl had tried to make Gillian talk about me, even after she had clearly been rebuffed. "I see," I said, abandoning the effort to keep the chill from my voice. "Do you know where she studied? How many people would have been with her? Do you have any of their names?"

Jocelyn's eyes got wider and wider until, finally, she burst into tears. "You're m-m-mad at me!" she wailed.

I winced. The human police might not be up here, but they were still in the house. If they came upstairs and found us interrogating Gilly's roommate, they would probably be suspicious at best, and angry at worst. "Please, calm down," I said.

"Let me," said Quentin. With a wry half-smile, he added, "I'm nobody, remember?"

Numbly, I stayed where I was as Quentin crossed the room and sat on the bed next to Jocelyn, putting one hand over hers. He might look human at the moment, but he was still Daoine Sidhe, among the most beautiful and most enthralling of the fae. He turned the full force of his attention on the girl, and for a moment, I thought she might swoon.

Literally. She seemed like the swooning type, all fluttering hands and overplayed fragility. How Gillian had been able to share a room with her for more than an hour without breaking her nose, I might never know.

No. I shoved the thought away, refusing to let it take root in the fertile soil of my fear. I would know, because I would ask her when I found her. That would be my payment for bringing her home. I couldn't ask her to let me be her mother again, couldn't make her let me into her life, but I could ask why she hadn't punched this simpering child the minute she'd refused to let the topic of Gillian's family drop.

"Hey," said Quentin, all teen idol earnestness. "I know this is probably overwhelming, and I get that you're scared. I'd be scared, too. But we need your help. We need to know where Gillian would have gone."

"I know you," sighed Jocelyn dreamily. "You're Quentin, her squire. You're in the Mists as part of a blind fosterage, but *everyone* knows you just have to be noble. I mean, nothing else makes sense, not with her being a hero and you being so handsome."

May and I exchanged a look.

Quentin, for all that he seemed increasingly uncomfortable, nodded. "That's right, I'm Quentin. It's a pleasure to meet you. But look, we're really worried about Gillian, and we need to find her as soon as possible. Is there *anything* you can tell us about where she would have been last night? Anything at all?"

The dreamy look in Jocelyn's eyes turned calculating. "I might be able to show you, if you took me with you to find her. I promise I won't be underfoot. I know how things work. I can be helpful. I can be useful. You'll see."

Madden, who had been snuffling at the space under Gilly's bed, pulled his head out and made a small woofing noise. He didn't like this idea.

Yeah, well, neither did I. But if that was what we had to do to get this girl to show us where Gillian and her friends would have been before the incident, I was going to go with it. "Do you know where they found her car?" I asked.

"It was near where her study group meets," said Jocelyn. She stood, pulling her hand away from Quentin's with obvious reluctance. "Let me get my coat and we can go. You won't leave without me, will you? Promise you won't leave without me!"

"Sure," I said. "We promise."

She beamed, bright as a Christmas tree, and ran out of the room, leaving the four of us alone. May and I exchanged another look. Quentin rose, wiping his hand on the side of his leg.

"I don't know whether to be terrified or impressed," he said. "Are all changelings like her?"

"You know better," I said mildly. "There's no such thing as 'all' when you're talking about people."

His cheeks reddened. "Sorry," he said. "I guess I do."

"Apology accepted," I said. "Now come on. We have maybe a minute to search this place without anyone watching us. Go."

I moved toward Gillian's side of the room, feeling simultaneously like I was invading her privacy and like I was finally entering a place I'd been standing outside for years. Her clothes were stuffed into a rickety dresser that looked like it had been purchased from one of those flatpack outfits, put together with a wrench and a lot of swearing. Cliff had never been the handy one in our relationship. He had probably bled all . . .

Bled all . . .

There was blood in Gilly's car. There was blood in my *daughter's* car. The police had found blood, and the blood was probably hers, and she hated me, and I was going to need to roll her memories across my tongue in order to see what she had seen in the moments before she bled. I would need to slide myself into her, into all the things she'd never wanted me to see, all the thoughts she'd never wanted me to share.

Under those circumstances, going through her dresser wasn't an invasion of privacy. It was a normal thing a frightened parent might do. What I was planning to do when we got to her car . . . *that* was an invasion of privacy. It was unforgivable. And I was going to do it anyway.

Gillian's clothes were neatly folded—surprisingly so for a college student; even Quentin didn't keep his dresser quite that organized— and smelled oddly herbal. I leaned closer, taking a deep breath, and coughed as I recoiled. May and Quentin turned away from their own investigations to stare at me. Madden flattened his ears with an inquisitive whine. I coughed again, signaling for them to stay where they were, and dug into the clothes.

I found what I was looking for at the bottom of the drawer, wedged into the far corner, where it was unlikely to get accidentally dislodged in the process of pulling out a pair of socks. It was a small mesh sachet, tied off with red-and-white ribbons, packed with herbs that made me want to drop the whole thing. Touching it made me feel dirty, slimy, like I had no business being here.

Breathing as shallowly as I could, I lifted the sachet and took another sniff. Grudgingly, my magic sorted through the individual components, naming and labeling them. Fennel and kingcup and St. John's wort; gorse and dill and kale. I blinked at the last one. "Kale?" I muttered and took one more sniff. Scots kale, to be specific, an old, almost heirloom strain.

"What is it?" asked May.

I dropped the sachet on the floor. Relief washed over me as soon as I wasn't in contact with the disgusting thing. Sadly, relief didn't come with a decongestant. "It's a marshwater charm," I said, voice thick with sudden snot.

May's eyes widened.

"What?" asked Quentin. "It's not wet."

"Marshwater charms are a class, not a specific description," I said, wiping my hand on my pants and glaring at the sachet. We needed to take it with us. I could see that. But I did *not* want to touch it again. "A lot of changeling tricks are considered marshwater. Small, simple, mostly self-powering if you put them together right."

"Like alchemy," said Quentin.

"Surprisingly, yes," I said. I looked around the room until I spotted a piece of tin foil in one of the trash baskets. "Get the foil. I don't want any of us touching this thing."

"But what *is* it?" he asked.

"It's a collection of herbs specifically designed to repel the fae," I said grimly. May and I exchanged a look. "There's no way she would have known how to make this without someone showing her."

"Lovely," muttered May.

"Yeah," I agreed, and went back to rooting through the dresser while Quentin wrapped the sachet in foil.

There was a sachet in every drawer. By the time I closed the last one, my nose was running and my eyes were burning, like the allergy attack I'd never particularly wanted to have. Even worse, my natural tendency to heal from every little thing didn't seem to be kicking in. If I wanted to go playing with unfamiliar magical items, I could just pay the consequences.

I was wiping my eyes and trying not to sneeze again when Jocelyn came thundering up the stairs, a denim jacket clutched in both hands. She stopped in the doorway, eyes going wide before her face fell in sudden, sympathetic sorrow.

"Oh, I didn't even *think*," she wailed. "She's your *daughter* and I was just talking about how amazing you are, not how much you must miss her and how scared you must be. Well, don't you worry. I'll take you right straight to where they found her car. You can find out everything you need to know."

"Here's hoping," I said uneasily. She must have taken my red eyes and runny nose as the aftereffects of weeping. Good. Better that than having her figure out the truth. Her blood was thin enough that the charms hadn't been bothering her, and I didn't want her to suddenly realize what they were or what they were supposed to have been doing.

There was nothing in the room to indicate who might have taken Gilly. I didn't like those sachets, and I desperately wanted to know where they'd come from, but they didn't feel malicious to me. Whoever had made those for Gilly had been trying to keep the fae away from her. Did that mean she had been in danger? Or did it just mean that she was going to a school where a certain amount of magical thinking was innate in the student body, and someone had managed to get lucky?

I needed to talk to Bridget. If anyone would know how many of the students had decided they needed to put up wards against Tinker Bell, it would be her.

Jocelyn continued to beam, smile only wavering for an instant when she saw Quentin slip the foil-wrapped sachet into his pocket. "What's that?" she asked suspiciously. "I don't think I'm supposed to let people take things."

I refrained from pointing out that she probably wasn't supposed to let people into the room, either, or leave them alone while she ran off to get her coat. It wouldn't do us any good to alienate the closest thing we currently had to a lead. "My lunch," I said. "The dog was getting way too interested in it, and he needs to keep a clear nose."

As if on cue, Madden walked over and stuck his nose against the crotch of her jeans in classic canine fashion. Jocelyn laughed shrilly and bent to start patting his head. While she had clearly been able to see through the illusions that made him look like a Golden retriever, she gave no indication she suspected him of being anything other than some kind of fancy fairy dog. The education her mother had given her on the fae had clearly skipped over a few places. Most people aren't that comfortable petting the Cu Sidhe.

I nodded toward Quentin while Jocelyn was distracted, signaling him to come forward. He grimaced but did as he was bid, stepping up and putting his hand on Jocelyn's shoulder.

"Hey," he said. "Lead the way?"

Jocelyn blushed and dimpled as she turned to do exactly that. Quentin followed. I picked up Madden's leash and looked to May.

"Don't-look-here and keep searching," I said tightly. "I'll text you with our location."

May sighed. "I thought you might say that," she said. Raking her fingers through the air, she gathered two handfuls of shadows and muttered something under her breath in a language I didn't know. The air rippled, folding around her. As soon as I looked away, I knew I'd lose track of her. Don't-look-here spells don't make people literally invisible. They just make them . . . difficult. Difficult to see, difficult to care about seeing. As long as May didn't break anything or otherwise call the kind of attention to herself that couldn't be ignored, she'd be fine.

"See if there's anything else around here like those sachets," I said. "I don't like them. Something's off about this."

If she answered me, it was quiet enough and far enough behind the spell that I couldn't make it out. I turned and followed the others down the stairs.

They had just reached the bottom—and more importantly, Jocelyn was just starting to look put out over my absence—when I got there. She relaxed at the sight of me. "I was afraid we'd lost you!" she said chirpily.

"I'm difficult to lose," I replied. "Lead the way."

Voices around the side of the house alerted me to the location of the missing police as we stepped off the porch and onto the lawn. Jocelyn made a shushing noise and motioned for us to follow her away from the house, waiting until we were a good distance down the sidewalk before she said, "I sort of didn't tell anyone you were here. How did you get in, anyway?"

"Magic," I said.

Predictably, her eyes lit up. "Oh, wow. Oh, gosh. I can't wait to tell Mom I met you. Did I tell you she used to know you, when she was my age? She—"

Jocelyn kept chattering as we walked down the sidewalk, Quentin and I looking carefully in all directions, Madden keeping his nose pressed to the ground like he could sniff out all of Berkeley, like he could solve any mystery if he breathed in deeply enough. I understood the feeling. More and more, my magic was leading me by the nose, telling me what I needed to know as long as I was careful not to catch a cold.

Of course, right now, my nose was so stuffed up from inhaling that weird herbal mix that I was sort of impressed I could still breathe at all. Gillian had been turning herself into a big walking allergen.

Allergen . . . "Hey, Jocelyn," I said casually, interrupting her explanation of this one time her mother had been in San Francisco and saw a real *kelpie*, "do you have allergies?"

Jocelyn wrinkled her nose. "I never used to, but they've been really bad this semester," she admitted. Then she brightened. "Why? Are there some sort of magic flowers that bloom once a century getting pollen everywhere? That would explain *everything.*"

The way she talked about Faerie was almost endearing. She had the sort of wide-eyed wonder I hadn't possessed since I was a very small child. It was definitely exhausting. Only the fact that we were at UC Berkeley—a campus which I knew for a fact hosted multiple live-action roleplaying games every week, as well as meetings of the Society for Creative Anachronism—kept me from slapping my hand over her mouth and reminding her, in no uncertain terms, that Faerie is supposed to be a *secret.*

Letting her chatter didn't hurt anything. Anyone who heard her would assume she was talking about something that didn't exist. Trying to convince her to shut up would draw a lot more attention to us. And maybe if I kept telling myself that, I'd be able to believe it. The habits of secrecy had been so ground into me, for so long, that this felt like I was breaking the rules, even though I wasn't saying anything forbidden.

"Not quite," I said. "I did smell something a little funny in your room, near Gillian's desk."

"Oh." Jocelyn's face shuttered itself, expression becoming unreadable. "She doesn't do drugs, if that's what you're asking. She doesn't do *anything.* She goes to class, she studies with her friends, and she refuses to talk about anything worth talking about. You know, I asked her about bringing you to campus to see our classes once, and she said she didn't want anything to do with you? Like anyone could mean that about a hero!"

My stomach clenched again. I was suddenly grateful for the burning in my eyes. It made it harder for me to tear up.

Quentin cleared his throat. "Maybe talking like that about Toby's *daughter* when she's missing isn't really very nice, you know? Do you think you could, I dunno, cut it out?"

"Oh." Jocelyn paled. "I'm sorry. I . . . I intended no offense." If we hadn't been walking, I'm pretty sure she would have dropped to her knees in her hurry to placate me.

The more time we spent with this kid, the more I wanted to shake her mother. It was one thing to encourage a thin-blooded change-ling to learn more about her own heritage. I had no objection to that. It was something else altogether to teach her just enough to mess her up and then leave her to figure out how to interact with the world. Some of the mistakes Jocelyn was making could get her killed if she made them around the wrong people.

Not for the first time, I genuinely regretted the decisions I'd made in the aftermath of Devin's death. He'd been a terrible person. There was no question of that. He had abused the trust of the kids in his care, all of whom had deserved better. I had deserved better. Dare had deserved better. But by Oberon's eyes, at least he'd given changelings a place to go and be with people who un-derstood. He had kept them safe from everyone but himself, and that had made him a monster, but it wouldn't have been able to happen if there hadn't been a need for the so-called "safety" he provided.

I should have done more to fill the void left when he'd died. I should have been there. All of us changelings who made it to adult-hood with our hearts intact should have been there. And we hadn't been.

"None taken," I said. "Breathe."

A faint trickle of color came back into Jocelyn's cheeks. She kept walking.

The route she'd chosen took us across a different slice of campus than our walk to the residence hall. Trees blanketed the path, their fallen leaves making our footing treacherous. I inhaled the good green scent of them, trying to chase those awful herbs from my nose. We came around a curve, and the lazily flashing lights of campus police cars ground my heart to a stop.

Gillian's car—a solid, dependable-looking sedan, the sort of thing it made perfect sense to send to college with a young woman living away from home for the first time—sat at the middle of a square of caution tape. That was a good thing: it hadn't been towed or impounded yet. It was also surrounded, first by the officers who were examining it, and then by a ring of onlookers.

"Hell," I muttered, coming to a stop. "This is a problem."

The residence hall had been the site of vandalism, but not kid-napping. There had been no blood on the glass there, no reason to suspect foul play. Gillian's car, on the other hand . . .

This was a real crime scene, not a mere nuisance, and there was no way the police were going to let us anywhere near it.

Jocelyn pointed at the building beyond the car. "That's Wheeler Hall," she said. "That's where the English Department is. Gillian likes to study in their computer lab. She says it's more peaceful than studying in our room." Her tone made it clear that she disagreed with this decision.

I swallowed my first response, which was to point out that she could have just told us to go to Wheeler Hall and spared us this entire awkward walk. I also swallowed my second response, which would have been considerably less polite. In the end, I forced a shallow smile and said, "Everyone learns differently. You've been very helpful. We appreciate it."

She beamed and seemed to be waiting for something. I exchanged a glance with Quentin. He shrugged.

I looked back to her, studying her expression more carefully. For all that she was smiling like a child who'd just ridden her bike without the training wheels for the very first time, there was a calculation going on behind her eyes.

"Yes?" I said finally.

"Aren't you going to thank me?" she asked. The calculation in her eyes grew stronger.

Understanding dawned. "No," I said. I didn't bother keeping the disgust out of my voice. It belonged there. "I'm not in your debt, and I'm not accepting any responsibility for you. You are not my vassal. This was a mean trick, and you should be ashamed of yourself for trying to play it."

Faerie's relationship with gratitude is . . . well, complicated. When so many of your citizens can be bound by a careless word or a casually given promise, saying something as simple as "thank you" becomes dangerous. So it's forbidden, or at the very least, discouraged. We don't thank each other. We praise. We say: "that was a nice thing to do." We flatter. We avoid the direct and inescapable display of gratitude. Naturally, this has caused some people— almost all of them either humans who've discovered the existence of Faerie or changelings who've been shoved so far to the outskirts that they lost the shape of their own heritage—to decide that saying "thank you" acknowledges an inescapable debt between the one who says it and the one who receives it.

Jocelyn's smile guttered out like a candle in a stiff wind, and the calculation in her eyes surged to the forefront, eclipsing everything else. "It was *not* a mean trick," she said mulishly. "I only want what I'm owed. That's all. Gillian's been sharing a room with me for *months*, and this is the first time I've even seen you. I should have been her best friend by now. We should have been sitting in your kitchen telling stories and learning important things, not standing in this mess, with these," the sweep of her hand encompassed the paths and buildings around us, and the mass of gawkers who thronged around the caution tape, "people." There was a sneer in her voice on the last word.

People. Oh, oak and ash, people. Jocelyn wasn't saying anything that was actually forbidden—she sounded like an ordinary college kid being weird rather than anything more dangerous—but she was going to get there, now that she was angry, and I didn't know what to do about it.

From the stricken look on his face, neither did Quentin. His eyes were getting wider and wider, and he was staring at Jocelyn like she was a nightmare he'd never considered could be real. Madden whined, pressing against my leg.

Jocelyn's eyes narrowed, her lower lip pushing out into a pout. "You *owe* me," she repeated.

"That strikes me as unlikely, Miss Lewis, but if you'd like to come see me during office hours, we can discuss the school's mechanisms for settling grievances." The new voice was female, haunted by the ghost of an Irish accent, like the speaker had been in California for so long that even her vowels were applying for citizenship.

My shoulders, locked tight with stress and fear, relaxed just the smallest bit, and I turned, a weary smile on my face. "Hi, Bridget," I said.

"Didn't expect to see you here this morning," she replied, giving me a quick nod while most of her attention remained fixed on Jocelyn. "Miss Lewis? Don't you have something else you should be doing? Something *elsewhere*?"

Jocelyn looked back and forth from Bridget to me, eyes wide and mouth hanging open. Catching herself, she closed it with a snap, and spat, "I should have known you were working together to keep me out. I should have *known*. I hope you *rot*."

She spun on her heel and stalked away before any of us could reply, hurrying to get the last word in. We let her. If it meant she would actually leave, she could have the last word, the last sentence, the last soliloquy. I didn't need it as much as I needed this to be over.

"Well," said Bridget into the pause that followed. "That was bracing. Now what in the world are you doing here?"

I stared at her, and I couldn't think of a single thing to say.

FIVE

SILENCE STRETCHED BETWEEN US. The students who'd come to watch the police at work talked and pointed, not noticing our dismay. The wind rustled through the leaves and the sound of cars drifted over from the nearby neighborhoods, but in that moment, I would have sworn that everything else in the universe had simply *stopped*. The world was frozen, or it should have been. It should have shown at least that much respect.

Slowly, Bridget frowned. "Toby? What's wrong?"

I shook my head.

Bridget had applied the fairy ointment to her eyes more lightly than Jocelyn had, and with a defter hand, blending it into her makeup so that it added a certain shimmer but didn't make her look quite so much like she had an addiction to glitter gel. It helped that her supply was almost certainly more refined than Jocelyn's. Her husband, Etienne, is Sylvester Torquill's seneschal, and as such, has access to the finest ingredients in the duchy. Even if he can't mix the stuff himself, he can give the components to Bridget, who can pass them along to Walther. Walther isn't just one of the best alchemists I've ever known, he's something of a social activist among the fae and has been working for decades to make simple alchemical tinctures accessible to changelings and fae who live outside the Courts.

It's an admirable thing to do. It's even more admirable considering that now that his aunt is back on the throne of Silences, he could easily go home and live the pampered, privileged life of a court alchemist, adored by his people for his part in getting their Kingdom back, wanting for nothing. Instead, he chose to stay in the Mists, to stay at UC Berkeley, and to keep supplying people like Bridget with the fairy ointment they need to be a part of our world.

Bridget isn't a changeling. She's as human as they come, a fact evidenced by the traces of gray at her temples. When she married Etienne, she got a special dispensation from the crown to continue working in the mortal world while also living with him at Shadowed Hills. It helped that she had made it clear that she wouldn't move to Shadowed Hills if it meant giving up her job, and where she goes, Chelsea goes. Etienne loves his wife, but he dotes on his daughter.

Bridget gets to be human and part of Faerie at the same time. She gets to have everything I used to think I wanted, and I can't even hate her for it, because she's too kind, and because I don't want it anymore. I haven't wanted it in a long time.

"Did Jocelyn call you here somehow?" she asked, in a slower, more carefully measured tone. "She hasn't got the authority to do that. I know her mum. I'll give her a call, remind her this is neutral territory—" Her voice dropped toward the end of the sentence, automatically shielding her words from prying ears.

I shook my head and gestured toward Gillian's car. "I'm here for her."

"The missing girl?" There was no recognition in Bridget's voice. She sounded curious, yes, but not concerned on my behalf. Maybe a bit on Gillian's. Bridget was a professor, after all, and she had to worry about her students. "Who called you?"

"Her father." My mouth was suddenly dry. I swallowed, fighting the urge to look away as I said, "My ex-boyfriend."

Bridget's eyes widened with sudden, if flawed, understanding. "Oh, my. He called you to help him find his daughter? It's kind of you to be willing. I know many people who wouldn't even try, in your position—"

"Our daughter."

"What?"

"He called me to find *our* daughter. Gillian's my child."

Understanding faded, replaced by momentary confusion. "How can that be possible? She's . . ." Bridget stopped, sobering. "Oh. I see."

"Yeah," I agreed.

Chelsea Ames was born a classic changeling: fae father, human mother. Half and half. Unfortunately for everyone involved—especially Chelsea—she got all her father's power and none of his control. She had been teleporting wildly, ripping open doors that Oberon himself had intended should stay sealed. In order to stop her, in order to *save* her, I'd been forced to give her a modified version of the Changeling's Choice: did she want to be fae, or did she want to be human? She had chosen fae. I had pulled the human blood from her veins and left her immortal and weeping and safe. Finally safe.

Chelsea was the inverse of my own daughter in more ways than one. Both had been raised by their human parents. Both had discovered Faerie in the most painful, traumatic ways possible. But Gillian had chosen to be human, to give up any trace of the fantastic in her heritage, and, because it was only a choice if I honored it, I'd done as she had asked.

"I'm so sorry," said Bridget, raising a hand to her mouth. "I had no idea."

"Most people don't. It's not exactly something I go around advertising." With no fae blood, Gillian had no protection from magic. If her abduction had anything to do with me . . .

I would carry that guilt for the rest of my life, and no one would ever be able to make it any lighter.

"No," said Bridget. "I can see where you wouldn't. I'm *so* sorry. When I heard it was Gillian who'd been taken—"

"Wait." I cut her off, staring. "You know my daughter?"

"She took my introductory folklore course this year," said Bridget. "She has a quick mind, and an excellent eye for detail. You should be proud."

I wanted to be. I *ached* to be. Somehow, all I could feel was a numb absence of surprise. A whole college campus, and of course Gillian wound wind up in a class with one of the two professors I actually knew, of course she would share something with one of the people around me, but never with me.

Never, ever with me.

"I need to get a closer look at that car," I said, stooping to collect a few smashed, muddy oak leaves from the path. It had been a long, dry December, without half the rain we should have had, but there was still mud. There was always mud. "Quentin, you and

Madden stay here with Bridget. Bridget, we have something we need you to look at once I'm done."

"My office isn't far from here, and I have a TA who can take my first class if needed," she agreed, without hesitation. "Anything I can do to bring your girl home, you know I'll do it, October. I owe you the world. I always will."

"I'll keep an eye on the crowd," said Quentin, taking Madden's leash. I offered him a quick, tight smile and walked toward the trees that ringed the area.

Berkeley is an urban campus with delusions of being some sort of pastoral paradise. For all that it's surrounded by city on all sides, the architects were careful to leave space for trees and long stretches of green lawn. They even worked to maintain the natural creeks that cut across the ground where they were planning to put their school. In that regard, it's one of the most *fae* mortal places I've ever been. They built with the land, accenting and acknowledging its features, rather than building against it. The end result was a school which, despite being surrounded by city on all sides, does its best to hide that city behind a veil of trees, bushes, and artfully designed structures that look like they belonged somewhere old-fashioned and wild. Squirrels run rampant across the campus, keeping company with less common raccoons, deer, and even hawks, which view the place as a glorious buffet. When trees fall, they're allowed to decay in place, as long as they don't block walkways, and even during the worst droughts, everything grows green, green, green.

Sliding down the nearest creek bank on the sides of my feet was commonplace enough to be unremarkable—people in Berkeley do that sort of thing all the time, as a shortcut, looking for a place to have a picnic, or just because they're goofing around—and put me at least six feet below the general ground level of the campus. In an instant and in plain sight, I had rendered myself hidden. I looked around, checking for lurking mortals, before I walked into the shadow cast by a nearby bridge. I would rather be safe a hundred times than sorry once.

Crumbling the leaves I had gathered in my hand, I chanted, "True, I talk of dreams, which are the children of an idle brain, begot of nothing but vain fantasy, which is as thin of substance as the air."

Illusions are hard for me. Having an incantation to hang them on helps. It's not the words that matter. It's the intent behind them, the familiarity and comfort with the idea they describe. That's why most of my verbal magic involves Shakespeare, song lyrics, or nursery rhymes. Right now, I needed the boost. Anger makes my magic easier, but fear? Loss? All they do is slow me down, muddy my thinking, and make it harder to cast anything concrete.

The smell of freshly cut grass and copper swirled around me, overwhelming the natural, earthy scent of creek and mud and shadowed places. I closed my eyes and concentrated on feeling the magic fill my hands, stretching and massaging it until I could drape it over myself and pin it fast. What I was casting had to be the best don't-look-here I'd ever spun, good enough to get me through the crowd in full sunlight, to get me to the car. To give me the time to look around, gather what I needed, and get away again. It had to be *perfect*.

The magic swirled through my fingers like ribbons crafted of air and shadow, slippery, trying to escape. I held it tighter, forcing myself to breathe. *I will do this,* I thought fiercely. *For Gillian, I will do this.*

There was a time when any don't-look-here would have been at the absolute edges of my capabilities. Now, only the scope and intricacy of this one rendered it so difficult. I bore down, grinding my teeth until there was a brief jolt of pain and the strengthening taste of blood at the back of my throat. The spell snapped into place. That pain faded—physical pain always does—and was replaced by an even sharper spike of pain behind my temples as the magic-burn settled in.

I used to think I got magic-burn because I was so weak. Now I understand that it means I've pushed myself too far, and it can happen to anyone. Oberon probably got magic-burn. As a consequence of raising a continent or something, sure, but that didn't matter. The experience itself is universal. That should probably be reassuring. Mostly, it's just tiring.

Opening my eyes, I tried to look at my own hands. They glittered and wavered, refusing to come into focus. It was an odd effect, and it would make walking interesting, but if the spell was hitting me, it would work on all of them up there. Maybe not Bridget, depending on the quality of her fairy ointment. That was fine. She could keep an eye on me.

Climbing up the embankment when I couldn't see my own feet

was harder than I expected. In the end, I closed my eyes and let memory guide me. That was easier than dealing with my sudden excision from the landscape.

I walked across the plaza in full view of the sun, and no one turned to watch me go, and I didn't cast a shadow. I was finally what my mother had always wanted me to be: totally invisible, absent from the world around me. Quentin didn't even glance my way as I walked past him, although Bridget's head turned slightly as her eyes followed me, and Madden sniffed at the air, more curious than cautious. Every spell has its loopholes.

None of the human authorities had access to the loopholes in mine. I walked a little faster, ducking under the caution tape and moving closer to the car.

The smell of blood hit me while I was still a few feet away. I stopped for a moment, staggered by the reality of it, and closed my eyes to reorient myself. Bad plan: cutting off visual input only made the smell of blood stronger, since now there was nothing to distract me from it. Human blood, yes, absolutely; Gillian's blood. It was mortal through and through, with nothing left in it for my magic to grab hold of and twist, but I could still taste the ghost of primroses on the back of my tongue when I breathed it in, the places where her magic could have been, *would* have been if only she had decided differently.

If only she had come home with me, and not gone running back to the safe harbor of her father's arms.

I opened my eyes, trying to look at the car with an investigator's eye. The driver's-side window was smashed in, although there was nothing nearby that looked like it could have done the job. A rock, maybe, or a metal rod. Whatever it was, it had been more than enough. There was a spray of glass all the way across the front seat, and some of the pieces were rimed red with blood. More had splashed across the inside of the windshield. I crouched to study it, trying to see it as just another case, and not my daughter's life.

One good thing: there wasn't enough blood to have killed her. Wherever she was now, she hadn't bled out in her car. That helped a little. Not enough.

Opening the car door was out of the question—no don't-look-here is good enough to keep that from attracting attention—and I didn't dare lean too far into the car. If I cut myself, I would heal almost immediately, but I'd still bleed, and any forensic tech worth their paycheck would find the evidence that someone related to Gillian had been near the car. I didn't want to become their prime suspect, not while there was still a chance that this was a mortal crime. But I needed that glass.

Something crunched underfoot. Glass. I paused before taking a step back and crouching, scanning the glittering debris. Gillian's attacker had clearly broken the window before opening the door, dragging her out—conscious or unconscious—and closing the door again. Why? Because a car with a broken window and no occupant was sadly not an unusual enough occurrence to attract attention, not unless someone saw the blood. At night, without a streetlight shining directly on the bloody windshield . . .

It could have taken hours for anyone to realize something was wrong. It was a sickening thought. I didn't want to have it. I couldn't push it away. I crouched further instead, squinting at the glass on the ground. That wasn't good enough. I closed my eyes and breathed deeply, following the scent of blood. Gingerly, I reached for the ground, and stopped the moment before I would have touched it. I opened my eyes.

A chunk of broken safety glass glittered less than half an inch from my fingertips, surrounded by identical chunks—almost. This one was stained, its edges rimed red with blood. Gillian's blood or her attacker's, it didn't really matter. Either would tell me things I needed to know. Reaching into my pocket, I pulled out a piece of tissue paper and wrapped it around the glass, careful not to wipe the blood away. I needed to protect myself until it was safe to bleed, but this would all be for nothing if I lost the evidence.

Once the glass was tucked safely in my pocket, I straightened and took a step backward, intending to get some distance between me and the car before I started breathing normally again. I collided with something.

"Hey!" said the something. "What are you doing here?"

Crap.

A good don't-look-here will do a lot to keep you from being noticed, but the invisibility spell that could prevent someone from noticing when they're walked into has yet to be designed. I turned to find one of the campus police staring at me, looking exactly as bewildered as I would have expected, given the circumstances. From his perspective, I'd appeared out of nowhere.

From my perspective, I was screwed. I forced a sickly smile, raised my free hand in a small wave, and bolted.

One of the nice things about a don't-look-here, as opposed to true invisibility, is that people still *see* you: they just don't notice you until you force them to, like, say, by backing into them while standing somewhere you're not supposed to be. I ran, and the students who were gathered to get a glimpse of the crime scene made space for me without even realizing it, shifting a step forward or a step back. Better yet, they returned to their original positions in time to keep the officer who was pursuing me from building up any real speed.

"Stop!" he shouted. "Come back here! Stop!"

Call me a cynic, but no one who shouts "stop" like that has ever had my best interests at heart. I kept running until I hit the edge of the creek. There wasn't time to skid down the side. Yes, it would have been safer, but it would also have slowed me down enough for the officer to see me before I hit the bottom, and I needed to break his line of sight.

I jumped.

It wasn't a long way to the bottom, maybe eight feet, but I wasn't braced for a solid landing, and jumping off of things has never really been my thing. My left ankle buckled as I hit the bottom, and for a heart-stopping second, I thought I was going to land face-first in the frigid water. It was shallow, a small, rushing creek rather than any kind of pond, but that would still be enough to wash the blood off my piece of stolen glass. I pinwheeled my arms frantically, fighting to keep my balance.

For once, in a battle between me and gravity, I won. Quickly, I limped across the creek and collapsed on the far bank, the precious bundle of glass and tissue still safe and dry in my pocket. I could feel the strained muscles in my ankle smoothing themselves out, knitting every little rip and tear, and it itched like fire.

The campus security officer ran up to the edge of the drop-off. I froze, muddy and bedraggled, on the creek's far bank. The spell was holding. I could feel it all around me, sticky as cobwebs. It *had* to hide me. It had to.

Seconds ticked by. The officer raked his eyes back and forth along the bank, never quite focusing on me. He scowled.

"Asshole kids," he muttered, and turned on his heel and stalked away.

I stayed where I was for another count of ten, holding perfectly still. When he didn't return, I gingerly rose, testing my ankle and finding it completely healed. There are some advantages to being my mother's daughter. Relative indestructability is one of them. It's not enough to balance out the part where she thinks she's better than me and wishes I'd died human, but hey, every family has its issues.

Still cautious, I moved into the shadow of the bridge and counted to ten again. When the officer didn't reappear, I released the don't-look-here, filling the air under the bridge with the cloying scent of cut grass and copper. Before it could dissipate, I grabbed it with both hands, twisting it back into my human disguise, modifying it until I no longer looked like the woman who'd been spotted crouching near the car. It didn't take much—a new hair color, red instead of barely blonde, slightly sharper features—but it would help if the officer was still on the lookout.

The pain in my head came back, even stronger. I was nearing my natural limit on illusions. Tough. I'd keep casting them until I had Gillian back in the safety of her father's arms, and my stupid skull could learn to cope.

Once I was sure the illusion would hold, I shook the shadows off my fingers and started down the bank, looking for a place where it would be easy to climb up, yet where I wouldn't attract unwanted attention for appearing where the officer was waiting. Every little bit helps when trying to evade the law.

I couldn't ride the blood yet. Not here, not when there was a chance it would overwhelm me and cause me to drop my illusions. It would need to wait until I was safely in Bridget's office, out of sight of casually prying eyes.

Bridget and Quentin were still on the walkway when I came back. Madden was sitting nearby, tail thumping, being cooed over by a group of students who seemed to think he was the best dog ever. Judging by the grin on his canine face, he agreed. The third bipedal member of the group was more relevant to my interests: May. I walked a little faster. Bridget and Quentin gave me guarded looks as I approached. May, on the other hand, snorted.

"You look *ridiculous* as a redhead," she said. "Mom did you a massive favor when she went off and found a new husband who didn't look anything like her old one."

"Sure did," I agreed—although having seen August, I suspected the problem wasn't my hair being red, it was my hair being as pigmented as a normal person's. I looked to Bridget. "I have what I needed. I'm assuming May does, too. Can we go to your office?"

"Yes," said Bridget, looking unsettled. "I . . . I wasn't aware you could do that."

"Do what?"

"That." She gestured vaguely toward my face before glancing toward Madden's little fan club. They were all human. She shook her head. "Follow me."

Madden came away with a small tug of the leash, and we followed Bridget from the crime scene, down the side of Wheeler Hall, and to a small, unassuming door painted a bland shade of tan.

"Faculty entrance," she explained, producing a ring of keys. "Not meant for student use at any time, always locked from the outside. Makes it easier when we need to avoid justifying our grading choices."

"Okay," I said.

"Sorry, sorry." She slotted a key into the lock. "I babble when I'm nervous. It's a dreadful habit, but that doesn't make it any easier to do away with. Come on." She pulled the door open. We followed her inside.

I never went to college, and yet somehow I've spent more time at UC Berkeley than any non-student has any business doing. The halls were strange and familiar at the same time, just enough like the chemistry department where Walther worked that I felt like I could understand the basic layout, just different enough that I knew I'd get lost if I took my eyes off Bridget for a moment. Madden's claws clacked against the tile. There were windows, but they were high and small and most of the blinds were drawn, casting the hall into a comfortable twilight.

"I thought there'd be classes going on," said Quentin.

"Oh, there are," said Bridget. "Mostly a floor below us. This is all offices and faculty space. It'll doubtless be gutted the next time someone gets it in their head to renovate and 'modernize,' replaced by some sort of commons that leaves us nowhere to do our work in peace, but for now, we can get about without treading on students every time we turn around. Love them, Lord knows we do; that doesn't mean they make the process of educating them any easier when they insist on being *present* all the time."

She stopped in front of a door that looked like every other door in the hall, save for the nameplate next to it, which announced that this was the office of Dr. Bridget Ames. "It's funny, you know," she said, as she unlocked the door. "My colleagues all think I've gone very modern and progressive, since I went and got married and didn't change my name. They approve, for the most part—my entire publication history is tied to my maiden name—but they didn't expect it of me. Hard to explain that my groom hasn't a surname to share with me."

"If he ever needs to do anything in the mortal world, he'll probably go by Etienne Ames," I said.

Bridget looked pleased. "Hadn't thought of that," she said, and opened the door. "Forgive my mess."

"Forgiven," I said, and stepped inside.

Bridget's office was small. Not quite cramped, but more than halfway there, especially thanks to the imposing bookcases that lined the walls, each one loaded until the shelves began to sag in the middle. In case that wasn't enough, piles of books and papers turned the floor into an obstacle course and the desk into a narrow strip of usable space. An avalanche seemed to be impending from all directions. I moved to the center of the room, trying to avoid touching anything. May, Quentin, and Madden all had the same idea. Madden even straightened up and returned to his quasi-human form, probably so his tail wouldn't take out a pile of papers.

Bridget blinked as she closed the door behind herself. "No matter how many times I see that, it never gets less jarring. Hello, Master Seneschal."

"Hi, Bess," said Madden, somehow managing to give the impression that his tail was wagging even when he didn't have one. "How's your husband?"

"Well as ever. Stuck-up and hidebound, but who isn't?" She smiled for a moment. Only for a moment. Smile fading, she said, "October, you had something you wanted to show me?"

"In a second." I looked to May. "What did you find?"

"More of those sachets in her drawers and under her bed—about a dozen, all told. There was even one hanging in the closet. Iron shavings and salt along every threshold in the house, and rowan twigs above the windows." May's expression was grim. "It's all low-grade stuff, charms and trinkets. The sort of thing someone could stumble across making by accident, almost. Not enough to actually keep fae out, but enough to make anyone with a measurable amount of fae blood uncomfortable in that house."

"It's the 'almost' that gets me," I said. "Were there sachets in anyone's drawers *apart* from Gillian's?"

May shook her head. "No, and I checked. I almost got caught a couple of times, too. If they'd been there, I would have found them."

"Right. Quentin?"

"On it." He pulled the foil-wrapped sachet out of his coat pocket, grimacing at the weight of the thing. He offered it to Bridget.

"What's this?" she asked, glancing to me before taking the sachet out of his hand. She peeled the foil carefully back and frowned as that sharp herbal smell wafted into the room.

I sneezed, my eyes already starting to water. Swell. Wiping them with the back of my hand, I said, "We found that in Gillian's room. You're the folklore professor. What can you tell us?"

"You're sneezing, and your eyes are red." Bridget looked at me sidelong. "First thing I can tell you is that you're definitely allergic to the stuff. All of you. More than that is going to take me opening it up, and that's going to release more of it into the air. Are you sure that's a good idea?"

I looked at the others. Only Madden seemed to be as bad off as I was: Quentin's eyes were red, and May was sniffling, but neither of them looked like they were going to be running for the Benadryl any time soon. Madden's nose was running. That made sense. No matter what shape he was in, his nose was better than any of ours.

I looked back at Bridget. "Would it help to know what's inside?"

"Yes, absolutely." Bridget weighed the sachet in her hand. "This would be easy enough to make. You can buy these little mesh bags at any craft store. They're used for making potpourri bundles, to put in with your clothes and keep them fresh."

"Humans are weird," muttered Quentin.

"No question about that," I said. I took a shallow breath, trying to avoid inhaling more of the smell than absolutely necessary, and said, "Dill, gorse, St. John's wort, fennel, kingcup—um, I think 'marsh marigold' is the more common name for that—and Scots kale."

Bridget's eyes grew huge. "Scots *kale*?" she asked.

"Yes."

"All right. I . . . oh, you poor things, you're all miserable. Hang on." She crossed to her desk, opened a drawer, and dropped the sachet inside. The air seemed to clear as soon as the drawer was closed. Bridget watched us closely as we stopped sniffling, although my eyes continued to burn. I rubbed at them, trying to be unobtrusive. Bridget frowned. "Normally, taking an allergen away doesn't change things that quickly. Something must have been done to the things."

"If whoever made those for Gillian were trying to keep the fae away from her, there are ways to make herbs and simples more effective for short periods of time," I said haltingly.

"How do you know she didn't make the bundles herself?" asked Quentin. "Maybe the Luidaeg left some memories behind and Gillian got scared and tried to keep the bad dreams away."

It ached to think I could be a bad dream for my own child. But he wasn't wrong. If she remembered anything about what had happened while Rayseline had her, she wouldn't be sleeping peacefully. Still, I shook my head. "It's marshwater work. Even if she went to someone and *asked* for the sachets, she wouldn't have been able to do the crafting. She wouldn't know how."

"Marshwater?" asked Bridget.

"Little magic. Hedge magic. It's sort of like alchemy, sometimes, in that it's as much about the ingredients as it is about the power behind them. And it's nothing like alchemy at all, because it's not about natural talent or being able to change what you're working with. I'm not an alchemist. I was pretty good at marshwater charms, back when they were all I had." I waved a hand, trying to encompass the scope of the differences. "If I tried to do most of them now, I'd burn them out. But there are things you could do, if someone walked you through the process of figuring out exactly how."

"Magic? Me? I thought you needed to be a merlin to be human and do magic." Bridget looked far too interested in the idea. Etienne's kitchen was probably going to be a very exciting place for a while.

That was fine. He needed more excitement in his life. "Big magic, yes. Merlins can cast spells I can't manage, and no matter what line of descent their fae ancestor claimed, they don't seem to follow any of the normal divisions—a Tuatha merlin might be incredibly skilled at flower magic, or a Tylwyth merlin might be an incredible blood-worker. They don't have the talents of their ancestors, but if they can put together a ritual for something, they can probably bully the universe into letting them have it. Marshwater work is . . . it's different. Some of it isn't magic at all, not in the inborn, automatic way that purebloods understand. But if you soak kingcup in moonlight for nine days, it lasts longer. That sort of . . . thing."

Everyone was watching me. Bridget looked fascinated. Madden looked appalled. I managed, somehow, not to squirm.

The purebloods have always liked to think they had the monopoly on magic. Quentin had spent enough time with me to figure out that not only did the purebloods not run as much of the world as they thought they did, thinking otherwise was likely to get him seriously injured, if not killed. In my line of work—and by extension, his, at least for the moment—underestimating an opponent because of old stereotypes is a good way to wind up dead.

Madden, though . . . for all that he was seneschal to a woman that some people called, sneeringly, "the Changeling Queen," for all that he worked in the mortal world and counted humans as friends, he was a pureblood raised by purebloods, with nothing to force him to see or sympathize with the changeling way of doing things. This was probably very confusing for him.

Tough. "Gillian doesn't know anything about marshwater charms, or at least not anything she could have learned from me. You're the folklore professor, Bridget. Does this look like something one of your students would have put together?"

"I won't say *no*, because I have students who come from all sorts of traditions. Some are religious people who happen to adore fairy tales, or theology majors picking up a bit of a grounding in what they call 'pagan nonsense,' or actual pagans." Bridget spoke slowly, picking her words with care. "The pagans, especially the Wiccans, do a great deal of herbal, ah, 'witchcraft,' although I've been careful never to form too firm an opinion on it."

"Better to stay neutral than to risk upsetting your students," said May.

"Exactly so," said Bridget. "There might be a few who'd managed to stumble on something that actually works, but if this is what you say it is . . . "

"This is the crafting of someone who knows the fae are real—and knows they can be kept away if you only weave the right combination of herbs and simples and rituals. I don't know how. I never wanted to learn. But it wouldn't be impossible knowledge to collect."

"Jocelyn?" asked Quentin. "She knew more than she should have, for someone too thin-blooded to see without ointment. Um. No offense, ma'am."

"None taken," said Bridget. "I know my place in Faerie is predicated on loopholes and bends in the rules, and I try to tread lightly, to avoid giving offense."

"Jocelyn wouldn't be attempting to keep the fae *away*, though, not when she's wearing fairy ointment and trying to get Gilly to talk about her famous family." I touched my pocket gingerly, feeling the piece of glass I had concealed there. "Not Jocelyn."

"She definitely wouldn't have put iron at the thresholds, not if her mother's a changeling," said May. "This wasn't her."

"Why didn't the iron harm any of you?" asked Bridget. "I always thought . . ." She stopped, shrugging. "When I was trying to protect Chelsea from her father, iron seemed the easiest way."

"It wasn't pure iron, for one, and none of us touched it, for two," I said. "If there had been more, or if we'd come directly into contact with it, things might be different."

"I see," said Bridget.

"It's been a fun day." I closed my eyes for a moment, trying to sort everything we knew so far into orderly categories, or at least into something that would be a little bit less confusing. It wasn't working. I opened my eyes again and pulled the glass out of my pocket. "I'm going to try to find a blood memory now."

May nodded, concern blossoming in her expression like a terrible flower. She knew the risks I was taking better than anyone, because she remembered taking them when she was me. Blood is where magic and memory live: blood is the key to a lot of questions that might otherwise go entirely unanswered. That's the good part. I'm not even taking much of a risk when I ride the blood these days, because I'm strong enough now that I can pull myself free before it can pull me down.

The bad part is that whatever the blood wants to tell me, I'll have to hear. That's the trade-off. If I taste someone's blood, I learn what they have to share. And, sometimes, that learning hurts.

I sighed, unwrapped the piece of glass, and turned it between my fingers, looking for the biggest stretch of stain. This would have been easier with more blood. It always was. Unfortunately, waiting until I could get unfettered access to the car—probably in some police impound lot, possibly after it had been photographed and sampled and disinfected—might mean waiting long enough for whoever had Gillian to get tired of holding her.

Assuming they hadn't already. And that, right there, was why I was hesitating. Some of my frantic forward momentum had bled off when I was sitting on the creek bank, waiting for my ankle to heal, and what had replaced it was a numb, resigned dread. I had freed my daughter from Faerie and walked away, trusting her father to keep her safe. I had given up any claim to the family I'd tried to make with the two of them, and moved on to making a new family, a new life, with Tybalt. Now Tybalt was gone, and I was facing the possible loss of my child. If she was dead, the blood would tell me. If she was alive, the blood would tell me that, too. I had to find out. I had to know which way I was running.

I didn't want to.

Quentin touched my arm. I looked at him, nodded, and placed the glass on my tongue. It cut me almost instantly, but I had been counting on that: while my blood would have confused the crime scene, all it would do here was make my magic stronger and make it easier for me to find the things I needed to know.

Blood—both mine and Gillian's—flooded my mouth.

Holding the glass shard between my teeth, I swallowed.

SIX

*T*HE PARKING LOT IS *dark around me, lit only by the distant glow of streetlights aimed to illuminate other things, other places. It's not safe to walk across campus alone at night—not fair, never fair, do they tell the boys it's not safe to go where they want, to be who they want to be? But this is the world we live in, and we can't trade it for a better one—but it's safe to drive, as long as I'm in my car. The dark can't take the safety away. The car means freedom. The car means I'm as good as anyone.*

Gillian's love for her car was an ache so deep it almost knocked me out of the memory. She was my daughter, and I was pretty sure she hadn't felt love like that for me in a very long time. I groped until I found Quentin's hand. He tightened his fingers around mine, grounding me. There wasn't time to acknowledge him: there wasn't enough blood on the glass for that. I bit down harder, slicing my tongue again, adding my own blood and strength to the working.

The blood memories reasserted themselves, veiling the world in red. *Check engine light is on. I pause to make a note for myself. Freedom only lasts if you take care of it, that's what Mel always says. I'm going to take care of it. I'm going to continue earning my freedom.*

Someone passes in front of the car. The lights are in the wrong place to let me see their face, but they pause and wave, and so I wave back, choosing to be friendly, safe behind my closed, locked doors. I can afford friendliness when there's no way they can get to me. I even feel a little smug about it. I'm safe. I'm free. Nothing can touch me—

Something hits the window. It shatters under the impact, there's glass flying everywhere, and it hurts, it hurts, there's glass in the air and my eyes are closed so the glass doesn't get in them and I can't see anything, and it hurts why does it—

An object harder and more substantial than shards of glass hit Gillian in the side of the head. There was a sound like bending bone, and the faint, inexplicable scent of cinnamon. That was where the memory cut off, extinguished along with her consciousness.

I snapped back into my own body with a gasp, turning to stare at my companions. There was blood on my lips, hot and sticky and almost entirely my own. I spat the sucked-clean cube of glass into my palm and used the back of my other hand to wipe my face.

"She was alive when they took her," I said, voice barely shaking. I wanted to be proud of that. I couldn't muster the energy. Gillian's pain echoed through every nerve in my body, reminding me of how much she had suffered. How much she could still be suffering. She didn't heal like I did. Any injuries she'd incurred during her abduction would remain, sketched on her skin like a memoir of trauma.

"Good," said Bridget firmly. "That means you have time to find her. Is there *anything* I can do to help you?"

I started to refuse, then paused, considering her offer and my options. "That sachet," I said finally. "Can you take it to Walther and have him see what he can make of it? It's better if none of us tries to carry it."

"Of course," said Bridget. "I'll call you as soon as I have answers." She sounded relieved. Belatedly, I realized we'd dumped all this on her without warning. She cared about us; she wanted to help; she was so far out of her depth that she couldn't find it with a map. Being given a task to perform that got her away from the rest of us must have seemed like a blessing.

I turned. "Madden . . . "

"I have Gillian's." He bobbed his head, doglike, eyes on me. "Between the room and the blood, I have her scent. If we go back to where the car is, I can follow it. Now that we know she's alive, I can follow."

I wanted to cry. I wanted to throw my arms around him and

thank him forever. I settled for nodding. "Then we go. Bridget, call me."

"I will," she said. "Open roads, October. And good luck."

Hearing such a traditional farewell from human lips was strange, but not unpleasant. "Kind fires," I said, and moved for the door, the rest of my motley little band trailing behind me, leaving Bridget to the remains of her morning. Madden dropped back onto four feet before he left the room, choosing efficiency. The makeshift leash and vest May had crafted for him didn't reappear.

Before I could point out that unleashed dogs were probably against school rules, Quentin waved a hand and muttered something under his breath, flooding the hall with the scent of steel and heather. The weight of the don't-look-here fell across us like a shroud, making my ears itch. I shot Quentin a glare. He responded with a silent, exaggerated shrug.

It was a good move. It was the move of someone who knew how close I was running to the limitations of my magic and wanted to be sure I wouldn't incapacitate myself before we knew what we were up against. It's a little scary sometimes how well Quentin knows me, how prepared he is to risk himself to protect me from my own decisions. He's been my squire for a long time. I didn't want him in the beginning. Now, I have no idea what I'm going to do with myself when he moves on.

Definitely not take on another squire. When Quentin—and by extension, Raj—were done with me, I was done with taking responsibility for random teenagers. They were an impossible act to follow, and so I wasn't going to try.

We made our way through the cool, quiet halls and back to the faculty door, which didn't require a key from this side. We didn't pass anyone. That was nice, if a little eerie. It was the middle of the morning, easing on toward noon. The human world was never more awake than it was right now. They should have been everywhere, and instead, we walked alone, isolated, a few feet to the side. It was like Gillian's disappearance had shifted the entire campus a few feet out of true, making it a twilight place even with the December sun beating relentlessly down.

Madden was the first one out the door, bounding ahead with his nose pressed to the ground and his tail held low behind him, like this was too serious a situation for wagging. It was odd. I was so accustomed to going through life escorted by cats that it was hard not to read that motionless tail as a sign of happiness, and he had no business being happy right now. None of us did. Not with Gillian missing.

No one looked our way as we moved down the path back toward the crowd of students and police surrounding Gillian's abandoned car. Madden trotted forward, nose still to the ground, sniffing and searching as he spiraled first in, toward the vehicle, and then out, away from it. Finally, he stopped, raised his head, and looked back toward the rest of us. It wasn't clear whether he could see us, or whether he was tracking the place his nose told him we were. It didn't really matter.

"Go," I murmured.

His ears perked forward. Then he turned and trotted purposefully away from the crime scene, past Wheeler Hall, toward the rest of the campus. We followed, sticking together so we wouldn't lose sight of each other, moving around the humans who, oblivious to our presence, went about their day.

Madden reached the edge of campus and stopped. My heart lurched until I realized he was only pausing because the traffic wasn't in his favor. Crossing a busy street as a dog is never particularly safe. Doing it as a mostly invisible dog? Seemed like a good way to become roadkill. Still, I walked a little faster, and May and Quentin matched my pace, until we were waiting on the curb next to Madden.

He glanced our way, eyes not quite focusing, and sniffed the air before barking softly.

"Yeah," I said. "We're here."

The light changed. We crossed the street, still hidden by the don't-look-here. Madden pressed his nose to the ground again, reorienting himself, and then trotted forward faster, leading us onward, away from campus and into the busy urban streets.

Berkeley is like San Francisco only in the sense that it's a Bay Area city, blessed with good weather and tolerably decent public transportation as long as you're only moving from city center to city center. The buildings are designed to stand up to earthquakes, or at least the newer ones are; older buildings tend to fall down a bit more easily, and the people who own them somehow never feel like investing in repairs is a good use of their money. That's where the resemblance ends. San Francisco is a city built on hillsides, in the shadow of the sea. Berkeley is surrounded by hills, and extends up into them, but for the most part, it's a flat territory.

Berkeley, unlike San Francisco, has *space*. It's a city that knows how to sprawl, how to give a store the floor space to carry as much as it likes without turning into a maze of aisles that collide and contradict. It's also a city that devotes a surprising amount of that space to tiny connecting roads and boulevards that are more like alleys with delusions of grandeur. Madden led us toward Shattuck Avenue and then farther down, to the vast artery of University Avenue. When the city planners were deciding whether to build "up" or "out," they chose the latter. Berkeley *sprawls*.

The cars were more frequent on University, sometimes ignoring the pedestrians they could actually see. People pushed up and down the sidewalk, a jarring density of humans. I've lived in cities for my entire adult life. I hadn't realized, not consciously, how much switching to keeping fae hours had insulated me from their populations. That wasn't good. That was pureblood thinking, and it needed to stop.

My thoughts were chasing themselves in circles, a sure sign that I was terrified. I've always found the very human tendency to take solace in the trivial and mundane to be . . . not soothing, exactly, but useful. It's hard to dwell when I can't focus. And it wasn't like there was anything else I could do. Madden was following the trail, and no matter how deeply I inhaled, I couldn't find any trace of it. The person who'd taken Gillian had also taken the time to stop the bleeding.

I should have been grateful for that, glad my little girl hadn't been carried through the streets of Berkeley with an open wound. All it made me feel was useless. Like I hadn't been able to raise her, and now I couldn't even be the one to find her.

May glanced my way and reached out to take my hand, giving it a reassuring squeeze. She didn't say anything. Attracting attention would only have slowed us down. No one was going to look at us and demand to know how we'd suddenly appeared in the middle of the sidewalk—don't-look-here spells are subtler than that—but as it was, when we walked toward people, they got out of our way. They created space for us to occupy. We wanted that to last.

We'd gone about three blocks when Madden stiffened, raised his nose from the ground, and barked before breaking into a run.

Several pedestrians turned to watch him go, a few exclaiming at the sight of the unleashed dog racing down the street. I didn't hesitate. I ran after him, dragging May with me, Quentin following close on our heels.

Madden didn't slow or look back to see whether we were keeping up with him. He just *ran*, until we reached a blank brick wall stretched between two buildings. Too blank: every other wall in sight had been plastered with advertisements or tagged by graffiti artists. This was just brick, a tempting target for every form of urban embellishment. So why hadn't it been tagged?

Madden whined, looking back and forth like he was confused. I mimicked the gesture, checking the sidewalk. Too many people could see us. We needed to keep the don't-look-here going for a few more minutes.

Somehow, I thought it was about to become irrelevant.

"Quentin, keep the spell going," I said. I let go of May's hand and my human disguise at the same time. Raising my thumb to my mouth, I bit down hard enough to break the skin. Fresh blood filled my mouth as the smell of cut grass and copper settled all around me.

The brick shimmered. I narrowed my eyes, biting even harder, coaxing more blood from a wound that was trying to heal even as I ripped it open. Blood magic has always been my strength, the one form of magic where I'm as adept as any pureblood. Given enough blood, I can reshape the world.

Gold-and-silver threads shimmered in the air in front of the wall. I reached out with my free hand, making a tugging gesture. Not enough to break them, since the disappearance of a brick wall would probably attract attention we didn't want. Just enough to . . . move them a little bit. To let me see what they were hiding.

The brick warped, not dissolving, but becoming momentarily translucent. I glanced at Quentin. He was still frowning at the wall, not seeming to see the change. That was fine. That was something I could work with.

"Grab my sleeve," I said, voice garbled by my mouthful of thumb.

He didn't argue. He just grabbed hold, reaching out to take May's hand for good measure. I bit down one more time, getting a fresh gout of blood. Then I pulled my spit-and-blood–covered thumb out of my mouth and started forward, grabbing the scruff of Madden's neck as I passed him. He yelped but didn't bite. Thank Oberon for that. I heal fast, but I feel pain like anybody else. I'd rather not walk into a brick wall while trying to keep an angry Cu Sidhe from ripping my arm off.

The wall was still shimmering, still shot through with those gold-and-silver threads. I swallowed the last of the blood and took a confident step forward, bracing myself against the moment when my face impacted with the brick.

It didn't. My first step carried us past the beginning of the wall, into a charcoal-colored void as disconcerting as it was intentional. Whoever had crafted this spell wanted to be absolutely sure that any humans who happened to blunder into it somehow—say at dawn, when almost all standing spellwork was weaker—wouldn't feel the need to keep going. Most people don't like being dropped into formless darkness.

It's not my favorite thing in the world. But the Cait Sidhe have access to the Shadow Roads, which are basically formless darkness with a side order of freezing cold, and Tybalt took me there with reasonable frequency. This darkness was room temperature. It was going to have to work a lot harder to get a rise out of me. I took another step forward, pulling my people with me through the dark, out the other side, into a place that shouldn't have been possible.

We were still in the mortal world: the sky was the slate gray characteristic of California winters, and the space where we stood was hemmed in on all sides by tall brick walls. Some of them had windows, and I wondered what the occupants saw when they looked out. An empty, inaccessible courtyard? Or the building on the other side of it, somehow rendered closer than the actual architecture allowed?

They couldn't see what we saw. They couldn't see *us*. If they had, there was no way Faerie would have been able to stay a secret, because this would have been enough, all by itself, to blow the doors right off.

"Whoa," said Quentin.

"Yeah," I agreed.

The courtyard was about the size of the surrounding buildings, maybe eighty feet wide by a hundred or so feet deep. It was *contained*, encysted into the architecture of the block like a worm inside an apple. Plants that had no business growing in the mortal world bloomed everywhere I looked, ignoring the fact that it was December in favor of putting out a riotous assortment of fruits and flowers. A moon-apple tree and a sun-apple tree tangled their branches together, forming a puzzle box lace of twigs and leaves, holding each other up under the weight of their dense harvest of gold-and-silver fruit. A line of goblin fruit bushes grew against one of the walls. I shuddered and looked away, toward the center of the courtyard.

The back wall was the only place where no vines climbed, where no trees grew. Instead, what looked like an old-fashioned human house huddled there, paint peeling and roof flaking, its porch slanted at a dangerous angle. In front of it, the most jarring thing of all waited, silent and motionless.

It was a house in miniature, the sort of house a particularly doting parent might build in their backyard for a beloved child. The walls were straight and sound, the roof was perfect; everything about it was perfect. The front door was large enough for a six-year-old, but not anything much larger. It was settled in the middle of a vast, tangled nest, its feathery chicken legs tucked up underneath its foundations. It had no eyes, but I couldn't shake the feeling that it was watching us.

"Quentin, drop the don't-look-here," I said tightly.

The scent of steel and heather overwhelmed the perfume of the flowers around us as the spell dropped away. Madden rose on two legs, a man once more as he moved closer to the group. I understood the sentiment. No one sensible would want to be here alone, not with that little chicken-legged house keeping watch.

"This shouldn't be here," muttered May. I glanced her way. She shook her head. "I have the memories of a dozen people who've lived in this town, and none of them knew anything about this sort of garden."

"And I used to work for a man who treated secrets like air," I said grimly. "If Devin had known about this place . . ." I let the sentence die.

If Devin had known about this place, he would have been trading the kids who depended on him to keep them safe for bushels of apples, for the carrots that poked out of the soft earth in front of the berry bushes. Earth carrots come in a lot of colors, but they don't glitter. There had to be some pureblood, somewhere, who was willing to pay the world for carrots that tasted the way they remembered carrots tasting when they were young and the doors to deeper Faerie were open.

"That house is looking at me," said Quentin.

"Which one?" asked May.

"Yes," said Quentin.

His tone was flatly confused, and somehow, that snapped me out of my own frozen contemplation. "Madden." I turned. "Where is she? Where does the trail go from here?"

"Um." He sniffed the air, then sneezed. "Too many scents. I'm sorry. I followed her this far, but this is where everything gets sort of fuzzy."

The little house stood up.

It was a quick, efficient gesture: it just got its feet under itself and pushed off, rising from its nest and revealing the full length of its scaled orange legs. It scratched a few times, like it was reassuring itself of its balance, and then it hopped out of the nest, strutting deeper into the courtyard. We all watched it go, momentarily united in our amazement.

There was something blue tangled in the branches at the edge of the nest. I barely had time to register the color before I was running, yanked forward by some intangible instinct. The little house ignored me in favor of continuing to strut away. That was a good thing. I had absolutely no idea how to fight architectural poultry.

Then I was at the nest, shoving my hands into the twisted branches and pulling out a pair of blue jeans with the knees ripped out. There was more fabric beneath them. I grabbed it, yanking until a red Berkeley sweatshirt came loose, followed by a full set of underthings. There was even a pair of shoes, shoved all the way down at the bottom. I stared at them for a moment before looking at the sweatshirt in my hands.

The fabric was dark, the same shade of red that I favored for my tank tops, because it hid the blood so well. A sob rose in my throat. I choked it down as I raised the sweatshirt to my nose, sniffing. I wasn't Madden. I couldn't follow a trail across a city. But when there's blood, I will always be able to find it. It calls to me. When the blood is so closely kin to my own . . .

My nose was still stuffy from the mysterious sachets we'd found in Gillian's room. This close, it didn't matter. The smell of my daughter's blood struck me hard, almost sending me reeling back.

I grabbed the edge of the nest with my free hand and breathed in deeper. The blood carried no magic, no memory, nothing but the irrefutable knowledge that my daughter had been hurt, and I hadn't been there to stop it.

"Toby?"

I turned. Quentin was a few feet behind me, an anxious expression on his face. Madden was walking in a slow spiral, his head bowed and his nostrils flaring as he tried to recover the scent without shifting back to his canine form. Only May hadn't moved. She was still looking around the courtyard in silent wonder, drinking in the sight of a secret that the Bay Area had apparently been able to keep even from the night-haunts.

Not just from the night-haunts. There were no pixies. I forced myself to breathe in and out, slow and easy, as I scanned the trees. There were *no* pixies, no bogeys, none of the other small and wonderful monsters that made Faerie a healthy ecosystem. The only things I could see moving were the bumblebees flitting from flower to flower—apparently as unconcerned about the actual season as the fruit-heavy trees—and the chicken-legged house, which was now pecking at the dirt. It didn't have a beak. "Pecking" consisted of tapping its roof against the dirt over and over again, like a foraging bird.

I looked back to Quentin. "Yeah?"

"I . . . I don't like to say this, and please don't get mad at me, but . . . "

"She was never here."

His eyes widened in shocked relief. "How did you—?"

"First, I'm the one teaching you, remember? If I couldn't reach that conclusion before you did, I'd be a pretty lousy teacher." Or a distraught mother holding her daughter's bloody clothes in her hands. That was also a possibility. "But no. There's too much blood and there's not enough blood, and the only way that isn't a contradiction is if she was never here."

The clothing woven into the nest was too deliberate a clue, and there was no way the house could have disrobed her. Someone who had known about this strange and secret place had laid a false trail to bring us here, and they had stripped Gillian naked and left her clothing as a red herring. I gave the sweatshirt in my hand another bleak look.

"She was never here," I repeated.

SEVEN

"MADDEN."
He turned, looking almost relieved to have something to focus on apart from trying to pick up a nonexistent trail. I thrust the sweatshirt at him.

"Someone stripped Gilly and put her clothes here for us to find." Probably someone who assumed I would be following the blood trail, or that Tybalt would be sniffing her out for me. For all that he liked to remind me that he wasn't a bloodhound, he had a remarkably good nose. Not as good as Madden's, but good enough that laying a false trail was only sensible. "They were smart enough to do it without magic: I'm not getting any spell traces. Can you see whether you can find any other scents on this? Anything at all?"

"Okay." Madden strode over to take the sweatshirt, adding as he did, "I have to call Ardy once I'm done. She needs to know what we found."

Berkeley is unincorporated territory, but the crown still has authority there. It's still part of the kingdom. I started to nod and froze, eyes widening. "Oh, sweet Titania, have I always been this stupid?" I asked.

"What?" asked Quentin.

"Hang on," I said, and dug my phone out of my pocket, pulling up my recent contacts. Raj was third from the top. I tapped his name and waited.

The Summerlands are outside the range of most cell towers. For a long time, one of the advantages the human world had over

Faerie was the reliability of cellular phones. Then April O'Leary, the cyber-Dryad ex-Countess of Tamed Lightning, got annoyed by her inability to call her friends whenever she wanted and started upgrading everyone's phones. At this point, they function across the Summerlands and even in the Court of Cats.

The phone rang three times before Raj picked up. "Hello?"

"Raj, I need you to come to Berkeley, find Shade—wake her if you have to—and bring her to University Avenue, between the organic gluten-free bakery with the bread braids in the window and the artisanal chocolatier."

There was a long pause. Then: "I'm hanging up and going back to bed."

"No, you're not. You want to act like you're my squire until it's time for you to become king? This is where you live up to the title. We found something that shouldn't exist, and Madden is going to call Arden, and she's going to swoop in and claim it for the Divided Courts. If you want the Court of Cats to have any say in this new mystery, you need to get Shade and get your fuzzy butts to University Avenue. Call me back when you're here."

I hung up. When I lowered my phone, Madden was staring at me, a hurt expression on his face.

"Why did you do that?" he asked.

"Because Shade is the local Queen of Cats, and by terms of the treaty between Oberon and the Cait Sidhe, she has as much claim to this place as Queen Windermere does," I said. "I'm not trying to take it away from Arden. I'm trying to make sure we don't have a diplomatic incident that could have been otherwise avoided. Did you find anything on the sweatshirt?"

"Only Gillian, and you, and Jocelyn," he said. "Nothing but those."

Gillian's blood was soaked all through the fabric; I had been holding it; Jocelyn was her roommate. That made—

Wait. Her roommate who handled her laundry for some reason, when she'd already admitted they weren't really friends? I frowned.

"How *strongly* does it smell of Jocelyn?"

"Pretty strongly." His frown mirrored mine. "That's a little weird, isn't it?"

"It's a lot weird." I gave the courtyard one more look, focusing on the decrepit old house at the very back. The smaller house had climbed up onto the porch and perched there, legs folded under its

foundation. "I'm going to look around inside. Quentin, here." I tossed him my phone. "When Raj calls, go out and get him."

"What if the wall is solid again?"

"Come in and get me, and we'll *both* go out and get him. Madden, I know you need to call your liege, but please make sure she's aware that the Court of Cats has already got their own Queen en route, and she'll need to share."

"Fine," he grumbled.

"I'll be right back," I said, and started forward.

There were still no pixies. There were rose bushes but no rose goblins. If not for the fact that we were surrounded by fae plants on all sides, some rare enough to be worth several fortunes, I would have thought this place was just a remarkably well-concealed human garden. It was wrong. Everything about it was wrong. Even the faint scent of cinnamon hanging in the air was wrong.

Cinnamon. Who did I know whose magic smelled like cinnamon? Or was I being paranoid, and the scent was a consequence of being so close to the organic bakery? Under the circumstances, I thought I'd earned a little paranoia.

The porch steps creaked when I stepped onto them, and for a moment I thought my feet were going to punch right through the rotten wood. But the planks held, and I kept going, climbing all three of the steps between me and the front door. The chicken-legged house made a soft sighing sound, like hinges creaking in the wind, and turned slightly to watch me as I tested the front door.

Locked, of course. Good thing I habitually carry lock picks these days, having encountered one door too many that seemed to think I could be kept out. I crouched, pulled the picks out of my pocket, and got to work.

There were no wards or countercharms on the door, only a lock so old that half its tumblers no longer latched the way they should. Getting it open was almost insultingly easy. If the day hadn't already been so long, I would probably have taken the time to gloat. As it was, I simply straightened, shoved the door open, and stepped inside, stopping to stare for what felt like the hundredth time since I'd been dragged out of bed by the sound of Cliff hammering on my front door.

The front room was small, quaint, and spotless, the sort of rose-

damasked parlor that felt like it belonged in a period drama full of British accents and quaint murders. Everything showed signs of having been dusted recently. The couch was overstuffed, inviting, and at least seventy years old, if the polished woodwork was anything to go by. I breathed in deeply, looking for any hint or sign of magic. I found nothing, only more cinnamon and the bizarrely modern scent of Lemon Pledge.

"What the hell," I muttered, and pushed deeper in.

For all that the house *looked* like it was going to collapse at any moment from the outside, the floors inside were smooth and stable, and the walls were straight with no hint of lean or sag. I paused to touch one of them, feeling the shape of the wood. It was all hand-planed, and there didn't seem to be any nails, just the wood itself, slotted together with an artisan's hand. How much of the outside was a lie, intended to keep people like me, who had somehow discovered a secret garden, from bothering to open the door?

A short stairway led to the second floor. I took it two steps at a time, no longer really believing Gillian was anywhere for me to find, but still hoping there'd be *something* that could tell me who owned this courtyard, this garden, this impossible detour on the all-important road to finding my daughter. Whoever it was, they were important enough to frame for stealing my child, and powerful enough to have woven an enchantment into the very foundations of the block. This wasn't a shallowing or a twist in the local geography: this place *existed*. I could feel it all the way down to my still-mortal bones.

The second floor was even smaller than the first, with only three rooms. An old-fashioned bathroom that looked like it dated from the dawn of indoor plumbing; a walk-in linen closet, the shelves almost bare, save for a few neatly folded towels and a spare set of sheets; and a bedroom with a single window looking out over a patch of garden I hadn't seen before, one that appeared to be almost entirely roses. There was a narrow bed, a dressing table, and a wardrobe. There was a spinning wheel. There was nothing to tell me who slept here, and no matter how hard I tried, I couldn't catch any traces of magic in the air.

It was like this entire place had somehow been made without any magic apart from the standing effects which kept it concealed from the mortal world. There are people powerful enough to set up those kinds of illusion and permanent barrier spells. I know some of them. I just couldn't for the life of me imagine *why*.

Someone shouted outside. I whipped around, forgetting the bedroom as I ran for the stairs and down them to the front door. The little house was standing on the porch, chicken-claws digging into the rotted wood as it looked attentively toward the growing crowd at the center of the courtyard. Arden had appeared next to Madden, probably after he somehow talked her through the process of opening a portal to a place she'd never been before. Nolan was with her, both of them gaping in open-mouthed amazement.

It was sort of nice to see the confirmation that Arden was still new enough to this "queen" thing that she could be impressed like this. I hopped down the porch steps and hurried toward her.

"Did Madden tell you the local Queen of Cats is on her way?"

"He did. I wish you'd talked to me before you called her."

"Why?"

"Because she's going to tell you the same thing I am: we're not supposed to be here." Arden took another look around, and for the first time, I saw the unease under the amazement. "My father knew about this place. I have his papers, remember? I've been trying to learn the secrets of my kingdom before they can be sprung on me."

"You never said," said Madden, sounding hurt.

"Because it was never your business." Arden gentled her voice as much as she could, trying to take the sting from her words. From the look on Madden's face, she didn't entirely succeed. "There are secrets queens keep, Madden. It's not personal. It's not meant to be cruel. It's how kingdoms work."

"How is it that we're not supposed to be here?" I asked. "This is your kingdom."

"Too bad you didn't think so when you called the cats," said Arden, shooting a sharp look in my direction. Then she sagged and sighed. "That wasn't fair. I'm sure they know about this place, too. They have to. It's their job to find the lost places, and this isn't a lost place, but it's got to be close enough to attract their attention, and this is their kingdom, too. There's no way they didn't receive the same message my grandparents did."

"Which was?" I pressed. Quentin was still holding the bundle of Gillian's clothing. I pointed to it. "Because whoever owns this place, someone wanted me to think they were the ones who took my child. Someone wanted to start trouble for them, or for me. I think I have a right to know."

"I think that's a very human approach to a very inhuman problem," said Arden levelly. "There are secrets in this world that you have no right to. Not every question you ask demands an answer."

"My *daughter* is missing."

"And Madden has already confirmed that she is not, and was never, here. The person who took her was laying a false trail."

I agreed with Arden, but in that moment, I couldn't say so. All I could do was stare at her, my heart in my throat and the blood pounding in my ears until I couldn't hear anything else. Quentin stepped up next to me, lending support through his silent presence. Only Quentin. May was nowhere to be seen. I glanced around and didn't find her in the shadow of the trees.

Quentin didn't seem alarmed, which meant May had told him where she was going. I returned my focus to Arden, trying to breathe levelly so as not to start shouting at the queen. That never ends well for me.

"Your *Highness*," I said, through gritted teeth, and watched Arden flinch from her own title like it was an enemy's blade. "I am a hero of the realm, named so by your own tongue. I am in pursuit of a missing child who was born of Faerie, even if she no longer claims it. You say there are secrets I have no right to. Well, by your own admission, I'm already standing in the middle of one of those secrets. Someone led me here, probably because they were trying to incriminate whoever lives here, and hence means them harm, which I think is sort of more important than preserving their privacy. I don't have a lot of time to waste, since I need to get back to *finding my daughter*. What is this place? Why is it here?"

"This place is an agreement," said a cool, unfamiliar voice with a strong Taiwanese accent. I turned. May had stepped back through the brick wall with a short, willowy woman at her side. The stranger's blazingly blue eyes and cat-slit pupils betrayed her nature even before I tasted her heritage on the breeze.

I bowed, showing her all the courtesy and regard I had denied Arden. It was an intentional snub, and from Nolan's small gasp, I knew it had been received. "It is an honor to stand before a Queen of Cats," I said.

"Yes, it is," agreed Shade mildly. "But we have met before, and this should be done quickly. Have you touched anything? Taken anything?"

"Only what was taken from me." I indicated the bundle in Quentin's arms. "We were led here by the blood trail of my daughter's clothes."

"There should be no objection to reclaiming lost property, as long as it is followed by swift departure." Shade looked to Arden. "Are we in agreement?"

In her feline form, Shade was a Blue Point Siamese, perfectly designed to blend into the fog that sometimes shrouded the city streets in the early morning. Her bipedal shape echoed that coloration, with snowy skin that darkened to a deep gray at her wrists, the points of her ears, and in an accenting stripe across the bridge of her nose. Her hair was black at the root, lightening slowly to that same blue-gray, and finally bleaching itself white for the last few inches. She could have chosen to look more like one of the Daoine Sidhe, as Tybalt often did: it was rare to see him with his stripes showing. The fact that she hadn't showed how little she cared for the good regard of the Divided Courts.

It was interesting, sometimes, being reminded of how unusual a King of Cats Tybalt was, and had been long before I'd come along to turn his world upside-down. He cared about things outside his Court. Not all Cait Sidhe bothered.

"Yes," said Arden.

I straightened. "I still want to know what this place is. Someone thought they could use it to hide my child."

"It is, as I have said, an agreement," said Shade. Maybe it was the fact that my own Queen clearly hadn't been telling me what I needed to know, or maybe she just didn't care about keeping secrets that didn't belong to her, but she continued, "When this city was still forest and field, still owned at least in part by those mortals who were here before the new Americans came and drove them out, an individual came before the rulers of our spaces, our kind. They held certain charms and a grant of land from Oberon himself. This, here, is what they asked for, and it was given. Did you never wonder why it is the Divided Courts claimed no authority here? There is a Court of Cats, for there must be to keep the shadows open, but the ones who should have demanded allegiance keep their distance."

"Because Oberon told you to." I glanced at Arden. She was glaring at Shade, her hands clenched. That, more than anything, confirmed Shade's story. "Do you know who the land grant was for?"

"No," said Shade.

"My father tried to find out before he died, but he never succeeded," said Arden. "This is the first time I've been here. We're breaking a dozen rules of etiquette just by breathing this air. We need to leave."

I thought of the absence of magic in the house, of the spare décor and the empty rooms. Whoever lived here was keeping an intentionally low profile . . . but apparently, they had still made at least one enemy.

"All right," I said. "But if I have to come back to save my daughter, I will."

Arden sighed. "I know. I couldn't stop you if I tried." She sketched an archway in the air with her hand. A portal opened, showing her throne room in Muir Woods. "Please be careful. I don't know who owns this land, but I know they were able to win it from Oberon himself. That's not a person to toy with." Then she was gone, Nolan behind her, leaving the faint scent of blackberry flowers and redwood bark hanging in the air.

I turned to Shade. "Did the Prince of Dreaming Cats come with you?" I asked. It would have been nice to see Raj, if only to confirm that *he* didn't know about this place. I knew Tybalt couldn't tell me everything about the Court. It wouldn't make sense to expect him to. But the hurt in Madden's eyes might well be mirrored in mine, if I found out he'd been hiding something that had been used to hurt my child.

"I dismissed him," said Shade airily. She studied my face for a moment before she smiled. "I see. You worry that he knew and did not tell you. That my opposite number knew and did not tell you. You forget that our fiefdoms are smaller than those of the Divided Courts, for we must deal much more closely with our subjects. This is a secret kept by those of us who rule here, over the Court of Golden Cats. Your mate did not keep a secret of this size from your ears. How is he?" There was actual concern in the question. "I have heard things that are . . . troubling to my ears. I would that he were well."

"I don't know enough about how your Courts function to be

sure I won't do him some political damage if I start answering questions now," I said. "But I appreciate you telling me he didn't know about this place, so I'll tell you this much: he's doing the best he can, and I'll be here for him when he wants me. I'm not going anywhere."

"Truth from the Liar's daughter; who would have thought I'd see the day?" Shade offered a small smile and a smaller bow. "If you have need while he is unable to assist you, call upon the cats of my Court. They may not come, but if I hear, I will do what I can." She stepped backward, into the shadow cast by a branch of the apple tree and was gone.

"Well," said May, after a long pause. "You've pissed off the Queen who's *actually* in charge of us and convinced a Queen who isn't that she should help us out. That's . . . pretty true to form. You're still you. I just checked."

"Ha fucking ha," I said. "Come on. We need to get out of here before the owner comes back, and we need to find another trail. One that actually gets us there. Quentin?"

"On it," he said, and wove his hands through the air, chanting the lyrics to some old sea shanty while the smell of steel and heather rose around him and burst, covering us all in the veil of his recast don't-look-here.

We walked to the false wall together, Madden returning to all fours and pressing his nose to the ground as he looked for a re-placement trail. I looked back only once, as we reached the exit. The little house was standing again, balanced on the edge of the porch, with its blank picture window eyes fixed on us, watching us go.

We stepped into the brick. The house, and the garden, and the impossible courtyard disappeared, and we just kept on walking.

EIGHT

GILLIAN'S CAR WAS GONE when we got back to campus. The police had probably towed it away to some impound lot for further study, and while I'd been anticipating its absence, expecting it and seeing it were very different things. I paused, taking a moment to catch my breath, before approaching the caution tape. It was still in place, campus security standing watch to make sure the students who loitered nearby, craning their necks for a glimpse of something forbidden, respected the fragile barrier.

We were less on the "respect" train than the "bring Gillian home" express. We ducked under the caution tape without hesitation, trusting Quentin's don't-look-here to protect us. Madden sniffed his way around the site while I gathered chunks of bloody glass from the ground, following the siren song of my daughter's pain. Some of the pieces had barely a drop clinging to their surface, but I found them all the same. I couldn't have missed them if I'd tried.

By the time Madden came back to the rest of us, my pocket was full of glass and my fingers had been nicked six times, forcing me to do some quick juggling to keep myself from bleeding on the ground. Strictly speaking, the campus was such a jumble of bodies and their associated fluids that it was almost certainly a forensic dead end: I could bleed everywhere, and it wouldn't necessarily point any fingers in my direction now that the car was gone. However, I preferred to be careful when I could.

"Well?" I asked Madden, voice pitched low. The student body

hadn't spotted us yet. I wanted to keep it that way. "Did you find a second trail?"

He hesitated before wagging his tail, once. So he'd found something, but he wasn't completely sure it was right or useful. That was fine. We could figure it out when we got there, and it wasn't like we had anything else to go on.

My phone rang.

"Shit," I muttered. Heads began to turn, and eyes began to focus as nearby students heard the sound. Empty air normally doesn't come with cell service. "Everybody move."

Quickly, we ducked back under the caution tape and hurried away from the crime scene. A few people tracked us, confused expressions on their faces, but most continued looking at the place I'd been when my phone began to ring. Magic has its uses.

My phone was still ringing. I pulled it out and swiped my thumb across the screen without checking the caller ID. No one has my number who shouldn't—literally. I'm not sure my number even *exists*. I got it when Devin gave me a phone, and I've held onto it through a dozen of April's "upgrades." I've never seen a bill. If there's a mortal cellular company that has my business, I don't know about it.

"Hello?"

"Is this a bad time?" Walther sounded weary, like he'd been pulled out of bed far too early for any civilized man. Given that it wasn't even noon yet, I couldn't fully blame him.

"No, it's not. Bridget got ahold of you?"

"Dragged me out of a department meeting with a story about a student in distress. I'd kiss her if she weren't married, not my type, and glaring at me." He audibly yawned. "Okay, I've had like, five cups of coffee and this is as awake as I'm getting. Are you still on campus?"

"Yes. Do you need me?"

"That depends. How's your nose?"

I paused for a moment, focusing on breathing. "A little stuffy, but mostly okay. My eyes itch more than anything. Quentin still sounds congested, and so does May."

"Got it. Yes, I need you. You should all come to my office as soon as possible."

"Why?"

"Allergy medication." He hung up with a click. I lowered my phone, staring at it. Something about his tone—

"Okay, everyone, come on; we need to hurry." I shoved my phone back into my pocket and started walking faster.

Quentin gave me a sidelong look. "Why?"

"Because Walther didn't tell me to."

His eyes widened. "Oh," he said, and matched me step for step.

Walther is a lot of things. "Overly dramatic" doesn't make the list. If anything, he has a tendency to downplay bad situations, acting like there's nothing to worry about when there's really everything to worry about. He already had the allergy medication ready for us. That told me it was something we needed to take.

"Drop the don't-look-here when you have a clear opportunity to do so," I said. Quentin nodded and, when we were briefly shielded from the rest of campus by the side of a building, snapped his fingers and let the spell go. There might be cameras. If there were, we wouldn't appear out of nowhere, more go from an unfocused spot on the film—or whatever cameras used these days—to a focused one.

May jumped when the spell dropped, shooting me a sharp look. "What's going on?"

"We're going to see Walther."

Her eyes hardened, but she only nodded, recognizing how exposed we were now. Placing her fingers in her mouth, she whistled shrilly. Madden's head whipped around, and he came bounding back to us.

"Okay, here's the deal," I said. "Walther needs to see us. Madden, can you find this trail again if we leave it here? Or do we need to split up?"

He whined once, but then he bobbed his head and fell in next to May.

"Okay," I said, feeling a wash of relief. If Walther had something to unclog our noses and make our eyes stop itching, that was good. That could only help Madden be better at doing his job and finding my daughter. Leaving him out could be seen as an insult to the crown—and after our little jaunt into the courtyard-that-wasn't, I didn't think Arden was that thrilled with me. Maybe she'd decide I was too much trouble and she didn't want my fealty after all. And maybe pigs would fly.

I snorted. May glanced in my direction, one eyebrow raised. "Something funny?"

"Pigs are flying," I said.

Quentin snorted as well, and May rolled her eyes.

"You are both twelve," she said, and walked a little faster. I didn't try to call her back. She knew the way to Walther's office as well as I did. Really, the only one of us who didn't was Madden, and since he was playing the faithful hound and sticking at May's heels, there was no need to worry about losing him.

People think searching for something—a knowe, a cheating husband, a child—is always a linear process. You start *here*, you go *there*, you find the things you're looking for and bring them safely home or back to their owners. Then you get paid and walk into the sunset, confident in a job well done. I blame television. Fitting something into an hour means cutting the wrong turns, the digressions, the complications. It's an easy first act, a twist in the second act, and a resolution in the third.

The reality is more complicated. Finding someone is legwork and research and watching the clock, always, always watching the clock, because time is never on your side. There are no acts, no commercial breaks, and no guarantee that when the search grinds to a halt, the person you're trying to find won't already be floating in a ditch.

Gillian had been taken. Fact. Gillian had been taken by someone who may or may not have used magic in the process. Normally, it would have been clear, but she'd been taken before dawn, which meant any minor spells had already been crisped to ash, while the major ones, eroded but intact, would be drowned in the soupy swamp of magical signatures that wreathed the campus. My sensitivity to magic is a good thing, especially in my line of work, but it could also be a liability in a place like this, where there was just too much to confuse the issue.

Gillian had been taken and stripped naked, and her clothes had been left in a place so secret it made queens pale to hear that people were inside it, a place I'd never heard of before. Devin should have been running a damn farmer's market out of a garden like that one. So who could have known it was there, and been willing to use it to throw me off the track like that?

It wasn't a comfortable question. It confirmed fae involvement as nothing else could have, and only the fact that the scent of oranges had never so much as put in an appearance kept me from being sure that Simon was behind it all. That, and the fact that I knew him. Lost or not, I knew him, and I couldn't believe he'd do this to me.

Then again, maybe I was being naïve. After all, he'd been willing to do this to his own brother. Why not me? But he couldn't have cast a single spell without leaving the scent of rotten oranges behind, and I wasn't finding any oranges. Just the strangely present scent of cinnamon, which didn't connect to anyone I could think of.

The chemistry building doors stood open, propped to let the morning air inside. Students lounged on the steps, some eating late breakfasts, others chatting with their friends until it was time to go to class. A few cast curious looks in our direction. I tensed before realizing their attention was mostly focused on Madden, who was, after all, a very handsome dog. I relaxed. I've always been more of a cat person, but that doesn't mean I can't appreciate the camouflage of a good dog.

Walther's office door was also open, thanks to a hefty brick that served as a makeshift doorstop. I still knocked. It was only polite. Walther poked his head out a moment later, stress showing in the tightly drawn skin around his eyes. It faded when he saw us. Not enough: there was still a shadow there I didn't like, something that seemed more concerned than it needed to be.

"Toby," he said. "Quentin, May. Please, come in." He didn't greet Madden. That made sense: Madden was a dog, after all.

Bridget was already in the office, sitting in the chair Walther used for visiting students, a paper coffee cup in her hand and a concerned look on her face that almost exactly mirrored Walther's. She waved, saying, "I'm glad you could make it."

"When Walther calls, we come," I said.

Walther shut the door, removing his glasses. "Good." He placed them on a convenient shelf as he started for his desk. "Stay right there."

Tylwyth Teg tend to fit a certain mold: golden hair, sharply pointed ears, and eyes of piercing blue too bright to be concealed by any simple illusion. Walther's glasses were designed to draw attention away from his eyes, and they generally worked, keeping his students from asking if he wore colored contacts. He was on the short side, with narrow shoulders and the quick, hurried posture of a scientist who was constantly afraid something in his lab was about to catch fire.

Once at the desk, he opened a drawer and withdrew four small plastic syringes, each filled with a virulently purple liquid that sparkled from within, like he had ground a pixie into dust and suspended it in the solution. "Each of you needs to drink one of these."

"What are they?" I asked, already reaching for one. Quentin and May did the same, while Madden shifted into his human form, shook himself, and took the last of them.

"I told you." Walther's mouth was a thin, grim line. "It's allergy medication."

"Walther—"

"Just drink it, okay? I'll explain after you drink it."

I gave him a suspicious look before raising the syringe to my mouth. It had no needle, just a small circular opening that seemed perfectly designed to slip between my lips. I drove the plunger home, and the sticky-sweet taste of pomegranate, pear, and what I suspected was artificial grape flooded across my tongue. That was the pleasant part. The kick followed half a beat behind the flavor, and suddenly everything was burning. I coughed.

"What did you *do*, mix fire ants and whiskey?" I wheezed. The burning sensation in my throat wasn't fading.

The burning sensation in my eyes, on the other hand, was gone. I stopped coughing in my surprise and realized I could breathe through my nose. Everything was clear. Everything was *fine*. Better than fine: everything was *normal*.

"Not quite, but you're probably not as far off as you wish you were," said Walther. He plucked the syringe from my hand. May and Quentin were still coughing. He took their syringes as well. Madden had yet to consume the contents of his. Walther stopped, eyeing him. "You need to swallow it if you want it to work."

"I don't know what sort of people you're accustomed to working with, Master Alchemist," said Madden, with a glance at me to make it clear that he knew *exactly* what kind of people Walther normally dealt with, "but I don't drink things that haven't been identified."

"I told you, it's allergy medication," said Walther. "You're not an alchemist. I have neither the time nor the inclination to explain exactly what it is to you. But you need to take it, and soon, or the allergic reaction you've been having since you touched that damn sachet is going to keep getting worse. There's a point past which I won't be able to help you."

Madden's eyes widened. "We've been *poisoned*?"

"In the sense that an allergic reaction is your body treating something that should be harmless as if it were poisonous, yes, and this is why I don't ever want to be a court alchemist, because when I give you something, you're supposed to *drink* it." Walther sighed. "Don't argue with me about it, don't try to make me explain things I've never had to explain before, do as you're told and drink it before I have to tell your liege, 'I'm sorry, but he needs to be put into a magical coma while he recovers from being stupid.'"

"And here I thought you were a teacher," said May.

"I teach *chemistry*. It's similar to alchemy, but it's not the same. If it were the same, humans would be turning lead into gold all willy-nilly, and I wouldn't need to brew half of what I spend my free time brewing." Walther looked at Madden. "The person who cured elf-shot is telling you to drink. So drink."

Madden drank.

"Mother of flowers preserve and protect me from the world," said Walther. He snatched Madden's syringe. "Toby, you were right. It was a marshwater working. You were also wrong, because it was the kind of marshwater work I don't think anyone's used for centuries. Old, deep, nasty stuff. The Scots kale was the key. It's still sold at farmer's markets and the like—good source of iron, humans are weird—but nobody uses it in charm work anymore."

"Why not?" I asked.

"It smells like a boiled fart for most of the drying process, and there are other plants that work just as well. No one's going to use Scots kale if they have any alternatives." Walther dropped all four syringes into a plastic bag and sealed it. "This one was designed to repel the fae, first off, and to blind them and stop up their senses, second off. So that burning in your eyes and stuffiness in your nose would have kept getting worse, and worse, and worse, until either something flushed it from your system or you temporarily lost one or more senses entirely. I've been dealing with changelings for *weeks* who were having this exact allergic reaction, and none of them could tell me what they'd touched. I'm betting that if we mapped their movements, they'd all touched your daughter."

I stiffened. "Maybe reword that a little bit."

"Sorry." Walther shook his head. "I mean, they'd all come into contact with your daughter. She's . . . imagine the entire fae population of this school is allergic to peanuts, and she's been washing her clothes in peanut butter every morning. She could kill someone if she's not careful. Do you have any idea where she might have gotten this recipe?"

I stiffened further, until it felt like my spine had been replaced by an oak tree, rigid and unyielding. "You think Gillian did this?"

"Honestly, I don't know what to think . . . but no one fae made this stuff." He held up his hands for the first time, showing me the vivid red rash covering his fingers. "It itches like poison oak. The herbs and vegetable components were blended perfectly, and then they were left under at least three full moons to cure. This is master class charm work. It's nasty and it's vicious, and I don't think even a thin-blooded changeling could have done it without hurting themselves so badly that someone would have heard about it. If only the night-haunts."

It was hard to stop myself from looking at May. The connection between Fetches and the night-haunts isn't widely known, and they don't really want it advertised.

"No." I shook my head. "This isn't my daughter's work. There's no way she could have learned how. I didn't teach her. Her father has no idea the fae exist. Someone did this."

"Why?" Madden turned to me, frowning as he spoke. He looked more solemn than he had since this day began. Now we weren't just looking at my missing child: we were looking at a threat to the kingdom, something that used magic so old and so small that there was no way to see it coming. I would have sympathized with his obvious dismay if it hadn't made me want to scream. "What possible reason would someone have to wreathe your child, who isn't fae at all, in charms designed to keep the fae away from her?"

The answer was simple and so, so obvious. "Jocelyn."

"What?"

"She's a changeling—she couldn't have made the sachets, but she could have found the ritual, gone to the Library and looked it up or bought it off some street-witch who cared more about money than they did about keeping something like this contained." If Jocelyn had done it all, if Jocelyn somehow had access to that impossible courtyard, she wouldn't even have needed money. A handful of fresh goblin fruit could have paid for anything she wanted in the world. "Pay a human to do it, and plant them all around Gillian."

"Why?" asked Quentin. "She was so excited to see you."

"Yeah, and she was sure fast to try to get me to thank her. She knows enough about the rules to use them, but does she understand them? And remember, changelings don't respond to things exactly like purebloods do. Iron doesn't hurt us as badly. Dawn hurts us more. Maybe she could clear up her allergies with actual, nonmagical Benadryl. Or maybe she thought it would only repel full fae."

"Why would she want to repel you, though?" Quentin's frustration was mounting. Being poisoned tended to do that. "She was so happy to meet you."

"Maybe she just didn't want us around *Gillian*," said May. "If we hadn't found the sachet, if we'd just encountered Gilly on campus . . . "

"You would have felt a strong compulsion to avoid her, probably because every time you got near her, you'd start sneezing," said Walther. "If this Jocelyn seemed immune, she might even have been able to position herself as a source of information. It's an unnecessarily complicated plan, but that doesn't mean it's a bad one, and these are college students. I watched one of them spend a semester trying to train squirrels to bring him Mountain Dew from the vending machine because he was too lazy to get up and press the button."

"Did it work?" asked Quentin.

"No, but some other kids broke into the squirrel nests later in the year and found twenty bucks in quarters."

We were all silent for a moment, considering that image. I shook it off. "Bridget, you know both of them. Any idea how they became roommates?"

"The house where they live takes applications at the start of the term," said Bridget slowly. "They don't accept everyone, of course, and once you're in, it can be difficult to get a new roommate. If I had to guess, I'd say Jocelyn greased a few palms to get the assignment she wanted."

This was beginning to look more and more damning. I took a breath. "Walther, can we get more of that allergy medication, just in case? If the herbal blend sticks to clothes, we might be reexposing ourselves by looking for Gillian."

Quentin gave the bundle of clothes he was still carrying an alarmed look.

Walther nodded. "I made some up in pill form. It doesn't work as fast, but every dose should last for about eight hours. If you think you've been exposed, take another pill." He picked up a clear bottle filled with violently blue gel caps and lobbed it at me. I caught it, shook it once to see how many pills were in there, and tucked it into my pocket. He tossed another bottle to May. I nodded approvingly. Never put all the life-saving medication in one basket.

"Overdose risks?" I asked.

"None." Walther paused. "Well. Some, but you'd need to take more than I've given you, and all you'd do is turn blue for a while."

"Swell." I turned to Madden. "I want you to take May and follow the second trail. If you find anything, *anything* that might tell us where Gillian's been taken, call me immediately, and I'll be right there." Sending them off without me ached. But if there was anyone this side of Faerie who loved Gilly like I did, it was May. She wouldn't let our daughter come to harm if there was anything she could do about it.

"What are you going to do?" he asked.

"Go and have a little talk with Jocelyn." I bared my teeth at him. He took a startled half-step backward. "She and I have so *much* to discuss, don't you think?"

"Don't kill the poor girl," said Bridget.

I looked at her. "And if she'd taken Chelsea? Would you be saying that?"

"No. I'd be telling you to bring me her entrails, so I could have a go at reading the future. But I am neither a knight nor a hero of the realm, and as Etienne would have me understand it, the rules are different for you." She looked at me levelly. "I'll not tell you to spare the girl if she doesn't deserve sparing. I *am* telling you to be sure before you do something that can't be taken back. It's a cruel enough world, Toby. There's no need for us to go and make it worse."

"Big words from a woman who tried to hit me with a cast iron pan when she even suspected I might have had something to do with her daughter's disappearance." Bridget flushed red and turned her face away. I tried to feel some sense of victory. All I felt was tired.

"Don't kill her so much that I don't get a chance," said May.

"That, I think I can promise." I turned to Walther. "I'll see you soon. Open roads."

"Kind fires," he echoed automatically.

With that I turned and walked out of the office, Quentin beside me, leaving the rest of them behind.

We made it out of the building and down the steps before he looked at me anxiously and asked, "You aren't really going to kill her, are you?"

"I don't know, kiddo," I replied. "I really don't know."

We walked on.

NINE

THE OFFICERS WERE GONE from the residence hall when Quentin and I got there. Several girls I assumed lived there were out front, hammering boards over broken windows with the resigned air of people who thought they were too good for basic, menial tasks. Only a few of them looked at us as we walked up the path to the front door, and no one moved to stop us from going inside or even ask who we were there to see.

"Nice security," I commented. Cliff was going to get an earful about this once Gilly was safely home, that was for damn sure. Maybe I didn't have any authority over her life at this point, but I could certainly make my feelings known. She needed to be living somewhere with a front door that *locked*. Maybe a doorman would be a step too far—in addition to being prohibitively expensive—but dammit, she deserved some sort of protection.

Quentin made a disgusted snorting noise. It was nice to know someone was on my side in this.

We reached the top of the stairs, walked to the room Gillian and Jocelyn shared, and stopped dead, both of us staring. Quentin found his voice first. He had fewer layers of shock and self-recrimination to work through.

"What the hell . . . ?"

Gillian's side of the room looked exactly the same as before. May's search, intensive as it had no doubt been, had left no traces. That was good. She lacked the muscle memory to do things like drive or fight, even if she could close her eyes and relive my lessons, but she knew how to toss a room without getting caught. Jocelyn's side of the room, on the other hand . . .

The bed was stripped. All her personal items were gone, from the books on the headboard to the small display of pictures on the wall. Even the desk was bare. I suddenly felt like I was choking, and it was no allergic reaction this time. She was gone, my daughter's room-mate was *gone*, and I couldn't breathe. I couldn't breathe.

Slowly, I stepped into the room, Quentin standing frozen behind me. The acrid scent of the herbal sachets lingered in the air. I realized I had no idea what Jocelyn's magic smelled like, or whether it was even strong enough to have a scent at all. The presence of so many hostile herbs had prevented me from sniffing it out while she was here, and now . . .

Now she was gone, and our chances of finding Gillian might well have gone with her.

"Oh, are you Jocelyn's mom? She told us you'd be coming by to make sure she hadn't forgotten anything."

I turned. A harried-looking human woman was standing in the hall, a clipboard in one hand, like something out of a college recruitment catalog. She flushed when she saw me staring.

"I'm Chloe, I'm the residence director," she said, almost apologetically. "I'm sorry. It's been a hell of a day."

My anger and confusion fell back as a mask of professionalism snapped into place. This woman might have answers, at least to the question of where the hell Jocelyn had gone. "I heard one of your residents went missing."

"Not from here, thank God." Her flush faded, replaced by a shocked pallor. "I'm sorry. That sounded bad."

"That's the second time you've apologized," I said, trying to sound gentle. I probably didn't succeed. Hopefully, I at least sounded like I understood why she might be tense. "Have they found the girl?"

"Not yet," she said. "Gillian was parked on campus when someone snatched her. No one noticed for hours because we'd had some vandalism here—wait. Didn't Jocelyn tell you all this?" Her eyes narrowed. "Can I see some ID?"

"Absolutely." I pulled a chunk of broken glass out of my pocket, intentionally slicing my fingertips on its edges, and murmured, "Baa, baa, black sheep, have you any wool? Yes sir, yes sir, but you can't have any, fuck off."

The smell of grass and copper swirled around us as a spike was hammered into my temple, the pain from before flaring up twice as brightly. Chloe's eyes went briefly unfocused. When they sharpened again, she was smiling.

"Sorry about that, but you know how it is," she said. "You can't be too careful where student safety is concerned."

A funny sentiment, considering that Quentin and I had just walked in. I shoved my hands into my pockets, hiding the blood on my fingers, hiding how tightly clenched they were. "Safety is the highest priority," I said. It was a struggle to keep my voice from wavering from the pain in my head. "Jocelyn was very upset about the disappearance of the Marks girl. She was a good roommate."

"Everybody loves Gillian," said Chloe. "I'm just sick at the thought of something like this happening here. We're going to set up a buddy system until she's found, to make sure the rest of the residents are safe. Please tell Jocelyn that when she decides to come back, I will be happy to *personally* be her buddy. Nothing is going to happen to any of my other girls."

"I appreciate that," I said neutrally. The spell I'd used to make her see an ID she would accept had also made her suggestable. That was a good thing, as long as I didn't push it too hard. "Did you have *any* sign that this was coming? Suspicious people hanging around the house, neighborhood kids throwing rocks, anything?"

Chloe looked uncertain.

Screw it. I'd push as hard as I had to. "If I'm going to allow Jocelyn to return to school, I need to know she's going to be safe."

"It seemed like nothing."

Jackpot. "What seemed like nothing?"

"Someone kept cutting the house internet. I know, that sounds silly, and at first we thought it was just our ISP being awful—it happens, people assume the Bay Area will have this incredible, super-fast service, and really, we're on decaying DSL lines and nobody wants to pay to upgrade them—but it kept happening, and one of our computer science majors managed to uncover an ongoing denial of service attack against us, specifically. Someone was flooding our Wi-Fi."

"All the time?" I didn't understand half of what she was saying, but I could tell Quentin did. He was frowning, looking thoughtful, not confused. He could explain this to me later.

"No." Her expression turned sorrowful, sheepishness and regret and hindsight warring for dominance. "Only when Gillian was home. Now, after the fact, it feels like . . . well, it feels like someone was trying to make sure she'd stop studying in the house. Maybe they were trying to get her to Wheeler Hall. I don't know."

I ground my teeth so hard it hurt, and I tasted blood. That was enough to center me, and I took a careful breath before I said, "I feel like someone should have called me, since she was rooming with my daughter." True enough, as long as the "she" in that sentence referred to Jocelyn.

The fae are great liars. They've had centuries to perfect their art. I've always found the truth to be more effective, especially when I'm already operating under false pretenses. It's harder to get caught in a contradiction when you never contradict yourself.

"We honestly didn't think it was anything dangerous." There was a defensive note in Chloe's voice now. I was approaching the end of her patience, even for a parent. "We would have notified all parents if it were."

"I appreciate your candor," I said, with a meaningful glance at Quentin. He nodded agreement, so vigorously that for a moment I was afraid his head would pop clean off his shoulders. "If you'll excuse us, I want to finish cleaning up in here and be on my way. My daughter is very upset about everything that's happened." Another truth—or at least I hoped it was. If Gillian was conscious, I had no doubt she was upset.

"I'll be in the kitchen if you need me," said Chloe, and retreated. For once, the natural human desire to avoid the fae—even if they didn't realize that was what they were doing—was working for me, not against me.

I turned to Quentin. "Check under the beds, behind the dressers, anywhere for signs of where she might have gone. If you see anything herbal, retreat and call me, got it? We have five minutes, tops, before that woman realizes we probably shouldn't be in here unsupervised."

"On it," said Quentin, and made for Jocelyn's bed.

I didn't want to come into contact with another of those dusty, deadly sachets, and so I turned away from the dressers, toward the room's single narrow closet. It looked barely big enough to contain my clothes, much less the clothing belonging to two girls in their late teens, when having a different outfit for every occasion still felt like it *mattered*. And it did matter, for some people. I'd never seen

Arden wear the same Court dress twice. I'd never seen my mother do it either. Depending on what they chose to do with their lives, Gilly and Jocelyn might need to have wardrobes large enough to contain worlds, packed with shoes and slip dresses, with silks and satins. Or they might wind up like me, barely filling a single dresser. That's the thing about time, about youth. It passes, and you become a bit more yourself with every day gone.

Nothing in the closet appeared to have been taken or even disturbed. I frowned thoughtfully. It was like Jocelyn wanted us to know she was gone but hadn't wanted to go to the trouble of actually *leaving*. Cautiously, I parted the hanging dresses. I knew when I touched something of Gillian's by the faint tingle it left on my skin and the acrid scent of dried fennel and kale. I was going to need more of those allergy pills before the day was done.

There was nothing of interest in the closet, and the sachet tucked into the far corner meant that sniffing out Jocelyn's magic wasn't an option. I closed the door and turned to her dresser, pulling the top drawer open.

There was a note there, neatly folded atop the balled-up socks and rolled underpants. I stopped, looking at it.

Quentin caught the change. He glanced my way. "Toby?"

"It's addressed to me." I poked the paper with one finger. There was no tingle. If Jocelyn had made the sachets, she had been incredibly careful to keep their contents off her skin.

I picked up the note, unfolded it, and read aloud, "'October, I bet you wish you'd been nicer now, don't you? I could have told you a lot of things, but you didn't want to listen. Good luck finding your precious brat. I guess you're pretty good at losing her. If you decide you want to play nicely, I'll find you in the place you gave away.'" I turned the note over. "That's all there is."

Quentin didn't say anything.

I sighed, allowing weariness to settle over me for a moment, letting it weigh me down. I was so damn tired. I hadn't slept, I hadn't eaten, my daughter was missing, and now it seemed we'd let one of the people responsible for her disappearance slip right through our fingers.

As if on cue, my phone rang. I pulled it out and swiped my thumb across the screen as I raised it to my ear. "Hello?"

"We're at Telegraph and Durant. Can you get down here? And hurry? There's something you need to see." May hung up. Either they'd found something terrible, or she knew we didn't have time to waste. Either way, we needed to move.

"Come on." I shoved my phone back into my pocket and tucked the note into my jacket as I turned for the stairs. Quentin followed behind me; thank Oberon, he didn't ask where we were going, or why we were going so quickly. He just followed, and when I hit the front porch and broke into a run, he did the same.

We raced down the sidewalk, the two of us, and this was such a familiar scene that it ached, because this had never happened before, not really, not like this. It felt like everything was crumbling around me. Gillian was missing, maybe hurt, and Tybalt was shutting me out, and Jocelyn had gotten away. Would I have recognized her as a threat if I'd still been closer to human, if I hadn't shifted toward thinking of people without magic as harmless? Would I have caught the signs that could tell me she was dangerous, not merely an annoyance, if I hadn't been distracted by worrying about Tybalt? Was Gillian going to pay the price for my hubris?

We ran and ran, and I tried to let the running become a distraction. If I could focus on the act of putting one foot in front of another, maybe I would be able to find something that would let me fight through this terrible situation to the other side.

A corner loomed ahead of us. We turned, running two more blocks, and there was Telegraph Avenue, artery of the city, running straight and clean from the highway to the quad where the clocktower loomed. We turned again, weaving through crowds of students, parents, and tourists, passing street vendors both human and otherwise as we made our way toward Durant, a cross-street that connected the surrounding residential neighborhoods with this bustling commercial chaos.

May and Madden were waiting for us there. Madden was back in his seemingly-human form. I couldn't decide whether that was a good sign. May elbowed Madden as we approached, and he swung his head around to face us.

"Hey," said May, once we were close enough that she wouldn't need to shout. "Did you find anything?"

"Not enough," I said. "You?"

"There's a second trail," said Madden. He rubbed the back of his neck with one hand. "It's not . . . it's not very strong. I don't track," he glanced around, and lowered his voice before continuing, "humans that well. They use such strongly scented soap that they all wind up smelling basically the same unless I can get a good starting whiff to work from. But I found it."

"Okay." I looked back and forth between them. "What are we waiting for?"

"It's better if you see," said May. "Come on." She started walking. I stared at the back of her head, confused. Then I followed her. I couldn't think of anything else to do.

We walked down Durant to a smaller, residential street and turned, going another block or so before we turned again. The houses grew smaller and deeper set into their gardens as we walked, the trappings of suburbia melting into a wall of green. I hurried to catch up to May, falling into step beside her.

"What aren't you telling me?" I asked.

She shook her head. "We're almost there."

"Dammit, May—"

"I need to know what you see, and I need to know you're not just repeating what I told you would be there." May gave me a pained sidelong glance. "Believe me, I'm not thrilled about this either, all right? Please. I need you to be patient. Can you be patient, just for a few more minutes?"

I took a deep breath, forcing myself to calm. "A few more, but that's it," I said.

"That's all I'm asking. Was Jocelyn there?"

"Gone. She left a note. I think she had something to do with Gillian's disappearance. But I still don't think the sachets were her doing. There wasn't any trace of them in her things, only Gillian's, and no one in their right mind fills their own living space with poison."

"Maybe." May stopped so abruptly that I almost tripped in my haste to do the same. She waved a hand, indicating the house in front of us. "What do you see?"

I turned and saw . . . a house. It was small and plain, with smooth plaster walls and a half-roofed porch overhung by a vast magnolia tree that didn't seem to care how far out of its own climate it was. There was a huge picture window—and that was where the problems began. When I looked at the window directly, it was smooth and perfect. But out of the corner of my eye, it was a cobwebby mass of cracks, all of them radiating out from a hole the size of a fist. I blinked. The window was intact once more.

"What the—?"

"So you see something wrong?"

I eyed May. "Don't you?"

"I can't make it past the bayberry bushes." She pointed to a pair of ornamental shrubs halfway up the path. "I just stop and forget what I'm doing. Madden can't even get that far."

"Quentin?" I turned to my squire. "What do you see?"

"It's a house," he said. He sounded frustrated and unsettled. Taking a half-step back, he said, "I don't like it. Is this where we're supposed to be? I don't like it."

I focused more fully on the house. This wasn't a normal illusion: there was no glitter in the air, no place where the normal became abnormal, or vice-versa. It was just . . . wrong, subtly so, with little flickers at the corner of my eye revealing the edges of the problem, but not the problem itself.

"Did the trail lead here?" I asked.

"It does," said Madden.

"Does it go inside?"

"I think so." He grimaced. "I can't go inside. I try, and it doesn't happen. So maybe it's yes and maybe it's no, but I think so."

"Right," I said, and started down the narrow pathway toward the house.

I had barely reached the bayberry bushes when an invisible force field started pushing me back. It was like I was walking into a wall of cling film somehow pulled tight across the universe itself, refusing to let me go any farther.

"I think not," I hissed. Pulling the knife from my belt, I ran it across my opposing palm. Pain flared up, sharp and reassuring and familiar in a way that made me think maybe everything was going to be all right. I raised my hand and slapped it against the resistance in the air, forcing my way forward—and to my profound relief, the invisible force yielded, allowing me to take one step, two steps, three steps past the line of the bayberries.

The resistance shattered, and suddenly I could see the house for what it really was: a decrepit, fire-gutted husk. The picture window was more void than glass, leaving shards to glitter across the ash-blackened porch. The front door was still there, but it was standing ajar, held on by a single hinge. I took another step forward, testing to be sure nothing would stop me, and turned to look back at the others.

They were standing where I had left them. Quentin's hand had gone to his hip, where I had no doubt he was carrying a concealed weapon of some kind. May looked mildly alarmed, and had her hand on Madden's shoulder, keeping him where he was. Madden . . .

Madden was growling, canine-style, his lips drawn back from his teeth in what would probably have been a terrifying display if not for the human disguise he wore. As it stood, the sight was strange.

"Toby, if you're there, we would *really appreciate it* if you would say something," called May. Her voice was shaking.

"I'm here. Can you hear me?"

May relaxed. Quentin's hand dropped away from his hip. Madden kept growling.

"We can hear you," May said. "What the hell?"

"There's some kind of repulsion charm mixed with an illusion covering this place up." I took a step back toward the bayberry bushes and paused. "I had to bleed to get through, but maybe I've weakened it. Can you try to come here?"

"Yes," said May and Quentin, in unison. They looked at each other.

"*Yes*," May repeated, with more force. Quentin looked like he was going to protest. She raised a hand to stop him. "I'm functionally unkillable, remember? You, however, are not, and the last thing we need right now is to add your pissed-off parents to the mix. So I don't actually care if you think it's your duty as her squire to help her with whatever the hell is going on here. I'm going to take the hit. Got me?"

Quentin wilted. "Got you," he said, sounding every inch the sullen teenager.

"Good," said May, and started down the path toward me. She made it as far as the bayberry bushes before she stopped dead, her feet suddenly seeming rooted to the stone. "Okay. I can't go any farther."

"Stick out your hand."

She did. I reached out and grabbed it, yanking her toward me as hard as I could. Her feet remained rooted in place. She cried out, high and pained. I let go before one of us fell.

May took a step back, rubbing her injured wrist with the opposing hand. "Unless you want to tear down the entire spell, we're not getting me through."

I looked at the burnt-out husk of the house behind me. "There's no way," I said. "This place has been on fire, the window's broken—there's just no way. It would attract way too much attention if I pulled the enchantment down."

"So don't," said Quentin. "Just . . . please be careful. If we have to wait out here, we will, but I don't want you getting hurt."

The shell was sealed with blood magic. Of everyone now waiting on the path, Quentin was probably the only one with half a chance of getting through it if he really tried. He didn't heal like I did. I didn't want him cutting himself if there was any other option available. I'd been able to teach him so much about being a good knight and more importantly, about surviving. I couldn't teach him how deep it was safe to drive the knife because, for me, there had never been a limit.

"I'll be careful," I said. "I have my phone. If the police show up to hurry you along, call me, and I'll come to wherever you are." Not out of the question. The police in Berkeley could be overenthusiastic about keeping the residential neighborhoods free of what they considered to be "riffraff."

"So call me," said Quentin.

I blinked. "What?"

"Right now. Call me."

It made sense. I pulled my phone out of my pocket and selected his number, dialing. His phone began to ring almost immediately. He produced it, answered, and raised it to his ear.

"You hear me?" he asked.

"Twice," I said, into my own phone. His shoulders relaxed. "I'm going in now. Wish me luck."

"Open roads," he said, and hung up.

There was nothing more for us to do outside. Turning on my heel, I walked away from my friends and toward the waiting house.

The closer I got, the more superficial the damage appeared. The fire had been bad enough to blacken the paint and warp the remaining glass in the window panes, but it didn't seem to have done much in the way of structural damage. I felt a pang of déjà vu as I stepped onto a porch I wasn't sure would hold me for the second time in a day. This one was brick and plaster, not rotting wood, and it didn't so much as shift beneath my feet.

A gentle push moved the door out of my way and I was inside, walking into a charred maze of damaged furniture and fallen plaster. The roof seemed to have mostly held, but the ceiling had partially collapsed, revealing beams and insulation. If not for the spell keeping intruders of all species out, there would have been raccoons living up there, taking advantage of the shelter from the weather and the lack of human occupants.

Moving into the center of the room, I took a shallow breath to acquaint myself with the scents of fire damage and mildew, filing them away as inconsequential elements of the atmosphere. Then, bracing myself, I inhaled as deeply as I could, sifting through every scrap of scent, looking for something—*anything*—that would tell me who had spun these spells, who had brought Gillian to this place. *Anything.*

The air seemed to chill. No, not really: it wasn't getting colder, but it *smelled* like it was colder, like the winter wind rolling across the surface of the sea. The scent of rowan wood was interlaced with that chill, the one feeding into the other, the tree blighted by a winter that would never, could never end. I gasped, and the air it brought into my lungs intensified both scents, until I was no longer sure I could keep my balance, until the urge to drop to my knees and weep was so strong that I could barely stand it.

"No," I said to the empty room. It was too small to carry an echo, but I felt like it should have, like it should bounce my voice back to me, magnify it, make it big enough to fill the world. "No, this isn't possible."

But when I breathed in again, the scent remained unchanged. Cold, and rowan, and the sea. It wasn't possible. It couldn't be possible. It was.

I pulled out my phone. Walther picked up on the second ring. "Hello?"

"Walther, does your sister have a phone?"

There was a long pause as he processed that question. Finally, he said, "Yes, Marlis has a phone. Also, hi. Also, what does my sister have to do with anything?"

"I need you to call her. I need you to ask her whether your family still has their sleepers safely imprisoned."

"Why are you—"

"Do it." I hung up and stuffed the phone back into my pocket before turning, slowly, to look at the room around me. I didn't want to be here. I didn't want to be doing this, didn't want to be searching this place like this was an ordinary case on an ordinary day. I wanted to scream. I wanted to run. I wanted my *daughter* back, and I wanted none of this to be happening, and I couldn't have any of the things I wanted. Maybe I never could.

Before Arden took the throne in the Mists, before I learned that queens could be kind—self-interested, yes, but still kind—a woman without a name had called herself our queen, had worn the crown and wielded her power like a cudgel, using it to crush anyone who would oppose her. She had been a puppet with no real claim to the position she held, put in place by Eira Rosynhwyr after the death of King Gilad. She was a mixed-blood, Siren and Sea Wight and Banshee all blended together in a soup so confusing and intoxicating that no one had asked how a Tuatha de Dannan king could have been her father until it had been too late to take the title away from her with anything short of a war.

Everyone's magic is unique. No two people have the exact same mixture of scents, the exact same balance between them. That's how I can use it as a way to track down the source and caster of a spell. Like blood, magic is unique. I had smelled this magic before. It belonged to the false Queen of the Mists.

And that wasn't possible, because she was elf-shot and sleeping away a century in the Kingdom of Silences. Her former lover, Rhys, had been their pretender king, and I had helped to depose him, too, leaving them both to spend a hundred years in an enchanted slumber where they couldn't hurt anyone.

Of course, I had also helped Walther develop a treatment for elf-shot. If she was free, if she had somehow woken up and escaped, I had no one to blame but myself.

I took a shaky breath, forcing myself to calm down, and breathed in again, finding the source of the scent. Holding it firmly in my mind, I followed it deeper into the house, stepping over the worst of the charred places, passing the burnt-out bathroom and what might have been a nursery once, going by the streaky pastel colors that still remained on the walls.

At the back of the house, almost untouched by the flames, was the master bedroom. It was still fully furnished. Mold had blossomed on the bedclothes and the bookshelves, painting them in a dozen soft shades of green. I barely noticed. I was too busy staring at the bed, struggling to breathe through the adrenaline and fear. It felt like my heart had come loose and was ricocheting around inside my body, never quite finding its rhythm.

Gillian was lying in the middle of the bed, sound asleep.

TEN

SHE LOOKED PEACEFUL, her hands crossed over her chest and her legs stretched out so that her sneaker-clad toes pointed toward the far wall. We could have been in her bedroom or at the residence hall, someplace where she had every reason to lie down for a nap without concern that something would happen. She was dressed in blue jeans and another UC Berkeley sweatshirt, and I was taking a step toward her, hand outstretched, when my phone rang loudly enough to jar me out of my brief fugue.

I stopped where I was and pulled the phone from my pocket, checking the display. Walther. With another longing glance at my little girl, I swiped my thumb across the screen and raised the phone to my ear. "What?"

"Marlis says she's still there. She wanted to know why I was asking. I told her I didn't know, but that's not going to hold my sister long. You know how paranoid they are in Silences. They have good reason to be, but—"

"Whatever they have up there, it's not the false Queen. She was here. She's the one who took Gillian." Gillian, *my* Gillian, was breathing easily, not in any visible distress. She was asleep, yes, but it couldn't be elf-shot, or she would have been dead before I reached her. Whatever this was, it would be something reversible, something temporary. I could have her up and back home with her parents before dinner. Maybe saving her twice would be enough to make them let me in. Maybe they'd set a place for me.

They wouldn't. But oh, it was nice to dream.

"How are you . . ." Walther paused, his breath catching loudly enough to carry through the phone. "Her magic. You found her magic. Did you find . . . ?"

"Gillian's right here, Walther. She's asleep. She's so beautiful, and she's *right here*."

There were no visible wounds on Gillian's hands or face. She could have just been taking a strangely peaceful nap in a deserted, fire-devastated house. Even her hair was relaxed, falling in perfect waves across the mold-speckled pillow. Her skin was a few shades darker than mine, a gift from her Italian father, but if she opened her eyes, they would be foggy blue, like mine had been when I pretended to be human, like my own father's eyes. He lived on in the granddaughter he'd never known, and if there was anything that kept me from mourning the loss of my human blood, it was the fact that it still flowed in her veins. I had given up the greater part of my own mortality in part so that when the time came, I would be able to preserve hers.

I hadn't seen her in so long, but I knew her. I would always know her. She was my child, she was *mine*, and I couldn't imagine anything more beautiful.

"October . . ." Walther hesitated. "Is anyone with you? I'm concerned."

I couldn't imagine what there was for him to be concerned about. "There was some sort of repulsion spell outside the house. I got through by bleeding. The others can't bleed the way I can." I laughed unsteadily. "Finally, that's a useful skill."

"So you're alone with your daughter right now?"

"Yes. I should wake her up. Her father is so worried about her." Cliff seemed like a small concern at the moment. More than anything, I wanted to see Gillian open her eyes and smile at me. She hadn't smiled for *me* in so long, not since she was so small, and I wanted to know what it felt like to have my adult child see me. I needed to know.

"Toby, hang on. Doesn't this seem a little easy?"

No. Nothing about this day had been easy. I wanted to hang up. But this was Walther, and he'd been a good ally to me; he was the reason so many of the people I loved were awake, not dreaming their lives away in some forgotten tower. I forced myself to keep the phone against my ear as I said, "I don't think so."

"And I get that. Look, do me one favor and I'll drop it, okay?"

"What do you want me to do?"

"You said you had to bleed to get wherever you are right now. That's all I want you to do. Bleed for me again. Bleed one time, enough to let you see any illusions that might be screwing with your perception. If I'm wrong, if nothing changes, you can wake her up. Okay?"

It was a reasonable request. The fact that it irritated me as much as it did was a sign that he wasn't wrong to make it. I swallowed my anger, trying to focus on the reason I didn't want to bleed. There didn't seem to be one. Walther was asking me to be careful, that was all. I'd promised Quentin I would do exactly that. So why was the idea infuriating me?

I drew my knife with my free hand. Keeping the phone pressed to my ear, I drew the blade across my lower lip, wincing as it parted delicate skin and brought blood bubbling to the surface. Quickly, I sucked at the wound, filling my mouth with the coppery new-penny taste of my own pain.

The room changed. I had time to register the shift—how much darker it seemed, how much more advanced the rot on the walls was—before the creature on the bed was howling her displeasure and lunging for me.

This wasn't the first time some terrible *thing* had pretended to be my little girl in order to get to me. I didn't know why it was such a surprise. But it was, and I was dimly afraid that it would continue to be, every time it happened. In the moment, my greater focus was on keeping myself alive. If there was any mercy to the situation, it was that she no longer looked like Gillian. I wasn't fighting my own little girl.

I brought my knife up, dropping the phone in my haste to block the attack. The creature howled again, dancing back from the touch of silver. She was emaciated, a husk of a woman, with skin the color of spoiled cream and hair like rotting gorse, a tangle of brown and gold and slimy, filthy green. Her eyes were holes leading into an abyss, and her mouth was a horror of teeth and hunger.

"Toby?" Walther was shouting now. "Toby, what's going on?"

"Little busy here!" I yelled, as the creature—the Baobhan Sith, sweet Oberon, this was a Baobhan Sith—lunged again, her howl like the rush of wind around the walls of a crumbling keep. Her outline flickered even as she was attacking, and I knew if I let it, the illusion that had made her appear to be my child would reassert itself. I wouldn't be able to fight back. I'd just stand there and let her rip my throat out.

I shoved the sleeve of my leather jacket up to my elbow and slashed my own arm, not taking any care to avoid the major arteries. Blood sprayed the room in a hot gush before the skin scabbed over, healing faster than I could cut. The Baobhan Sith paused, sniffing the air with a speculative look on her face. She was hovering easily three feet off the floor, because what I like in an opponent is the ability to fly.

"Hi," I said. "I am Sir October Daye, Knight of Lost Words, and I command you to stand down, in the name of Duke Sylvester Torquill of Shadowed Hills and Queen Arden Windermere in the Mists."

That got her attention. The Baobhan Sith shrieked and dove for me, mouth open and aimed at the thick smear of blood coating my arm. I danced backward, bringing my knife up to block her. It wasn't as good as a sword, or a shield, or running the hell away, but the door was somewhere behind me, and I didn't want to turn my back on her. In my experience, letting something with that many teeth get the jump on me was a good way to lose more skin than I liked.

She slapped my knife to the side, hard and fast enough that I barely had time to parry, and then her mouth was clamping down on my arm, her sharp, serrated teeth reopening the closed wound and making dozens of new wounds at the same time. I shrieked in surprise and pain, slashing at her shoulder in an effort to make her let go.

The blow landed, my knife slicing into her arm and embedding itself against the bone. She didn't let go. If anything, she bit down harder, suckling at my arm like an infant. I struggled to pull my knife free as a wave of dizziness washed over me, nearly dropping me to my knees.

The smell of blood permeated the room, somehow enhancing the faded magical scents that were already there rather than overwhelming them. The cold and rowan remained: I wasn't wrong. No matter what Walther said, I wasn't wrong. The smell of mold and char also remained, and I realized through the growing dizziness that it was the scent of the Baobhan Sith's magic. She was an ambush predator, and this trap had been set specifically for me, putting her in a place where her magic would blend into the environment, making her impossible to detect unless I was actively looking.

My arm was going numb. I twisted and slammed my head into hers as hard as I could, hearing the distinctive sound of bone cracking. She howled as she ripped herself away, leaving blood to cascade freely across my skin. My knife was still embedded in her shoulder. I grabbed for it, and she jerked away, taking the knife with her.

The skin was already beginning to knit itself closed at the edges of the ragged, terrible wound she had made in my arm. That was good. It was happening more slowly than I expected, and I was losing a lot of blood in the meantime. That . . . wasn't good. Something crunched underfoot as I lunged for my knife again, and I knew without looking down that I had just stepped on my phone.

There would be time to worry about that later, when I wasn't covered in blood and fighting for my life. The Baobhan Sith lunged again, her hands outstretched in front of her like talons. The smell of her magic was getting stronger the more she flew, almost as strong as the smell of my own blood, which seemed to be enraging her.

She was no longer as emaciated as she had been. She was slim, not skeletal, as if something had melted away the worst of her hard edges, smoothing increasingly healthy-looking skin over increasingly well-padded bones. Her hair was growing lusher, less like dead, rotting flowers gone to brown in the winter and more like the first delicate flowers of spring. She was rebuilding herself by devouring me.

I can recover from almost anything, given time. According to some people, I've risen from the dead at least once. But magic is in the blood, mine even more so than most. What would happen if, when I collapsed, I had no blood left to raise me?

I wasn't in the mood to find out. As the Baobhan Sith lunged, I grabbed her by the hair and swung her, hard, for the wall. She shrieked as she slammed into it, and shrieked louder as she ploughed right through it, taking out chunks of waterlogged plaster and fire-damaged beams on her unplanned journey to the hall.

This was it: my one opportunity to run. But run *where*? There was a window. Getting it open and getting myself out it would take too long, and my throw had put her between me and the front door.

And she still had my knife.

I'm not all that hung up on material possessions, but I need my leather jacket, and I need my knife. They were gifts. They matter.

I shook the sleeve of my jacket back into its normal position, hissing as it touched the slowly-sealing wound. The leather was thick enough that if she bit down again, she'd have to chew hard to get to my skin. That was good. She was probably going to have the opportunity. That was bad.

Howling, she came at me again. Her hands latched onto the collar of my jacket, jerking me toward her, and I realized what she was about to do too late to get my elbow up, too late to do anything but shriek as she clamped her surprisingly strong mouth down on the side of my throat, biting through the skin and burying her teeth deep in the flesh. I tried to scream. I couldn't find the air. Everything was pain, pain, *pain*, and for some reason, it wasn't fading at all. It was like my body wasn't even trying to heal while she was biting me. That was . . .

That was not good. I had been stabbed in the heart and kept healing. Now some flying fairy leech was trying to drain me dry, and I couldn't even breathe.

I tried to push her away, hands slapping futilely against her shoulders. My fingers brushed the pommel of my knife. I groaned and focused on grasping it, trying once again to pull it free. The activity seemed to have jarred it loose, at least a little, because I yanked, and it shifted. I yanked again. It came free in my hand.

Hesitation was only going to weaken me, and Arden wouldn't prosecute me for violating Oberon's Law when it was so clearly self-defense—I hoped. Without stopping to ask myself whether this was the right move, I brought the knife around and stabbed the Baobhan Sith in the neck, feeling the blade sink home.

She stiffened, hissing hard around the seal her mouth had made against my skin, but didn't pull away. I worked the knife free, drawing back to stab her again—

—only to swing wildly as hands grasped my shoulders and yanked me away from her. She didn't let go without a fight, biting down harder as I was pulled from her embrace, so that her teeth shredded what felt like half my neck. Then I was flying, flung away from her so hard that my back slammed into the far wall before I could fully register what was happening. My skull hit the wall a bare second later, and the world became a dancing blur of light and shadows, undercut by the sound of a tiger roaring in full-throated rage.

No. Not a tiger. There couldn't be a tiger in here, there wasn't any room. I tried to get my eyes to focus, to see what was going on as the tiger roared and the Baobhan Sith shrieked. Blood was still oozing down my neck, hot and sticky. I put my hand over the wound, trying to keep at least some of the blood inside. That seemed like the sort of thing I should be worrying about, since I needed blood to live. Applying pressure seemed to help, somewhat, even as it made the pain worse.

Oddly, that pain made focusing easier. It was like my mind was so desperate for a distraction that it was willing to seize on whatever it could get. I blinked, and there was a man in the room with me, lean and fast and dark-haired, leaping to avoid a blow from the Baobhan Sith. She was bleeding now, too, from vast claw slashes that ran across her chest, leaving holes in the tattered gown she was wearing.

The man—I squinted, trying to see his face. The Baobhan Sith lunged for him, teeth gnashing, and he danced back with another roar. The motion turned him so that his face was half in profile, turned toward me just enough to let me see the familiar slope of his cheekbones, the curve of his lips. I gasped.

Tybalt glanced toward me for barely a beat, only long enough to be sure I wasn't in danger. Then he was slashing at the Baobhan Sith again, the battle continuing as he tried to drive her back, away from him, away from me and the so-tempting smell of my blood.

The wound at my throat felt like it was starting to heal. I risked pulling my hand away, wincing as another gout of blood oozed free. I was going to need to eat a hamburger after this. Maybe two. Or twelve. I staggered to my feet, knife gripped firmly in my hand, blood running down my arm inside my leather jacket, so that I felt like I had been utterly doused in the stuff.

"Hey!" I snarled. "Get the *fuck* away from my fiancé!"

The Baobhan Sith turned, hissed, and launched herself in my direction. Tybalt let her get past him, stepping aside to let her gain momentum before he grabbed her by the feet and used that same momentum to slam her, hard, into the bedroom floor. She howled. He stomped on the small of her back, scowling at me.

"Can't you seize an opportunity for escape when it's offered to you?" he demanded.

"Excuse me for not wanting to leave you to get eaten!" I snapped and kicked her in the head as she tried to raise it. "What are you even doing here?"

"Entertaining as it would be to repeat your own words—" he began, then faltered when he saw the way I was looking at him. "Quentin called me."

There was a lot in that sentence to unpack. I settled for kicking the Baobhan Sith in the head again. She tried to bite my foot. "I had things under control."

"You'll forgive me if I doubt you."

I stopped looking at the Baobhan Sith to look at Tybalt instead— normally one of my favorite activities, and now, suddenly, something I wanted to avoid for as long as possible. He looked back at me, and I didn't know whether it was trust or exhaustion that allowed me to see the shadows in his malachite-banded green eyes. He looked haunted. His hair, always dark brown, was streaked with darker stripes as his natural tabby patterning carried over into his human form. That wasn't normal. His stripes only showed when he was comfortable, or when he was under too much strain to properly design his human form, which was a far more voluntary thing than most people realized.

Young or weak Cait Sidhe sometimes carried aspects of their animal shapes over into their human ones, tails or actual cat ears, markings more blatant than the usual cat-slit pupils and retractable claws. Tybalt wasn't that far gone, but he looked more animal than I had seen him in a very long time, with an aura of wary skittishness around him that made me think of stray cats glimpsed at the mouth of alleyways, there one moment and gone the next.

"Tybalt . . ." I began.

The Baobhan Sith struck.

Launching herself away from the floor with a single convulsive shove of her wiry, well-muscled arms, she knocked us both backward before lunging for my throat and clamping down. She moaned triumph as she began to suck, teeth grinding against my windpipe. I tried to grab her shoulders, but all the strength had gone out of my arms. I couldn't get a grip. I dropped my knife, to no avail; my fingers refused to close.

"Forgive me."

Tybalt's voice was barely louder than a sigh and was all the warning I had before he wrapped his arms around my waist and dragged us—me, and the Baobhan Sith—backward, into the darkness of the shadow roads.

ELEVEN

WE FELL LIKE STARS, plummeting into the freezing cold waiting on the other side of the light. I couldn't breathe. That wasn't much of a change. I already hadn't been able to breathe, thanks to the Baobhan Sith crushing my throat. The blood covering my neck and arms froze almost instantly, becoming an icy shroud that wrapped around me and worked the cold even deeper, driving it all the way to my bones.

There was a sudden sharp heat as the Baobhan Sith's hold on my throat broke and she tumbled away into the darkness. That heat faded as well, becoming another layer of cold as the blood stopped flowing. Everything was freezing. Everything was falling.

There was a sudden jolt beneath me, and I realized Tybalt still had his arms wrapped around my waist. I could barely feel them due to the cold. He swung me up and around, settling me into a bridal carry before he broke into a run. I didn't fight. It might have been more accurate to say that I *couldn't* fight. There was no strength left in me, no capacity to do anything other than huddle where I was and let myself be carried.

It was such a familiar position that it would almost have been pleasant if not for the blood drying at my throat and the knowledge that the Baobhan Sith was still out there, lurking somewhere in the dark of the Shadow Roads. It had been so long since Tybalt had carried me like this that I had almost forgotten how *normal* it was. Somewhere between my return from the pond and his proposal, this had become ordinary. I had probably spent more time in the shadows than any other non-Cait Sidhe in a hundred years.

"Almost there, little fish," he murmured, and I didn't try to argue. Between the cold and the blood loss, a pleasant lassitude was stealing over me, leaving me utterly relaxed. If we were attacked again, he would need to be prepared to defend us both.

Belatedly, I realized I no longer had my knife. It had fallen in the room where the Baobhan Sith had pretended to be my daughter, a perfect trap, perfectly laid for me. I would have to go back for it. I couldn't lose it. I refused to lose it.

Tybalt leapt, clutching me to his chest as he jumped into the blackness. The shadows broke around us, and we emerged into a deserted classroom filled with potted lavender and rosemary plants. They covered every surface, encroached on most of the floor, so that we were utterly surrounded. Knotted ropes coated in flame-retardant wax hung from the ceiling, their lengths dotted with candles that glowed with flames like the sun.

In case that hadn't been sufficient warning of our location, Tybalt said, in a tone nonchalant enough to scream concern, "We are in the Court of Cats. Shade may not care for our presence, as this is technically her territory, but if she objects, I will explain. Are you awake? Can you hear me?"

For a moment, I considered refusing to open my eyes. Let *him* be the one to deal with the fear of his lover not responding to him. I dismissed the petty, pointless idea as quickly as it had come. He hadn't been answering when I called for him. I was injured. The two situations were completely different.

"Yeah," I rasped, and raised a hand to feel my throat, dislodging icy sheets of blood with every motion. There were still toothmarks there, smaller than they had been, but enduring despite the length of time since my injury. "What the . . . ?"

"The saliva of the Baobhan Sith slows healing. Their prey generally bleeds out rather than recovering and leaves them with a trail they can follow to a feast. Can you stand?"

"Try me."

Gingerly, Tybalt lowered me to my feet, keeping hold of my arm as he straightened and let me test my balance. My legs wobbled but held. I clutched his arm, finally raising my eyes to meet his.

He must have seen the recrimination there, because he winced, glancing guiltily at the floor. "Quentin called me," he repeated.

"I feel like there's a chain of events you're leaving out."

"Raj had . . . informed me you were in Berkeley, investigating the disappearance of your child. I was attempting to convince myself that my presence would be welcome when he returned to say you had found something which should not exist and were planning to parley with my opposite number." He rubbed the back of his neck with one hand, still not looking at me. "Then he threw his phone at my head and told me to behave more like a cat than a coward, and he left before I could scold him for his insubordination. When you began screaming, Quentin called Raj to ask if he could use the Shadow Roads to enter the house. He seemed quite surprised to get me instead. He called me some *fascinating* names. I was not aware he knew so many ways to belittle a man."

"That's my boy." I flexed my fingers, popping off a sheet of frozen blood, and placed it in my mouth with barely a grimace. There was a time when even the sight of my own blood would make me light-headed. Now I swear the stuff makes up more than half of my diet.

The blood-ice melted on my tongue. A bit of the cloudiness in my head cleared. I straightened, feeling stable enough to stand on my own, and took my hand off Tybalt's arm. His face fell immediately. I almost put my hand back, deciding against it only when I realized it wasn't going to do any good.

"I should have been there before you could be hurt," he said, voice soft. "I should have been there from the beginning."

"Yeah." There was no point in lying to him. He was smarter than that, and more, I respected him too much to litter the ground between us with falsehoods. We were past that point. We'd been past that point for years. "You should have been. But you're here now."

He paused for so long that I began to be afraid that no, he wasn't here. That he'd been willing to save me, but that was where it ended: he was going to return to his self-imposed seclusion, and I was going to be going on without him. Again.

That wasn't how things were supposed to be. They had changed, for the better, and I didn't want them changing back. I never wanted them changing back.

"Only if you want me to be," he said, in a small voice. "I am— damaged, October, I am hurt in ways I have never been hurt before, that I can barely put name to, much less chart in their healing.

I flinch from my own shadow. How is that fit behavior for a king? How is that fit behavior for your love?"

I stared at him for a moment, unable to believe what I was hearing. My arm ached. My neck throbbed. Blood, both frozen and beginning to sluggishly thaw, coated more of me than I liked to consider. And none of that mattered as I raised my hand to brush his cheek, and stepped closer, and kissed him.

In fairy tales, a kiss can fix anything. My life is not a fairy tale, and a kiss has never been enough to save my life. But a kiss can change things in any version of reality; a kiss can reorder the world. Tybalt's eyes widened. Then he closed them, arms going around my waist and pulling me close. I closed my own eyes, letting the moment exist without observation. His lips, as always, carried the pennyroyal and musk flavor of his magic. My lips, I knew, would taste mostly of blood right now, and he kissed me anyway, kissed me like a starving man, like he'd believed the time for kissing was somehow over.

We were both panting slightly when he pulled back, staring at me again. I immediately grabbed the front of his shirt—rough linen, like something out of a BBC Shakespeare production, and now irrecoverably stained with blood—and kept him from going any further.

"I don't care," I said. "I want you here."

"Your mother—she trapped me, and a King who cannot run, cannot fight, is a danger, I would attract danger to you, and be unable to help—"

"I'd like to see anyone who wanted to hurt you get through me," I said.

Tybalt blinked, looking too startled to reply.

That was fine. I could talk for both of us. "If you're hurt, you let me help you heal," I said. "If you're damaged, we learn the ways around it together. I don't care whether you can be fixed. I don't care whether you flinch at shadows. All I want is for you to be with me—and let me be a part of whatever 'getting better' looks like now."

"Perhaps refrain from using 'fixed' as a descriptor with your betrothed, the common cat," he said weakly, a flicker of a smile crossing his lips. "It is unsettling at best."

I beamed, bright and earnest and unable to stop myself. "There you are. Root and branch, I've missed you."

In answer, Tybalt put his arms around me again, enfolding me in his embrace, and pressed his face into my hair. Voice so soft it was barely a whisper, he breathed, "I have missed you, too, my little fish. More than you can see or know."

It was tempting to remain in that embrace forever, to stand surrounded by flowers and let myself breathe in the scent of him until the broken places in my heart began to reluctantly heal. There wasn't time. The rest of the world wasn't pausing while we dealt with our problems. If only it would.

I pulled away, letting my arms rest against his chest for a moment more as I said, "We have to go back."

"Back?"

"To the house where you found me. I dropped my knife. The one Dare gave me." And my phone, which would probably raise questions if the human insurance companies ever discovered the burnt-out old house.

There was nothing I could do to collect the blood that had liberally painted the walls. That would be fun. The local kids would get a new "murder house" to talk about at school, and all the local parents would get a new reason to drink heavily.

Tybalt frowned. "There are other knives."

"But there isn't a Dare anymore, and everyone else is trapped outside waiting to find out if I'm all right." I paused. "How did you get in?"

"The barrier you found was normal for a Baobhan Sith's denning place. They spin the world into a shell to protect themselves. They lack the authority of Oberon, and it's a wild magic, not an intentional warding; the Shadow Roads allow the Cait Sidhe to slide through as a wind blows through a keyhole. They are . . . not fond of us, shall we say."

The casual nonchalance with which he said that lifted my heart. Who would have thought that one day I'd be yearning for the arrogance of the Cait Sidhe? "Is she going to attack us when we go back into the shadows?"

"She's no doubt escaped by now." I stared at him. Again, he smiled, barely broadly enough to be worthy of the name. "Baobhan Sith that have recently fed have little need for breathing. She need only move through the dark until she sees the flicker of someone coming or going, and then push past them. She won't attack, not until she's free. It will be a grand opportunity for one of my subjects to test their wits."

"Okay," I said slowly. "So can you take me back?"

"I . . ." He paused. "I don't want to."

"Not the question."

Tybalt stood silently for a moment before he hung his head and said, "Yes. I will return you to the monster's lair. Why were you there to begin with?"

"Madden picked up Gillian's trail. It led to the house." The image of the Baobhan Sith disguised as my daughter flashed through my mind. I shuddered. "When I got inside, she looked exactly like Gillian. *Exactly*. Why . . . ?"

"If someone brought her the girl, a taste of her blood would have been enough to manage the mimicry, and she could then have lain in wait for better prey."

My eyes widened. "Baobhan Sith can imitate their victims?"

"Yes." Tybalt frowned before his eyes widened in turn. "She had far more than a taste of your blood."

"We need to *go*."

"Yes, we do," he said, and swung me back into the bridal carry. For once, I made no effort to fight or resist him. This would be faster. My legs were still shaking, and I was in no condition to run an unknown distance through the freezing dark.

"Hold fast, my love," he said, and then he was plunging into the dark, carrying me with him. I screwed my eyes closed, holding the last breath I'd been able to take like it was the most precious thing in the world.

The Shadow Roads are different for the Cait Sidhe than for their passengers. There's no other way Tybalt and Raj could use them the way they do, racing from one place to another without coming out choking and wheezing for breath every single time. For me, they are always featureless, unforgiving, and cold, like running through a void that chooses to hold me up, except when it chooses to let me fall.

It felt like he ran for less than half as long as he had run before. The shadows shredded around us, and we emerged into the mold-and-ash-scented room, now spattered with great streaks of my drying blood. I sucked in a great, gasping breath and pushed against his chest, wordlessly indicating that he should put me down. He did so, with reasonably good grace, and watched as I recovered my knife and broken cell phone from the floor.

"What possessed you to think you should enter such a place alone?" he asked.

"I've never met a Baobhan Sith before," I said. "I thought it was some sort of warding spell. We all did. And if Gillian was in here, this was where I needed to be." I looked around, in case Gillian might somehow have appeared while I wasn't looking. The closet had no door, and pieces of the mattress had rotted away, making it clear that she wasn't under the bed. I scowled. "Another damn dead end."

"Someone is laying traps for you. Someone too aware of your limitations."

"Isn't that great? I love it when the world decides to kick me while I'm down." I took a breath. "Can you . . . can you *smell* anything here? Any magic?"

Tybalt inhaled. "The Baobhan Sith's," he said. "Yours, although less so, and mostly, I think, because of the quantity of blood you've lost. This room has been practically painted."

"Fortunately, I don't have to pay the cleaning bills." I looked at him solemnly. "The false Queen's magic was here when I arrived. I think . . . I think she's involved."

His eyes widened. "But she sleeps—"

"Maybe. Maybe not. This is *Faerie*, Tybalt. You know things aren't always what they seem." I raked my blood-sticky hair out of my face before I turned and started toward the front of the house. "Get a human disguise up. We don't want to scare the neighbors."

"Perhaps you should do the same."

I stopped, reaching up to feel my ear. Good illusions are tactile as well as visual. They have to be. I could never have managed to sleep with Cliff if every time he'd touched me, he'd discovered angles that weren't supposed to be there. My fingers found a tapering point.

"Oak and ash," I muttered. "I didn't even feel the spell break."

"You lost a great deal of blood."

"I didn't lose it," I said. "I know exactly where it is."

I didn't need to turn to feel Tybalt glowering at me. "Ah, yes," he said. "I begin to remember why I missed you so. The glorious spectacle of watching a woman do her best to bully the universe into rearranging itself according to her utterly self-destructive whim."

"A girl needs a hobby," I said, and grabbed a handful of shadows—or tried to, anyway. They slipped through my fingers like, well, shadows, refusing to catch or cling. I frowned. "That's weird."

"Not really. Again, you lost a *great* deal of blood, and what remains is preoccupied with putting you back together." Tybalt stepped around me, stopping so that we were face-to-face in the char-covered living room. "May I?"

I wanted to tell him "no." Other people's illusions always make me itch, and I hate not having control over the spells I wear. Instead, I nodded, and said, "Please."

The smell of musk and pennyroyal rose as he leaned in and ran his thumb along the line of my cheek. Then he kissed me again, soft and slow and achingly mine. I kissed him back. The spell took shape around us, solidifying and bursting into being. He pulled away, a smile on his suddenly-human lips. I raised an eyebrow.

"What?"

"It's nice to see you," he said. "Especially when I don't have to look at quite so much of your blood."

I couldn't think of anything to say to that, and so I punched him in the shoulder. To my surprise and delight, Tybalt laughed.

Even a human disguise couldn't conceal the fact that he was a handsome man, although it rounded his ears and his pupils, took the impossible malachite green out of his eyes and the dark stripes out of his hair. He looked like the sort of man who belonged on a stage or in a magazine, and he was right there in front of me, smiling at me like I was the most amazing thing in the world.

There wasn't time to appreciate him now, but oh, I wanted to. "When this is over, when Gillian is safe at home with her father, come home with me," I said. "Don't leave me again."

His smile faltered. Then, gravely, he nodded. "As my lady wishes," he said.

"Good." I kissed his cheek, quick and glancing, and walked out of the house. To my relief, Tybalt followed.

Quentin, May, and Madden were waiting on the sidewalk, and had been joined by a fourth: Walther, his hair in disarray and his glasses askew as he threw what looked like table salt at the bayberry bushes. He stopped when he saw us emerge. "Toby!"

"Hey." I hurried down the path toward them, Tybalt at my heels. I had scarcely passed the barrier before Quentin slammed into me, wrapping arms around my waist and pressing his face to my leather jacket. Then he pulled back, expression going from relief to suspicion in an instant.

"I smell blood," he said. "How drenched are you under that illusion?"

"I genuinely appreciate your squire's focus on the important aspects of life with you," said Tybalt dryly.

Quentin's eyes flicked to him, suspicion becoming irritation. "I'm mad at you," he said. "We all get messed up sometimes. Running away isn't the answer."

"Understood," said Tybalt. "I will endeavor to win my way back into your good graces. Now, you were asking the lady about her injuries . . . ?"

Quentin's attention swiveled back to me. I swallowed a groan. "Dirty pool, cat," I said.

"A man does not reach my ripe old age without learning the better part of the art of distraction," said Tybalt.

Walther cleared his throat. "Can we get back to the blood, please? You screamed, and the call dropped. I thought . . ." He stopped. "I thought you were in real trouble."

"I was." I looked back at the house, which seemed so perfect, so untouched. It wasn't hard to make my decision. I turned to the others. "Madden, you need to go back to Muir Woods and let Arden know a Baobhan Sith has been nesting here. She made this her den."

His eyes widened. "What? There haven't been Baobhan Sith in the Mists since before King Gilad took the throne. That's not possible."

"She tried to chew my arm off. I'd say she's here. I can help clear her out *after* I find Gillian, but right now, I need to get back on the trail of my daughter, and you need to tell Arden there's a threat hiding in Berkeley." The Baobhan Sith could have been there for years. This was unincorporated territory, no Count or Duke or Marquis to report to when someone disappeared. Most of the fae of Berkeley treasured their independence. They wouldn't necessarily have gone running to the crown when they had a problem.

Or maybe they had, and the Queen they'd found had seen an opportunity where they saw a monster. The smell of cold and rowan had been so damn strong, and after Jocelyn's note . . .

"We need to move," I said. "All the false trails have been here in Berkeley, which means Gillian *isn't*. They're trying to make us waste as much time as possible. Walther, if you can keep your eyes open, talk to your kids, anything. I don't think she's here, but if she is, I'm hoping you can find a lead."

"I'm not an investigator."

"I'm barely one," I shot back. "We need to go to San Francisco."

May frowned. "Why?"

"Jocelyn left me a note. She said I'd find her in the place I 'gave away.' That describes two places I can think of, and they're both in San Francisco."

"What?"

I turned. Quentin was staring at me.

"One of those places is Goldengreen," he said. "Dean's there, and he's going to be asleep right now. Why aren't we there already? We need to warn them." He dug for his phone, already dialing without waiting to hear my excuses.

I couldn't blame him. I didn't have any excuses. I just had a lot of fear—and the driving need to bring my daughter home. I started walking, and the rest of them moved with me, a little knot of strangers traveling through a residential neighborhood where we had no business being. It felt like eyes watched from every window, twitching curtains aside and making notes about our suspicious behavior. I knew that wasn't really happening—if it were, the police would have come for Quentin and the rest while I was inside the Baobhan Sith's house, fighting for my life against a terror made of teeth and hunger.

Quentin lowered his phone, looking at it bleakly. "He's not picking up," he said.

"I'm sorry."

"I'll decide whether I believe you once we get there and he's okay," Quentin snapped.

I couldn't blame him for that, either. Not even a little. I just kept walking.

We stopped when we reached the parking lot, Madden giving me a doleful look. "Are you *sure* you don't want me with you?" he asked. "I have her scent now."

"You need to stay here and show Arden to the house," I said. "It should be under constant supervision, for when the Baobhan Sith comes back. If she doesn't need you standing guard, you can keep looking for more trails. I bet we find every monster in Berkeley by finding all the places where my daughter isn't."

"I'll call you if we find anything," said Walther.

"Call Quentin," I replied. "I sort of killed my phone."

"Of course, you did," he said. "Open roads, October, and good luck."

"Kind fires," I replied, and unlocked the car.

Tybalt settled in the front passenger seat while May and Quentin took the back. It was strangely comforting having so much of my weird little family around me. I hadn't realized how big a hole Tybalt's absence made until it wasn't there anymore.

"Quentin, before you call Dean again, can you don't-look-here the car?" I asked. "I need to check my injuries, and that means making sure no one can see how much blood I'm wearing."

"I wish that were a surprising request," he muttered, and waved his hand, mumbling a verse of a song I didn't recognize. As was usually the case with him, it was about boats. The air thickened, and the don't-look-here dropped on us with the force of a wave.

I started the car. "Tybalt?"

"Remind me what attracted me to your side in the first place because, at the moment, I have a difficult time bringing it to mind," he said. He snapped his fingers. The illusion shattered into the smell of pennyroyal and musk.

In the back seat, May gasped. "October Christine Daye, *why* is there a *hole* in your neck?" she demanded.

"It's never a good sign when you use my full name."

It was difficult to see my own throat in the rearview mirror while driving, but with a little twisting around, I managed it. The sight wasn't pretty. The wound was fairly superficial at this point, consisting mostly of some tears in the skin surrounding a raw spot that was barely larger than a hickey. That wasn't the alarming part. The alarming part was that it existed at all. I should have healed long since, wiping everything away except for the blood, which would always remain to betray me.

"What *happened*?" she demanded, leaning forward.

"The Baobhan Sith tried to eat me. She got more blood than I like to think about. That's probably going to be a problem later. Right now, I just need something to eat and I'll be fine."

"Wait." The note of alarm in May's voice wasn't fading. If

anything, it was getting stronger. "You're telling me there's a Bao-bhan Sith out there running around with a stomach full of your blood? That's . . . that's not *good*, Toby."

"Tell me about it," I muttered. Like the Daoine Sidhe, the Bao-bhan Sith are blood-workers. Unlike the Daoine Sidhe, that's *all* they are. They don't do flower magic, they don't do blood magic, and unlike the Dóchas Sidhe, they don't generally use their own blood for castings. They do it all with the blood of others. That's also what sustains them. Some people think the human vampire legends began with the Baobhan Sith, and honestly, I can't say those people are wrong.

As long as she had my blood, the Baobhan Sith who had at-tacked me would be able to access powers that mimicked my own—meaning she'd be able to recover from supposedly mortal wounds and track people by the scent of their magic. Not good.

"Why did she attack like that?" asked Quentin uneasily. "I'm a blood-worker, and I don't try to chew people's throats out."

"She looked like she was starving," I said. "If she'd somehow been held there, unable to hunt . . . it could have been pure hunger that had her going for me like that." It didn't make me feel any warmer or fuzzier toward her, and I sure as hell wasn't going to be inviting her over for dinner any time soon, but at least there was a chance there had been no malice in her attempting to eat me.

That didn't explain why she'd looked like Gillian when I'd first found her. Nothing was going to explain that. Nothing good, anyway.

"Your throat—" insisted May.

"It's healing," I said brusquely.

"You're not supposed to be *healing*," said May. "You're sup-posed to have already healed, past tense, no delays. This isn't nor-mal, and I don't like it."

"Nothing about today has been normal," I countered. We were nearing the bridge. I glanced at the rearview mirror. "Quentin, try Dean again. If he still isn't picking up, try Marcia. She's thin-blooded enough to be mostly diurnal."

"She stays up as late as she can so that she can do her job as seneschal correctly," said Quentin, even as he started poking at his phone. "I've tried her twice. No one's picking up."

Tybalt and I exchanged a glance.

Goldengreen is the name of both a County and the knowe that

serves as its heart. They were founded at the same time, by the same woman: Evening Winterrose, also known as Eira Rosynhwyr, Firstborn of the Daoine Sidhe. Being part of the local nobility made it easier for her to control them . . . at least until she "died" and the false former Queen gave Goldengreen to me in order to discharge the Kingdom's debts. Oh, and shift my fealty from Sylvester Torquill to her, thus ensuring that when she wanted to charge me with treason, my liege wouldn't be able to do anything to save me.

Nice lady, our former Queen. So nice she almost killed me. "Almost" only counts in horseshoes and hand grenades, as Devin used to say, and when I wasn't put to death for crimes against the crown, I offloaded my title and lands as quickly as I could, using them to avert a war between the Kingdom in the Mists and the local Undersea. As the son of a Merrow Duchess and a Daoine Sidhe Count, Dean Lorden was perfectly positioned to hold Goldengreen and make it a symbol of peace and cooperation.

Of course, that also meant that if anything ever happened to him, his mother, Duchess Dianda Lorden of Saltmist, would march her army right up our beaches and start swinging. Dean was a great kid. He seemed to be a good first boyfriend for Quentin; the boys were happy, and that was all I really cared about. But if he was actually hurt, things were about to get a lot worse.

"Drive faster," advised May.

I did.

It was a testament to how urgent things were that Tybalt didn't complain, at all, about how my driving was likely to get us killed; he just hung onto the handle above the door and closed his eyes, doing his best to endure this madcap modern transportation without making a fuss. That was a good thing. Normally, I found his disdain for cars cute, endearing even. Right now, I needed to floor it.

I made it from the toll booths to the city in what felt like record time, tearing through several red lights and several more near-misses as I raced toward the San Francisco Art Museum. Knowes require an anchor to stay connected to the mortal world, and Evening had always liked to be thought of as someone who was cultured, connected to the most modern developments in human art and music. Having a museum built atop her connection point must have seemed perfect.

There were several cars in the lot when we arrived. A glance at the clock confirmed that the museum had already opened for the day. I grimaced. There are entrances to the knowe located outside the museum—there have to be, given how often people need to come and go after operating hours—but most of them aren't exactly subtle, and we needed to get in unseen.

I pulled into a space under the eucalyptus trees that circled half the lot, turning off the engine and announcing, "We need to go for the cliffside entrance. The shed's too visible this time of day."

"Perhaps you have forgotten, but the last time you went over a cliff in this place, you nearly drowned," said Tybalt.

I didn't correct him. I was pretty sure I *had* drowned, and that sort of thing isn't soothing to announce. "That was when the wards had been locked down and the doors had been sealed," I said. "There's a chance that's happened again, so May can go first. She's indestructible."

"Here's a song we've sung before," muttered May.

"You know you're my favorite sister."

"Because your only other sister is a raving—"

"We're wasting *time*," snapped Quentin as he got out of the car, forcing the rest of us to hurry if we wanted to keep up with him and hence stay within the sheltering confines of the don't-look-here.

Evening had a vicious sense of humor when she designed the knowe. The easiest, most secluded entrance is straightforward, as such things go: all you have to do is walk the right path to the right spot on the towering cliff that is the museum's thin slice of coast, and step over it without hesitating. Do it right, your feet hit the floor of the hall and you're home free. Do it wrong, it's a long fall to a cruel sea, and most people don't survive that sort of thing.

May caught up with Quentin right before he was about to step over, grabbing him by the shoulders and pulling him back. "No," she said. "Fetches first." Then she turned, stepped off the cliff, and disappeared into thin air.

"Oh, thank Titania," said Quentin, and charged after her.

Tybalt and I were close behind, his hand clasped so firmly over mine that it ached a little. I didn't mind. He was scared, but he was trying. He was staying with me. Right now, that was all I could have asked and more.

We stepped over the edge of the cliff together. The world twisted and bent around us, spinning wildly for a few precious seconds before it settled into the hallway of Goldengreen. I staggered, and Tybalt held me up. No matter how far I pushed myself toward fae, as long as I was holding onto the shards of my humanity, that kind of transition was going to be hard on me.

I got my breath back and straightened, looking around. I don't think Evening would recognize her own knowe if she saw it. That's a good thing. Under her, Goldengreen had been sterile and static, devoid of clutter, of people—of life. She had grown herself a perfect flower and then she had frozen it like a rose in ice, keeping it exactly the way she wanted it to be. That had started to change while I held the County, if only because I'd taken in the displaced residents of my friend Lily's knowe after she died. The presence of people always changes things.

Now, under Dean's leadership and Marcia's gentle hand, the knowe was blossoming. The hall seemed to have grown wider, accommodating the bookshelves and low tables lining the walls. Some of the shelves were laden with sunken treasures, no doubt dredged from the bottom of the San Francisco Bay. Tapestries showing scenes from the surrounding Summerlands hung above the tables, interspersed with the coats of arms of the people who resided here, when applicable. Not every resident of Faerie has their own crest, but those who do are often very proud of them.

Multicolored lights glimmered from the tops of the shelves. The knowe's pixie population was asleep, dreaming the day away. I relaxed when I saw that. If the pixies were still sleeping peacefully, there probably wasn't anyone here who shouldn't have been.

At the same time, much as I would have liked to know that Dean was in no danger, I would have been equally happy to find and save my daughter in these familiar halls, where I knew the territory and it knew me. Knowes are alive. Goldengreen might not be mine anymore, but I like to think I was kind enough for it to remember me fondly.

Quentin exhaled, his own relief mirroring mine. Then he started swiftly forward, not pausing to see if the rest of us would follow. We did, of course, hurrying behind him until a noise from one of the rooms caught my attention. I stopped, pulling Tybalt to a halt, and pointed. He nodded, understanding what I was signaling, and we turned away, leaving May to follow Quentin toward his final destination.

I just hoped Dean liked to sleep clothed, or May was probably about to see a bit more than either of us had any desire to.

Tybalt and I moved closer to the noise. It was coming from the main kitchen, I realized, and it wasn't the only thing: I smelled cinnamon rolls and fresh-brewed coffee. My stomach rumbled, reminding me that I had been hauled out of bed, hadn't stopped for breakfast, and had lost a remarkable amount of blood at the hands of the Baobhan Sith.

Marcia looked up as we stepped into the room, blinking at us blearily but without surprise. She was wearing a green housecoat with reeds and rushes embroidered around the edges, turning it into a cloth recreation of a swamp, and her always tangled blonde hair was piled atop her head in a messy bun, giving her the overall air of a slightly flustered cockatoo.

"Toby," she said. "Tybalt. To what do we owe the honor at this uncivilized hour of the day? My cinnamon rolls aren't *that* good."

My stomach growled audibly, as if in argument. "How long have you been up?"

"I don't know. Not long. Long enough to bake, but I made the dough yesterday and had one of the girls put it under a stasis spell." Marcia's gaze sharpened as she looked at us, taking in Tybalt's discomfort and my overall condition. She frowned, looking more bewildered than upset. "Why are you covered in blood?"

Trust Marcia to treat my exsanguination as another minor inconvenience. "I got into a little argument with a Baobhan Sith. She thought I was a breakfast buffet. I thought it was rude to eat someone to whom you hadn't even been introduced. I guess we both sort of won. She got a good meal, I got away with all my limbs."

"Your definition of victory will never cease to shock and horrify me," muttered Tybalt.

"You need cinnamon rolls," said Marcia, and grabbed a spatula. "You probably also need bacon, but I'm not safe to fry anything until I've had another cup of coffee. I think there's some sliced beef left from last night's dinner. I can check the pantry."

I raised an eyebrow and waited. Marcia dished out two cinnamon rolls, then paused.

"You didn't tell me why you were here," she said. "Toby, why are you *here*?"

"My daughter's been kidnapped from her college." The words

didn't become less painful with repetition. If anything, they got worse. Someone had my daughter, and I wasn't saving her.

Marcia's eyes went wide and round. "Gillian's missing? Again?"

"Yeah. We think her roommate, a thin-blooded changeling named Jocelyn, may have been involved." I paused. "Actually, that reminds me. Marcia, do you know how to make anti-fae charms? Herbal sachets and the like?"

She shook her head violently. "No, I don't, and I wouldn't want to learn if someone offered to teach me."

"Why not?"

"You think changelings are only allowed to be a part of the community on the sufferance of their 'betters'?" It was impossible to miss the sarcastic twist in her voice. "Talk to the thin-blooded sometime. They're a step above merlins, but there's a lot of prejudice there, and they're not covered by the Law. In fact, some people think the Law should be interpreted to mean all thin-blooded changelings should be killed on sight, *because* they're so close to being merlins. If they marry human, the bloodline goes into the mortal world, almost undetectable, and magic emerges later, dangerous and unpredictable and not within the purebloods' control. Too many of the old ones remember the war against the merlins. They remember how many purebloods died. Thin-blooded changelings are only a part of Faerie because it would be too much trouble to kill them all. Learning how to work magic that actively repels the fae is a good way to make it seem worth the trouble after all."

I frowned. "Are you in touch with any of the other thin-blooded fae in the city? Do you know if any of them might not agree with you?"

"I have more power and more privilege than any other person I know who wears the fairy ointment," said Marcia. There was an unusual chill in her voice. "Half the thin-blooded changelings in the city are *here* in Goldengreen, Toby, because I've asked them to be, and the Count is happy to have me handle staffing if it means he doesn't need to think about it. They sweep floors and polish furniture and sleep in real beds and eat real food, and they're *happy*. There's no conspiracy brewing."

"I didn't think there was," I said firmly. "We found anti-fae charms in Gillian's things, and the letter Jocelyn left for me said she'd be in the place I 'gave away.'"

"And Goldengreen fit the bill," concluded Marcia. Her cheeks reddened. "Sorry if I jumped to conclusions a little bit there."

"There's no need to be sorry," I said. "I didn't mean to sound like I was accusing you of anything. We just needed to be sure everything was okay. We needed to be . . ." I faltered. With everything happening so fast, I had yet to tell anyone but Tybalt what I'd smelled in that burnt-out old house. I wasn't sure I wanted to open that can of worms without more evidence. Awkwardly, I finished, "We needed to be sure."

"I'm sure I'm going to need to make more coffee, if your squire is waking Count Lorden," said Marcia wryly. "I know you don't drink coffee anymore, Toby, but what about you, Tybalt? Would you like a cup?"

"Much as I would love to linger over your hospitality—and see my lady consume a good breakfast to replace what she's lost—I doubt she'll allow that sort of indolence under the circumstances," said Tybalt, with what sounded like genuine regret. "Another time, perhaps? You can explain the art behind your fabulous icings, and I can look attentive and ask unclever questions."

"Flatterer," she said. Then she looked to me and sobered. "You were the first people to come through the wards since sunrise. I don't know where your daughter is, but she isn't here, and neither is this 'Jocelyn' girl. I'm sorry."

"Don't be," I said. My stomach snarled again. I finally picked up my cinnamon roll. "We'll find her."

Footsteps behind us heralded the return of my Fetch, who walked into the kitchen, picked up Tybalt's cinnamon roll, and announced, "Dean has an incredible fastball for a guy who grew up on the bottom of the sea."

"Patrick must have played catch with him," I said. "What did he throw?"

"Conch shell. They're pointy." She took a bite of cinnamon roll before saying, around her mouthful of dough and icing, "Quentin's behind me."

"Jocelyn isn't here. Neither is Gillian. If Quentin is satisfied of Dean's safety, we need to move along."

"To where?" asked Marcia. I glanced at her. She was watching me anxiously. "What other places have you given away?"

"Depending on how you want to interpret it, a lot." I had given up my apartment when I moved into the house Sylvester provided for me; I had given up Home when I left Devin for Cliff. I had even given up Amandine's tower when I ran away from her to start my own life in the mortal world.

The thought of Gillian's kidnappers taking her to Amandine would have been chilling if I'd believed, even for a second, that Amandine would have allowed them to approach her tower. She was enmeshed deep in her reunion with my beloved older sister, and no one who wasn't welcome was going to get through her wards. Give it a year or two and she might be a threat to me and mine, but right now? She was a monster on the horizon, worthy of fear and respect, but not coming to cause problems. Not yet, anyway.

Sometimes I feel like my life is turning into one long game of chess with the Firstborn. Every time I manage to get one of them out of the way for five minutes, another one pops up to take their place. It's enough to make me want to crawl into bed and stay there.

Quentin appeared in the kitchen doorway, making no effort to conceal the relief on his face. "Dean's fine. He says good morning, and begs your indulgence, but he was up late, and he needs to sleep a little longer."

"Did he *really* beg our indulgence, or did he tell us to go piss up a rope?" I asked.

"He didn't do either of those things," said Quentin stiffly. "I'm allowed to interpret. You do it for Tybalt all the time."

"She does?" asked Tybalt, with a sidelong glance at me.

"You talk like a romance novel," I said. "I'm doing you a favor. The cinnamon rolls are excellent, Marcia, but we need to get moving. Gillian is out there somewhere. I have to bring her home."

"Open roads, Toby," she said.

"Kind fires," I replied, and started for the door. Then I paused, darted back, and grabbed a second cinnamon roll.

Her laughter followed us all the way to the exit. Quentin pulled a don't-look-here down over the four of us, and we were gone, heading back into the world, back on the trail of my daughter.

TWELVE

THE CAR WAS UNDISTURBED when we reached it. One small mercy for a day that didn't contain many of them. Quentin started to open the right rear passenger door. I grabbed his arm, stopping him.

"Do you feel better?" I asked.

He nodded, slowly. "Yeah. Sorry if I was sort of pushy before, but . . . yeah."

"You don't need to be sorry. I need to think about other people." I paused, wincing as I released him. "Including Cliff and Miranda. We need to stop by their place before we go wherever it is we're going next."

May frowned. "Why?"

"Because my phone is dead, and I was the only one with Cliff's number. Even if we found something right now, we wouldn't be able to call and tell them about it. I need to update them on what's happened so far, and I need to get Cliff's information again, so we can call them if we need to."

"I'm going in with you," said May flatly.

"I don't think—"

"She is going in with you," said Tybalt. I shot him a wounded look. He shook his head. "They consider me your shiftless swain, and while I would normally find accusations of roguishness charming at best and delightfully inaccurate at worst, they are parents in distress, and do not need the additional strain of having you walk in with a suitor in tow. As for Quentin, I ask, are they aware you have a teenage ward who has no blood relation to your house? Among humans, such arrangements are no longer common unless formalized under the law, and I am sure they'd be aware if you had done so. Our presence would raise too many questions. We will remain in the car. And yet, all that being true, I am not comfortable with the idea of you facing them alone."

I sighed. "Remind me again why I missed you?"

"Because I am the only man who adores you as fully as you should be adored, covered in blood or no."

It was a good line. I still rolled my eyes as I got into the car and started the engine.

Marcia's cinnamon rolls were excellent, but they could have been made of paste and putty, as long as they contained calories. Every bite settled the roaring in my stomach and the aching in my head, which had become so status quo I had actually stopped noticing it. My neck itched, and I knew that it was finally healing.

"Dinner tonight needs to involve roughly ten pounds of steak," I said.

Tybalt smirked. "That can be arranged."

Quentin leaned forward, his own cinnamon roll in his hand, and eyed Tybalt. "So are you back?" he asked bluntly. "Or are you going to run away again as soon as we're done with this? If you're going to run, I'd like to know."

I stiffened. Tybalt looked at Quentin solemnly.

"You are a prince, and you are my lady's squire, and for both those reasons, you believe you are owed an answer," he said. "Please understand I privilege the latter far above the former. Princes of the Divided Courts are owed nothing from the Court of Cats. Yes, I am back. October has requested I not leave her again, and after being reminded how much trouble she can get into in my absence, I believe it is best if I acquiesce. If you are asking if I am better, the answer is, sadly, a different one." He turned to look out the window.

He didn't stop talking. "I am afraid of small spaces. For a cat, that is a devastating thing. I cannot seek the comfort of my feline form without fear I will be trapped that way, unable to cry out for those I love, unable to protect them should they cry out for me. I cannot walk among my subjects as I should. Not all Cait Sidhe are capable of transformation. A King should meet those who are bound to four legs in the same fashion, that they may feel they are truly of his Court. I cannot do so. I fail my people, and I fail myself. I have unquiet dreams. I am not a well man, Quentin, and I would not blame October if she bid me not to darken her door until I had recovered. I only pray that she will not, for I think I could not bear to lose another piece of my heart before the last one has come home."

Silence fell across the car, lasting only until Quentin punched Tybalt in the arm.

"That's for being stupid," he said. "There's nothing *wrong* with being hurt. We all get hurt. But you shouldn't have been hiding from us. We're your family, and you're stupid if you think we would judge you for needing help. We help each other."

"You are going to make a fascinating King when your time comes, with the people you have chosen to surround yourself with," observed Tybalt mildly . . . but he sounded pleased.

I decided that was probably a good thing and drove on.

After my disappearance, Cliff had quit his feckless artist's ways and gone into a career in finance. Something stable, dependable, that would allow him to take care of the daughter he was now struggling to raise alone. He'd done well for himself. The tiny apartment of Gillian's infancy had been replaced by a large two-story brownstone in one of the nicer residential neighborhoods. Not as nice as my Victorian, maybe, but Cliff didn't have an ancient fairy lord playing patron. It was more than nice enough, all things considered.

I pulled up and into their private driveway, parking so I blocked the garage. That's normally a cardinal sin in San Francisco, city of hills and limited parking spaces, but under the circumstances, I didn't think Cliff was going to mind. I twisted in my seat, so I could address the car.

"All right," I said. "Tybalt and Quentin, you wait here. If anyone questions you, tell them you're waiting for someone inside. You're both pretty charming. I believe in your ability not to get arrested for lurking."

"Your faith is staggering," said Tybalt. "Go. We will be here."

I blew him a kiss and grabbed for the shadows, intending to weave myself a fresh human disguise. They refused to come. I blinked.

"Um," I said.

"Your blood has yet to return," said Tybalt. He wove his own fingers through the air, and I felt the weight of illusion settle on my shoulders. He smiled, sweet and a little shy. "Much improved."

"Flatterer," I said, and got out of the car, meeting May at the base of the front steps. She looked around with undisguised interest.

"Not bad," she said.

"Nope," I agreed. We walked together to the door. I had barely raised my hand to knock when it was wrenched open, revealing Miranda.

"Did you find her?" she demanded.

"Not yet," I said. "May we come in?"

She stared at me, and for a moment, I thought she was going to refuse and that I would have to do this standing on the porch. Then she sagged and stepped to the side, making room for us.

"Of course," she said.

"Is Cliff here?" I asked, trying not to stare as I stepped into the hallway. The walls were covered in pictures of Gillian as I had never seen her, toddler becoming small child becoming gawky adolescent. It was like a museum of my dreams and failures, and I wanted nothing more than to explore every inch of it, memorizing and committing it to heart.

Miranda was in more than half the pictures. She looked like she was Gillian's mother in blood as well as legality: they fit together. She looked, I realized, like me—dauntingly so. Just blonder and better fed. Was that part of what had drawn Cliff to her in the first place? I wasn't sure whether the thought was flattering.

"He's at the police station, following up," said Miranda. She shut the door, focusing on May. "I'm sorry. I'm afraid I didn't catch your name."

"Oh," said May. She smiled wanly and extended her hand. "I'm May Daye, October's sister. It's a pleasure to make your acquaintance. I just wish it were under better circumstances."

Miranda's eyes narrowed. "I don't think so," she said. "Who are you *really*?"

Oh. Crap.

When Cliff and I first met, I'd been a walking cliché: the teenage runaway living in a den of poor choices and poorer morals. The fact that I'd actually been substantially older than I looked hadn't exactly been relevant. I *was* a runaway, after all, and my upbringing hadn't prepared me for the mortal world. The Summerlands are a great place to grow up if you want to know how to charm a unicorn or host a Midsummer's Ball. They're not so useful if you want to understand human money or how to make macaroni and cheese without setting the kitchen on fire.

The man who'd initially taken me in had understood the difficulties faced by fae-raised changelings escaping from their sometimes overly-protective parents and trying to make a go of things in the mortal world. Devin had always been patient, perfectly understanding of my unique and sometimes difficult circumstances. Of course, that had been because he was using me, like he'd been using all the other "kids" under his care. We were his thieves and his spies and his attack dogs. We were his own private army of Lost Children, and he was our Peter Pan—even now, years and miles away from Home, he was our Peter Pan. Devin had been dead for years. Part of me was always going to be waiting for him to call me back.

Cliff had been my escape from that life, the human man who looked at me and didn't see my mother or my heritage, but *October*, a scrawny, pale kid with a funny name that was simultaneously too silly and too big for her. No matter how hard I try, I can't think of a single person before him who loved me completely for who I was and not for the shadows around me. Not even Stacy. Not even Sylvester. There was no question that they loved me, but they'd started by looking at me through the mirror of my mother, and I had never been enough to eclipse her.

Only problem was, Cliff knew about my family—the dead father, the estranged mother. And he knew I didn't have any siblings. Which meant Miranda knew that, too. She'd needed to know, if she was preparing to challenge me for custody.

"Really," I said. I cleared my throat, buying myself a few precious seconds, and decided to go with as much of the truth as I could afford to risk. "May is my younger sister."

"You don't have a sister," said Miranda with a scowl. "You told Cliff you were an only child, and our investigators haven't found anything to contradict that."

Lying to someone who'd been investigating me. How fun. "I thought I *was* an only child." Dig for the truth. Use it to spin a convincing lie. "Mom never told me about her. She showed up on my doorstep a little while after I got away from my kidnappers. Said she wanted to be a family. I didn't have anyone else. I decided it was worth giving her a shot. What's the worst that could have happened? She kills me and gets me out of your hair forever? I gambled. I won. She's been an incredible help to me these past few years."

"Plus, I pay half the rent," volunteered May. "Isn't this sort of beside the point? We're supposed to be worrying about Gillian, not debating whether I'm actually related to the woman I look almost exactly like. Either I'm her sister, or she's the victim of a long con that required a lot of plastic surgery, and I'd expect you to be happy about that second one. Now can we focus? We have things to do."

"Yes. Gillian." Miranda returned her attention to me. "Why are you here if you haven't found her yet?"

"My phone got broken," I said. "I need to get Cliff's number again, and I wanted to update you on what we've done so far. I went to the school, searched her room, spoke with her roommate—"

"You must not have searched very thoroughly," said Miranda.

I frowned. "Why not?"

"You just don't . . . I would have expected you to find something if you'd searched thoroughly. If you didn't find anything, you can't have done a very good job."

"If you don't think I know how to do my job, you can find someone else to work for you," I snapped. "I'll still keep looking for Gillian, I'll still do everything in my power to find her, but I won't keep you updated, and when I find her, I may or may not inform you. Does that sound like a better plan? Because we can march right the hell out of here, if it does."

Miranda scowled. I looked neutrally back, trying not to let her see how much this entire situation flustered me. I knew Miranda didn't like me. That was a good thing, in its own way, because I didn't like her either. It was better when neither of us was trying to pretend. That didn't explain why she was being openly hostile. With Gillian in danger, we should both have been willing to set our differences aside, at least until the girl we both loved came home.

As if she could follow my thoughts, Miranda sighed and said, "Follow me. I need a pen and paper." Unspoken was the fact that she wasn't willing to leave us alone in her house. Some things don't need to be said. She started down the hall. May and I exchanged a look, and both of us followed her.

The hall ended at a large, open kitchen with a greenhouse window in one wall, the protruding glass panes creating a perfect growing environment for a variety of herbs and houseplants. They grew with joyous abandon, filling the air with sweet and spicy scents. I sniffed appreciatively, and then sneezed.

I blinked. I don't normally have allergies. I was about to comment when I sneezed again, and again, barely covering my nose in time.

"Sorry about that," said Miranda, not sounding sorry at all as she opened a drawer and rummaged for a writing utensil. "My St. John's wort is having a very exciting pollination season this year. I may need to cut it back before the next blooming."

I stiffened. Out of the corner of my eye, I saw May do the same. Then I turned, with exquisite care, to consider Miranda's window garden.

It was artfully planned. At first glance the plants looked like they'd been shoved in wherever they would fit, but a few seconds' consideration confirmed it wasn't so. Each had been potted precisely, positioned to receive the exact degree of sunlight it needed to thrive. She gardened like a scientist, like someone who knew precisely what she was hoping to achieve.

I didn't know the plants by sight, but I knew them by scent. She was growing the usual herbs, rosemary and basil and thyme. She was also growing fennel, and kingcup, and St. John's wort. She was growing hemlock, and gorse, and dill, and kale.

She was growing everything we'd found in Gillian's room and more. The only thing she wasn't growing was cinnamon.

"Here." Miranda turned to offer me a slip of paper. "My number, and Cliff's. Call if you find *anything*." Her tone made it clear that she didn't expect me to. She was playing along, grasping at any straw she could find.

I looked at her, searching her face for any sign of inhuman heritage. There was nothing, no smear of fairy ointment around her eyes or glitter of illusion in the air. But those herbs . . .

I took a breath. I've been following my instincts for my whole career, and while they've led me wrong a time or two, they've been right far more often than that.

"Okay," I said. "I have just one question before we go. Why are you warding my daughter's room against the fae?"

Miranda froze, staring at me. Then, taking a step back, she hissed, "Get out."

So I wasn't wrong. That might have been reassuring, if I hadn't been so damn confused. "I found the sachets in Gillian's dresser. The smell is all over her clothing. What do you know that I don't?"

"I know you're all liars and thieves, and you'd take her in the night if you thought you had half a chance at holding her." Miranda took another step backward. "It doesn't matter whether you're mother or monster; you'd steal her all the same. So I kept her safe. I kept her away from those who might have harmed her. How dare you raise your voice to me, as if you had ever done a damned thing to protect that child?"

The image of a meadow that never existed flashed before my eyes. There had been three versions of Gillian there, three versions of my perfect changeling child: the one who was, in that moment, and the two who had the potential to rise from her ashes. I had given her the Choice. I had protected her in the only way I had, in the only way I had known how. If it hadn't been enough, how was that my fault?

"You have no idea what I've done for her," I said stiffly. "You have no idea what I might still do for her. You're not her mother. You have no right to act like you are."

"I'm more mother than you ever were," Miranda snarled. She turned, apparently intending to grab a knife from the block next to the sink.

Oh, *hell,* no! I was trying to be nice. I was trying to be reasonable. Neither of those things required me to stand idly by while Cliff's new wife stabbed me. "Not happening," I said, and lunged, grabbing her around the ribs. The action pinned her arms to her sides, which was a nice bonus.

Her response—slamming her head back so that her skull impacted with my forehead—was less of a bonus, and more of a predictable problem. Blood gushed from my nose, clearing my head almost instantly. I squeezed harder.

"Calm *down,*" I spat. "You think I care if you're not human? I don't care. I only care that you were apparently trying to keep me away from my own daughter."

Miranda jerked away from me. She was surprisingly strong, and

I didn't want to hurt her, not when I was going to have to explain it to Cliff. "Hi, I beat up your wife because she likes to play with herbs . . ." wasn't the sort of thing that was exactly going to fly with him. I fell back, wiping my bloody nose with one hand, and watched her warily.

"I am *entirely* human," she snarled, and grabbed her purse from the edge of the counter, rummaging through its contents with one hand. I expected her to draw a knife, given what she'd been lunging for before. Instead, she produced a wicked-looking rose thorn with tin foil wrapped around its base. It was half the length of my thumb, its surface glistening like it had been dipped in something viscous and terrible. She pointed it at me, then at May, continuing to move it back and forth between us.

"You stay back." Her voice was low, tight, controlled. "You stay back, and I won't have to use this."

"Do you regularly carry super jumbo thorns in your purse?" asked May. "Aren't you afraid of stabbing yourself when you go for your checkbook?"

Miranda scowled at her. "Who uses a checkbook anymore? I do all my banking online."

"How progressive of you," I said. "What happens if one of us gets stabbed with your little gardening project?"

"Pray you don't find out," she said.

"Yeah, okay," I said, and grabbed her.

As expected, she stabbed me with the thorn, embedding it in my wrist. A wave of dizziness passed over me. I stepped back, letting her go in order to pull the thorn out and jam it into my jacket pocket. The dizziness passed as quickly as it had come. If there was any charring or blistering of the skin, my human disguise hid it.

May rolled her eyes. "You're not immune to poison, you asshole," she said.

"Yeah, but I'll recover." I drew my knife, holding it in front of myself in a defensive position. "Drop the purse, Miranda."

She dropped the purse, eyes gone incredibly wide. "How are you still standing?" she demanded. "That should have felled anything even partially fae."

I considered lying to her, but I didn't see the point. She knew too much. Somehow, she knew too much, and this was going to have to be dealt with.

Cliff would break if his wife disappeared right after his daughter went missing. He would never recover, and even if he never knew enough to blame me, I would know that I had done this to him. I'd never been Miranda's biggest fan, but it wasn't until that moment that I began to hate her.

She raised her hands, showing us that they were empty, that her inexplicable thorn had been the only weapon she possessed—or at least, the only weapon she had had access to. We were still in her home. We needed to proceed with caution.

"May, get her purse," I snapped. "I don't want her going for whatever else she might have in there."

"Lip balm," said Miranda dully. "Throat lozenges, painkillers, some tampons. No weapons. I have nothing else in there that can hurt you."

"You'll forgive me if we don't take your word for that," I said, while May grabbed the purse and retreated out of Miranda's reach, starting to rummage through it. "What the hell are you? What did you do to Gillian? What did you try to do to *me*?"

"I didn't do anything to Gillian. I love her. I've raised her like she was my own daughter, and I've never harmed her, not in the slightest." Miranda looked at me, eyes pleading, like my understanding suddenly mattered to her. Like she needed me to believe her more than she needed anything else. "Whoever took her, they didn't take her because of me."

Oddly, I did believe her, at least about that. Whoever took her was much more likely to have taken her because of me. "How did you know to ward her room against the fae? What are you?"

"'Who' might be a better question," said Miranda. "I—oh, God, I didn't want to have this conversation today. Or ever. Honestly, I was aiming for 'never' as a good time. I'm so sorry."

"Maybe you have good reason to be," I snarled. "You were using something that could *kill* people to keep the fae away from Gillian, while she was on a *college campus*. You've made a lot of people sick."

"They wouldn't get sick if they kept their distance," she said. "It's just hedge magic. Really, October, I expected you to recognize basic charm design, after everything I know you've gotten up to." The corner of her mouth twitched. I realized, shocked, that she was smiling. "I was always impressed by your marshwater work. I don't understand why you stopped. It's not like those pure-blooded bastards would ever see it coming."

May and I both stared at her.

"Lady, what the hell *are* you?" I asked. My voice didn't shake. I was proud of that. "I know you're not a changeling, so are you a merlin? Are you one of the Firstborn? *What*?" They were two different extremes, but both were more feasible than anything else. I would have spotted a changeling or a pureblood the second Cliff had introduced me to his new wife. As a merlin, she would know about magic while having so little fae blood in her that I wouldn't necessarily be able to detect her through my usual means, especially when I wasn't looking for anything out of the ordinary. As one of the Firstborn, she would have the necessary strength to hide herself from me without difficulty.

"Neither," said Miranda. "I was hoping things wouldn't come to this. I didn't think you'd identify the sachets. That was my fault, and I take responsibility for it. I got sloppy."

"You're still not answering my question."

Miranda sighed, looking away. "I suppose you're right, and I suppose you've the right to know," she said. "I really *am* human. I never lied about that, although I may have omitted a few things. But my name isn't Miranda. It's Janet. I'm your grandmother."

THIRTEEN

EVERYTHING FROZE. IT FELT like my heart stopped working properly, each beat thudding through my body like a hammer blow. I couldn't move. I couldn't do anything but stare at this woman—this utterly *human* woman, with her golden hair and her eyes like blue heather growing in the Scottish hills, with her frizzy braid and the freckles across the bridge of her nose—who was claiming the impossible.

"Janet" is a common name. It has been for centuries, falling in and out of fashion but never disappearing. And humans change their names all the time. They don't share the fae reluctance to have a name someone else has already used. There were plenty of explanations that didn't have to *mean* anything.

None of them explained why she was claiming to be my grandmother, or why she said the name "Janet" like she knew what it meant. This wasn't possible. It didn't make *sense*.

"I *thought* I recognized you," said May. Her voice was shrill, even filtered through my hammer heartbeat and overwhelming confusion. "I told myself it wasn't possible, that it was just that you look sort of like Toby—which is creepy, by the way, and says bad things about your relationship with Cliff—and I was seeing things that weren't there, but I wasn't. I recognized you. I saw you in Oberon's hall the season before he disappeared. You were dressed like one of his handmaids, and no one questioned your right to be there, or explained why the father of us all would want some random mortal woman in his knowe."

"You demand to know what *I* am, but what are *you*?" said Miranda—Janet—sounding dismayed.

"Like we said before, I'm her sister. I'm also her Fetch," said May. She glanced at me. "I thought I was seeing things, Toby, I swear. I would have told you if I'd realized there was actually something strange about her."

I believed her. I still couldn't take my eyes off Janet, my mortal lover's mortal wife, standing there with raised hands and a strangely hopeful glimmer in her eyes, like this conversation somehow meant that we could come to an accord.

"*Fetch*?" demanded Janet, the hopeful glimmer dying, replaced by horror. She turned her attention on me. "Do you know what that means? She's a death omen, she's—"

"My sister," I said flatly. "She's been more family to me than any of the people I'm actually related to. Don't worry about her. She's none of your concern."

"If she's riding with you while you search for Gillian, she's entirely my concern! A Fetch is a harbinger of doom! You'll die, and you'll leave that sweet child stranded in some hell she had no part in making!"

"You don't even know the fae took her!" I countered—even though I was fairly sure, by this point, that no one else could have done it. The smell of rowan. The house with the chicken legs. There were just too many impossible elements. "With as much poison as you packed into her dorm room, all we'd need to do to find a fae kidnapper is look for the person in the coma with the backpack full of Benadryl! May is not. Your. Concern. She is my family. She's the only real family I have, since you swept in and stole my daughter."

Janet's face fell. Root and branch, why was that name bothering me so much? "It was a mean trick, coming in while you were gone and taking Gillian for my own; I'll own that." Her voice took on a pleading note. "But please, try to understand. No one knew where you were. I thought you'd taken your mother's example and run away rather than facing your responsibilities. Anyone with eyes could see the girl was mostly human. She was never going to be offered that spiteful bargain your people call a 'choice.' I thought you'd thrown her away. I was trying to do right by the blood of my blood, and you were gone so long, I truly came to love her as if she were my own child, and not my great-granddaughter. Then you came back, and I . . ." She spread her hands. "I couldn't handle losing another child to Faerie. I told myself it was the right thing to do. That she deserved a mother who could stay, who wouldn't be led astray by a society she would never belong to."

I stared at her. "That sounded almost like an apology."

"Because it was." She looked me squarely in the eyes. "I am not sorry to have been her mother, but I am sorry I didn't make room for you. I'm so sorry."

"What the hell is happening?" My lips were numb, but my voice was working fine. That was good. I suddenly had a *lot* to say. "You can't be my grandmother! You can't know *any* of this! You're a human! You—"

"I was Oberon's lover," said Janet. Time seemed to stop again. "There's a long story as to how that happened, and I'll be happy to tell it to you. Later. This isn't the time. He loved me, and we had a daughter, and we named her 'Amandine,' because he knew I missed the almond trees that grew in my father's orchards. He knew how much I missed my father, and Oberon was always kind, when the world gave him room to be. That's what I hold to most, so long after. That he was kind, even when it wasn't necessary. But then he had to go away, and he decided it wasn't safe for me to be associated with our daughter, not with my history. He had her placed in a blind fosterage. By the time I found where he'd put her, it was too late."

"Too late for what?" I whispered, horrified. It was like listening to my own story turned on its head. The missing parent, the child removed and raised by someone else . . .

"Too late for me." Janet tipped her chin up. I saw my mother in that gesture, stubbornness and pride mixed up together until they became indistinguishable. I saw my mother, and August, and Gillian, and myself.

That was the moment when I started to believe her.

"Amandine didn't need a mother. She certainly didn't need a *human* mother, and the implications that carried. She didn't need a family at all, apart from the fosterage her father had arranged. She had no place for me, and I'm not foolish enough to go against one of Oberon's Firstborn, even when that Firstborn is my own daughter. Maeve's curse aside, she would have crushed me."

"Maeve's . . . ?" Once again, I was starting to feel like I needed a flowchart to keep up with everything. I realized I was still holding my knife in front of me. Grudgingly, I lowered it. Somehow, I didn't think stabbing her was going to do me any good. It might make me feel better, but it wouldn't *help*.

"Oh. Did I leave that part out?" Smile turning wry, Janet tucked her hair behind one ear and said, "Until she returns, until she re-leases me, I don't age, and I don't die. At least not of anything I've been able to discover thus far, and believe me, I've discovered a lot of things. Plague, blood loss, poison—I recover. Until Maeve lets me go, here I am, preserved like a body in a bog."

"Most people would go for the 'mosquito in amber' metaphor these days," said May.

Janet shrugged. "Most people haven't been through a hundred years of speech therapy to stop sounding like they belong in a part of Scotland that barely even exists anymore." She paused and cleared her throat. Her next words were draped in a brogue so thick it should have sounded like a parody. Instead, it sounded like the world finally coming clear. "They forbade us maidens all who wore gold in our hair to come nor go near Caughterha; said young Tam Lin was there. More fool me, who never once learned how to listen."

The floor seemed to drop out from under my feet. "You're *Janet*," I whispered.

Janet looked relieved. "Yes," she said, brogue vanishing back into her carefully-schooled California accent. "I am."

I didn't say anything. It didn't feel like there was anything left that I could say.

"Wait." May held up her hands. We both turned to her. "You're really Amandine's mother?"

"Yes," said Janet. Then she frowned. "You swear you're not here because October is marked for death?"

"She was, once, but she got better," said May. She glanced at me. "I mean, she still runs into danger like it's her damn job, but it's not because she has some predestined fate waiting in the wings to eat her."

"That's because it *is* my damn job," I said. "I'm pretty good at surviving, though. May's been living with me for years. Since just before I took down Blind Michael."

Janet blanched, becoming so pale she looked like she was on the verge of passing out. There couldn't have been any blood left in her head. "Blind Michael?" she repeated. "The horror of the hills, and you stopped him?"

"I had to," I said simply. "He hurt my family."

Janet blinked. Then, bitterly, she laughed. "As have I, is that what you say next?"

"You know, for someone who's presumably been shopping on Amazon and yelling at the cable company for the last decade or so, you sure do talk like a romance novel," said May.

"My apologies." Janet shoved her braid back, grimacing. "It's a bit automatic when speaking to the fae. Even when Oberon was here to protect me from his own people, I was human. I always have been: there's no changing that. I learned the best way not to get hexed or hurt was to be as polite as possible."

"You weren't polite when you shoved your way into my home and accused me of kidnapping, or when you covered my daughter in something that would *literally poison me*," I said. My frustration was starting to get the better of me. I stopped, forcing myself to take a deep breath.

Janet was the source of the sachets. The sachets were one of the only clues we had. Therefore, Janet needed to answer some goddamn questions.

"When did you start dipping my child in herbal toxins?" I asked.

"After she was stolen by your world for the first time," she replied. "She came back changed. I assume that was your work?"

I nodded, the words catching in my throat until I swallowed them and said, "I offered her the Choice. It was the only way to save her life."

Janet sighed. "I thought . . . when that happened, I thought that was you ceding her to me. You pulled Faerie from her blood. I thought you were saying I was her true mother, and it was my responsibility to keep her safe. So I kept her safe. I started making teas for her to drink and scents for her to wear, anything that would keep Faerie just that little bit at bay. And it worked! For so long, it worked."

"Except for the part where anyone fae who touched her got sick, which meant they could figure out something was up with her," I countered. "Best case would have been her getting reported to the local nobility as a human who knew about the fae—and I say 'best' because that would have been run up the chain of command to the queen, and I might have heard about it before she wound up turned into an apple tree or something. This wasn't subtle."

"She attends Berkeley," said Janet. "There *is* no local nobility."

May and I both stared at her. Finally, carefully, I asked, "How do you know that?"

"Before he left, Oberon promised me that wherever I chose to settle would have no one watching over it, no ruler tied to the land more directly than whatever king or queen claimed it as part of their domain." Her lips twitched, like she was trying not to smile. "He wasn't quite ready to make a queen of me. Said it might send the wrong message, given everything that had happened, and given I'm immortal solely because his absent wife decreed I should be. A pity. I would have been fetching in a crown."

It took me a moment to find my voice again. "The people who stole Gillian used her clothing—her *bloody* clothing—to lay a false trail into a courtyard that shouldn't have been there, full of things that shouldn't exist. No one had used magic there since it was created, and apparently, all the local royalty know about it but don't tell anyone, because there's an agreement that predates any of them. Is that . . . ?"

"Not aging is a problem in the human world, and I don't have your hand with illusions: once cosmetics stop doing the job, I'll have to fake my own death and disappear for a decade or so," said Janet. There was genuine regret in her tone. "I settled here to be close to my daughter, and later, to you. Oberon himself granted me that land. No one should have been there."

"Someone was. Someone wanted whoever went looking for Gillian—meaning me—to find the place, which means someone not only knew about the courtyard, they knew about *you*. They wanted me to . . . find . . ." I stopped. "We have to get you out of here."

"What?" asked May.

"What?" asked Janet.

"I've been acting on the assumption that whoever kidnapped Gillian was trying to get to me. Maybe I'm looking at things the wrong way. Maybe they're trying to get to *you*." I shook my head. "We have to get you out of here."

Janet stared at me, eyes wide. "You can't be serious."

"Someone violated your space, which was apparently granted to you by Oberon himself. Someone stole a human child most people would assume was your daughter and yours alone." The false

Queen knew Gillian was mine. The false Queen was aiming for us both. I couldn't say that until I was sure, and not until I had Janet out of harm's way. "They're trying to hurt you, either by setting us against each other, or by ignoring my part in things entirely. You can't stay here. You're in danger."

"I can't be killed," said Janet.

"Cliff can," I said.

She went still.

"You think I put him in danger by loving him and being fae? I was a changeling, I was barely more than a child, I had no power and no position and nothing to lose. You? You're a legend and a monster and an impossibility. You need to come with me, or you're going to get him killed." I shook my head. "Leave a note. Say you're looking for Gillian. Say whatever you want. But I'm not leaving you here."

"Dear God," breathed Janet. My earlier assumptions about how pale she could get were clearly not good enough, as even more blood drained from her face. "I . . . how long do you think this will take?"

"However long it has to," I said. "May, you stay here and help Janet get whatever she needs. I'm going to go and tell the boys what's going on."

"Wait!" Janet took a step back, visibly alarmed, and stopped only when her hips hit the counter. "Who are 'the boys'? You're not going to tell them who I *am*, are you?"

"Lady, I don't think you have any right to ask me to keep secrets after what you've done to my family, but I'm not going to put that same family in danger by broadcasting your identity all over the Mists." I made no effort to keep the weariness out of my voice. I was exhausted. A few cinnamon rolls weren't enough to counteract the amount of blood I'd lost, and I was going to need real food soon. "At the same time, yeah, I'm telling my squire and my fiancé. We don't keep secrets in our house." Not anymore. Not with the way every secret we'd tried to keep had ended up playing out.

Some things aren't worth risking. My family—the one I had made for myself, the one I was going to fight for until the end of the world—was on that list.

"I don't suppose I have a choice here, do I?" asked Janet.

"Not really," I said.

"Nope," said May, with malicious cheer. She glanced at me.

"Go. I'll make sure she doesn't do anything any of us will regret later."

Leaving the two indestructible women alone seemed like a dandy idea. More importantly, I wanted to be away from Janet, at least for a few minutes—at least long enough to get my head together. This was all too much. My daughter was missing; her stepmother, the woman I had spent so much time envying and despising for taking my place, was my grandmother. It was enough to make my head spin, and I wanted a moment to wrap my mind around it.

I practically bolted for the front door, not allowing myself to look back. That isn't just a bad idea in Bible stories and Greek myths: it's what leads to a simple course of action getting complicated or disrupted, and things never getting done. Janet's revelation was . . .

Janet's revelation was a problem, and it was going to take me days, if not weeks, to process all the way through it. I needed to talk to the Luidaeg. She could explain what this meant, how it was possible for my mother to be a human's daughter, whether it had somehow affected me even two generations down the line. And that was fine, that was absolutely great, because where could I go to hide someone who shouldn't have existed, someone who stood at the center of the story that broke the world?

To the sea witch, of course.

Quentin and Tybalt both turned when I yanked the car door open and dropped myself into the front seat. Human disguises can mimic all the little parts of living, the blushes and the pallors, the changes of mood. The one Tybalt had woven for me wasn't good enough for any of that. It let me pass for human, and that was about all it could manage.

Tybalt frowned, sniffing the air. "What's wrong?" he asked.

I frowned. "How did you—?"

"You're sweating. And you've been bleeding again, which is something you can't afford to be doing right now." His eyes narrowed. "Where is May? Did that former lover of yours strike you? I would take the greatest pleasure in taking him apart, if he did."

"No. No, it's nothing like that. It's nothing . . ." I laughed unsteadily. "It's nothing that *normal*. We're about to have another passenger."

"Who?" asked Quentin.

"Miranda. She's coming with us. And her name isn't Miranda,

it's Janet. And she's my grandmother." The words sounded ridiculous when I put them out there like that. I tried again. "I mean, she's my mother's mother. She's human, and she's my mother's mother."

"That *does* happen," said Tybalt, carefully not looking at Quentin.

As far as either of us knew, my squire didn't know his own mother had been born a changeling, or that her human heritage had been the price of marrying the Crown Prince and eventually ascending to her own place in the nobility. It wasn't our place to tell him. I shook my head.

"Mom's Firstborn, and her mother is human. Oberon loved a *human*."

"Wait," said Quentin. "That would make her at least—"

"Five hundred years old," I said. "I know."

Quentin shook his head. "That's not . . . no. That's just a story. It's not real. She can't really be that Janet. Can she?"

"I don't know." I paused. "I think so."

"Root and branch," breathed Tybalt. "How is this possible?"

"A second ago you were the one reminding me that human ancestors happen," I said.

"Yes, and a second ago, you were not intimating that Janet of Caughterha was going to be in your car." He shook his head. "This can't be so. She spins a story well enough to ensnare you."

"May remembers seeing her in Oberon's Court. She's from Scotland. She fits the description. She knows things she shouldn't. I don't want to believe it either, but I think maybe I should. Maybe not believing is a luxury we don't have time for right now." I took a deep breath. "She owns that courtyard we found. It's hers. She's been here since Gilad's parents held the throne. Whoever took Gillian may be trying to hurt Janet as much as they're trying to hurt me."

"Is that why she's joining our merry band?" asked Tybalt. "Because you fear for her safety?"

"In part, yeah," I said. "Also because I fear for Cliff's. She's indestructible. He isn't. And doubly also because I want to question her further, and I don't want Cliff walking in on us. So we're taking her to the safest dangerous place I know."

"Where's that?" asked Quentin.

I smiled. Tybalt raised his eyebrows.

"I am suddenly grateful that I can't see the blood," he said. "Your expression is frightening enough without it."

"Yeah, well, I've learned from the best," I said. "We're taking her to the Luidaeg. Let's see how many questions we get answered *now*."

FOURTEEN

IF I'D THOUGHT the atmosphere in the car was uncomfortable before—with Tybalt brooding and Quentin exhausted, and me and May trying to deal with Gillian's disappearance—it was nothing compared to what happened when we added Janet to the mix. She sat in the middle, crammed between Quentin and May, both of whom eyed her mistrustfully all the way across the city. It would have been funny if it hadn't been so damn tense. Janet looked like an ordinary housewife, rumpled and out of place. May had returned her purse, and she clutched it like she feared it was going to be taken away again. Quentin watched her warily, not saying a word. May slumped against the window on her side of the car, obviously exhausted, making no effort to conceal her hostility.

"Where are we going?" Janet asked, after we'd been driving for ten long, silent minutes.

"To see a friend of mine who may be able to clear up some of what's going on, and better yet, who makes an excellent babysitter for unexpected grandmothers in need of temporary protective custody," I said tightly.

Janet's eyes widened. "What? I thought you were taking me with you."

"No, we're taking you away from your unwarded, indefensible home, so Cliff doesn't get hurt when whoever may or may not be messing with you shows up." Keeping my voice level was more difficult than I'd expected. "You're not coming with us. We need to be free to go anywhere the trail leads, and I don't feel like you'd be welcome in most places, especially if you want to play 'innocent little mortal woman' and not have us broadcast your identity to anyone who wants to know why we're hauling you around."

"Where are you—"

"To my favorite aunt. She can answer a lot of questions for me, and I know she has space. I mean, her guest room is currently full, but she has a couch. You can probably sit on it, assuming she doesn't make you stand in the corner and think about what you've done."

Janet stared at me, expression hurt. "I haven't done anything to you."

"You've done *everything* to me. To all of us. You broke the Ride, if you are who you say you are. That means this world is your fault." I pulled to a stop on the street in front of the Luidaeg's alley. Technically, it wasn't a legal parking place, thanks to the combination of red curb and fire hydrant. I wouldn't get a ticket. No one who came to see the Luidaeg ever had to worry about anything as mundane as the police.

Being turned into something unpleasant and chucked into the bay, on the other hand . . .

There was a moment when I thought Janet might bolt. I took one elbow. Tybalt took the other. With her safely pinned between us, we marched on, Quentin in the lead, May ready to tackle her if she somehow broke free and tried to run.

The Luidaeg's door looked like it always did: rotten wood and peeling paint, set so far back into the wall that it would have been easy to miss if we hadn't already known where we were going. Quentin hopped onto the stoop and knocked without any sign of hesitation. He's known the Luidaeg since before he formally became my squire, and while he appreciates that she's terrifying and all, he also seems to consider her as much his aunt as she is mine. He adores her. She returns the favor. With as long as she's been one of Faerie's greatest monsters, it must be nice for her to have someone who just loves her, no qualifiers, no strings attached.

Seconds ticked by. Janet squirmed.

"Your friend isn't home," she said. "We should go."

"She's here," I said. "Wait."

Janet was still glaring at me when the door opened and the Luidaeg appeared.

As always, when not trying to make a point, she looked like a human teenager, somewhere in the baby-faced range between puberty and college. The ghosts of acne scars dusted her cheeks, and her thick, curly black hair was pulled into twin pigtails, one over each shoulder, both tied off with electrical tape. She was wearing a pair of denim overalls, her feet and shoulders bare, and the expression on her face was somewhere between annoyance and relief.

"I was wondering whether you assholes were going to come bother me today," she said without preamble. "It's been a week. I was starting to think you . . . had . . . forgotten . . ." Her voice slowed, finally trailing off as she stared at Janet. She took a step forward, stopping when her toes struck the edge of her threshold. She froze there, still staring.

"Hi, Luidaeg," I said. "I finally met my grandmother."

"October." Her voice sounded hollow. "Do you know who that is? Do you know . . ." She stopped, swallowing hard. The blue was bleeding out of her eyes, replaced drop by drop with clear glass green. That wasn't a *great* sign. Better than if they had been going black, but still, not *great*. "Do you know what she did?"

"Can we come inside?" I asked. "This doesn't feel like the sort of conversation we should be having in the street."

She looked at me with honest, raw confusion. I had never seen her at such a loss for words, not even when I had used blood magic to bring her back from the dead and loosened some of the geasa on her in the process. "Inside?" she asked. "Inside my *home*?"

"Yeah. I'm sorry to ask you to do this, but we don't have anywhere else to go, and Janet may be in danger."

The Luidaeg looked at her—scrawny mortal woman with her messy hair, sandwiched between me and Tybalt, both of us holding an arm so she couldn't get away if she tried—and laughed. "In danger? Her? She *is* danger, and make no bones of that. But if you came all this way, I suppose you may as well come in." Her gaze swiveled to Janet. "We'll discuss the rest of this behind closed doors."

Janet blanched, twisting in our hands as she tried, futilely, to break away. Tybalt and I both tightened our grips—I, at least, was still trying not to bruise her; I couldn't necessarily say the same for him—and pulled her into the apartment, following Quentin and the Luidaeg. May brought up the rear, closing the door once we were all inside.

It latched with a sound loud enough to consume the world. Janet moaned, small and tight and, yes, terrified. I gave her a sidelong look.

"Why are you so afraid?"

"Why aren't you?" she demanded, turning to face me. "Do you know whose door you've darkened?"

"Yeah. The Luidaeg is a friend of mine." You couldn't have told it from her apartment. The illusions that made it look like something that had washed up with high tide were back in place. Streaks of mold in a dozen virulent colors smeared the walls, all of them clashing with one another, and clashing even worse with the wallpaper behind them. The carpet was worse, seeming to squirm under its thick layer of slime and debris. It squished under our feet. Maybe it was just illusionary water, but the Luidaeg is a master of her craft, and the muck still felt like it was seeping into our shoes.

Janet wasn't resisting anymore. She allowed us to drag her toward the living room, her eyes rolling wildly as she took in everything around her.

"You know, it's pretty common knowledge that the Luidaeg is in San Francisco," I said, tone light, almost conversational. I would have been lying if I'd tried to say I wasn't enjoying seeing her so uncomfortable. This was the woman who had *known* I was fae, had *known* my disappearance was related to the world Cliff couldn't touch, and rather than helping me make peace with my daughter, had used her knowledge as a lever to keep me even further away. "What the hell are you doing here, if you didn't want to risk running into her?"

"I wanted to be near my Amy," she said. "And I knew the sea witch was here, but she didn't know about me. That made all the difference in the world. She'd never see me if I didn't want her to."

Tybalt and I exchanged a glance over her head. He looked baffled. Cait Sidhe sometimes seem to have a monopoly on arrogance, but this was a class above.

The Luidaeg was already seated in her favorite overstuffed armchair when we pulled Janet into the living room. She raised a hand and pointed imperiously to the couch.

"Put her there," she said.

"Where's Poppy?" I asked, as Tybalt and I led Janet to the couch.

"Sleeping, like all sensible fae should be at this hour. Which is how I knew it was you people on my porch. You can be accused of having many things, October, but 'sense' doesn't even make the list." The Luidaeg's expression softened for a fraction of a second. Then it slammed down again, turning to ice as she looked at Janet. "Do you know what she did?"

"I know the story. Sort of. I was never sure how much of it was accurate and how much of it was people who weren't there making things up."

Everyone knew the story. Maeve's last Ride, the night that broke Faerie forever. It was history and legend and cautionary tale, it was the moment when an empire fell and became an afterthought, all because of one human girl and her outstretched, grasping hands. It was the end. It was the beginning.

It was where we got lost.

"Then let me tell it to you," said the Luidaeg, voice like high tide rolling across the beach. "Let me tell you about a time when Faerie was open to her children, when my father and his Queens still kept Court and counsel. It was my mother's turn to host the Ride, and she had chosen her sacrifice, a mortal man by the name of Tam Lin. He was a liar and a poet and a sybarite, and he'd been more than happy to take his side of the bargain. For near seven years he'd feasted on the fruits of Faerie, growing fat and happy and rich beyond mortal measure at our expense. And then, when time was almost up, he decided he didn't want to die for us after all."

"Die for us?" blurted Quentin. "Why would he need to die for us?"

I kept my mouth shut for a change, glad that he'd asked before I could. It was nice to look like I knew what the hell was going on.

The Luidaeg looked briefly uneasy. "Things were different then," she said, finally. "Every seven years, we made an offering to Faerie, to keep us healthy and strong. Tam Lin was to have been the latest in a string of brief, bright lives, stretching all the way back to our beginning."

"You were going to murder him," snarled Janet, seeming to forget her fear.

"He was destined for the gallows when my mother found him," said the Luidaeg. "We gave him seven years that might as well have been stolen. We gave him everything he asked for."

"Except for his freedom," said Janet.

"Who among us is *free*?" The Luidaeg spread her hands,

indicating the apartment walls. "We're all bound by promises and obligations and fealties we had no say in. No one's *free*, not unless they've slit a hundred throats to get that way. He made a promise. He took a vow. He said he'd die for us, and when he didn't—when you broke my mother's Ride—Maeve had to go in his place or throw everything out of balance. Only it turns out that taking one of my father's queens away throws everything out of balance in a whole different way. Everything we've suffered, everything Faerie has suffered in the last five hundred years, it's all down to you."

"I didn't know," said Janet.

"Oh, didn't you? They told you not to go to Caughterha, didn't they, Jenny?" The Luidaeg's lip curled as she looked at Janet. "They told you what you'd find there wasn't yours to have. But you went anyway. Greedy little girl. Had to have it all."

"I've paid for what I did, and not everyone said to stay away," said Janet. There was no fire in her voice. "I was a child."

"You were a thief."

"I was a *child*." Janet shook her head. "I paid for what I did. I paid, and I paid, and I paid, and no one came to save me from the consequences of my own actions. No one even said I deserved saving. You can be as angry with me as you like, but there's no way you can pretend I haven't suffered."

"You don't know what it means to suffer, *human*," said the Luidaeg. "You have no idea."

"Maybe she does and maybe she doesn't, but we brought her here because we need you to keep her safe," I said. "Please, Luidaeg. Can you protect her?"

The Luidaeg turned and stared at me. Then she sniffed the air. "Blood," she said, sounding disgusted. "How much blood are you wearing right now?"

"Some," I said. "That's not the point."

"Oh, isn't it?" She snapped her fingers. The air briefly became a haze of conflicting scents as our illusions—all of them—were ripped away, leaving the four of us with something to hide fully revealed.

Janet gasped. Whether because of the blood or because she was suddenly in the presence of four unmasked fae, it was difficult to say. Quentin and May made almost identical noises of displeasure.

"Do you have any blood left *inside* your body?" Quentin demanded.

"I asked her much the same," said Tybalt.

"Dad's eyes, Toby, sometimes I wonder how you've lived as long as you have." The Luidaeg stood. "I'm making you a sandwich before you fall over. That'll give me a minute to calm down, and when I get back, you're going to eat, and you're going to tell me exactly what the fuck you think you're doing. If I like what you have to say, maybe I'll let you keep all your limbs."

"They'd grow back, and you know it," I said.

"That's what makes threatening to pull them off so much fun," she said, and swept out of the room.

Janet started to rise. "Now's our chance. We can run."

May pushed her back down. "No," she said coldly. "We stay."

Janet gave her a wounded look. "You're a Fetch. You're new to Faerie. You shouldn't share their preconceived notions of who I am."

"You seem to have some preconceived notions of what a Fetch is, so I guess we're even," said May. "I should have known who you were the second I saw your face in October's memories. It should have been the first thing I said when she and I met. 'The woman who condemned us all is here, in San Francisco, and she has your child.' I should have *known*. But memory fades when it gets over-written. A Fetch is a palimpsest of people they aren't anymore, because every new life removes pieces of the old one. I didn't know you, and I'll be carrying that forever, *especially* if Gillian has been hurt to get to you."

"You don't know why I did what I did," said Janet. "You weren't there."

That wasn't always a safe assumption to make, with May, but under the circumstances, it was a reasonable one. No one had been there. "So tell us what happened," I said. It was a way to keep her talking and calm until the Luidaeg came back; it was a way to keep the squirrels in my mind from chasing each other down dark holes. Gillian was out there somewhere. She needed me to find her, to bring her safely home. But if I left while the Luidaeg wanted me to stay, I would have more problems added to the pile I was already carrying.

Janet looked at me defiantly. "You won't listen," she said.

"Try us," said Quentin.

Janet looked at him. Looked at me. And took a breath.

"It was a very long time ago . . ." she began.

FIFTEEN

"MY FATHER WAS A landholder in Scotland. He had fields such as stretched nearly to the horizon, and he could have been a king, if he'd wanted to call himself such. He didn't like the idea of a crown, though, nor the thought of people coming to take it from him, and so he contented himself with land, and hall, and the knights that helped him hold it. We were comfortable, and content, and happy enough. He loved me." Janet paused, lips curving in a small, secret smile. I felt like an intruder, looking at that smile. "I was his eldest daughter, and I looked so much like my mam, and she gone to the grave after the birth of my little brother, and he loved me so. With a son in line to inherit his lands, and set to care for me no matter what, he could afford to love me. I didn't have to be handed off to the first wealthy man to come along and promise to fill my stomach. I could be his pretty girl, and all the world was mine to have."

"Spoiled little rich kid," I said. "Got it."

Janet's lip curled as she looked at me. "Things were different then. Being able to love your children when they were no longer children was a luxury most men never had."

"Very few of the people in this room were permitted by circumstance to enjoy the company of a doting father," said Tybalt blandly. "You will please forgive us if we are not as sweetly touched by your tale as you believe we ought to be, and hunger instead for the meat of the thing. We have a child to find, after all, and linger here only so long as we must."

Not entirely a child, to the rest of the world, but forever a child to me. Not only me: Janet winced, nodding.

"My apologies," she said. "I was . . . as I said, I was not an only child, not set to be his heir, but well enough treated and spoilt as to believe the world was mine by right. He set a patch of farmland and forest on me as my dowry, a place called Caughterha, where the grass grew as green as the sky was blue, and the river ran heavy with fish throughout the year. It was a rich place. Any man who married me would have it for his own, and if I never married, it would keep me fed even if my brother tired of me or had a wife who would see me set aside. Legally, it was complicated for a woman to own such, but my father was well-loved among the local landowners and his men alike, and he was fairly confident no hand would try to wrest it from me. No mortal hand did."

Janet's lip twisted again, this time not in my direction. The look of disgust seemed to be turned inward, at someone who wasn't here. "The fae knew a good piece of land as well as we humans did, and they anchored one of their parasitic halls in my wood, near my river. They even spread the word through the towns nearby, said 'I forbid you maidens all as wear gold in your hair to come nor go by Caughterha.' As if that *ever* worked."

"It would work on us," said Quentin. She turned to him and raised an eyebrow. I almost jumped. How had Cliff missed how much his new wife's expressions looked like mine? He shrugged. "I know you may not believe it, but I'm only as old as I look. I'm a little younger than Gillian. And if someone said, 'don't go in that one, specific forest, bad things will happen if you do,' I wouldn't go. Ignoring that kind of warning gets you killed. Unless you're a hero, you wouldn't."

Tybalt nodded agreement. I frowned.

"I think this is where the changeling experience differs, guys," I said. "I would *absolutely* have gone to see what all the fuss was about."

"If you had, if you broke that rule, I hope what would have happened to you would have been different from what happened to me," said Janet. "I went. I had to. I needed to *know*. I tied my skirts above my knee to keep them from dredging up the dew, and I braided my hair to keep it free of the trees, and I went to Caughterha with all the arrogance I was heir to. And I met a man." Her voice and face softened. For a moment, she looked so young it ached. "I met a beautiful, charming man who came out of the trees and told me not to pick his roses. Me, who had planted them, tended them, known them as my own for my entire life! I laughed in his face, told him if he wished to deny a girl her pleasures, he'd best hie himself out of my wood. And I left."

We were quiet, waiting. We didn't have to wait long.

"I left, and then I went back, again and again, over and over, until spring melted into summer, until he kissed me among the roses. He didn't know I was a local landholder's daughter. He knew I claimed to own the wood, but he had laughed and said his mistress would be mightily interested to hear that, and I never felt, even for a moment, that he believed me. To him, I was nothing but a human woman, and to me, he was a human man."

"A human man who had sold himself, body and soul, to the Queen of Faerie," said the Luidaeg. I turned. She was standing in the doorway that led to the kitchen, a plate in her hand and a weary expression on her face. "Don't forget that part. I know he told you, because he didn't have a choice. That was part of the agreement. Seven years of everything he wanted, no matter how extravagant, no matter how depraved. Seven years of paradise, his needs met, his belly full. And at the end—"

"A tithe to Hell," snapped Janet hotly. "How could any man be expected to honor such a bargain?"

"Because he made that part up," said the Luidaeg. "We geased him to tell anyone human he encountered that he was in the service of the fae, and they needed to keep their hands off if they didn't want to incur our wrath. He said he needed some freedom to stay healthy and happy and we believed him, or, rather, Mother believed him because she always wanted to think the best of you humans."

"You never did," said Janet.

"Because I had actually paid attention to more than a few humans. I knew, even then, how much trouble you could cause."

"Will you deny that you intended to sacrifice him?"

"No. He was the tithe. But it wasn't to Hell, and he came to us willingly. Seven years of everything he wanted, and at the end, a peaceful death. That's more than most men got in those days. Hell, that's more than most men get now." The Luidaeg walked over and shoved the plate at me. "Cold chicken and cheddar cheese with strawberry jam, just the way you like it."

Janet blinked. "You . . . like that?"

"If you're going to be disgusted, go for it," I said, taking the plate. "Cliff used to make gagging noises and think he was the cleverest man alive."

"Gillian eats her sandwiches the same way."

I nearly dropped the plate.

"Her father told her they were 'mommy sandwiches' when she was, I don't know, four or so. He and I weren't married yet. She tells people they're my favorite, but we both know that isn't true. He wanted her to have something of yours, even if he could never admit it." Janet looked to the Luidaeg. "So my Tam lied to me. He was trying to save his life. You'd have done the same."

"I would never have agreed to Mother's bargain in the first place, and if I had, I would have kept my word," corrected the Luidaeg. "He made a promise. He swore to die for Faerie's sake. We kept our side of the bargain. All you ever were to him was a chance to turn his back on his obligations."

"You think I don't know that?" Janet's laugh was bitter. "I know perfectly well what I was to him. He didn't want to die."

"All mortal flesh dies." The Luidaeg shot me a sharp look. "I know you want to hear the end of this, but I want you eating that sandwich. Now."

I took a bite. As with all the Luidaeg's cooking, it was balanced and delicious. Having seen what her apartment looked like without the illusions, I wasn't even worried about eating something I didn't intend to. Much.

"Not all mortal flesh," said Janet. "Mine's still here."

"Only until Mom comes home and releases it."

Janet smiled tightly. "And won't that be a day? Yes, I went to Caughterha. Yes, I fancied myself in love with a man who said I was beautiful, said I was perfect, said I could save him from the fae. I wanted an adventure. I got one."

"It really happened. You really did it," said Quentin, horror and awe in his voice. "You were the one who broke Maeve's last Ride."

"It was the only way to save him," said Janet. "On Halloween, when the fae Rode, I had to pull him from his horse and hold him fast. I had to refuse to let him go, or everything would be lost forever. I did it. God help me, I did it, and the fairy queen had to go in his place."

"This is the good part," said the Luidaeg. "I mean, ignore the part where she's trying not to brag about going out to the forest with the express intention of killing my mom. Look at the rest of it. The way the humans tell the story, Tam Lin told her how to save him from us, because he didn't want to die and we were going to condemn him to Hell and how dare we. But you know how well we can stop a tongue that might say things we don't want said. Do you honestly think my mother—my *mother*—would set her little pet free to wander the woods with the key to her downfall ready to tumble from his lips and into the hands of the first pretty maid to happen by? She was smarter than that. She was better than that. Who gave you the key you needed, pretty maid? Who told you how to break us?"

I looked from the Luidaeg to Janet, and I knew what she was going to say, and I didn't want to hear it. Five hundred years. That should have been long enough that the villains of the piece would change, and yet . . .

"She said her name was Eira, and that it wasn't fair for an innocent man to die for Faerie's sins. She told me what to do."

"There we go." The Luidaeg toasted the air with an imaginary glass. "My sister's greatest crime. Shattering our world. And the stories call *me* a monster."

"I think I'm going to be sick," muttered Quentin.

"I lost the baby," said Janet quickly, like she could sense her time to speak was coming to an end. "All that magic, all that effort, holding onto my lover as he became beast after beast—it was too much. I lost the baby, but my father already knew I'd been touched, and he demanded Tam marry me. I suppose I should have known he wasn't the kind of man to keep his promises, but I thought . . . I thought I was different. We were both human, and Maeve's curse was so fresh on my skin that I didn't realize yet what it would do. When Tam ran, I did the only thing I could think of. I tied my skirts and I braided my hair and I went back to Caughterha looking for the fae. They were the ones who had ruined my life. I wanted them to restore it."

"We told you," said the Luidaeg. "We *told* you. 'Don't go to Caughterha.' When that didn't work, 'don't touch the favorite of the queen, the man condemned to die.' We *told* you, over and over. You ruined your own life."

Janet ignored her. "It was easier to find the fae in those days. They were less hidden, less secretive. I found their Court, and I found their King, and I demanded he do right by me. So he did. He took me into his service, and he took me into his confidence, and one night, after too much wine and too much conversation and too many regrets, he took me into his bed. Not against my will—never that—but still, we both knew we shouldn't have done it. Amandine happened not long after that. My pretty, perfect Amy. The best thing Faerie ever made."

Tybalt shivered and turned his face away. I took a step to the side, still cramming sandwich into my mouth, and leaned over so my shoulder rested against his. He glanced at me and relaxed, very slightly. That was enough. That had to be enough.

"We know the story from there," I said brusquely, and turned toward the Luidaeg before Janet could resume singing Mom's praises. "Gillian's missing. Whoever took her used her clothes to lay several false trails, including one to a courtyard Janet owns that no one's supposed to know about, and another to the lair of a Baobhan Sith. She bled a lot when she was taken, but the blood I was able to retrieve didn't contain a death. I think she's alive. She's being held captive, and I need to get her back as soon as I can. Can you help me?"

"With your debts where they are, I doubt my father himself could help you," said the Luidaeg, grimacing. "She's a mortal girl, October. She's outside my reach."

"Can't blame a mother for asking."

"That is one of the things I would never try to blame you for." She tilted her head, looking at me. "You're calmer than I'd have expected. Is this the blood loss speaking, or do you know where you have to go next?"

"I know who took her." I kept my eyes on the Luidaeg, not wanting to see my companions react. If any of them looked like they didn't believe me, I was going to start swinging. "I caught a scent in the Baobhan Sith's lair. Nothing I could follow, but enough to give me an identity."

The Luidaeg raised an eyebrow.

"I don't care if it's impossible. I don't care if it doesn't make sense. The false Queen was in that room. She knows about Gillian. She *met* her, when Gilly was a baby. I took her to Court to present her as my daughter." Even then, with Gillian's fae blood as thin as it was, I'd wanted her to be taken care of. I had wanted the purebloods who barely allowed themselves to see *me* to see her as someone worthy of protection if something happened to me. "Rowan and ice. That was what the room smelled like. And it was fresh. This wasn't a trail from before she was deposed."

"I thought you left the imposter queen sleeping in Silences," said the Luidaeg mildly. Her eyes flicked toward a point behind me, and I knew she was quizzing me for the sake of the others, the ones who hadn't been there, who didn't *know* the way I did.

I could have kissed her, if she wouldn't have ripped my head off for doing it. "We did. I even had Walther contact them. He says she's still there. I say she's not. We can find out what they have in their basement after I bring my daughter home."

"Home to *me*," said Janet. I turned. She was still sitting, but her hands were balled into fists, and she was glaring at me with every ounce of fury she could muster. She locked her eyes on mine. "This changes nothing. You don't get to take her."

"She's a person," I said. "An adult person, who gets to make her own choices. But yes, I am bringing her home to you, and to Cliff, because she chose to be human, and he never asked to get this tangled up in Faerie. Even though his human wife might as well be one of us." I paused. "He doesn't *know*, does he?"

"Never," said Janet. "I would never."

"Good." I looked back to the Luidaeg. "It's her, and she has my child, and I don't know how or why she took her, but I know it's her."

"Do you know where she is?" prompted the Luidaeg.

I opened my mouth to answer. Then I paused and dug Jocelyn's note out of my pocket, unfolding it. "Gillian's roommate is a thin-blooded changeling. Thin enough not to be having a violent allergic reaction to Janet's 'protection charms,' but strong enough that fairy ointment works on her. She knew more than she should have, and she left me this note." I shoved it at the Luidaeg. "The old knowe. They're at the old Queen's knowe."

The Luidaeg looked at the note. Then she looked at me and nodded.

"I think you're right," she said. "You'd better go."

I started to turn. Then I hesitated, and said, "Promise me."

The Luidaeg lifted an eyebrow. "Excuse me?"

"You haven't said that you'd protect Janet. That means you don't intend to. I need her safe. Promise me, Luidaeg." I paused. "You're my aunt. You're my blood. Apparently, so is she. I need time to figure out what that means."

The Luidaeg pinched the bridge of her nose. "Dad preserve me in the face of all his damn heroes. Yes, October, I will protect the woman responsible for *my mother* being lost to me. Happy now?"

My stomach twisted. I hadn't really considered that part. "No," I said honestly. "I'd be happier throwing her in the Bay. But I can't do that to Gillian. I'll be back as soon as I can."

"See that you are."

I turned then, and bolted for the door, accompanied by the footsteps of my friends as they ran after me. The Luidaeg's patience wasn't infinite, and neither were Gillian's chances.

It was time to bring my daughter home.

SIXTEEN

BEFORE THE POND, before Luna and Rayseline disappeared and Sylvester asked me to bring them home, before my life fell apart, I had been a wide-eyed innocent rambling through the Bay Area, somehow—despite parental neglect and accidental, predatory apprenticeship to a man who never met a pair of hands he didn't want to exploit—holding on to the idea that Faerie was wonderful and we were lucky to live in a world made of magic. I had been looking for my place in that world, seeking the combination of talent and skill that would make me indispensable to the Courts.

What I had found was that purebloods are, by and large, not curious people. There are exceptions, of course, but those exceptions almost always seem to come after too much exposure to the mortal world, where things happen fast and don't leave room for introspection. For most purebloods, taking a hundred years to solve a riddle is perfectly reasonable, because they have a hundred years to *take*. For me, a hundred years was out of the question. I had started off like the Nancy Drew knockoff I believed myself in my heart to be, finding lost things and solving little mysteries. By human standards, I'd been bumbling at best, untalented and inept at worst. But by fae standards, I had been a miracle worker from day one, because I was willing to *try*. The lost could be found. The broken could be fixed.

And then the Queen—the Queen! The actual Queen of the Mists, the pureblood to end all purebloods, even if her heritage was more mixed than some of the courtiers seemed to think was appropriate—the Queen *herself* had put out the word that she was seeking a new knowe. The one she had was collapsing in on itself as the shallowing that sustained it rotted away.

Now, I could see that for the warning sign it had been. Her knowe had collapsed because it hadn't been properly rooted and she didn't have the power to sustain it, and King Gilad's knowe was sealed, inaccessible until Arden was found. At the time, though, it had seemed like the greatest opportunity of my short life. All I had to do was find a new knowe for the Queen, and I would be in her good graces, finally accepted as an equal to the purebloods who surrounded me—and best of all, finally able to be sure Gillian would be safe.

Then a woman named Dawn had been found dead by her "sister," Evening Winterrose, and somehow a simple real estate search had turned into a hunt for a murderer, following the trail through hidey-holes and dead ends all across San Francisco. In the end, I'd found the man who held the knife, and better yet, I had found a place in the mortal world where the veil between Earth and the Summerlands had been worn thin as paper, ready to be punctured by a steady hand.

That hand could never have been mine. But when the Queen had followed me to the shore, I had felt invincible. I had felt like I could do anything, forever. She had touched the weak spot I had found, and it had torn wide, revealing a hall with marble floors and a ceiling like the sky itself. Whoever had constructed this knowe had long since abandoned it, and I was the one who brought it back to Faerie. Me.

I had earned a knighthood for that week's work, and the eternal enmity of a woman who had been unable to make herself accept that changelings could do anything of use. She had demanded a ceremony—archaic even for Faerie—during which I gave up all claim to the knowe in exchange for letting my title go uncontested. Sylvester had shaken his head and said she reached too far, that as a Duke, he could knight anyone he pleased once they showed themselves worthy, but my eyes had been full of stars, and they had been blinding me. The Queen knew who I was. The *Queen*. How could anything ever go wrong for me again?

Sometimes I wish I could travel back in time and shake myself briskly until all the stupid falls out. Except that if I hadn't been such a fool when I was younger, I wouldn't have the life I have now. Warts and all, it's mine, and I love it.

Tybalt had his eyes closed and was clutching the handle above the door, a clear response to the fact that I was driving at unsafe speeds through the streets of San Francisco. I glanced at him, asking conversationally, "The Court of Cats is where the lost things go, right? Whether they're part of Faerie or not?"

"We have access to the lost places, yes," he said, not opening his eyes. "If you are about to tell me we have become lost, you should get a map. I refuse to open my eyes until we exit this traveling death trap."

"Did you have access to the false Queen's knowe before I found the door?"

He hesitated before saying, "Yes."

"Is that part of why you used to be so pissed at me all the time?"

He sighed. "Can discussion of our past relationship struggles please wait until the current situation has been resolved, and we are *not* about to die?"

"Um, this is Toby," said Quentin. "We're always about to die. When we're not about to die, we're still about to be about to die. She's like a Rube Goldberg machine whose only job is generating life-threatening situations."

"And I want to know the answer," said May.

Tybalt sighed again, harder. "Yes, October. Your 'discovery' of a lost piece of real estate cost my subjects several very comfortable denning places and forced the entire Court to rearrange itself. Cats do not like being ousted from their territory. I disliked you for a great many reasons, but your actions did not help. Happy?"

"Ecstatic." An opening appeared between two cars. I slammed my foot on the gas, hurling us through it before it could close again. Quentin, whose driving lessons were recent enough that he understood exactly how dangerous a maneuver that was, whimpered. "So here's a riddle for you: when the false Queen was removed from her throne and the knowe was sealed, it started to fade back into the shallowing the same way Lily's did, the way it had been when I found it for the first time. Right?"

"Correct," said Tybalt carefully, feeling out the word. He knew I was getting at something. He just didn't know what it was yet. At least he knew me well enough to be fairly sure he wasn't going to like it.

Clever boy. "Does that mean the deeper parts of the knowe are lost again?"

Surprised, Tybalt opened his eyes and stared at me. Then, slowly, he smiled.

Knowes are fascinating things, half-alive, half-aware, crafted from a combination of real architecture and raw magic. They can sprout rooms like mushrooms after a rain, expanding and contracting to meet the demands of their residents. But every knowe has its anchors, points of absolute reality driven deep into the fabric of the Summerlands and holding the rest of it in place. Bigger knowes, like Muir Woods or Shadowed Hills, may have five or six anchors, in addition to whatever seed point was originally used to "spark" the knowe.

I've never built a knowe myself. I wouldn't know where to begin. But I knew enough to be sure that even as the more publicly accessible parts of the building had started to fade, those anchors would have remained, lost until someone came to open them again.

"Do you have a plan?" asked May. "Or is this one of those situations where you charge in half-cocked and count on things to work in your favor?"

"A little bit of both," I said. "Feel up to punching me in the nose?"

"Always," said May.

"Um," said Quentin.

I grinned and hit the gas harder.

The old Queen's knowe is anchored to a stretch of San Francisco coastline that has yet to be fully gentrified, meaning there's even less parking available there than there is elsewhere. I circled the block three times before giving up and cramming the car into a stretch of sidewalk left open in front of a fire hydrant. As long as nothing actually burst into flames, Quentin's don't-look-here would mean my car remained unnoticed. If a fire truck needed to access the hydrant, I'd have a whole new set of problems.

At the moment, I felt like I'd welcome all of them. Tickets and towed cars were ordinary things, human things, things that were so much better than immortal grandmothers and impossible enemies. Let me worry about whether the milk has expired and how much the electric bill will be this month. Let me go back to fighting with May about wedding planning and how much I didn't want to do it. Let this be done.

Let us bring my daughter home.

I undid my seatbelt and twisted to face May and Quentin. "I don't know how much magic the false Queen can detect, but we know Jocelyn is limited to whatever her fairy ointment can unmask," I said. "That gets her through most illusions. We're not identical anymore, but we look enough alike that if you walk in with my squire, covered in my blood . . . "

"That buys us time," said May. "What are you going to do with it?"

"Ask Tybalt to carry me into one of the lost parts of the knowe, so I can approach them from behind," I replied. "They're not going to expect anyone to be deeper in the structure than they are. The old Queen is too arrogant, and Jocelyn is too ignorant. It can work."

"Why do I have to go with May?" asked Quentin. "I'm *your* squire. I'm supposed to be there to support you if you get into trouble."

"Because May can't fight, and being impossible to kill is not the same as being invincible," I said. "She needs someone who knows his way around a blade by her side, in case the false Queen has more support than we realized." It didn't seem likely. The members of her Court who had supported her during the coup had either been exiled or stripped of lands and titles as punishment for their crimes, and most of her staff worked for Arden now. They seemed much happier under the leadership of a queen who didn't treat them like expendable cogs in a beautiful machine. Funny, that.

Quentin looked unconvinced. "I don't like splitting up. Why can't we all go with Tybalt?"

"Charmed as I am by your confidence in my abilities, carrying three people through the shadows is a bit beyond me at the moment," said Tybalt. "I have the strength but lack the conviction. In the shadows, conviction is everything."

Quentin frowned. "But you can take Toby?"

"The day I cannot carry my heart along the Shadow Roads is the day I am a King no longer, but only a man who has failed himself so profoundly that his days of peace are done," said Tybalt.

We were all quiet for a moment, staring at him. May shook her surprise off first.

"If you ever want to go into the greeting card business, we can make a *mint*," she said. Turning to me, she asked, "So what, I just punch you?"

"In the nose," I confirmed. "It's the easiest way to make me bleed." I shrugged out of my leather jacket, leaving it on the seat. "If we're right, and this really *is* the false queen, I'd give even odds she transforms your clothes into something she thinks is more 'suitable.' In this case, hope for it. Her magic will obscure yours and make it even harder to tell us apart. You need to distract her as long as poss—"

Her fist caught me square in the face, snapping my head back and bringing a hot gush of blood flowing down my lip. I straightened, staring at her, and she punched me again. There was more blood this time, May's cupped hands under my chin to catch it. When the blood slowed, she took her hands away and ran them down the front of her shirt, leaving gory handprints behind. She looked at them and beamed.

"Now we're twinsies," she said.

"Oh, root and branch, what is wrong with you people?" moaned Quentin.

"More than we have time for," I replied. "My sword's in the trunk if you wanted to take it, May. For show." My own swordsmanship lessons had reached the point where I mostly didn't stab myself—mostly. The weapon was too big and too unwieldy for me after a lifetime of smaller tools, and the majority of problems in the mortal world can't be solved with a sword. That's the sort of thing that gets the cops called.

"Got it," she said. She grabbed a handful of air. Her human disguise shimmered, becoming identical to mine. "Quentin, you're with me."

"So I heard," he muttered, and gave me one last, anxious glance before following her out of the car.

Tybalt and I stayed where we were as May retrieved my sword from the trunk, belting it to her waist. She and Quentin hurried away down the street, toward the cave-side entrance to the false Queen's knowe. That was the one anchor point she had shored up herself. If any of them was still holding fast, it would be that one.

Tybalt touched the bare skin of my arm. I glanced at him.

"I am loath to admit this, but I'm afraid," he said. "What if I can't keep you safe?"

"Then you let me keep you safe for a change," I said. I pulled my keys out of the ignition and pocketed them, offering him my best hopeful smile. "I've had some practice. Now let's go bring my daughter home."

"Indeed," he said.

We got out of the car, one of us on either side, and met on the sidewalk. Tybalt took my hand, leading me to the narrow alley between two shops. We stepped into the shadows together, fingers tangled in a lover's knot. The darkness parted like a heavy curtain, allowing us to pass through into the freezing dark beyond.

The Shadow Roads are always cold and airless for me, but this time, when Tybalt ran, I ran with him, my feet pounding against ground I could neither see nor fully identify. It was too yielding to be stone and too firm to be wood, some unknown substance that existed only in the deepest dark. Trying to figure out what it could be was a distraction, something to keep me from focusing on the fact that I was running blind as my lungs began to ache, warning me of the lack of oxygen.

Tybalt could breathe here, somehow, if not as well as he could in the real world. That was part and parcel of the Cait Sidhe connection to the Shadow Roads. Knowing that helped me keep running. If I ran out of air, he would pick me up and carry me the rest of the way to the exit. Dignified? No. But when has survival ever been about dignity? He would never let me die in here. He would never let me go. As long as I held onto his hand—

Something slammed into me from behind, furious and screaming through the infinite dark of the shadows. I fell, my hand wrenched out of Tybalt's. Whatever the ground was made of, it was rough enough to scrape my cheek as I slid across it, half the remaining air knocked out of me on impact.

I rolled onto my back, instinctively covering my face with my forearms. Just in time, too: my attacker glanced off them, what felt like talons biting into my flesh. The Baobhan Sith. Tybalt had been wrong when he said she had made her escape by now. She'd been here the whole time, lurking in the shadows, waiting to attack whoever happened across her.

Lucky me, it had been us. I could feel the ice forming on my eyelashes and in my hair as the tips of my ears and fingers started going numb. I didn't know how the Baobhan Sith had been able to survive in here for as long as she had, but I knew I couldn't pull off the same stunt. If I didn't get pulled back into the real world soon, I was either going to suffocate or freeze. Maybe both.

The speed with which I heal means that most forms of death are somewhat impermanent for me. Break my bones, slit my throat, drown me, I'll get back up again as soon as I've had a chance to knit myself back together. Kill me in the Shadow Roads, though . . .

If I suffocated and froze to death at the same time, would I recover? Would I want to? I could be lost here forever, freezing and choking, only to wake up and do it all over again. Maybe dying here would mean dying for good. And then Gillian would be lost forever, and Tybalt would . . .

Tybalt would break. After what Mom had done to him, if he lost me in a place that should have been his to control, he would *break*. I couldn't let that happen. I needed to survive for so many reasons, and only a few of them were me.

The Baobhan Sith shrieked, the sound thin and reedy in the attenuated atmosphere. That was all the warning I got before she charged again. *This is a bad idea,* I thought, and held my ground, waiting for the sound of screaming to draw close. When I judged that she was only a few feet away I dropped my arms, giving her free access to my throat and chest.

She slammed into me with all the force of a cannonball, her fangs clamping down on my shoulder, ripping me open like it was of no consequence. Unlike her, I bore the assault in silence. I couldn't scream without air.

But I could bleed.

Ice formed on the blood trickling down my chest and arm, turning the hot liquid sharp and painfully cold. I closed my eyes. It changed nothing, but I was counting on that blood, and I needed to offer no resistance. The Baobhan Sith drank, and I bled, and the edges of my awareness started to get fuzzy, like the world was slipping away.

Tybalt roared in the distant dark, furious and desperate. That was all the warning either I or the Baobhan Sith had before he ploughed into her, ripping her teeth out of my shoulder and freeing another hot gout of blood.

So much for the Luidaeg's sandwich, I thought, among the blank spots that were starting to colonize my mind. Freezing to death isn't supposed to hurt much. Neither is bleeding to death, or suffocation. If I was shooting for "painless," I had managed to find the trifecta.

Arms slid under my butt and shoulders, scooping me up and cradling me close. I was still bleeding heavily enough that Tybalt's shirt was going to be ruined. I was willing to bet he wouldn't mind, under the circumstances.

"Hold on, October, for the love of Maeve, hold on," he said, and broke into a run.

I tried to count the seconds, but they slipped away like eels, darting off into the dark. I settled for struggling to remember not to breathe. There was nothing here for me. If I exhaled, all I would be doing was losing the last of the air in my lungs, and the freeze would follow. I couldn't let that happen. So I held my breath, and Tybalt ran, and then we were breaking into the light, into the bright and burning light. I cracked my eyes open, dislodging the ice on my lashes. We were in a deserted ballroom with cloth over the furniture and cobwebs covering the ceiling.

Tybalt ran for the nearest sheet-draped couch, an overstuffed thing like something out of a Regency romance, and all but threw me onto it, his hands fluttering from my face to my frozen hair to the wound on my shoulder. He didn't quite touch it, but pulled back, looking even more anxious. I took a shallow breath. It was good.

"It'll heal," I rasped.

His eyes snapped back to my face. "You must *stop* doing this, little fish, unless you intend to be the death of me."

"You saved me." I lifted one hand to trail my fingertips against his cheek. His skin was warm. It was almost impossible to believe we had been in the same place. "I wasn't scared. I never am, when you're there to save me."

"My October," he said, and turned his head to kiss my palm. "The death of me."

"You should be so lucky." I sat up, sending more ice cascading away from my body. My head spun. Even I have limits, and I was finding them fast. "Ow. Okay. Are we in the knowe?"

"We are, but you need time to recover. We should—"

"We should get moving. May and Quentin didn't stop to play with the Baobhan Sith. They're already inside, and the false Queen is only going to believe that May is me for so long." If she believed it at all.

Without her Siren blood, she couldn't compel them to fight each other—she was Banshee and Sea Wight now, and nothing else—but she could hurt them. She had run the kingdom for over a century, and she had always demonstrated powers that none of her bloodlines possessed. Meaning she was a borrower, using charms and tinctures to access the magic of others. We might have driven her from her knowe and into the Kingdom of Silences, but we'd never found her store of potions. I hadn't even thought to look. We had been dealing with the ascension of a new queen and the collapse of the old queen's knowe.

Now she was back, and there was no telling what she had access to, or what she could do if we gave her the chance. I stood by the choice to send decoys. That didn't mean I was going to leave them without backup.

"You should lie still," Tybalt snapped. "I don't know how much blood you lost in there."

"I still have blood in my body," I said. "I'll be fine."

He stared at me. Then, to my surprise, he smiled.

"You will never change, will you?" he asked, offering me his hand.

I took it, sliding to my feet. The outline of my body remained on the sheet, etched in pinkish ice-diluted blood. "I wasn't planning to," I said. "Now come on. We need to find Gillian and get to our people."

"The knowe is not fully awake," he said, following me across the ballroom floor. "Pieces may be missing."

"We can work with that," I said. When we reached the doors, I paused, putting my hand against them, and said, "My name is Sir October Daye. This is my friend, Tybalt, King of the Court of Dreaming Cats. I'm the one who found you after the last time you'd gone to sleep. I'm sorry I helped a bad woman claim and hold you. I didn't mean to. We can let you rest after this, until no one remembers that she ever had any power over you. But right now, we need to find my daughter. A human girl. The bad woman has taken her. Can you help us find her?"

"You're talking to the walls again," said Tybalt.

"Don't knock what works," I said. Returning my attention to the door, I added, "Please?"

The door swung open.

The hall on the other side was too plain to have been the

approach to a ballroom of this size. It was more suited to use by the servants, helping them to move through the knowe without being seen. I shot Tybalt a smug look and hurried down it, with him at my heels, until we reached another door.

This one led to an abandoned kitchen. The fires were dead, the chopping tables were deserted. It was a strange, silent world. I paused, darting into one of the pantries, and emerged a moment later with a turkey leg the length of my forearm. Tybalt raised a brow.

"How . . . ?"

"Stasis spell," I replied. "I've been raiding the kitchens at Shadowed Hills since I was a kid. The big knowes *always* keep the pantries full, in case someone important wants to demand, I don't know, roast cockatrice at three o'clock in the afternoon." The fae equivalent of the middle of the night.

The wound on my shoulder itched as I started gnawing on my prize, the edges finally starting to heal. Tybalt shook his head.

"Sometimes I forget the depths of your misspent youth," he said.

"I was never the best thief in the Mists, but the best trained me," I said.

We kept walking. Beyond the kitchen was the library, and beyond that was a spiral staircase, winding downward. The "windows," such as they were, provided crystal portholes into the ocean beyond the shore. The water glowed a pale, pearlescent blue, and through the glass we could see all manner of strange fish, both fae and mortal, swimming idly by. Tybalt frowned again, eyeing them.

"The Undersea must have been very eager to curry favor, to have allowed such an intrusion into their territory," he said.

"That, or they really, really wanted to be sure they'd have a weak point to attack if it actually came to war." I pointed to the nearest "window," shaking my head. "Dianda could punch that thing to shards in under a minute, and she's their duchess. Imagine what an actual soldier could do."

It felt strange not to be running. But there was no blood trail here, and Gillian had no magic for us to follow. Letting the knowe lead us was the best option we had. If we were walking into a trap, we would find a way out of it. We always did.

There was a door at the bottom of the stairs. I hesitated. Then I handed Tybalt my turkey leg, grasped the knob, and opened it.

The hallway on the other side was familiar, stretching out for what looked like forever. The walls were mist-colored marble; the ceiling was a blue so dark that it became virtually black, blending into the shadows at its edges. White marble pillars held the whole thing up, as much for show as any architectural reality. My breath caught in my throat, choking me.

This was the first place we had seen when the false Queen had pried the knowe open, calling it back from whatever sleep waited for our hollow hills when we didn't need them anymore. The walls had started to bleed fog as she had led the way along the hall, softening the lines of the pillars and blanketing the floor, erasing it. So why weren't they doing it now?

The answer was obvious, when I stopped to think about: they weren't bleeding fog because it would have attracted attention, and I had done something the old Queen would never have thought to do. I had asked the knowe for help.

Knowes don't always like the people who hold them. They don't have to. Power keeps them open, and power keeps the throne. But the king is the land in Faerie, and when the king is the land, the land gets to have opinions just like a person would. The false Queen's knowe liked me, even though she didn't. Buildings have always been among my biggest fans.

I reclaimed my turkey leg from Tybalt, caressing the nearest wall with my free hand as we resumed walking. I was eating as fast as I could, bolting down roast meat without doing more than the most cursory job of chewing. Taking time to eat in this sort of situation felt frivolous, but the wound at my neck still itched, and there was enough blood on my clothing to make it clear that I needed to replenish my veins before I was forced to open them again. Even my body can't build something out of nothing.

"Please don't choke to death," said Tybalt, voice low. His feet made no sound on the marble floor, unlike my own. If anyone heard us coming, it wouldn't be because of him. "I would be distraught if I had to contend with your corpse before I could even call myself a decent widower."

"Sweet talker," I said, around another mouthful of turkey.

He smiled faintly. We walked on side by side until we reached a closed, filigree-laden door. The patterns were abstract as ever, the echo of wind and waves and the distant rolling lines of what could have been hills or dunes. They might have held the secret of who had opened this knowe in the first place, whose hands had done the crafting and whose tears had sealed the doors. There wasn't time to worry about that now.

"Sorry about this; I'll come back and clean it up if I can," I said, bending to set my turkey bone in the corner with as much respect as I could muster. "If I can't, if I'm dead or something, maybe you could let some pixies in? They'd be happy to clean it up for you." They could also keep the knowe open, assuming it wanted to be. They're always looking for safe places to build their houses and raise their children, and while much of Faerie might think they're vermin, they love their homes. They defend them.

I glanced at Tybalt. He nodded. I opened the doors.

The central receiving hall was a fairy-tale nightmare of white marble and vaulted ceilings, everything shrouded in thick, cloying mist. The scent of rowan and ice hung over everything like a warning. We were behind the central dais. Voices drifted in our direction, one raised in irritation, the other cool, calm: the voice of a woman who thought she had everything under control.

"You promised me they'd be here by now! Why aren't they here?"

"Patience, Jocelyn. One would think you had been raised by wolves and not by mortals. Even humans understand the importance of manners."

"I'm tired of this. I want what I was promised."

"You'll have it. You'll have everything."

I looked at Tybalt and pointed to the right side of the dais before making an exaggerated shooing motion. His eyes narrowed as he nodded understanding. He didn't like splitting up, but he saw the sense in it.

Where were May and Quentin? The seaside entrance led directly to this room. They should have been here by now, taunting the false Queen, throwing her off-balance. The fact that they weren't here was bad.

My foot hit something buried in the fog on the floor, and the situation went from bad to worse. I knelt, trying to be as quiet as I could, and fanned the fog away from May's sleeping face. She was wearing a ballgown I'd never seen before, a confection of heather gray and soft lilac, and any hope that the false Queen might have mistaken her for me died at the sight of those colors. The false

Queen always dressed people as she considered suitable. She had never dressed me like a cloud. Usually, she dressed me more like an abattoir.

The pallor of May's gown made it easy to see the arrow protruding from her abdomen, short and blunt and dangerous. Her chest was rising and falling in the easy rhythm of the sleeping: elf-shot. The false Queen had hit her with elf-shot.

Even now that we had a cure for the stuff, I was still damn tired of it.

I straightened and resumed my cautious forward movement. Quentin was probably asleep somewhere in the mist on the other side of the dais, similarly dressed for a party that was never going to happen, that he was never going to attend.

"They should be here by now." Jocelyn again, her voice descending into a whine.

The false Queen sighed heavily. "They'll come. We have something October can't possibly resist. Don't we, Gillian, dear?"

There was a sound, like flesh striking flesh, and a whimper. I hadn't heard it in years. It didn't matter. The sound bypassed my brain and lanced straight for my heart, breaking it and lacing it back together in the same moment. All thought of stealth or subtlety fled my mind as I drew my knife and broke into a run, flinging myself around the front of the dais.

The false Queen of the Mists turned her head, looking at me with moonstruck eyes as cold as light reflecting off the water, and smiled.

"Hello, October," she said. "So nice of you to join us."

SEVENTEEN

THE FALSE QUEEN HAD clearly put a great deal of time and thought into this moment, staging everything to make the biggest possible impact. She was standing at the center of the dais, dressed in a gown of dark blue silk that darkened to black where it pooled at her feet, shimmering with oil-slick rainbows that almost distracted from her skin, which was as pale and faintly blue as the flesh of a drowned sailor. Her hair—fine, straight, and white as sea foam—was pulled over her shoulder and allowed to fall in a tangled line all the way to her feet.

Jocelyn stood behind her, dressed in a blue linen version of that same gown, looking for all the world like a child playing in her mother's closet. She was beaming, triumphant and cruel, as if she had finally been given her heart's desire.

And on the ground, at the false Queen's feet, was Gillian.

She was on her hands and knees, panting, a red mark on one cheek where the false Queen had slapped her. There was blood on her clothing, and one sleeve of her sweatshirt was torn, revealing the scrapes beneath. She looked . . .

She looked amazing. She was injured and terrified, surrounded by things she didn't know or understand, and she was still struggling to keep herself upright, refusing to give in to fear. My brave, beautiful girl.

"Let her go," I snarled. "You have no right—"

"*She* has no rights, thanks to you," purred the false Queen.

"The rights of changelings may be negotiable, but the rights of mortals? Those are nonexistent. I could slice her into pieces and hang them from every tree in the Mists, and I would have done nothing wrong in the eyes of anyone who matters. Even your precious pretender queen can't claim I've broken the Law by taking her, because the Law was never intended to protect her. She's no better than a beast in the field, ready for the slaughter, and *you* did this to her."

She grabbed Gillian's arm, wrenching it behind her back. Gillian moaned, pain and exhaustion in equal measure, and my heart broke again. If this didn't stop soon, there was going to be nothing left of me.

"But I am a merciful Queen," continued the false Queen. "I understand that everyone makes mistakes. Everyone lies. I'll give her back to you, if you return what you stole from me."

"Do it, Mom," moaned Gillian, seeming to see me for the first time. The desperation in her eyes was something no mother should ever have been forced to see. "Whatever you took, whatever you stole, just let her have it. Please."

"I can't," I whispered. Louder, I said, "I *can't*. What you're asking for is impossible."

The false Queen narrowed her eyes. "Oh," she said. "You can do better than that."

I shook my head, hoping desperation would convey my honesty. "I *can't*. When I pulled the Siren blood from your veins, it was lost. I don't have it to restore to you. I'd give it back if I could, I swear I would. Please don't take this out on my daughter. Please let her go."

"You simply need the right incentive to unlock your abilities," said the false Queen. She reached into the cascading folds of her dress and pulled out a blunt arrow, no longer or thicker around than a pencil. Someone had tied a bundle of owl feathers to the end in a vague attempt at fletching. The point gleamed, as oily and shimmering as the base of the false Queen's gown.

I stared and continued staring as Tybalt stepped out of the shadows at the back of the dais, his eyes glowing green, his hands hooked into claws.

"You took as much from her as you did from me," said the false Queen, and moved before either of us could react, jamming the "arrow" into Gillian's shoulder. My heart lurched as a veil of sudden déjà vu engulfed me, making it difficult to breathe. Gillian shrieked, the sound cutting off as she slumped forward, already unconscious.

Tybalt roared, lunging not at the false Queen, but at my child. He swept Gillian into his arms and leapt to the floor, stopping when he reached me. I reached for the sides of her face, lifting her head, checking for her pulse. She was still breathing. Her heart was racing, hammering so hard that it felt like it was going to burst, but she was breathing.

"What did you do?" I moaned. I turned. The false Queen was gloating, seemingly unconcerned by the loss of her hostage. "What did you *do*?"

"Either you're a liar and you'll restore your child, proving you can do the same for me, or the human brat will die, as she should have done the moment she rejected our world," said the false Queen. "I have done nothing wrong."

Jocelyn frowned at her. "What about me?" she asked. "You promised me."

"Hush," said the false Queen. "You'll get your turn."

I ignored them both, pulling the arrow from Gillian's shoulder—thank Oberon that it had a smooth point, and not a proper arrowhead—and dipping my finger into the blood. I didn't dare taste it, not with the elf-shot running through her veins, but I only needed to sniff it to know there was nothing left in her but humanity. I couldn't change what wasn't there.

Elf-shot kills humans. My daughter was human.

I moaned, low and agonized and unthinking. "Walther," I said, raising my eyes to Tybalt's, seeing my own despair mirrored there. Tybalt didn't know Gillian, didn't love her like I did, but he had buried his first wife and their child, and he knew what it was to feel the ground crumbling beneath his feet. "The cure."

"She won't make it as far as Berkeley," he said, voice hushed. "I could carry her, but not alive, Toby, I'm not fast enough."

I stared at him and knew two things for the absolute truth: that he would never lie to me, and if I ordered him to carry my daughter's corpse through the Shadow Roads, even with the added danger of the Baobhan Sith lurking somewhere in the dark, he would do it. For me, if I asked him to try, he would do it.

And I couldn't. There had to be another way, there had to—

I leaned in close, close enough to whisper, "The Luidaeg, and then Dianda. Save my child and then save my ass. *Go*."

He pulled back, understanding clear in his banded green eyes. Then he turned and ran for the wall as fast as his legs would carry him, diving into the shadows, taking Gillian with him. She wouldn't know to hold her breath. She wouldn't know anything, because she was asleep, and she was dying, and he was running a race against the impossible.

I turned, slowly, back toward the false Queen and Jocelyn. The false Queen looked thoughtful. Jocelyn was pouting, actually *pouting*, like a child denied a treat they really, really wanted to have.

"I see," said the false Queen. "So committed to your lies that you'd let your own child die rather than give back what is rightfully mine. I thought better of you. You call yourself a hero, and yet you behave like the very basest of villains."

"You kidnapped my daughter." I took a step toward the dais. "You tried to lure me into a forbidden place." Another step. "You elf-shot my friends and my *little girl*, knowing the potion would begin to kill her as quickly as it could. You want a villain? Look in the mirror." I held up the elf-shot arrow I'd pulled from Gillian's shoulder. "It's time for you to go back to sleep. You shouldn't be here."

"But I am. Don't you wonder who woke me?"

I froze. The false Queen smirked.

"You aren't as adored as you think you are, and not everyone loves this brave new world you struggle to create. Changelings have no place in polite society. Elf-shot is a tool to be used, not a disease to be 'cured.' You overstep in every possible direction, and then you wonder why anyone would react poorly." The Queen leaned forward. "Oberon made you and your ilk to be tools, living hope chests for the masses, because even he could see that Faerie needed to be cleansed. The mortal taint should never have been allowed to take root the way it did. You're a *thing* playing at being a hero, and it's time you learned your place."

"And you're a fool who never learned to throw a damn punch," I said wearily. The false Queen's eyes widened.

I rushed the dais.

She was a small, frail-looking woman. I knew that to be at least partially a lie—all Sea Wights look like they're on the verge of collapse, and most of them can sling sunken ships around like pebbles. I also knew that she'd been a queen for a full century, and queens don't fight their own battles. Queens sit back and let other people do their fighting for them.

My shoulder caught her in the middle of the chest, sending her careening back against her throne. She hit with the distinctive snapping sound of breaking bones, and I was furious enough to feel a small thrill of triumph at that noise. I might not be able to hurt her emotionally the way she'd hurt me, but I could—by Oberon—hurt her physically. That would have to be enough.

Jocelyn screamed, shouting, *"Get away from my godmother!"* before slamming something sharp and cold into my side. I staggered away from the false Queen, looking down in shock to see my own sword jutting out of my abdomen.

Jocelyn was glaring at me, cheeks flushed and arms shaking as she struggled to keep her grip on the sword. She had swung it like it was a baseball bat, and I couldn't fault her technique: it was damned similar to my own.

"You get away from her," she repeated with less heat. She was starting to sound uncertain; she was starting to sound scared. Whatever she had expected when she agreed to this little adventure, she wasn't getting it.

I looked from her to the sword and back again. Finally, gritting my teeth against the pain, I asked, "Was it you who told her where Gillian was? Did you tell her where the car would be, when it would be safe to touch my daughter? Is this all your fault?"

"You rejected my mother because she was too human, like she *chose* that," Jocelyn retorted. "You acted like she could have been anything she wanted to be, and decided to be less than fae, when you could have fixed things for her any time you wanted to. And then you never even gave me a chance. You never came to me. You went Home, and you closed its doors before I was old enough to go. You made sure I had nothing."

I started to respond, and paused, hearing a capital letter where it didn't belong. "Your mother was one of Devin's kids?"

Jocelyn's response was to grab the hilt of my sword and twist. I gasped, trying to take a step backward, away from the pain tearing at my guts. The way I heal has saved my life a dozen times, but it also means I've experienced injuries that should have been the worst things I'd ever feel, and they keep getting topped by the next one to come down the wire. Feeling my insides sliced to bits while my daughter was somewhere far away, dying in the dark? Was a new topper for the list.

"My *mother* is Tracy Wilson," hissed Jocelyn, through clenched teeth. She twisted the sword again. The world flashed white with pain. I dropped to my knees on the dais.

The sudden change in my position was enough to wrench the sword from her hands. That was a nice change. It was in too deep to be pulled free, but at least she wasn't twisting it anymore. I gasped and scrabbled for the blade, trying to grasp it and yank it out of me.

The false Queen's foot caught me in the middle of the back, shoving me forward, driving the sword deeper. I would have been embarrassed to be caught this flat-footed by two noncombatants, but I was too busy trying not to vomit or black out from the pain.

"Someone else you failed to save," she taunted blithely. There was a ragged edge of pain in her words. I had put that there. Whatever I'd broken in her chest was digging into her flesh, maybe puncturing a lung, and she didn't heal the way I did. No one heals the way I do. All I had to do was stall, and eventually she'd have to stop tormenting me in order to seek medical help.

Of course, that would leave Jocelyn and the sword, and that assumed she'd need to go for help before my guts were on the ground, but sometimes it's nice to be an optimist.

"I don't believe they call you a hero," said Jocelyn. "You're just a coward who doesn't want to do what she was made to do. Your *Queen* is asking you to help her, and you keep saying 'no,' like that's even allowed. You make me sick. I'm *glad* I helped her snatch that worthless bitch you pretend is your daughter. She's as mortal as they come. I don't know what happened to your real baby, if you ever even had one, but I'm a hundred times better than *her*."

"A thousand times," said the false Queen, the smooth purr of her voice only slightly broken by a wheeze. "You, at least, hold Faerie in your veins. Remember that. You are, for that alone, her superior."

I tried to focus on my breathing. Unlike the wounds dealt by the Baobhan Sith, the wounds my sword made were healing the way I usually did, fast and unrelenting. I could feel the skin knitting around the blade. That was bad—there was going to be no way to pull it out without slicing myself up again—but it was also good, since Jocelyn was going to have one hell of a surprise if she tried to go for the sword a second time.

"So make her do what you promised." The whine was back in Jocelyn's voice. I was extraneous to the scene the two of them were playing out, I realized: I was part of the scenery. That was normal, where the false Queen was concerned. For her, I had only ever been a means to an end, a tool to be used or a danger to be disposed of.

Keep her busy, kid, I thought, and closed my eyes, breathing through the pain.

Tracy Wilson. Sweet Titania, it had been years since I'd thought about her. She had been—presumably still was, since Jocelyn spoke about her in the present tense—a Gwragen changeling, a little less than half-blooded, the result of a marriage between a Gwragen half-blood and a Gwragen quarter-blood. Her parents had believed their commonalities would outweigh their differences. They had been wrong. She had been bitter even for one of Devin's kids, unforgiving of the smallest slight, ready to pick a fight on even the slightest provocation.

The only reason he hadn't thrown her out was that she'd left of her own accord, heading down the coast with a human musician who'd promised her a life of adventure, excitement, and free beer. We'd all been glad to see her go. Of all the people I felt I'd failed during my own somewhat misspent youth, Tracy Wilson didn't make the list. She didn't even come close. That was reassuring, honestly, even as I was trying to stop myself from bleeding out in a deposed monarch's knowe.

Oh. Blood loss. Yes, that was probably part of the problem. Even I can't bleed forever. But I was bleeding enough. I bit my lip. The plan that was forming in my mind was a terrible one. It wasn't going to work, and if it did, it was going to get me hurt worse than I already was. It was still a plan, and it was the only thing I had.

I grabbed the sword, making an exaggerated moaning sound as I tried to pull it free, slicing my palms in the process. Another gush of blood poured out on the dais. It was getting to where I couldn't smell anything else. For what I was trying to accomplish, that was a good thing. As long as I could actually survive it.

How long had it been? Long enough for Tybalt to carry an unresisting mortal through the Shadow Roads to the Luidaeg's door? Long enough for him to come back? There was no way he'd leave me here to deal with this by myself, not when he had a doorway and a breath left in his body. That helped me keep going, keep yanking on the sword and trying to pull it free.

A hand gripped my hair and yanked my head up. Jocelyn met my eyes and smiled, too brightly.

"You don't like having that sword there, do you?" she asked. "I can fix it. And all I need is for you to do one teeny little favor for me."

"I don't do favors for people who hurt my family," I wheezed.

Her hand caught me, hard, across the face, splitting my lip and setting my nose bleeding again. I swallowed a mouthful of blood, letting it warm and stabilize me. The taste was cloying, filling the entire world, but I didn't let that stop me from swallowing again, trying to draw every drop of strength I could from it.

Jocelyn's smile vanished, replaced by a scowl. "I wouldn't have had to *hurt* her if she'd just been willing to *call* you," she spat. "I asked her over and over again, why won't you make up with your mom? She sounds nice, you should let her come to visit, you should try to forgive her, you should make things right. I *tried*. But she didn't want to listen, and so I had to find another way."

There was something I was missing, something to connect a thin-blooded changeling with an ax to grind to the former Queen of the Mists, who should have been sleeping her years away in another state, another Kingdom. Their alliance didn't make *sense*. The false Queen should never have realized Jocelyn existed. Jocelyn didn't have the resources to brew or steal Walther's elf-shot cure—which any good alchemist could replicate now that the formula was out there in the world—and even if she could have, there was no way she'd have been able to get into the palace in Silences. What was I *missing*?

"Look at me!" Jocelyn's voice rose into a shrill scream. I wrenched myself out of my thoughts and focused on her face. The fairy ointment around her face was smeared and thinning, slowly being absorbed into her skin.

I smirked. It was the one thing I could think of that was most likely to enrage her, and the longer we could keep this show going, the longer the false Queen would stay focused and gloating over my helplessness. "I'm looking," I said. "How long before you can't return the favor? Looks like the world's going to get real blurry for you, real soon."

Her hand flew to her face, fingertips stopping just shy of the skin around her eyes, which were suddenly wide with alarm. "That won't happen if I'm here. I'm safe if I'm here."

"That's not how fairy ointment works, kiddo," I said. "Maybe you've never been in a real knowe before. But a place like Home, that's built in the mortal world and concealed with illusions, that's not the same as the *Summerlands*. Where you are now, it's not real to the human part of you. That ointment wears off, you're flying in the dark. Hope you brought a flashlight."

Jocelyn made a wordless sound of frustration and dismay, letting go of my chin and turning to run for the back of the dais. I barely had time to relax before the false Queen's foot bore down on my back again, her heel grinding into my spine. The motion forced me forward, driving another few inches of steel into my gut. I made no effort to stifle my groan.

"You can't talk your way out of this one," she hissed. "You're going to give back what you stole from me. You may be willing to let your daughter die—but then, you already proved that, didn't you? When you made her mortal, you condemned her to the grave like every other human. You threw her away, and now you pretend at anger because I picked up what you no longer wanted."

She leaned closer, her breath hot against my ear. "She's trash. She was always trash, and all you did was prove it."

Thoughts of plans, of waiting for help to come and make this easier, of patience . . . they flew out of my mind, replaced by raw and burning rage. I slammed my head back as hard as I could and was rewarded with a shriek and a loud cracking noise as my skull impacted with hers. I shoved myself to my feet, grabbing the hilt of the sword in the same motion, and attempted to draw the blade from my own body.

Pulling a sword from a scabbard can be difficult, depending on the angle and the seal between blade and case. A scabbard is *designed* to house a weapon. Everything about it is meant to make the process of drawing the sword as easy as possible.

My body is not a very good scabbard.

The false Queen staggered backward, one hand over her bleeding nose to keep the mess from spraying everywhere. Then she saw how much trouble I was having getting a good grip that wouldn't require me to slice myself open lengthwise, and she laughed. Really laughed, loud and joyous and utterly unforgiving.

"You're no hero," she jeered, voice rendered thick and burbling by her bruised lips and broken nose. "You're a joke. You've always been a joke. It's a miracle you were ever able to cause me any trouble at all."

I yanked the sword free, ignoring the pain that accompanied the motion, and was rewarded with her shocked expression in the instant before I swung it, hard, toward her throat. She vanished in a cloud of rowan-scented smoke. Rowan . . . and cinnamon, again. Cinnamon mixed with cardamom. Those had never been elements of her magic. Who was *helping* her?

"Oh, come *on*!" I shouted, recovering my footing. I turned on the dais, sword held defensively in front of me. "I thought I was a joke. Why are you running, if I'm such a joke? Come back here and face me like a queen!"

"Queens fight to win," she hissed, from behind me, and shoved what felt like a blade of ice into my kidney.

The pain was immediate and electric, racing through my body, paralyzing me where I stood. I dropped to my knees again, the sword clattering harmlessly from my hands. Jocelyn darted forward to grab it, her eyes once more shrouded in rings of glittering fairy ointment. She was smirking. Of course, she was smirking. Somehow, I had come to represent everything she'd never been able to have, and she was seeing me cut low. This was probably one of the best moments of her life.

I tried to reach behind myself and grab the knife I could feel jammed into me, freezing and burning me. My hand passed right through where the hilt should have been. The false Queen kicked me again, in the back of the head this time, and I went sliding across the dais.

"No human hand will ever touch a Folletti blade," she said, sounding smug. "You should have been quicker at cleaning out my armories if you didn't want them to be used against you."

We had cleaned out the treasury, the main armory, as many of her storerooms as we could find. But the knowe had already been folding inward on itself, shutting down and fading in the absence of an owner to keep its doors open, and none of us had been interested in claiming it. Arden had the knowe in Muir Woods, her father's knowe, and she had been determined to move the seat of the Mists back where it belonged, away from the pretender's throne.

Looking for hidden secondary armories hadn't been on anybody's list of things to do.

Belatedly, I realized the false Queen had a dungeon full of iron to go with whatever other delights she might have hidden around the place—and that Jocelyn's fae blood was weak enough to let her wield iron without any immediate consequences. If the false Queen remembered that little fact, I was going to be in even more trouble than I already was.

But I was still bleeding. There was still a chance my plan, hurried and incomplete as it was, might work.

Come on, Tybalt, I thought, gasping and shivering as the ice lanced deeper into my flesh. Everything was freezing, and everything hurt. *Come back for me.* I pressed my forehead against the dais, hair dangling in the blood that surrounded me.

"Do you feel like being a good girl now, October?" asked the false Queen. "I think Jocelyn has been patient for long enough."

"Fuck you," I managed.

Someone's foot—I wasn't sure whose—caught me solidly in the ribs.

"You'll do it!" snapped Jocelyn. "You'll make me perfect!"

I struggled to lift my head, squinting at her through my blood-tangled hair. "She had a hope chest the whole time she had the throne," I said, voice raspy and weak. "She could have shifted your blood any time. She could have made every changeling in the Mists fully fae. She didn't. She never even offered. So maybe if you want to be mad at somebody, you should try being at least a little bit mad at her."

Jocelyn paused, confusion written on her face.

And behind me, the Baobhan Sith screamed.

It was a haunting, triumphant sound, the cry of a predator that had finally broken free of a trap. It echoed through the room, spreading until it seemed to come from every direction at once. A hand grasped my hair, yanking me up until I was looking at the wide-eyed, horrified face of the false Queen.

"What did you *do*?" she demanded.

"Nothing," I said. I closed my eyes. The dark was soothing and tempting. This would all go so much faster if I never opened them again. "Tybalt, on the other hand, may have freed your pet. Bet she's not happy about you bringing people to her den."

The Baobhan Sith howled again, much closer this time, and the false Queen was ripped away from me, going ass-over-teakettle as she rolled off the dais. I pushed myself to my hands and knees, prepared to bolt—

—and froze as Jocelyn pointed my own sword directly at my face. Well, shit.

EIGHTEEN

"*N*O," SHE SAID, anger and fear battling for dominance in her voice. "You stay right where you are. You have to fix me."

"I'm not going to change the balance of your blood," I said, unable to take my eyes off the blade. I've died at least twice, probably more, but I'd never died of brain trauma. Would it grow back? Would I still be myself if it did? Or would I be someone new, someone like May, who had most of my memories but no longer saw them the way I did, who could hold herself at arms-length from my life and not miss what she'd never really had.

"You *have* to," she said, sounding like a child on the verge of a tantrum. "You owe me."

"I don't owe you anything." The Folletti knife was still embedded in my kidney, freezing me slowly from the inside out, and the Baobhan Sith was no doubt going to lose interest in the false Queen eventually, choosing to go for the juicier meal—me. I needed to move. "You hurt my daughter. You woke a despot. If anyone's in debt here, it's you."

"I didn't wake her," said Jocelyn, looking startled. "I wouldn't even know how to start. She got in contact with Mom. She said she wanted to be my godmother, to make everything better for me. Mom pulled some strings with the residence hall to get me moved into Gillian's room. Mom got paid, and I'm going to get a new life, a better life. The life I should have had from the beginning. But I didn't wake her. Her friend did, the man with the green hair."

I stared, the bottom dropping out of my stomach as everything suddenly, horribly, started making sense. I only knew one man with green hair who would have any reason to work with the false Queen . . . a man who smelled like cinnamon and cardamom.

Sweet Maeve forgive me, but I'd thought he was dead.

I was still staring when Tybalt stepped out of the mist behind her, reached down, and wrenched the sword from her grasp. Jocelyn cried out in pain. It looked like the act of breaking her grip may have also broken a few of her fingers, or at least sprained them.

Good. Anyone who pulls a sword on me deserves to hurt. Doubly so if the sword they're holding is my own. That's adding insult to potential injury, and I won't stand for it.

"How many of your bones shall I break, kitten, to make clear that no one threatens my lady without some payment being demanded?" His hand engulfed both of Jocelyn's, pinning her in place. He was making no effort to seem human, or even Sidhe: his pupils were wide ovals, consuming more than half of his irises, and when he spoke, he showed canine teeth too long and sharp to belong to anything but an apex predator. Stripes slashed down his cheeks and across his forehead, his tabby coloring carrying over onto the skin.

That was a bad sign. That was a *very* bad sign. Tybalt is powerful enough that he experiences that sort of slippage only when under extreme stress, and seeing it made me want to run to him and pull him away from her before he could do something he'd regret. Killing Jocelyn wouldn't be a violation of Oberon's Law. It would still hurt him, deep inside, and while I might not care about her life, I cared way too much about his.

And I didn't know whether Gillian was alive. If she wasn't, my ability to intercede on Jocelyn's behalf might go way, way down.

The false Queen was still screaming somewhere in the fog. That was a good sign, in that the Baobhan Sith hadn't torn her throat out yet. I wanted her alive to stand trial for her crimes. She may not have broken the Law, but all that meant was that I couldn't demand her life. I could demand a hell of a lot else. I was planning to do exactly that.

Later. Right now, I had bigger problems. Like Dugan. Oh, Oberon, Dugan. "Tybalt, you have to let her go," I said, struggling to my feet in order to make it easier to attract his attention.

He turned to me, and there was almost no rationality in his eyes.

He looked like a feral creature, like he was ready to bolt with his kill.

"She *hurt* you," he said, as if I might somehow have failed to notice.

I nodded. "I know. I was there. But I need you now, and she's not going anywhere. She couldn't get out of here if she tried. The doors won't open for her without someone to help her. Let her go."

He hesitated. "I came back," he said finally.

"I know. I'm so grateful. But I'm kind of in a lot of pain right now, so if you could please let her go and take care of me . . . "

Tybalt blinked, some of the blankness fading from his expression. "October?"

I turned, intending to show him the knife protruding from my back. The motion left me dizzy, and my legs buckled, sending me crashing toward the dais. I was almost getting used to hitting it face-first. I braced for impact.

Tybalt's arms wrapped around my waist and pulled me back, scooping me against him. He searched my face with wide, worried eyes. "What have you done to yourself now?" he asked, voice low.

I blinked. He was blurry. "Jocelyn . . . ?"

"I didn't kill her."

"Good. She's . . . patsy. Queen not working alone." I closed my eyes. "There's a knife. My left kidney. Can't touch it. Still too human. Can you . . . ?"

"As the sword from the stone," he said, and rolled me over in his arms. I went limp, allowing him to move me. I trusted him. Out of everyone in the world, I trusted him.

The blade sliding out of my kidney was an indescribable pain, followed by an absence that ached for a moment before the agony of thaw set in. I think I screamed. I know I convulsed, and only Tybalt grabbing me and refusing to let go kept me from taking yet another tumble.

When I was done screaming, when the cold had died to a manageable level and my legs were willing to hold me, I shuddered and leaned against Tybalt, trying to open my eyes. That was when I heard the silence, or rather, didn't hear it.

The false Queen wasn't screaming anymore. Neither was the Baobhan Sith. The only sound was Jocelyn sobbing somewhere nearby, the thin, reedy wails of a child who had been denied her favorite toy.

Unsteadily, I pushed myself away from Tybalt and looked around. The cut in my back still ached, healing slowly—assuming it was healing at all. The existence of one thing that could hurt me for more than a few seconds implied the existence of other things, things that might be a little more permanent than the bite of the Baobhan Sith.

"That's why I have two kidneys," I muttered, mostly to myself.

The mist covering the floor had grown higher, turning everything not on the dais into a sea of eddying white. I turned slowly. Jocelyn was standing in the shadow of the false Queen's throne, cradling her hand against her chest and weeping. I dismissed her. She didn't have a weapon, and judging by the glassy expression on her face, this was the first time she'd been seriously hurt in her entire life. She would be processing her way through the pain for a while. Once she did, she might become a threat again. Until then . . .

I stooped to retrieve my sword, taking a careful step in the direction where I'd last seen the Baobhan Sith. "Hello?" I called. "Is there anyone out there who can talk right now?"

"I call for truce," said an unfamiliar voice. A woman stepped out of the mist.

Her hair was still the color of gorse, but blooming, yellow and green tangled together until she looked like a meadow going out for a stroll. Her eyes were an odd blend of the two, almost chartreuse. Her skin was clear, and her flesh had filled out until she could have been any woman on the street, assuming the women on the street had pointed ears and teeth like daggers, ready to slice through flesh to find the blood beneath. She was wearing plenty of that blood— maybe even more than I was, which was no small trick—in dried tracks down the front of her winding white gown.

"Why do the blood-workers always wear white?" I asked, almost dazedly. "It makes us look like the sloppiest eaters ever."

"I was bound and buried, and a shroud is appropriate for that sort of thing," said the Baobhan Sith, watching me warily. Most of her attention was on my sword. "Is truce granted?"

"For the moment, yes," I said, lowering the weapon slightly. "You'll forgive me: I don't have a scabbard on me. Did you kill her?"

"No," said the Baobhan Sith. Her lip curled in disgust. "She tried to push me into a violation of the Law, but as it seems I have avoided it, I refuse to waste the crime on *her*."

I nodded. "You got a name?"

"Kennis. Yourself?"

"Sir October Daye, Knight of Lost Words. This is—"

"I remember the King of Dreaming Cats, even if we never had direct acquaintance with one another." Kennis offered Tybalt a polite nod. It was strange, having her converse so calmly when only a little while ago, she'd been trying to kill us both. "The year must not be so very late, if you're still the one leading the Cait Sidhe of this place."

She had been emaciated when I'd first found her, as if she hadn't eaten in years. I gave her a measuring look. "What year do you think it is?"

"I was taken by surprise in my bed, pinned and prisoned while the house burned around me, in nineteen seventy-four," said Kennis. "I knew my captor by the smell of her, ice and rowan, but I couldn't fight—not with as much magic as she'd poured into the room before the match was lit. I've woken twice since then, once when a man came to me with a cup of blood from a human girl, and again when you entered the room where I was tethered. You have my sincere apologies for what happened next. I was not entirely myself."

"Meaning the false Queen starved you to use you as a weapon," I concluded grimly. Not against me, necessarily; in the seventies, I'd still been in the Summerlands, following my mother like a good little shadow, trying to do everything within my power to make her proud of me. But the false Queen had always been fond of her weapons.

How many more traps were scattered throughout the Mists? How many more citizens of Faerie, people like Kennis, were bound and waiting to be triggered, reduced to their basest impulses by hunger, or isolation, or a dozen other factors? We had been careless. We had put Arden on the throne, and not followed the regime change by immediately beginning to ferret out every scrap of danger the false Queen had left behind.

"*False* Queen?" Kennis asked, eyebrows raised in surprise. "She's not the rightful holder of her throne? Oh, *naughty* girl. Have I brought a fugitive to justice, then?"

"You've helped," said Tybalt mildly. "I am sure Queen Windermere will be glad to reward you by not punishing you for attempting to devour a hero of the realm."

Kennis had the good grace to blush. "I was starving. I would apologize, but I had no control over my actions."

"You said there was a man," I said, pulling her attention back to me. "What did he look like? Did he have green hair?"

Tybalt's head whipped around, eyes narrowing as he put two and two together and came up with an unhappy five. Kennis shook her head.

"Plain. Inconsequential. He stank of Daoine Sidhe beneath his illusions."

So it could have been Dugan, or it could have been somebody else. Swell. I frowned as I stepped off the dais, wading through the mist until I found the false Queen, curled into a ball with her eyes tightly closed. Kneeling, I felt the side of her neck, relaxing only a little when I found her pulse. "She's alive. Weak, but alive."

"I said as much," said Kennis.

"You also tried to kill me multiple times, so I wanted to confirm it for myself." I jerked my head toward the sobbing Jocelyn. "Can someone grab her before she runs? I really don't feel like playing spoiled brat scavenger hunt today."

"Of course," said Tybalt. He moved toward her. Jocelyn screamed and tried to dodge. Deftly, he snaked an arm around her waist, grabbing her wrists with his free hand as he pulled her close. "Where do you think you're going? We need to have a conversation, you and I. It will hurt less if you don't struggle."

He grinned, showing the full scope of his inhuman dentition. Jocelyn screamed again before collapsing in a dead faint. Only Tybalt's grip kept her from falling to the floor. He turned to look at me.

"Will this do?" he asked.

I nodded. "That's fine."

"October—"

"No." I moved through the mist until I found Quentin's slumbering form. Kneeling next to him and beginning to go through his pockets, I said, "I don't want to know. Not yet. As soon as I know one way or the other, I'm going to fall apart, and I can't do that until we get someone here to take this whole mess over. So I don't want to know. Even once I do know, we have to deal with the fact that the false Queen wasn't working alone. I think she had help. I think Dugan was helping her."

"Dugan *Harrow*? But wasn't he—"

"Arrested? Yeah. And then he vanished into the dungeons, and we all figured it had been taken care of. Surprise, surprise. We were wrong." He'd been with Raysel when she kidnapped Gillian the first time. He'd betrayed his liege, and when he'd tried to assassinate her, she'd locked him away.

Stupid me—assuming that out of sight and out of mind meant no longer my problem.

Dugan Harrow had been a courtier in service to the false Queen, a landless Daoine Sidhe noble sent to the Court from Deep Mists—and since Deep Mists was in Marin, he might have grown up with stories of how once, the royal court had been located in Muir Woods, well away from the human city, in the trees where it belonged. It would certainly explain why he'd been willing and eager to help Rayseline Torquill kidnap both the Lorden boys and my own daughter, holding them hostage in an attempt to start a war. Kidnapping was his go-to move, the only thing he could be absolutely sure would get the reaction he was looking for.

He'd been arrested after drawing a cold iron knife on the false Queen, and when we hadn't found him in her dungeons, we all assumed she'd just done the inevitable and made her problem . . . disappear. The Law forbids killing. It doesn't forbid transforming an enemy into a stone and dropping them into the ocean, even if you know that when the spell wears off, they'll drown before they can make it to the surface. There are always loopholes for people vicious enough to look for them.

The thought that she might have slapped him on the wrist for failing at his coup and released him to go home had simply never occurred to me. He'd tried to *kill* her. But he was working with her now, and he hadn't been there when we'd taken her knowe. Her letting him go was the only thing that made sense, and it didn't make sense at all.

And I didn't have time to worry about what did or didn't make sense right now. Too much was going on. As usual, Quentin's phone was in his jacket pocket. He had a lock screen, but the day I can't remember my squire's combination is the day I tell him his training is finished. I keyed in the code, revealing a picture of him and Dean sitting on Dean's private underground dock, their shoulders touching, neither of them in a human disguise. It was an adorable moment. I dismissed it with a sweep of my thumb.

"Dianda's on her way. We won't have to hold the scene for long."

"Good." Dianda was a natural disaster, but she was a natural disaster on our side. She would keep things together. I pulled up the address book on autopilot, dialed, raised the phone, and waited.

What time was it? We'd been running hard since the early morning. Was it afternoon yet? Were people going to be awake? The phone rang, and I held my breath, until there was a click, and Etienne's familiar, somewhat puzzled voice said, "Hello? Who is this?"

"Etienne." I closed my eyes. Maybe I should have called Arden. Maybe this was a matter for the Queen in the Mists. But I was tired, and I was scared, and I wanted my family. My *real* family, the one that had always been there for me. "It's October. I . . . is Sylvester awake?"

"He could be." Etienne's tone turned gentle. "Bridget told me she saw you on campus this morning. She told me why. October, is . . ." His voice trailed off. It was clear he didn't know how to ask the question, and that he wouldn't have wanted to ask it if he could.

"I don't know," I said, honestly. "I'm in the false Queen's knowe. The receiving hall. It's currently open. Can you please get Sylvester and bring him here? I . . . I need him."

There was a long pause. The last time I'd seen Sylvester Torquill was when I'd told him that his brother, Simon, had managed to escape from my custody. Sylvester was still my liege. He still held my loyalty, in more ways than one. But until I found Simon and brought him back, I didn't feel like I'd earned the right to go home. Even bringing his niece back from the dead—a pretty impressive trick, if I do say so myself—hadn't felt like enough.

Besides, January deserved some time with her uncle without me sniffing around the edges, trying to intrude. Where I went, chaos followed. They had the right to ask for better than that.

Etienne didn't seem to share my opinion about keeping my distance. Without hesitation, he said, "Stay where you are. We'll be there as quickly as we can." The phone went dead. I lowered it, staring at the screen.

Then I raised it again. This time, I pulled up Walther's number. He picked up on the second ring.

"Hello? Quentin?"

"October. Do you have the elf-shot cure mixed and ready to go?"

"Um." He hesitated. "Yes? How much do you need?"

"Two doses. Quentin and May are down."

He made a noise somewhere between a groan and a grim chuckle. "You know, I don't know how much of that stuff it's safe to take. You can't keep running into arrows and expecting that nothing will go wrong."

"Believe me, I'm aware. Sadly, they weren't really consulted."

"Got it. Where am I delivering the stuff?"

"I'll send Tybalt to pick it up as soon as he has a free hand." From the dais, Tybalt gave me a dubious look. I shrugged exaggeratedly. If he didn't want to play courier service, he could . . . he could nothing. This was what I needed from him right now. "Okay?"

"Okay. Be careful, please. I can't wake you all up."

"Hopefully you won't have to. Open roads."

"Kind fires."

I hung up the phone and tucked it back into Quentin's pocket. When I straightened, Kennis was eyeing me oddly.

"What is that device?" she asked.

I smiled despite myself. "You're going to really enjoy some of the advances in modern technology," I said.

In the distance, a door banged open, followed by the sound of running feet. Kennis tensed, while Tybalt relaxed. I glanced back to the Baobhan Sith.

"You might want to hold very, very still, and keep your hands where people can see them," I said. "The folks who are on their way don't like it when they run into strangers covered in blood."

"You're covered in blood," she said.

"Yes, but they know me."

Dianda was the first into the hall, running remarkably well for a woman who only had legs when she really wanted them. She was wearing a thigh-length tunic, belted at the waist, and carrying a trident that looked like it had been designed to disembowel her enemies. Knowing her, it probably had been. Half a dozen Undersea soldiers were behind her, most of them the octopus-legged Cephali, although I spotted a few other Merrow.

Patrick, her Daoine Sidhe husband, brought up the rear, strolling while the rest of them rushed. He wasn't here for combat. He was here to stop his wife before she killed anyone they were going to need later. It was nice to see someone looking so calm about the situation.

Dianda caught sight of me and pivoted, stalking in my direction. "Where?" she demanded.

"Over there." I pointed toward the unconscious body of the false Queen. "You can't keep her. Arden's going to want to handle sentencing, whatever that's going to mean. But you can kick her a few times, if it looks like she's going to wake up."

Several of the Cephali had surrounded Kennis—people with the lower bodies of octopuses and the eight associated arms could do a remarkable amount of surrounding—and were watching her closely, their spears and short swords trained on her. To her credit, she was holding very still and keeping her hands visible, as I had requested. Spending four decades locked in a burnt-out house seemed to have instilled a strong sense of self-preservation.

"That's Kennis," I said, indicating her. "She's a Baobhan Sith. The false Queen had her locked in a house in Berkeley and used her as a pit trap to try to murder me. She's bloody because she at-tacked me, but she was starving at the time, and she and I have worked it out." That was a bit of an exaggeration. Somehow, I didn't think Kennis was going to mind.

"I see," said Dianda. She looked to the dais and frowned. "Who's the child?"

"Her name is Jocelyn, and she helped the false Queen abduct my daughter."

Dianda, who had never met Gillian, only heard about her in context of the kidnapping of her own children, stared at me. "Your girl is missing again? October, I'm so sorry. What can I do to help?"

Sometimes it's nice to know that people have my back. "Noth-ing," I said. Before Dianda could object to my refusing her help, I explained, "She's with the Luidaeg. I'll know something soon."

Both statements were technically true, even if I couldn't bring myself to look at Tybalt as I made them. Gillian was with the Lui-daeg. Alive or dead, awake or asleep, I'd know something as soon as I was ready to ask, and I let him answer. For now, I needed to keep moving.

She was in the best hands she could possibly be in. If anyone could save her, it was the sea witch.

Please.

Dianda nodded, accepting my words at face value, and shot a venomous look at the false Queen. Patrick was kneeling next to the woman, one hand extended as he presumably took her pulse. It was nice to see him being thorough.

"I could overpower you," she said. "She's allowed crimes to be committed against my people. I could have her halfway to the Undersea before you had a chance to stop me. If you think Queen Windermere is going to be lenient . . . "

"I don't," I said. "This woman took her father's throne. She left Arden as an exile in her own kingdom for a century, and she had Nolan elf-shot. I think the false Queen will end up wishing she'd stayed asleep up in Silences." Which raised the question of where we could find Dugan Harrow, and how many times I was going to punch him before he stopped fighting back. I glanced to Jocelyn, who was still slumped, unconscious, in Tybalt's grasp. We were going to have a long conversation after she woke up, and she wasn't going to enjoy it.

Etienne's scent of limes and cedar smoke drifted through the air. I whirled in time to see a glowing portal appear behind me. My liege, Duke Sylvester Torquill of Shadowed Hills, stepped through. I didn't think. I dropped my sword and broke into a run, flinging myself into the comforting familiarity of his embrace. He didn't hesitate before folding his arms around me, surrounding me with the scent of daffodils and dogwood flowers that permeated his skin. I inhaled deeply. His magic had meant home and safety to me for as long as I could remember.

"October," he said, resting his chin against the top of my head and holding me closer still. I started to shake, all the fear and trauma of the day bubbling to the top. "Calm, my dear, calm. I'm here. It will be all right."

I didn't look at Tybalt. He was the only one who knew whether my liege was lying. I *couldn't* look at him. Not yet.

"I'm sorry," I said, pressing my face against Sylvester's chest. "I couldn't, I couldn't . . . I'm sorry. I couldn't do it without you."

"Nor should you have to. I'm your liege. That means something, October. Even when you feel you can do things on your own, you shouldn't have to. I'm always here when you need me. Always." Sylvester lifted his head, and I knew he was looking at the dais, at Tybalt, waiting there for me to be ready for whatever terrible thing was coming next.

I was almost prepared when Sylvester pushed me out to arm's-length, his golden eyes grave as he searched my face.

"October," he said, "where is your daughter?"

"With the Luidaeg," I said, voice small.

"You should go to her. Duchess Lorden and I will see that Queen Windermere takes custody of these ruffians."

I nodded, unable to speak. Then I knelt, retrieving my sword from the floor. "Tybalt will be back with the elf-shot cure," I said, finally finding the words now that they weren't about me. "Please don't let any harm come to Quentin or May."

"I would never," Sylvester assured me.

Dianda looked at me sympathetically, but didn't speak, as I walked back to where Tybalt waited. He shoved Jocelyn at her. She caught the changeling easily, locking her trident across the smaller woman's body, so that there was no chance she could wake up and break away.

"I'll be back for them," I said, and stepped into Tybalt's embrace. He drew me close as he stepped into the shadows, and we were gone.

NINETEEN

THE SHADOW ROADS WERE as dark and cold as ever, and somehow no less terrifying for the lack of a Baobhan Sith lurking somewhere in the blackness. Tybalt swung me into a bridal carry, a move that was sweetly, painfully reminiscent of the way we always used to run together, back before I had a prayer of keeping up with him. I closed my eyes and did my best to relax against him, feeling the blood that covered my clothing freeze and flake away.

I didn't know what we were running toward. It was by my own choosing, and I understood that, I accepted that, but it didn't change the fact that I didn't know. Were we running toward a consequence or a miracle? I didn't *know*. What had seemed easier in the pale light of the false Queen's knowe seemed like a dire mistake now, as we ran through the dark and the consequences of my choices loomed ahead of me.

Gillian. My Gilly. I didn't know her as an adult, had barely known her as a child, but I knew her so well as a baby, and those were the images my heart raced for. The first smile, the first word, the first time she'd tried to grasp a pixie in one pudgy fist and I had known, for sure, that she was fae enough to see the magical world around us, not safely insulated from it like her father. The way she'd scowled when she didn't want to do something, whether it was eating her broccoli or going to bed. The way she'd laughed every time I crossed my eyes. She had been the most magical thing in my world, and if she was gone, she was gone forever. I didn't know how I was ever going to move past the reality of her absence.

But I'd been moving toward that reality for years, hadn't I? Since the moment I'd kissed her forehead and pulled eternity from her veins, I had known that one day she would die and leave me. There had been a chance before that—a slim chance, given how thin her fae blood had been, but a chance all the same. When I had asked her to choose which world she belonged to, I had kept my word. I'd listened. I'd given her what she asked for, and in the process, I had taken away her chance at forever.

Maybe things would have gone differently if I'd been able to explain what it meant to be fae, what it meant to be mortal . . . or if Janet hadn't already been burrowed into Gillian's life, quietly poisoning her against Faerie. I shuddered, nestling more tightly against Tybalt. So much of this came back to Janet. She had been there all along, and somehow I had failed to see her. Because she was human, and humans didn't matter in Faerie.

I was becoming as prejudiced as any pureblood, assuming I hadn't been already.

Tybalt tensed and leapt and the shadows fell away, brightness lancing at my closed eyes. I cracked them cautiously open and blinked when I saw we were in the Luidaeg's actual living room, rather than in the alley outside.

"She modified the wards for you?" The question sounded stupid even to my own ears. Of course, she'd modified the wards. How else could we have been where we were? Tybalt was a King of Cats, but no King apart from their Firstborn could possibly have the power to tear through the Luidaeg's defenses.

"She volunteered it; I did not ask," he said gravely, lowering me to my feet. "I would not waste her favors on such a petty privilege."

"Which is why you get to have it, kitty," said the Luidaeg. I turned. She was standing in the kitchen doorway, wiping something thick and black off her hands. The washcloth's original color was unknowable, thanks to the muck. She smiled wanly as she looked at me. "Covered in blood again, I see. I suppose it's your signature look. Maybe think about getting a hat or something instead."

I opened my mouth, intending to make a snide comment. Nothing came out. My lips moved soundlessly, my voice trying to find purchase on the air. The ice on my lashes was still melting, gluing them together, filling the world with a prismatic gleam.

The Luidaeg sighed. "Breathe, Toby. You need to breathe. She's alive. But we need to talk about what that means."

I barely heard her final words. "Alive" echoed in my ears, drowning everything else out. I took a step forward, staggered, and collapsed, saved from impact with the floor by Tybalt, who wrapped his arms around my chest and hoisted me back to my feet.

"Can you get her to the couch?" The Luidaeg sounded very far away.

"I can carry her to the ends of the earth." Tybalt was there with her. I hoped they were having a nice time in whatever strange new land they had discovered. I hoped they would come back and get me.

Alive.

"That won't be necessary," said the Luidaeg, with a hint of amusement. "All you need to do is get her to the couch."

Tybalt half-carried, half-dragged me across the room to the Luidaeg's couch, an overstuffed antique blotched with mold and leaking stuffing from every seam. He settled me on a cushion, and there was no weakness in the frame or scent of decay. Like so much else about the apartment, the rot was an illusion.

Sitting upright suddenly felt like too much trouble. I allowed myself to sink into the cushions, that single word—alive, alive, *alive*—still echoing so loudly that it drowned out almost everything else.

The Luidaeg sighed. "She's in shock. What fun."

"Will she be . . ." Tybalt hesitated. "Gillian. Is she . . ." Both times he stopped before the question could fully form, leaving his words to hang in the empty air.

"That's a conversation I need to have with October, and just because you're planning to marry her, that doesn't make you her surrogate for this sort of thing. Don't you have somewhere to be? Somewhere that isn't here?" When Tybalt hesitated, the Luidaeg sighed again, angrier this time. "She's not going to come to harm while she's in my keeping. You have my word about that. On my own ground, this close to the sea, there's none among my siblings both living and awake who could take her from me."

"Quentin and May were elf-shot in the false Queen's knowe," he said reluctantly. "October contacted Master Davies before we came here, to ensure he would have his cure prepared for me to collect and carry to them."

"There you go. Shoo. Go wake the rest of your little gang of fools, and we'll be here when you get back."

There was a long pause. Then the smell of musk and pennyroyal washed through the room, and I knew that he was gone. Someone settled on the couch next to me.

"October. Look at me."

I turned my head, forcing my eyes to focus. The Luidaeg appeared, studying me gravely. Her eyes were green as glass, green as the eyes of the Roane who had been her children, before almost all of them were killed. Evening's doing. She had already hated her sister, even so long ago as that. The Luidaeg understood what it was to be a mother and bury her children, and more importantly, the Luidaeg couldn't lie. I seized on that thought with everything I had. The Luidaeg *couldn't lie.*

And yet . . . "Alive?" I asked, in a very small voice.

"Yes," she said. She put her hand, nails still dark with whatever that substance had been, over mine. "October, can you understand what I'm saying right now? We need to have this conversation—we need to have it as soon as possible—but I'm not going to try to explain this to you while you're checked out. Are you here for this or not?"

"I . . ." I hesitated, trying to figure out my answer. Finally, slowly, I nodded. "I'm here."

"Good girl." She reached into the pocket of her overalls, producing a small cut-glass bottle filled with a cherry-red liquid that glittered in the light, catching it and flinging it back in prismatic shards. She held it out to me. "I want you to drink this."

"What is it?" I asked, already taking the bottle and worrying at the stopper. When the Luidaeg tells me to drink something, I've found it easier to just agree. Maybe this explains the amount of time I've spent transformed into something I'm not or marooned on roads that were never supposed to be accessible to me, but it's also the reason I've managed to survive for as long as I have. There are worse allies to have in my corner than the sea witch.

"It's something that will make you feel better."

I gave her a sidelong look. "Because refusing to tell me what I'm drinking is the way to calm me down."

"It's already working, if you're being sarcastic," she said. "Drink."

Arguing with the Luidaeg is like arguing with a mountain: in the end, all you wind up with is a sore throat and an implacable landmark. Only in the case of the Luidaeg, she might wind up turning you into a toad for your impertinence. I drank.

It tasted like cherry syrup mixed with steak sauce—not a pleasant combination—and although it was cold, it sent a wave of warmth through my body, relaxing my limbs and draining the tension from my back and shoulders. I slumped further into the cushions, blinking, as the Luidaeg reached over and plucked the vial from my suddenly limp fingers.

"The paralysis will pass," she said pleasantly. "Not that you were moving that much before, but this way I know you'll hold still and listen to me, with the added bonus of helping you regenerate some of the blood you've lost."

"'S not lost," I managed, through lips that didn't want to cooperate. "Know exactly where it is."

"Again, sarcasm. You're still in there." She touched my arm. "I'm glad."

The concern in her eyes was clear enough that my own eyes started to burn with tears. I tried to turn my face away. I couldn't move. She had locked me into facing her, and despite her insistence that Gillian was alive—despite her inability to lie—it felt like I was standing at the edge of a very high cliff, waiting to step off into nothingness.

"You're going to start asking questions and demanding proof in a second, and I'd like this to be over before that happens, so let's go," she said. "Yes, she's alive. I want you to understand what a miracle that is, all right? I want you to *comprehend* how impossible it is for your daughter to still be a part of this world. When my sister created elf-shot, she did it to curry favor with our parents—'look, see, we don't have to kill each other anymore. Aren't I clever? Aren't I the absolute *best*?'"

Her voice spiked on the word "best," becoming the sound of glass breaking. She paused, catching her breath. When she continued, she sounded calmer . . . and sadder.

"It didn't have to be fatal to changelings. That was her little extra twist, her way to make sure that when there was a war, only the 'right' people would come off the battlefield. We can't go to war the way we used to when the world was younger, when there was more space for us both in and out of Faerie. Back before we decided to go into hiding from the humans, we could fill valleys and cover mountains, and every kingdom with changeling citizens would send them to the frontlines, because why shouldn't they? A changeling couldn't be a landholder or a noble or an alchemist or a court seer, but they could take an arrow like any pureblood. And if they didn't come back, after my sister's work was done, that added a sense of . . . of reality to the wars. A hundred fatalities were a hundred fatalities. Never mind that the hundred bodies you'd buried were the hundred you never wanted in the first place."

I frowned, and managed to ask, "What does . . . ?"

"Peace, October." She touched my arm again. "I'm getting there. Please let me get there. I need you to understand what happened here today."

I couldn't nod, but I could stop fighting to speak and lean into the cushions. She smiled a little, clearly seeing this for the acquiescence it was.

"In order to make elf-shot fatal to changelings, she had to make it fatal to mortals. One follows the other. And that would have been enough, but she also wanted it to hurt, October, she wanted it to hurt *so badly*, because how dare we? How dare we bring humanity into our world, in however dilute a form? How dare we waste love that should have been reserved for better things on finite creatures? She never had a lot of love in her to spare. She didn't understand how the rest of us could spend it so freely. She never understood a lot of things. So she didn't just make a poison. She made a work of art." The Luidaeg paused. "It kills changelings and it kills humans. But it kills changelings because it attacks everything in them that's mortal, while the parts of them that are fae struggle to fight back, to go peacefully to sleep as the potion intends. It takes its time. That's why changing the blood allowed your mother to save you and allowed you to save Gillian the first time she was elf-shot. The potion moves so slowly that any half-competent blood-worker can challenge it in a changeling. Even my sister had her favorites. Even my sister understood the value of being able to save a grandchild whose parents had never intended for them to be there. Changelings happened early in Faerie, and they kept happening, and she needed to be able to save them. Humans . . . "

The Luidaeg paused again. This time when she continued, her voice was harder. "Humans have always been disposable, and she had no interest in being called upon to save them. Elf-shot was designed to look for traces of fae blood and, upon failing to find them, to rip through the body as quickly as possible. To shred and tear and destroy. Her ideal would be a world in which it was literally impossible to cure elf-shot poisoning in a human, because there wouldn't be *time*. Did you ever wonder why I never cured elf-shot? Why none of the people who've come to me across the centuries ever thought to say 'oh, sea witch, why don't you give me a way to wake my loved ones from their enchanted sleep'?"

I took a deep breath and managed to nod, very slightly. Her answering nod was deeper.

"It's because they did ask me. And I couldn't do it. There aren't many limits on what I can accomplish if I'm being paid, but that is one of them. I can't counteract my sister's work, any of it. I could never have been the one to unmake elf-shot. So when you sent your lover to me with your child dying in his arms, I didn't have a cure that would work for her, human child that she was. The alchemist's cure couldn't work without something fae to latch onto."

I closed my eyes. She'd been lying to me after all, somehow breaking all the rules in an attempt to be kind. I should have been expecting it. I should have known we'd never make it through this intact.

She touched my arm. "She was dying, and there was nothing I could do, and then I stopped thinking about what was possible and started thinking about what was right. Letting her die wasn't right. She's family. You're only my niece—not much, compared to all the siblings and children I've buried—but it's been a long time since I've had even that much. You're my niece and she's your child and letting her die was wrong. I don't like to be wrong."

I opened my eyes and stared at her. The feeling was coming back into my limbs, accompanied by a new strength, as if I hadn't been bleeding for most of the day. I sat up, resisting the urge to grab and shake the most powerful individual I knew. "What are you saying?"

"My youngest daughter's name was Firtha." The Luidaeg looked at me with calm, steady eyes. "She was clever and cunning, and she died without having children of her own because my sister—my damned sister—put knives in the hands of humans and told them they could find their route to immortality through the bodies of my babies. Unlike me, she can lie. She was hoping to kill my children and see me kill the humans who wore their pelts in my rage, so she could paint me extinguisher of my own descendant line. She knew there'd be no immortality for the killers of the Roane. But I am . . . I'm not nice, October. I was never made to be nice. I've still tried, all the long days of my life, to be kind when I can. I have striven for mercy. I was merciful. I was . . . perhaps more merciful than anyone knew."

She turned her face away, looking out the window on the other side of the room, the window that showed a ceaseless view of the surging tide. "My sister's patsies killed my children, and their children killed them, when they came home with bloody hands and sealskins thrown across their shoulders. The children of my children's killers saw their own deaths in the blood running down their parents' backs, and they tried to save themselves. My sister thought I would be unable to show enough kindness to find my way to cruelty. She thought I'd kill them. And instead, I kept them, as many of them as I could. But there were . . . losses, especially in the first years, when the Selkies were still learning what it meant to be what they had become. The man who wore my Firtha's skin broke his own neck jumping from a cliff. The woman who inherited the skin was caught and killed by human fishermen. The girl who inherited from *her* chose not to have children at all, so when she died, there was no one waiting for the skin to pass to them. It came back to me, instead. A few of them have, over the years. A few of them have come home." The Luidaeg looked back to me. "Do you understand?"

This time, the numbness in my lips and tongue had nothing to do with any potions. "She has no fae blood left in her," I said. "What you're saying . . . it's impossible."

"I'm the sea witch. The ocean in my veins and the ocean in yours is so similar as to be identical. I can't do what you can do, because the blood all looks the same to me. Such small adjustments are beyond what I can narrow my magic to achieve. But when I poured the blood price of my children into their skins, I wasn't doing anything *narrow*, anything *small*. I was refusing the remaking of the world. So, no, it's not impossible. It's not easy. It's well within my power."

My mouth felt like a desert. My head spun. "She's . . . she's really alive?"

The Luidaeg rolled her eyes. "Mom's teeth, didn't I say that to begin with? You know I can't lie. You're lucky I don't get insulted and turn you into a coral reef for the next thirty years. Yes, she's really alive. She's not the same. She can't be the same for at least a century, which is going to put a crimp in any plans she had for a human life, but she's alive. That's more than anyone else could have done."

I burst into tears. I wanted to ask for details, to ask where she was, to ask anything that wouldn't run the risk of offending the Luidaeg, but I couldn't do it. All I could do was sit on the couch and sob brokenly, my vision going blurry and my chest going tight.

Then arms surrounded me, pulling me close, and the Luidaeg's voice was in my ear, whispering, "Shh, Toby, shhh, it's all right. You can cry for her without mourning for her now. It's going to be all right."

The tears, now that they'd been set free, refused to stop coming. They were a hot flood of misery, and I was being swept away. I grabbed hold of the Luidaeg's sheltering arms and held on for dear life, trusting her to be my rock against the terrible tide.

Lips still pressed against the curve of my ear, she said softly, "When you feel better, when you're ready to stop crying and start coping, I need you to remember this: you are still in my debt for so many, many things, but you are not in my debt for this. You didn't ask me to save her. Even your kitty didn't speak the words. I saved her because I know what it is to bury a child—a hundred times over, I know—and because I'm selfish, Toby, I'm so much more selfish than any of you ever give me credit for. I would have swallowed the sea if they'd let me. I wanted someone who could carry Firtha's skin into the world again, and you gave me that. You owe me for every favor I've ever done you. You owe me nothing for your daughter."

My tears, which had been tapering off, redoubled. Whatever she had asked for saving Gillian, I would have paid it without a second thought. I would have returned to the pond for another seven years; I would have put a dagger through my own heart. I had never considered that this might be something she could, or would, do for free.

The Luidaeg stroked my hair and murmured soothing words, some in English, some not, until I calmed down enough to sit up and wipe my eyes, chasing the prisms from the edges of my vision. I looked at her and blinked, swallowing a gasp.

She still looked more like a human teenager than anything else,

and her eyes were still a clear driftglass green, like pieces of a broken bottle that had been tumbled by the tide. But her hair was an
oil slick, filled with shifting rainbow colors painted over the black,
and her clothes had changed, becoming a ruffled white shirt like a
cascade of foam and a pair of dark blue hose. She quirked an eyebrow when she saw me looking.

"Yes?" she asked.

"How do you do that?" I blurted. Her eyebrow climbed higher.
I continued, "The clothes thing. The false Queen always used to
do that to my clothes, but even when she was part-Siren, she never
should have had transformation magic like that."

"Your brain is a fascinating place," said the Luidaeg dryly. "It's
old sea magic. Not common on the land, I'll grant you, although
the Hamadryads might be able to teach you a thing or two."

"So Sea Wights can do it?"

"No," the Luidaeg admitted. "But it would have been easy enough
to buy from one of the Asrai or Fuath. Easy as it is for land fae to
borrow from the blood of one another, it's a hundred times simpler
for those born to the water."

"Sometimes you talk like a riddle," I grumbled, wiping my eyes
again. "If transformation magic isn't something native to her bloodlines, why would she be so obsessed with using it? Where's the ben-
efit?"

"I really hope you're not planning to sit here and use me as a
sounding board for all your half-baked theories," said the Luidaeg
blandly. "I would have thought you'd be asking to see your daughter
by now. I'm tired of taking in your refugees, by the way. If this
doesn't stop happening all the damn time, I'm going to start charging
you rent."

"And I guess I'll pay it." I stood, my knees still wobbling like
they weren't sure they wanted to hold me up. Then I paused, looking around the empty living room. "Where's Janet?"

"Given everything, I think I'd be justified in saying 'hanging out
with the other cockroaches,' but no. She's in the parlor. I wanted
her to have some time to herself to think about what she's done,
and to not be under my damn feet. And thank Dad for that. If
she'd been here when your kitty came running in with the littlest
Carter . . ." The Luidaeg shuddered theatrically.

I frowned. "What do you mean, 'Carter'?"

"Fae don't have surnames," said the Luidaeg. She looked at me like she was waiting for the other shoe to finally drop. "Why would we have a family name when the shape of our ears tells people who we're descended from? And then there's the issue where every member of any given descendant race is technically related to all the others but keeps marrying them *anyway*, and the more time we've spent with humans down the centuries, the less we've wanted to think about that. So where do the family names come from? The Torquills and the Sollys and the Lordens? Humans bring their names with them, and they leave them behind when we strip their blood away. Dad's idea. He didn't think it was fair to change people's heritage and not let them keep *something* of where they'd come from."

The thought of a human marrying into the Lorden family was as terrifying as it was delightful. Humans can't generally breathe water. Then again, neither could Patrick, and Dianda was doing a reasonably good job of keeping him from drowning. "So 'Carter' is because . . . ?"

"Family names have changed since Janet's day. She'd be a Carter now. Place names and all that." The Luidaeg stood. "We're getting distracted again. Do you not *want* to see your daughter?"

I hesitated. Then, in a voice so small I barely recognized it as my own, I whispered, "I'm afraid to."

"Oh, *mo laochain*," she said, voice twisting around the unfamiliar syllables like a rose through a trellis. She put her arms around me and drew me close, into the sea-salt smell of her, until my face was pressed to the cool skin of her shoulder. "We're all afraid. That's what it is to be a mother. We're all afraid."

I started to cry again. She held me until I was done, and then she pulled away, her hand still grasping mine, and led me down the hallway toward my daughter.

TWENTY

THE LUIDAEG'S APARTMENT ISN'T a knowe in the traditional sense. The door is easy to find, and I've never had the feeling that I was crossing between worlds when coming and going. And despite all that, the more I've learned about her living arrangements, the more I've been convinced that *something* is going on that violates the usual laws of topology.

The layout seemed simple the first time I was there: a long hallway lined with doors, the whole thing usually cloaked in an illusion that made it seem like a polluted shore at low tide, ending in a foul-smelling living room with a kitchen off to one side. Since then, I've discovered a back door leading to a patch of swampland in the Summerlands and the existence of at least one additional hall connecting to a guest room. So it wasn't as much of a surprise as it could have been when the Luidaeg opened a door to reveal a staircase winding gently upward, like something from a tower in a fairy tale. There was no way it could have been accommodated by the architecture of her actual building. As I followed her onto the steps, that didn't seem to matter.

There were windows located on both sides of the stairwell as we climbed, filling the air with a gentle, shifting light. No matter how hard I squinted, I couldn't see anything beyond that light. Everything was a colorless gray that could have been mist, or clouds, or even frothy water. I was still squinting when the Luidaeg put her hand on my arm. I glanced up at her, startled.

She shook her head. "Don't," she said. "The things you could see aren't things you *want* to see. Just keep walking."

"Sometimes I think spending time with someone they used to write cautionary tales about is bad for my health."

The Luidaeg laughed. "Honey, if you knew how many of those stories I'm in, you'd never leave your house again."

"Sometimes I don't want to leave my house anyway," I admitted. I glanced over my shoulder. The curvature of the stairs meant the door at the bottom was long since out of sight. "The wards will still let Tybalt in, right?"

"As long as he doesn't abuse my charity, I won't close them against him, and that man could track the scent of you across an ocean if he had to." The Luidaeg kept walking. "He'll be back. As soon as he's finished taking care of whatever mess you've made so that you don't have to, he'll be back."

I wanted to feel bad about that, about running out on my friends and allies while there was still work to be done. The false Queen needed to be taken to Arden and forced to stand trial for what she'd done—and we still didn't even know the full scope of what that was. Dugan was out there somewhere, unseen and only half-suspected. Kennis was a living citizen of Faerie who'd been used as a booby trap. I wanted to believe she was the only one. Somehow, I couldn't quite manage it.

I couldn't quite manage feeling bad, either. Losing Gillian had long been one of my greatest regrets, a shining centerpiece in a long chain of things I'd failed to protect, or do, or be. Now she was waiting at the top of this staircase, her life changed forever by something she had never chosen, something I'd tried to protect her from. It didn't matter that I wasn't the one who'd forced her into Faerie. This was still my fault. She already hated me. What if this was the moment when I *really* lost her forever, and we were trapped in the same world, unable to go back to the polite distance that had kept my heart from breaking up until now?

The Luidaeg smacked me on the shoulder. I turned to her, eyes wide and startled.

"Stop," she said, not unkindly. "You're chasing the tide again, and you're never going to catch it."

"Excuse me?"

"Your head. It's got its own undertow, you know, and if you

swim too deep, it can suck you down. You can't chase the tide. You need to stay on the shore and let it come to you." She shook her head. "I'm not going to tell you that everything is going to be fine. I wouldn't do it even if I was still allowed to lie. Some things are too cruel even for a sea witch. But I will tell you that what's on the other side of that door is never going to be as bad as the undertow in your own mind."

I blinked. We had reached the top of the stairs. A closed door with a rounded top and a seashell design subtly worked into the wood waited in front of us, set into a frame that gleamed faintly in the light, like it had been dusted in pearl. I reached for the handle, then hesitated, looking back at the Luidaeg.

"Where are we?" I asked.

"You're stalling," she said. "We're in my home. I live here. I've lived here for a very long time. Now go and see your child. Do what I can no longer do. Be a mother."

I swallowed, and it felt like I was forcing a stone down my throat, something hard and unyielding that scratched my flesh as it passed. Then I grasped the handle, which moved easy under my hand, pushed the door open, and stepped inside. The door swung closed behind me.

The Luidaeg didn't follow.

The room was small and round, as befitted a room at the top of a tower. The windows looked out on the San Francisco shoreline from an angle that I knew for a fact matched nothing in the part of the city where the Luidaeg's apartment was located. There didn't seem to be enough light pollution out there, as if the windows were somehow pointed at the past. Stranger things have happened in Faerie, and I knew that. I also knew that I was stalling. Taking a deep breath, I pulled my eyes away from the window and considered the rest of the room.

The furniture was old, heavy oak that should have seemed like it was too much for the space, but it was saved by the combination of its own delicate carving and the gauzy curtains that softened and blunted the walls. A wardrobe; a dresser; a desk; a bed. The curtains around the bed were thicker, allowing the occupant to shut out the better part of the light, and they were drawn, transforming her into an outline that could as easily have been a pile of pillows in a comedy as my daughter. My heart hammered. My head spun. I took a step forward.

That first step seemed to break the seal on the rest of them. It wasn't easy to move, but it was possible, and once I'd done it, the next step came a little easier, and the one after that, and the one after that, until I was standing next to the bed. I pulled the curtains aside, and there she was. My girl. My Gillian.

The Luidaeg had changed her clothes, dressing her in a simple blue sweater and a pair of dark pants. I should have been annoyed, but all I could manage was gratitude. I wasn't sure my heart could have handled seeing my daughter soaked in her own blood. Her chest rose and fell in a slow, easy rhythm, the breathing of someone sunk into a deep slumber.

There was a seal's pelt draped around her shoulders, burnished silver dotted with patches of deeper gray. She would be beautiful in the water, like all the Selkies were, like Connor had been. I put a hand over my mouth, smothering any sound I might have made. Elf-shot had taken my Selkie lover from me, reduced him to so much meat for the night-haunts to claim. And now elf-shot had, however unintentionally, given my Selkie daughter back to me.

The signs of her renewed fae heritage weren't in her face yet, but they would be. Her eyes would darken; her ears would take on subtle points. Maybe she'd have spots in her hair like Connor had, or speckled rosettes ghosting along the skin of her back and arms. The change would come on slowly, keeping pace with her ability to disguise herself from human eyes.

Not for the first time since I'd learned the true origin of the Selkies, I thought the Luidaeg had been kinder to them than she'd had any cause to be. She needed them to keep the skins of her dead children alive, yes, but she could have punished them far more severely than she had. In her own way, she still loved them. In her own way, she still tried.

I knelt, taking one of Gillian's hands in mine, and paused at the first real sign of change. A thin membrane of skin had formed at the base of her fingers, connecting each of them about halfway to the first knuckle.

"It's a good thing you weren't studying to be a surgeon," I murmured, and laughed unsteadily. Somehow my laughter turned into tears, great, racking sobs that rose up from my toes and traveled through my body in waves. I bent forward, forehead to the mattress, and wept.

A hand touched the crown of my head. I sat up with a start.

Gillian's eyes were open. The edges of her pupils were beginning to bleed black into the foggy blue of her irises, washing the color away, making it something else for her to mourn. I wondered, for an instant, whether she would ever be able to look at her recolored eyes without hating me a little, the way I hated my own mother for changing me to save me. Then the moment passed, and I was staring at my daughter, and she was staring back at me, and there were no illusions between us. No illusions at all.

"M . . ." she started, and stopped, swallowing the syllable. It was such a familiar gesture that it ached. She tried again: "Toby?"

"Hi," I whispered.

"I . . . your ears." Her eyes widened as she struggled not to stare. "I thought I dreamt it. I thought I dreamt . . ." She started to shiver, sitting upright and clutching the blankets over her chest. "This is a dream. I am dreaming right now."

"You're not, honey. I'm sorry, but you're awake." I stood, taking a step back and giving her as much space as I could without leaving the room. "This is all really happening."

"No, it's not. This *can't* be happening." She clutched the blanket tighter. The motion caused her fingers to brush against the edge of the sealskin wrapped around her shoulders. She flinched away from it, and my heart broke.

Hearts are resilient. They can heal over and over again. That's the good part. The bad part is that having a resilient heart means it can be broken so many times that it feels like it should never recover, like it should be nothing but a pile of shards in my chest. I forced myself to keep breathing as I took another step back, putting even more distance between us. Making it clear that I wasn't trying to pressure her.

"Gillian . . ." I stopped. What was I supposed to say? That she'd lost her humanity, but it was okay, she still had her life? How well had that line worked on me? I was more human than my own changeling daughter, now. A Selkie is either a Selkie or they're not, and if she set her skin aside, she wouldn't be a Selkie anymore. She'd just be a dead girl.

"That woman, that *awful* woman, she stabbed me." Gillian looked down at her hands and flinched again at the sight of the webs between her fingers. She closed her eyes, looking at nothing as she continued, "She stabbed me with an arrow and I thought I was going to die, and why can't I remember what she looked like? She nearly killed me. Why can't I remember?"

"She's a pureblood, and humans have trouble looking at the fae," I said. "You were too human before. Your head couldn't handle looking at what she really was." The false Queen's beauty had always been the kind that tore people down, rather than building them up. Looking at a pureblood as a human or a thin-blooded changeling could be dangerous, because the mortal mind was never intended to behold things that far outside the natural world.

Gillian froze. I reviewed my words and winced as I realized what I'd said wrong.

"What do you mean, I was too human before?" she asked.

I counted carefully to ten before I replied with a question of my own: "What did they tell you when they woke you up?"

Gillian opened her eyes. The black had progressed in just those few seconds, slithering across the blue like smoke, clouding and concealing it. Soon enough, it would be gone forever. "The other woman, the one with the green eyes, she made me drink this stuff that tasted like seawater, and then she said, um." She paused before reciting, "'This isn't a perfect solution, and I'm sorry, but you deserve better, and so does your mother, and some debts are too old to ever be paid.' Then she tied this thing around my shoulders and told me to go to sleep again, and I couldn't keep my eyes open. I wasn't even tired, and I fell asleep."

"That was the Luidaeg," I said. "You may hear people call her the sea witch. She needed you to sleep so you could get used to the skin."

"The . . . skin?"

Oh, oak and ash, I didn't have the vocabulary for this. Maybe no one did. The Luidaeg had told the Selkies what they were going to be and then they had told their children, but the knowledge had been passed, over and over again within a closed loop, parent telling child, everyone expecting it. This was new. I took a deep breath.

"Faeries are real," I said. "Fairy tales get a lot of things wrong, but faeries are real, and when you were born, you were part-faerie, because I was half-faerie. Do you remember a few years ago, when the woman with the red hair snatched you from your bedroom?"

Gillian's face tightened. "I have nightmares about it."

"Do you remember the dream you had, before the police found you and brought you home?"

"I . . ." Gillian stopped, staring at me with sudden understanding. "I was in a meadow, and you were there too, only you didn't look the way you looked in pictures. You looked like you were something else. Like you were my fairy godmother."

Not exactly the description I would have used for myself, but I nodded anyway. "Yes. Exactly. What happened in the meadow?"

"There were two more versions of me. One of them who looked like you, and one who looked like Daddy." She hesitated, her face screwing into a look of deep concentration. "You told me I had to choose, because you could only save me if I chose. You looked so sad, and I wanted to be the kind of person who could choose to stay with you, but I couldn't do it. All I wanted was to go home. I wanted my dad and Miranda. I wanted my room and my things, and I guess that's why I'm being punished now, isn't it? Because I chose wrong."

"Oh, baby, no. No, you're not being punished. You're not . . . you did nothing wrong. The choice was yours to make, and you asked for what you needed. No one should ever be angry with you for that. I'm not. I never was." I'd cried myself to sleep because she hadn't wanted to be with me, but I had never been angry with her. "That meadow, though, that choice . . . I was there with you. It wasn't a dream. It was the magic letting you see what you needed to see in order to understand what I was asking. You had been shot with a sort of poison that only kills mortals, whether human or changeling—um, fae who have some human blood in them—and in order to take it out of you, I needed to be able to change your blood. When you asked me to make you human, I did."

She looked at me with wide, bruise-colored eyes. "That's why my skin stopped breaking out when I helped Dad work on the car, and why I stopped being so tired in the mornings. Because you took the alien out of me."

"Not alien: fae," I said. "And yes. My kind of fae is . . . we're a little odd. We work with blood. We can make it do what we want. But we can only work with what's there. When I took the fae blood out of you, I couldn't ever put it back again."

"And you took it out of me to save my life. Because I asked you to."

"Yes."

Gillian lifted one hand, fingers spread to show the soft new webbing between them. It would thicken and get tougher as it spread, until it connected her fingers all the way to the first knuckle. If the other Selkies I'd known were anything to go by, her manual dexterity wouldn't be that affected, but all those other Selkies had been raised knowing that one day, if they were lucky, they might go to the sea. They might earn a skin. Gillian . . .

Hadn't.

"So what the fuck is this?" she asked, voice small and wounded. "Why does everything feel wrong? Why is there fur tied around my shoulders, and why can't I take it off? What did your weird monster friends do to me?"

I took a sharp breath, forcing my tone to gentle before I said, "The woman whose face you can't remember stabbed you with the same stuff you'd been shot with before. The stuff that kills humans. It's called elf-shot. It was tearing you apart, because that's what it does. You were dying, Gillian. So my friend Tybalt brought you here, at my request, to find out whether there was anything that could be done to save you. I was hoping . . . I don't know what I was hoping for. I was hoping for a miracle. What I got was a loophole. That skin you're wearing, it belonged to the youngest daughter of my aunt, the Luidaeg. The woman with the green eyes. When her children . . . died, she put powerful magic into their skins. Anyone who bonds with one of them becomes what's called a Selkie. A kind of fae. Not the kind you were before you asked me to change you, but still fae, and if you're fae, the elf-shot can't kill you."

She stared at me. "You're lying."

"I'm not."

"You—you orchestrated this whole thing! You *wanted* this to happen! You wanted me to have to come and live with you!"

"That's not going to happen." She was my daughter, I loved her, and I would have been lying if I'd said I had never dreamt about it, never closed my eyes and seen her sitting across the table from Quentin, the two of them close as siblings, arguing over who had stolen whose toast and who had to go make more. But dreams were exactly that: dreams. "You may need to take a little time off from school to adjust to the change, and I apologize for that. It's still better than dying. And you're not coming to live with me. You won't even have to see me if you don't want to. Your . . . "

My voice caught in my throat, lodging there like a stone. I couldn't speak. Gillian narrowed her eyes, looking at me warily.

"What?" she asked.

I swallowed the stone. It settled heavy in my stomach, and I said, "Your mother is here. J—Miranda. She knows about Faerie. She's always known. She'll take you home and tell you how to hide yourself from your father until someone can teach you how to spin illusions, and she can take you wherever you need to go." Probably to Half Moon Bay, to the rambling house occupied by Elizabeth Ryan and her small clan of Selkies. She'd be able to help Gillian adjust to her new reality, and I'd be able to stay far away, missing yet another milestone in my child's life.

But my child was going to *have* a life. Maybe not a human life, and maybe not the life she'd been expecting, but a life all the same. That was so much more than I'd expected. I wasn't going to complain about it.

Gillian sat up a little straighter, some of the worry going out of her face. "Miranda is here? In this weird place?" She paused. Her eyes widened. "Miranda knows about fairies?"

She wasn't pronouncing the word quite right yet—there was a subtle wrongness to it that told me she was still thinking more Tinkerbell than Blind Michael. She'd have time to learn the difference. I nodded.

"She is," I said. "When the bad woman took you, she tried to make us think Miranda had done it, that she was the one who'd hurt you. I think she wanted us to fight, to give her more time to get you into hiding." But that didn't make sense, did it? The false Queen hadn't made any effort whatsoever to hide Gillian: if anything, she'd been disappointed that it had taken me so long to follow Jocelyn's note.

Dugan was playing his own game. Every piece we found made me more certain of that. I just didn't know what that game *was* quite yet, and until I found out, none of us were safe.

"Gillian," I said carefully, "I'll get Miranda for you, and I won't come around unless you ask me to. You have my word on that. But I need you to think very hard. Apart from the woman you can't remember clearly, was there *anyone* strange around the residence hall in the last few weeks? Anyone at all who didn't feel like they should be there?" If she'd seen him . . .

Gillian began to shake her head. Then she stopped, and asked, very carefully, "Did I really see Jocelyn in that place with all the fog?"

"I'm sorry, honey, but yes, you did."

"That *bitch*." Her expression hardened. "She was always trying to suck up to me, you know? Always asking questions about you, like you were some kind of hero, and not a deadbeat who ran out on her family when things got hard."

I didn't say anything. Gillian was part of Faerie now. She would learn the truth soon enough, and this wasn't the time to try arguing the case for my redemption. "She said something similar when I came looking for you," I said. "Why do you ask?"

"Because she had a new boyfriend hanging around this past week. I mostly noticed because he was really cute, and I thought he might make a good model for our life drawing class."

My heart was beating too fast again, and I felt faintly sick to my stomach. If Simon had done this after all—if this was my fault for waking him up—I was going to crawl into my bed and never come out. "What did he look like?"

"Cute," she repeated. "Um. Tall, skinny, sort of a hipster vibe, like he did all his shopping at vintage stores for 'the aesthetic,' but didn't really know how things went together. He pulled it off, it just didn't look *right*, you know?"

"I do." It was a complaint I had made myself, more than once, when talking about purebloods who didn't have much contact with the human world. Fashions changed too quickly for them to keep up. Some, like the Torquills, settled on an era and stayed there, dressing well but noticeably dated. Others tried to keep up, with mixed results. "Was there anything else about him that caught your attention? His hair, maybe?"

"Oh, yeah, his hair!"

My heart sank.

"It was this amazing shade of emerald green. I really wish I'd been able to get the number of his stylist. My hair's so dark that I can't ever seem to find anyone who can get it to take color." Gillian hesitated before plucking at a strand of her hair, relaxing a little when she saw that it was still black.

She'd be unhappy when the gray started to appear. But that was a problem for later. "The man you saw with Jocelyn was tall and pretty and had green hair. Are you sure?"

"I notice a good dye job."

"Okay." I took a step back. "I need to go. I'll ask the Luidaeg to let Miranda come up here and talk to you. Please don't try to take the sealskin off. I'm not sure you could, yet, but if you did, I think you'd probably die. Please promise me you won't."

Gillian blinked slowly. Then she nodded. "I won't."

"Good." I turned to go.

"Mom?"

I froze.

"I . . . I'm really angry with you. For leaving, and for being something you never told us about. It impacted my life and I never knew why, and that's not fair. I don't know if I'm ever going to stop being angry with you. But thank you. For coming to save me when I needed you. I don't know what I am now, and I don't know if I'm going to like being it, but I know I didn't want to be dead. So thank you."

I looked over my shoulder, managing the sliver of a smile. "You're welcome."

Then I looked away from her and walked, as quickly as I could, to the chamber door. When I let myself out, the Luidaeg was there, waiting for me on the stairs. Her eyes were still sea-glass green, and she was making no effort to conceal her concern. She was just looking at me. Silent, patient as the tide, and equally as eternal.

I burst into tears and threw myself at her, trusting, just this once, that she would catch me. She was my friend and my family, and she would catch me.

And she did. She wrapped her arms around me, murmuring a language I didn't understand against the curve of my ear, surrounding me in the smell of the sea. I cried into her shoulder until I felt like all the tears had been wrung out of me, leaving me dry as a bone. Only then did I pull away, to find her still looking at me gravely.

"Better?" she asked.

"Yes." I wiped my cheeks with the back of my hand. "Tybalt?"

"Here. Waiting for you. He's anxious, but he never tried to go up the stairs. He knew you needed time." A smile ghosted across her lips. "You should keep this one. He has a good sense of boundaries."

"I'm planning to," I said. "Gillian needs her mother. She needs Janet."

If my statement surprised the Luidaeg, she didn't show it. She merely nodded and said, "I'll fetch her. They can stay here a little longer, while you finish doing what needs to be done, and then I'll take them to see Liz, so she can start explaining what it is to be a Selkie in this world. I'd do it, but I don't understand them the way I do the Roane, and the bargain has yet to be brought due."

"It's been more than a year."

"I know." She looked at me coolly, a thread of black wiggling across her right iris like a worm working its way deeper into the flesh of an apple. "You're almost ready, and by giving them a year, I forced them to start putting their house in order. They should be prepared to pay by now. They should be grateful I gave them as long as I did. Now. Your cat is waiting for you, and I suppose I should go rouse the traitor, shouldn't I?"

"Yeah," I said. Impulsively, I grabbed her hands and squeezed them hard before starting down the stairs, leaving her on the landing, leaving my daughter in the tower room. The world had changed. The world wasn't changing back.

What remained now was trying, in whatever way we could, to set things right.

TWENTY-ONE

I STEPPED INTO THE LIVING ROOM to find Tybalt perched on the absolute edge of the couch. He knew most of the filth was illusionary, but that didn't stop him from being disgusted by it. The carpet squelched under my feet. He turned toward the sound, relief washing over his face as he stood in a single, fluid motion and began walking toward me.

He waited to speak until there was barely a foot between us. "Your daughter . . . ? I know she lives, but at what consequence?"

"She's a Selkie now," I said, and laughed, tears and hysteria both threatening to break through the sound. "Can you believe it? A Selkie." A small, terrible corner of my mind reminded me that if Connor and I had stayed together—if his family hadn't come between us, if I hadn't chosen Cliff over chasing after him—Gillian might not find any of this strange. She could have grown up knowing that one day a skin would come to her.

But she wouldn't have been Gillian. Even if I'd given an imagined daughter with Connor the same name, she would have been a different little girl, growing up in a different world. Hindsight is twenty-twenty. That doesn't mean the things it shows are always better.

"Perhaps she'll be the first of them the sea witch can allow herself to love, as she didn't choose it," said Tybalt, and lightly touched my cheek. There were still shadows in his eyes. The damage my mother had done wasn't the kind that could be washed away in a single adventure, no matter how hard we both wished it could be. "I am glad she is well."

"Me, too." I took a breath, letting myself relax into his touch. It was only for an instant. That instant was enough to make me feel like the rest of this might be something we could survive. "Quentin and May?"

"Awake, and in Muir Woods with the rest. The pretender Queen has been arrested for her crimes, as has her changeling accomplice. The Baobhan Sith who tried so industriously to devour you has been given a nice new robe and a place to stay while she adjusts to the decade." He frowned. "I recognize she was a victim here, acting entirely on instinct, but still it galls me that someone with such a taste for your blood should be kept as a guest in your monarch's halls."

"Just don't invite her to stay at the Court of Cats, and we'll be fine," I said. I took a step back, less to create distance between us than to make it clear that the moment had passed: we needed to move. "She'll digest my blood and lose the ability to disguise herself as me soon enough. Are you feeling up to carrying me to Muir Woods?"

"You live, my love, and your daughter lives as well. Right now, I could carry you to Mag Mell if you asked it of me."

"I'd rather you didn't. Having the groom collapse from exhaustion before the wedding does no one any good."

The look of surprise on his face would have been amusing, if I hadn't known he was, on some level, worried that I wouldn't want to marry him when he was anything less than perfect. I put my hand on his arm.

"Come on, Tybalt," I said. "Take me to see the queen."

"It would be an honor." He swept his arm under my legs, lifting me into the bridal carry that seemed to be the easiest method for conveying me through the dark, and stepped into the shadows before I could say anything else.

Most of the time, I preferred to run the Shadow Roads by his side, when we had to use them at all. It was easier on him if he wasn't trying to carry me while he ran, and I preferred to know that I was at least technically in command of my own fate, even if a simple fall could mean being lost forever in the darkness. He could see. As long as I could hold my breath, he'd be able to backtrack and find me. Or at least I liked to tell myself that, since it made the whole experience a little less upsetting.

Ice formed on my skin and in my hair, gluing my eyelashes together, caking on my lips. I snuggled closer to the comforting warmth of him—the man I had chosen, who had chosen me; the man I was going to marry, no matter what the world threw at us— and tried to focus on the sound of my heartbeat, which thundered in my ears.

I should have put the pieces together sooner. I blamed my concern for Gillian and my rapid blood loss. Even for me, it had been a hard day. But the false Queen didn't have many allies left. Rhys— I wasn't sure of the title for a deposed puppet King, other than maybe "loser"—was still asleep in Silences. Her guards worked for Arden now, who treated them better than her nameless predecessor ever had. Her courtiers were scattered throughout the Kingdom, retreating to their home demesnes in disgrace. It would be a long time before any of them could gather enough influence to win themselves a place in Arden's Court. Really, Dugan had been the only logical person to have been helping her.

The signs had been there all along. The scent of cinnamon and cardamom; the involvement of secrets that were meant to be kept at the royal level, which his time with the false Queen could easily have revealed to him. Gillian's description of Jocelyn's supposed "boyfriend" only confirmed what I'd already been virtually certain of.

"Almost there," murmured Tybalt. "Brace yourself."

I did, snuggling closer still, and held my breath as we burst into the warmth and light of the mortal world. The scent of redwood trees assailed my nose; we were in Muir Woods. I took a deep, whooping breath, cracking the ice on my lashes as I opened my eyes and beheld a strip of late afternoon sky framed by redwood branches. In the distance, someone laughed, a warm, comfortable sound. The sound of tourists in a state park, who saw no reason to worry that anything might go wrong.

I blinked. There was no weight of a don't-look-here on us, and I hadn't been wearing a human disguise while I was at the Luidaeg's. "Oh. Shit."

Tybalt blinked in turn. "What do you—"

"Illusions. *Now.*" His eyes widened in understanding. He didn't quite drop me, but he put me down with more vigor than was technically necessary, both of us grabbing for the strands of shadow running through the air. His gestures were more refined than mine, elegance in motion, like he was dancing. I, on the other hand, was a magical wrecking ball, grabbing at whatever power I could find and yanking it down over myself like a shroud.

The smell of cut grass and bloody copper rose around me, twining and tangling with Tybalt's musk and pennyroyal. A verbal spell would have risked attracting too much attention: the sun wasn't down yet, and while the path where we'd emerged wasn't on the main thoroughfare—thank Oberon—Muir Woods is a popular tourist attraction. The place was probably thronging with mortals who'd have serious questions about why our ears were pointy and our eyes were funny if they happened to come around the right corner at the wrong time.

The spell crashed down to cover me, knocking more ice loose without chasing the freeze from my skin. I gasped, as much from the strain of casting a silent illusion as from the shock of its presence. Shaking the shreds of magic from my fingers, I turned to Tybalt.

He was watching me with what I could only call fond indulgence, his features blunted and his eyes dimmed by the illusion he had designed for himself. "I will never tire of watching you do that," he said.

"What? Panic?"

"No. Enchant yourself in my presence. It is a small vulnerability, but as it's what our circumstances allow to us, I shall accept it for the gift that it is."

"Weirdo," I said fondly. Then I sobered. "We need to get to Arden."

"Indeed, we do," he said, and offered me his arm. Together, newly apparently human and no more out of place than any other tourists, we stepped out of our isolated corner of the park and started down the path toward the far wall.

Muir Woods is what so much of California used to be: lush and green and virtually untouched by human hands. The paths that wind through the ancient trees have been designed to be as unobtrusive as possible, allowing humans to see the redwoods without necessarily damaging them. When a sequoia falls, downed by time or rot or forest fire, it's allowed to stay where it lands, slowly rotting and feeding the living world around it. Everything smells of good green growth, of running water, of the sea. If the entire mortal world were like Muir Woods, we would have no need for the Summerlands. We could just stay in the trees and be happy.

Of course, the entire mortal world *was* like Muir Woods, once, and look where that got us.

The humans I'd been worried about running into strolled along the main boardwalk, some in couples, others in family groups. A small child pointed in awe at a bright yellow banana slug while a park employee watched unobtrusively off to one side, ready to step in if the animal were put into danger. A woman pushed an older man in a wheelchair. Several people pushed strollers. The only unusual thing about me and Tybalt was the way I had my hand resting on the crook of his elbow, rather than tucked into his hand.

I could fix that. Loving a man several hundred years older than me has meant adjusting to a little anachronism in my daily life, but he still knew how to hold hands. I tangled my fingers into his, and he glanced at me, first startled, then smiling.

"Your hands are cold," he said.

"Yours aren't."

"The shadows have learned to love me in their own way. I apologize that they may never feel so very generous toward you."

"I'm not Cait Sidhe." I shrugged as we walked, as fast as we dared, toward the wooden stairway that would take us to the path toward Arden's knowe. "I'm okay with the idea that the shadows won't love me, as long as you do."

"The act that could strip away my love for you has never yet been committed, nor is its commission a thing I have any cause to fear," said Tybalt.

I snorted. "Now you sound like a romance novel again."

"Sometimes it is the best of ways to sound." He glanced at me. "My recent absence has been . . . "

"I know why you were gone."

"Your knowing doesn't change the fact that I've allowed precious hours to slip by without spending them in your company. I am ashamed of how afraid I am. Still, I am afraid. It seems I should have shaken this concern away, as I have shaken off so many others, but . . ." He shook his head. "My people. Raj. You. It has been a very long time since I feared failure for any reason other than the damage to my pride. Your mother showed me that I am vulnerable, and I did not much care for the feeling."

I squeezed his hand. It was the only thing I could think of. I did wonder whether our appearance in the mortal areas of the park, where we would have to walk quietly and without attracting attention to reach the knowe, had been due to the road ending or due to some possibly subconscious desire on his part. Sometimes it seemed like our lives never left much room for serious conversation that didn't include someone trying to kill one or both of us. Quentin and May were awake; Gillian was safe with the Luidaeg; the false Queen was in custody. This might be the last real pause we got.

But Dugan was still out there somewhere, and Arden didn't know about him, or how dangerous he could potentially be. We could walk slowly enough to be overlooked. We could steal a few minutes to talk about our feelings. Anything more than that was for later, when our enemies had, however temporarily, been subdued.

Sometimes I really miss the days when my biggest concern was whether I'd be able to afford fresh milk for my coffee. Then I consider the gains I've made—my home, my friends, my weird and chosen family—and I remember that the past is only rosy because of all the blood that was in my eyes.

"Something will have to change," he said softly. "I fear it might be me."

We had reached the stairway. We climbed it in silence, still holding onto each other, until we reached the hard-packed dirt trail that ran around the edge of the basin containing the tallest of the trees. Side by side, we walked to the base of an ancient redwood whose roots had carved a series of natural "steps" out of the hill. After that, it was a simple matter to wait for the mortals around us to pass. Once we had a clear moment, I dropped Tybalt's hand and started upward.

As we walked, I wove my hands in and out of the air, tugging on it, teasing it, making it clear who I was and where I was going. Some knowes, like Shadowed Hills, require complicated rituals to find the door. Others, like the false Queen's fading home, only need people to make it past the repulsion charms and general environmental unpleasantness. Arden's knowe split the difference. She didn't want humans wandering in unwittingly—obviously— but she also didn't want to be inaccessible to her subjects. There were several approaches, some easier than others, and all of them required a certain series of gestures or syllables to tell the boundary that you were approaching with the queen's own approval.

The world shivered around me, illusions adjusting themselves to show me what I needed to see. Glowing mushrooms appeared among the underbrush, and some of the banana slugs took on an even brighter glow, the consequence of eating both the fungus and the leaves dusted with pixie sweat. A flock of pixies swirled by overhead, wings chiming. I waved at them.

Behind me, Tybalt snorted. "I fully expect a battalion of them to appear at our wedding to hold your veil and demand shares of the cake."

"It's cute how you think I'm going to wear a veil," I countered, and he laughed.

That sound was more encouraging than anything else could have been. It put a spring into my step, and in what felt like no time at all, I was cresting the top of the hill. The doors to Arden's knowe were standing open, flanked as always by two guards in her livery— including, I was pleased to see, Lowri.

She waved when she saw us. I hurried across the clearing, waiting until I was close enough to talk to her without shouting before I said, "Tell me everything you can about Dugan Harrow."

Lowri blinked. "I . . . what?"

"Dugan. Do you remember him?"

"Um, yes." Her chuckle was dark and caustic. "I don't know about you, but I tend to remember it when people try to stab my liege with iron knives. I was part of the band that arrested him and threw him into Her Maj—I mean, the false Queen's dungeons."

It occurred to me that I had no idea what the group noun for a bunch of guards was supposed to be. That had never seemed like a hole in my education before. "Was he one of you?"

"Him? No." Her nose wrinkled. "The false Queen didn't want her guards to be knighted. Most nobles, they can't *wait* to show off this bunch of wee titled fools they have carrying swords in their name, but her? She was happier if we served only at her convenience and couldn't go running off somewhere else even if we'd wanted to. He was never the type who wanted to get his hands dirty, but even if he had been, she'd never have allowed him to join the guard, because he came with a title. He'd never have needed her enough for her to believe his loyalty."

"What was his title?"

"Baron." She wrinkled her nose. "No land, no manners, but oh, he could lord it over us like anything—begging your pardon." The last was a hasty addition as she finally seemed to register that the man behind me, in his jeans and plain green shirt, was Tybalt. "Not everyone with a title is terrible. Please don't assume I meant yourself."

"I try never to assume anything other than praise is a reference to me," he said mildly. "It prevents misunderstandings."

I rolled my eyes but kept my focus on Lowri. "So he was a jerk."

"Even before he tried to stab his mistress in the heart, yes." Her expression turned wistful. "Far be it from me to wish harm on another, but we might be in a better place, as a kingdom, if certain events had occurred more quickly."

"I don't know," I said. "If she'd died without an heir, High King Sollys would have been forced to name someone else to take the throne, and we would never have gone looking for Arden. Awful as it was getting here, I sort of feel like this may be the best-case scenario."

Lowri's cheeks flushed. "I hadn't considered that."

"It's okay. What happened to Dugan? After he was arrested, where did he go?"

"The false Queen had him taken to the dungeons. You remember the dungeons."

Did I ever. They'd been so soaked with iron that both Tybalt and I had come close to dying. He'd actually reached the point of begging me to shift my own blood away from fae, so I would be human enough to survive. He'd expected me to do it, too, to take an escape hatch that was only available to me and leave him to die. We'd gotten out. We'd been lucky, and we'd had access to magic that Dugan, as a pureblooded Daoine Sidhe, could never have accessed.

"Yes," I said tightly.

"She left him there for a fortnight. Long enough for him to soften, for him to start listening to what she had to say." Lowri shook her head, expression clearly disapproving. "It's torture. You know, the humans forbid it? They have more laws than we do, and half of them are about not hurting each other. Sometimes, I think they have the right of it."

"You're not alone in that," I said. "What happened after a fortnight?"

"She let him go." Her expression twisted, going from simple disapproval to outright disgust. "He tries to kill her in full view of the Court, and she lets him go. Like it was nothing to be concerned over; like it was *ordinary*. He's a Baron, yes, but he's not from a powerful family, he doesn't stand at the center of some great web of obligations. She let him go because she wanted to, and not because she had to."

"That's about what I thought," I said.

Iron is poison, in every sense of the word. It kills magic. It burns fae flesh. It distorts the world, making time slow down and then dissolve like sugar into water, so that everything that happens has been happening forever, and anything that came before the iron seems inconsequential. I don't have many regrets about the increasingly fae balance of my blood, but my increased sensitivity to iron is one of them. The mortal world can be *dangerous* for someone who can't stand the touch of a major metal.

After almost two weeks in the false Queen's dungeon, Dugan would have been willing to agree to anything if it meant he got to walk away. *Anything*. Like eternal loyalty, the kind that can be compelled with an oath or geas. The fact that he was helping her now made sense when I saw it in that light. And if she'd somehow convinced him she had a shot at retaking her throne . . .

Too many people had seen him attack her. The only way he was ever going to rise to true power was if she was the one to lift him up. As a Daoine Sidhe, encouraged by his Firstborn to ambition, the temptation to try must have been too great to resist.

"Where's Arden?" I asked.

To her credit, Lowri barely flinched at my use of the queen's proper name. "In the salon with your people. I believe they're waiting for you."

"Got it. It was good to see you."

"Open roads," she replied.

"Kind fires," I said, and walked through the doors with Tybalt by my side. This was almost over. I just had to hang onto that. This was almost over, and soon, we would be going home.

We walked along the length of the receiving hall. The guards flanking the door motioned to the left when they saw us coming, and we reoriented ourselves, walking on. It seemed to work like that every time we came to a juncture: we would approach and a servant or guard or courtier would appear, quietly indicating the way we were supposed to go. It was all running smoothly, and I thought I could see Cassandra's hand in the elegance of it all.

As Arden's seneschal, Madden was in charge of serving as her good right hand when she couldn't be present to make a decision pertaining to her kingdom. As chatelaine, Cassandra filled the same role on a smaller level, making decisions for the household. Cassandra had grown up in a house full of younger siblings, all attending human schools during the day while their parents were asleep. She was very good at organizing things as unobtrusively as possible.

One silent turn at a time, we came to a part of the knowe I had never seen before, a wide, sunny parlor with panes of colored glass in place of a ceiling and bright carnival sheeting on the walls. Couches and loveseats dotted the floor, and household servants moved between them, offering sandwiches and cups of lemonade.

Arden and Nolan were seated together on one loveseat, while Madden sat in an oversized armchair, his feet tucked up under his body. May sprawled across an entire loveseat by herself. Quentin, who had been stalking a serving girl with a tray of sandwiches around the edges of the room, broke into a broad smile when he saw us.

"Toby!" He trotted in my direction as the others were still turning to look our way. His smile faded as he got closer. "Gillian. Is she . . . ?" He stopped.

The room seemed to be holding its breath. May, especially, looked like she was on the verge of breaking down in tears. I shook my head in quick negation.

"No," I said. "No, she isn't dead, no, she isn't dying, no, she isn't going to spend the next hundred years asleep. She's . . . she's going to have some adjusting to do, but she's going to live."

Even the servants had stopped moving as they listened to me. I kept my focus on Quentin and May, my family, the ones who needed to know this.

"She's going to be a part of Faerie now," I said.

There was a crash. We all turned. One of the serving men had dropped his silver tray, scattering drinks and appetizers across the floor at his own feet. He was staring at us, eyes wide and angry. His hair was brown, his eyes were green, and there was a glimmer in the air around him, like he was hiding something, like he was hiding himself.

I smelled cinnamon.

"I *knew* you were a liar," snarled the servant. "I knew you just didn't want to fix what you had broken. Well, you're going to fix it now." He lunged, grabbing Nolan around the neck and flinging a small vial at the floor in the same motion. Then he stepped backward, jerking the prince into the hole that had opened in the air, and was gone.

TWENTY-TWO

ARDEN SCREAMED. I IGNORED HER, rushing for the place where the hole had been and breathing in as deeply as I could. The smell of Dugan's magic—cinnamon and cardamom and how had I been so *stupid*, how had I not considered that he was a courtier born and bred, fully capable of observing protocol well enough to conceal himself in a noble court—swirled around me. I breathed it in, searching for the shallower scents beneath it.

"What are you *doing*?" Arden's hands grasped my shoulders, spinning me around to face her. "Who was that man? Where is my *brother*?"

"His name is Dugan Harrow, he works for the false Queen, and I'm trying to figure that out," I snapped. "Tybalt?"

"Yes," he said, and took Arden's arm, pulling her back. She stared at him in shock. His smile was quick and cool. "I think you'll find, my lady, that as a King, my title is equal to yours, and so while my setting hands upon you is rude, it is not a proper insult, nor have you the authority to punish me. Let her work. She does her best under pressure."

He was still talking as I turned back to the place where Dugan had opened the door, doing my best to tune out everything but the thin scent of cinnamon and cardamom. The false Queen and her people had always been fond of borrowed magic. They had cultivated it, hoarded it for occasions just like this one. I had always wondered where they could get so many tricks—it wasn't like the Luidaeg had been brewing for them—but things had started making a lot more sense when I discovered that Eira had sponsored the false Queen to the throne. Eira was the mother of the Daoine Sidhe. Of course, she could bottle blood and magic together. There was nothing to stop her.

Reaching under the cinnamon and cardamom scent of Dugan's magic, I strained until I caught the faint hint of some sweet, half-familiar fruit. "It's not pear," I said aloud. "It's close, but it's . . . quince." I breathed in again. "Juniper sap and quince. Whose magic is he using?"

Arden gasped. I looked over my shoulder. She was staring at me, looking even more stricken than she had before.

"My father," she whispered. "That was his."

"Your father's magic? Are you sure?"

The look she gave me could have split stone. "I'll never forget my father's magic."

"Okay. That's . . . that's good. He's been dead a long time. There shouldn't be anything confusing his trail." I turned back to the trailhead, such as it was, and inhaled again. "Arden, what are you willing to do to find your brother?"

"Anything." There was no pride in the word, no anger, only the earnest need of a woman who was no longer willing to be alone in the world.

I understood the feeling. "Good," I said, drawing the silver knife from my belt. There was a gasp that ran around the room as the real servants realized I'd drawn a weapon in the presence of the queen. Madden even growled, the sound cut off quickly as he realized what I was doing.

It was good that they were loyal to her. It was good that they were willing to get angry on her behalf. She was still going to bleed for me. Maybe this was what it was like for the Luidaeg: she always knew why she was asking me to let her hurt me, but she didn't have the vocabulary, or the time, to explain it all.

I held out my free hand. Arden slipped hers into it, and I ran the edge of my knife across the back of her knuckles, cutting as shallowly as I could. Blood welled up fast and red and all too tempting. There was a time when I couldn't stand the sight of blood. Now I couldn't take my eyes off of it.

"Think about your magic," I said, and raised her hand to my mouth.

Her blood tasted like her magic, like blackberries and the trees, and her memories slammed down on me like a hammer.

He's gone Nolan is gone he's gone and she isn't going to be able to get him back, I'm going to lose him forever and it's all my fault, I should never have—

I broke the connection with a gasp, blinking away the red-tinged veil of Arden's fear. "Arden, please. Think about using your powers. I know it's hard to stop focusing on your brother, but this is how we follow him." I could feel the trail and she couldn't. She had the magic to follow it, and I didn't. By borrowing her magic, I could bridge that gap and try to bring him home.

"I'm trying," she said in a small voice.

"Try harder," I said, and took another mouthful of her blood.

This time, the memories slammed down harder, carrying with them the effervescent joy of using her magic freely after spending so many years concealing herself from Faerie. Images of Arden opening a gate to get from one side of the gardens to the other, all for the sheer delight of doing so, danced across my mind. I grasped them as firmly as I could, swallowed one more time, and *reached*.

An archway appeared in the air, smelling of her magic but also of mine, a blend that should never have been possible. My head spun, pain lancing through the space behind my ear in quiet warning that even when I was using someone else's blood to set the shape, it was my own power fueling the enchantment. That was fine. That was *dandy*. I didn't need to stay on my feet for much longer.

"Quentin, watch her," I snapped, and jumped through the arch, the knife still in my hand.

I landed heavily in the mists of the false Queen's receiving hall, my legs buckling beneath me. I turned my fall into a roll, remaining low to the ground, where the mist would have a chance of concealing me. Something moved near me in the gray. I didn't think. I just turned and swung, aiming for what should have been the center mass of anything human-sized.

Tybalt grabbed my wrist, stopping me before I could actually stab him, and raised an eyebrow in silent question. I grimaced and shook my head. If he didn't want to be stabbed, my expression said, he shouldn't sneak up on me in foggy rooms full of potential enemies.

It said something about how well he had learned to read me that after a beat he sighed silently and let my wrist go, ceding the point.

"I know you're there," called Dugan. "Did you *really* think I wouldn't hear you? You walk like an ox, Sir Daye. It's a wonder you're allowed shoes, with as loudly as those mortal feet of yours seem determined to tread."

I remained low to the floor, even going so far as to press one finger to my lips and signal Tybalt to silence. He gave me a disgusted look. I shrugged. Yes, he'd been taking care of himself for longer than I'd been alive, but this was my show, and I needed him to take his cues from me.

"You lied, Sir Daye. You told my mistress you couldn't restore what wasn't there anymore, and then you turned around and gave your daughter her eternity back. Naughty girl." He sounded almost amused. "My lady doesn't care for liars, but there's still a chance for you. Anything can be forgiven, if you're useful enough. If you're willing to work for the privilege of returning to her good graces."

Dugan paused, clearly expecting me to say something. When I didn't, he stomped his foot, making an audible huffing noise.

"You've done your best to ruin everything, but you're just one woman, and you can't be everywhere. You'll always be vulnerable. You'll always be a target. Why not give it up now and join the winning side?"

He was somewhere ahead and to the right. I began crawling through the fog, keeping my head low. Tybalt matched me, moving with a little less grace than I was accustomed to seeing from him. The sight woke a strange, out-of-place ache in my chest. He should have been in cat form by now, slinking along on four legs and ready to pounce. Instead, thanks to my mother, he was stuck like this. It wasn't fair.

This wasn't the time to dwell on past damage. I rolled closer, grabbing the collar of Tybalt's shirt and pulling him as close as I could. Pressing my lips to the curve of his ear, I breathed, "Get the others," before shoving him away.

He looked at me for a moment with wide, startled eyes. Then he nodded, silently agreeing to follow my commands, and rolled into the fog, disappearing from view. That must have been enough to qualify as a shadow. The scent of pennyroyal and musk rose, and I knew he was gone, leaving me alone with Dugan.

Dugan Harrow: Daoine Sidhe. Blood magic, illusions, and

whatever tricks he might have borrowed from the false Queen. His loyalties were first to power, second to himself, and third, ridiculous as it seemed, to her. He was still trying to be loyal enough to earn her good regard. What he thought that would get him was less clear—although with Daoine Sidhe, it's so often about what gets them a path to the throne. The false Queen had no spouse, no heirs. Her relationship with the deposed King Rhys of Silences was the closest I'd ever seen her come to caring about another person. Staying close to her, letting her think he was sorry for his attempted betrayal and had become faithful . . . that might seem like a way to one day add "king" to his list of titles.

It was never going to happen. Even if he killed Nolan, Arden would still have her throne, and there was no way she was going to name her brother's murderer as her heir. But if he didn't understand the legitimacy of her claim, or if he somehow believed that he could override the decision of the High King and put his own nameless figurehead back in charge . . .

When all else fails, count on the arrogance and corruption of the purebloods. It almost always carries the day. And if there's one thing I've learned about the arrogant, it's that they really, *really* don't like to be mocked.

Tybalt was on the Shadow Roads. He'd be halfway to Muir Woods by now, where he could gather forces to help him help me. Quentin and May, at minimum; Arden and her guards. I only needed to stall for a few minutes.

I pushed myself away from the floor and rose out of the fog, holding my knife in front of me as I turned to sneer in what I guessed was the correct direction. Dugan was standing at the base of the dais, Nolan kneeling in front of him with his hands bound behind his back. Nolan's eyes were bright with rage. I guess no amount of temporal displacement will make kidnapping seem like anything but what it is.

There were no illusions on him now. Dugan Harrow stood before me revealed, from his dark green hair to the planes of his cheekbones, sharp enough to slice glass. He was handsome, there was no denying that. He was also horrible, rendered such by his own choices, which had stripped every scrap of decency away.

It was hard not to look at him and see exactly what Eira had been hoping to make of her descendants. He was here for power. Everything else was secondary.

"There you are," said Dugan, sounding satisfied. He held up a rowan sheath, large enough to hold a blade slightly longer than mine. "Do you know what this is?"

"I have a bunch of guesses, but most of them aren't fit for polite company, and the prince, at least, is polite." I nodded toward Nolan. "Your Grace. Has he hurt you? I'll cut off his ears if he's hurt you."

"Nothing I can't recover from, Sir Daye," said Nolan. "A few bruises. A few scrapes. Some wounded pride. Have you come to take me home?"

"That's the plan."

Dugan scowled. "Your attention should remain on me, if you want your precious prince to remain among the living."

I lifted one eyebrow. "Why? Are you going to threaten stabbings? I love it when people threaten stabbings in front of witnesses. That makes it self-defense and means I'm much less likely to get in trouble for kicking the crap out of you."

Dugan curled his lip and removed the sheath from his blade. My blood went cold. Nolan paled, leaning away as much as his current position would allow. Naturally. He was closer to the knife. He could probably feel the poison rolling off of it.

Dugan smirked, holding the iron knife up to make sure I saw every cold, pitted inch of it. It looked almost raw, like it had barely been touched by the blacksmith's hammer. Every inch of me wanted to turn and run, fae instincts kicking in at the worst possible time. "Not so cocky now, are you, Sir Daye? Are you ready to negotiate? Or shall I slit this poor princeling's throat, and remove one more pretender from the line of the throne?"

"Iron knives are sort of your thing, aren't they, Dugan? Where do you keep *getting* them?" My own knife was silver. It would be no match for his. Silver is a soft metal. Fae metalworkers imbue it with layer upon layer of enchantment, making it harder and more capable of holding an edge. Iron would cancel all that out. If his knife hit mine, it would slice through the silverwork like it was butter, and I would be unarmed.

Since I wasn't willing to attack him with what I had, I already functionally was.

"Only a fool refuses to use every tool available to him," said Dugan.

"A fool, or a man with honor," I snapped. Muir Woods wasn't

that far from the false Queen's knowe. Tybalt had to be there by now. He had to be explaining. Arden wouldn't want to wait—she would want to rush out and rescue her brother as quickly as possible—but Madden would be cautioning her to move slowly, to consider her actions. I didn't know how much longer I would need to stall. "Does iron make you feel important? Does it make you feel big? I don't care how much rowan you put between yourself and that shit, it's going to eat you alive. You're playing with fire. Or enriched uranium, assuming you even know what that is."

Dugan sneered. "You talk a good game for someone who's staying out of range. Not everyone has that privilege." He grabbed Nolan by the hair, pulling his head back and laying the iron knife across his neck.

Nolan cried out in shock and pain, a look of raw embarrassment washing across his face on the heels of the sound. He didn't want to show how badly this was hurting him. I wanted to tell him I didn't think less of him for this, that no one could stay silent in the presence of iron, but I didn't dare. Anything I said to him, instead of to Dugan, could make things even worse.

"What do you want, Dugan?" I asked, taking a step forward. "Do you want me? I'll come to you if you'll let him go."

"What, so that your little friends can sweep in here and rescue you? No deal, Daye. I've heard the stories of what you've been up to since the last time we met. I could stab you a hundred times and you'd still get up and walk away. You're no hostage, especially not against your own good behavior."

"So what do you *want*?"

He looked at me, utterly arrogant and utterly calm, and said, "I want you to restore my lady to her former glory. Return to the pretender's knowe, release the true Queen from her prison, and pour the sea back into her veins. When she stands before me, whole and hale, I'll let this little liar go. He and his sister can live a happy life in exile, far from our shores. I have my lady's word that no harm will come to them if they agree to go."

"I can't do that, Dugan."

He pressed the knife harder against Nolan's skin. Nolan whimpered. Eyes gleaming, Dugan looked at me and spat, "You can, and you will. If you can restore your whelp, you can restore a *queen*."

"I didn't restore Gillian!"

I hadn't intended to shout, but the words came out of me barely shy of a scream, echoing through the room, stunning both of us into silence. Nolan held himself rigidly still, clearly struggling to maintain the dignity of a prince while under the touch of the iron knife. I kept my focus on Dugan, hoping he would believe me, knowing that he probably wouldn't. Believing me would mean admitting that he had failed—that this, all of this, had been for nothing.

"I'm not the one who saved her," I said, more softly. "I'm not the reason she's alive. The Luidaeg did that. She wrapped my daughter in a Selkie skin to keep her alive. They can be bonded to humans, if there's someone to start the process. Gillian isn't human anymore, but it's not because I was clever, or quick, or powerful. It's because the sea witch took pity on her. I can't save your queen. I never could."

Dugan stared at me. "You're lying."

"I'm not. You have an iron knife to the throat of the Crown Prince in the Mists. If I could do what you wanted, I would do it. If I thought I could lie convincingly enough to make you let him go, I'd do that, too. Why would I stand here saying exactly what you don't want to hear if it wasn't the absolute truth? Let Nolan go. If you run, no one but me can follow you. Release him and run, and as long as you don't come back to the Mists, I won't help anyone track you down. I'll swear on the root and the branch and in Oberon's name, if that's what you need."

Dugan wavered, the knife in his hand dipping slightly—enough that I could see the blisters forming on Nolan's throat. I swallowed hard, trying to keep my chin up, so neither of them would see how frightened I was.

"You're lying," Dugan said again, with less confidence this time.

"I'm not," I said again. "If you let him go, you have my word, I won't be the one who brings you back here."

Nolan closed his eyes.

"You have no right to decide who is and is not fit to rule," said Dugan. "You're just a changeling. You have no authority to do what you've done."

"And your queen is just a pawn, chosen by a woman who wanted to destroy everything King Gilad had built," I said. "We could play this game all day. Your time is running out. Go. Once the others get here, this deal is off the table."

Dugan opened his mouth to reply and froze as the scent of

blackberry flowers and redwood bark wafted through the air. I didn't turn. I didn't need to.

"Time's up," I said, as Arden and her guard moved into position behind me. "Put down the knife, Dugan."

He looked at me with the calm, resigned face of a man who knew he had nowhere left to go. He had backed himself into a corner. The odds were good that he was going to die here—or worse. The Law only forbade killing, after all. The purebloods were capable of doing so much worse than that, especially when they felt their families were threatened.

"No," he said calmly. "I don't think so."

He pulled the knife away from Nolan's throat and shoved him forward into the fog. I had time for an instant of relief before I realized what he was going to do.

"*No!*" I shouted, dropping my knife and breaking into a run, bolting toward him as fast as I could.

I wasn't fast enough to stop him from slashing the knife across his throat. He fell, the blade still clutched in one hand, and I fell with him, clasping my hands over the wound to keep his blood as contained as possible. It wasn't enough to stop that same blood from drenching me before I got it damped down, spattering on my cheek and lips.

So much blood. I closed my eyes and licked my lips, tuning out the sound of the people rushing all around me. The red haze of his memories descended, showing him creeping up on Gillian's car with a potion in his hand, ready to attack and abduct her. I fought my way past it and saw him carrying her clothing into the walled courtyard that belonged to Janet. There was no sense of familiarity there. He was baiting a trap he had been told about by the false Queen, a secret from her reign that she was trying to use against me.

I licked my lips again, struggling not to laugh bitterly. He hadn't known. He hadn't *known*. He hadn't known Janet was my grandmother, or that she was masquerading as Gillian's stepmother, or that she owned the courtyard at all. She hadn't told him, if she even knew. It had been a secret his Queen had been instructed to kccp at all costs, and he'd been trying to use it to hurt me. Not stop me, no. Kennis, the courtyard, none of it had been intended to *stop* me. It was all a game, meant to slow me down and weaken my resolve, to panic me so much that when I finally found my daughter, I'd be willing to do whatever they asked in order to save her.

Save her. We had saved her. She wasn't the same anymore, would never be the same again, but she had a future now, even if it wasn't the one she had wanted. Dugan was captive. Nolan was safe. The false Queen was in Arden's custody, with no allies left to help her get away and come after us again. It was over.

It was over.

Someone pushed me aside, Arden's people rushing to do what they could to save a man who shouldn't be saved. I dropped to my knees in the mist, put my hands over my face, and cried. Tybalt knelt beside me, putting his arms around me, but that didn't change anything. The tears kept coming. He buried his face against my hair, and he cried, too, and everything was over, and everything was different, and I no longer knew what safety was, or what "home" looked like.

I didn't know anything at all.

TWENTY-THREE

"ARE YOU SURE you want to do this?" May looked across the street to the house where Cliff and his family lived. My family, too. My daughter; my grandmother. Root and branch, had things always been this *complicated*?

Yes. I'd just been better at pretending they weren't.

"The Luidaeg says she'll be able to let Gillian and Janet come home in a few more hours," I said. "I need to start getting our story straight." Because that was the problem, now, wasn't it? Gillian hadn't made the Changeling's Choice, not really, and she wasn't a changeling anymore. She was a Selkie. She had the right to play fairy bride, and if she wanted to change the rules to make it a game of fairy daughter instead, she was allowed.

Cliff could never know what had happened to her. Like his lover and his wife before her, his daughter was going to spend the rest of her life lying to him, and one day, the three of us would stand at his funeral, draped in illusions that made us look older and other than we were.

"Do you want me to go in with you?"

"Who would you tell him you were? He knows I don't have a sister." I offered her a shaky smile. "Besides, I need to get this done so that Tybalt and I can get back to Muir Woods. Wouldn't want to miss the train to Silences."

May looked unsure. "I guess."

The false Queen of the Mists was definitely *not* asleep in the Kingdom of Silences, no matter what Walther's family said: she was in one of the towers at Arden's knowe, awake and under constant guard. Lowri had been placed in charge of that particular duty, since there was no concern she had any lingering loyalty to her former mistress. Really, the only concern with Lowri was that she might "accidentally" spit in the false Queen's food. Once I was done talking to Cliff, I was going to be accompanying Madden, Tybalt, and a small detachment of Arden's guard to Silences to find out what they actually had in their custody.

Big fun. Bigger fun, by far, than talking to the man I had once believed was the love of my life about why his daughter wasn't home yet.

I took a deep breath. "Here goes nothing," I said, and started across the street.

The doorbell was still echoing when Cliff jerked the door open, panting slightly with the exertion of running from wherever he'd been in the house. His eyes flicked from me to the empty spaces on either side of me, and his face fell, fleeting hope dying before it could bloom.

"October," he said.

There was a time when he spoke my name with love. There was a time when he looked at me like I was the most beautiful woman in the world, like I was Helen of Troy and he was ready to launch a thousand ships to save me. That time passed years ago, and as I looked at him now, all I felt was pity, and a little regret that he no longer believed he could lean on me.

Then again, when I'd needed saving, he hadn't exactly broken out the fleet. "Breathe, Cliff," I said. "Gillian is *fine*."

He froze. Every inch of him seemed to have been transformed suddenly to stone, leaving him incapable of anything beyond standing there and staring at me. "How . . ." he managed. Then: "Where. Where is she? October, where is my daughter?"

"*Our* daughter is with Miranda, receiving a medical examination from my Uncle Sylvester's private physician." I looked at him steadily. "She's fine. She's alive, she's relatively unhurt, and she should be home soon."

Cliff sagged in the doorway. My "rich Uncle Sylvester" has always been a constant in our relationship: a man of unclear relationship to my family whose money was virtually infinite, and who allowed me to do odd jobs for cash when necessary. The fact that

Uncle Sylvester had never paid my bills or put me through college had seemed more like tough love than cruelty, back then, and even now, Cliff was clearly prepared to believe I had access to a man who could afford his own private doctor.

That was good, because I was lying. Janet and Gillian were still with the Luidaeg, and it was going to be quite some time before I felt like reintroducing my daughter to my liege, much less to the members of his Court. Sylvester *was* family to me, in his sideways Faerie way. I wasn't ready for Gillian to look at him and judge what she didn't understand.

"She's all right," he said, words slow and heavy and deliberate.

I nodded. "She's all right."

"She's . . . you're sure?" He stepped forward, grabbing me by the shoulders, his large hands engulfing the curve of my upper arms. "You're not lying to me to soften the blow. You're sure she's all right."

"She's *fine*," I said firmly. "Shaken, yes, absolutely. She had a real scare, and she's probably going to need some time to recover. I've turned everything I found over to the authorities, and I'm sure they're going to find the jerks who thought this would be a funny prank."

Cliff's expression hardened. "Prank," he echoed.

"They'd heard about her being kidnapped while she was still in high school." This was the hard part. This was the part that cast blame, however deserved, on me.

If not for Jocelyn's burning need to be a part of Faerie—with blaming Gillian for not wanting to be—there would have been nothing for Dugan and the false Queen to grasp hold of. They might still have been able to get to Gillian, but with Janet's anti-fae charms everywhere, it would have been a lot harder, and a lot sloppier. The dangerous side of hero worship is stalking and obsession, and I had been Jocelyn's hero.

Jocelyn and Dugan were awaiting trial. They could make things easier on themselves if they testified against the false Queen. Dugan might never speak again, thanks to the damage he'd done to his throat, but he was alive despite the damage, and he could still hold a pen. If he was willing to tell everything, he might see the moonlight through something other than bars in a century or two.

"How . . . ?"

"I guess Gillian talked about it in one of her classes." I shrugged, trying to express my ignorance of all things collegiate. Bridget would absolutely back up any claim that Gillian had mentioned the kidnapping, and Gillian had already been advised to agree that anything Professor Ames said was the full and absolute truth. "Some of her classmates thought it would be funny to pretend to be a terrorist group, kidnap her, and tell her that they were the same people who'd taken her before. They told her they were going to make her disappear so completely that her family would never know what had happened to her. She'd just be gone. So you can understand if she's a little messed up right now, given our history."

That last part had been my addition to the script. I no longer wanted Cliff to take me back—hadn't wanted that for a long time— but that didn't change the fact that what he'd done when I'd returned from the pond had been shitty, and small-minded, and wrong. He needed to accept that. Especially now that Gillian was going to, of necessity, start falling deeper into my world. Even if I still wasn't a major part of her life, she was going to be a part of my world forever.

His cheeks reddened. "Are you saying that this is somehow my fault? That she wouldn't have been kidnapped if I'd taken you back?"

"No." I kept my eyes on his, trying to ignore the way his hands were tightening on my shoulders. I was suddenly glad Tybalt was at the house bringing Raj up to speed and making sandwiches, which he swore upon his honor he was going to make me eat. "This is the fault of the kids who kidnapped her. This is the fault of people not getting the full story. You asked me to find her. You came into my home and all but accused me of being the one who'd taken her. I found her. She's with her stepmother now. She's coming back to you. Do you think you could maybe, *maybe* find it in your goddamn heart to finally forgive me for something I never intended to do? Because every time you have come to me for help, I've given it to you. Every time you've asked me for *anything*, I've been there for you."

I took a step back, twisting my shoulders and breaking free of his grasp. Cliff stood frozen where he was, hands grasping empty air. For a moment, I almost felt sorry for him. He was only human. He was just the man who had grown out of the boy who'd seen a

girl on the sidewalk, two runaways looking for a better life together. It wasn't his fault I'd never been able to give him what he
needed.

And it wasn't my fault, either.

"Let go of whatever it is you think I did to you, Cliff," I said,
voice soft. "I am the mother of your child. I am the woman who
used to love you, who never meant to leave you, and I am asking
you, let it all go. This is how you pay me for finding her. You stop
fighting to keep me out of her life."

"Miranda—"

"Miranda and I have already talked." That was stretching the
situation a bit. She had confessed, and I had listened. Still, she
wasn't going to argue when he said I needed to be allowed to hang
around. There was a lot left that we needed to discuss.

He hesitated before saying, finally, "What if I don't want you
around?"

"What if I don't care?" I looked at him flatly. "I broke your
heart. I get that. I genuinely do. I didn't mean to, but you're never
going to believe me, so whatever. You broke my heart when you
slammed the door in my face. There's a lot of bad blood between
us, and from where I'm standing, you put most of it there. I didn't
have a choice. You did. Gillian needs to know me. I am her mother.
No matter how much she wants to judge me or dislike me, she
needs to know where I come from, because that's part of where she
comes from, too."

Cliff glared for a long moment before he sagged, becoming nothing more than an aging mortal man whose world stubbornly refused to stop changing. He looked away. "You say I had a choice. I
didn't. You left me alone with a little girl who wouldn't stop asking
about you. Where you were, why you'd gone, why you weren't coming back. Whether it was her fault you'd left us. I let you go because
I had to, if I wanted to save her. Yeah, I slammed the door when
you tried to come back. I had finally found a way to make things
good again. You wanted to change all that. I couldn't risk it."

"So we both made mistakes. I let myself get lost. You refused to
let me be found. Our daughter's coming home, Cliff. Be glad of
that and stop trying to turn me into your enemy. It's never going to
happen. Her existence means it can't."

"I . . ." He took a deep breath as he looked back to me. "Yeah.
Okay. I'll try."

"That's all I wanted." I stepped backward, preparing to go.

"Toby?"

"Yes?"

"Thank you."

I smiled. Really and sincerely smiled. "Not a problem. Maybe next time ask before you accuse, though, okay? She'll be home soon." I turned and walked away.

The sound of the door closing behind me felt like an ending. A good one.

May looked up from her phone when she heard me coming. "Well?"

"We're okay." I opened the car door. "How's Jazz?"

"Mad that we didn't call her before we went chasing a kidnapper around Berkeley, but glad Gilly is safe." May got in on the passenger side. "She says bring home donuts."

"We're going to Portland to find out how a deposed, elf-shot monarch was able to escape, make it back to the Mists, and arrange for the kidnapping and attempted murder of my daughter, and I'm supposed to stop for donuts?"

May shrugged. "I guess she figures you'll have some free time."

I had to laugh at that. It felt good to be relaxed enough that I *could*. Things were beginning to knit themselves back together. Maybe they'd even make it all the way back to normal.

We drove back to the house singing along to the radio with off-key gusto, and nobody tried to kill either of us, and no one wound up drenched in blood, and it was awesome. Technically, I spend more time not being threatened than I do running for my life. It's just that the moments of extreme stress and peril tend to loom large on my mental landscape.

May looked over at me as I pulled into our driveway. "You going to talk to him? Now that he's halfway out of his head? Because he's just going to crawl back in and refuse to come out if you give him a chance."

"You don't know that."

"I know you." She tapped her temple. "I remember. I know a *lot* of people the way I know you. Healing takes more time than anyone wants to think it will, and it takes more than one big gesture to be finished. He needs time. He needs you even more."

"I have a plan," I said.

She looked at me. "In Portland?"

"In Portland."

"Good." She got out of the car, leaving that as the final word of our conversation. I shook my head, smiling as I followed her to the kitchen.

Tybalt was putting the finishing touches on what looked like an entire picnic basket full of sandwiches when we walked in. We both stopped in the doorway, blinking. May spoke first.

"Are we feeding the neighbors?" she asked. "Because I don't even *know* most of the neighbors. There's that old guy two doors down who always glares at me like I kicked his dog. I don't want to give him a sandwich. I'd be happy to give it to the dog, though."

"You may have two," said Tybalt imperiously. "The rest are for October."

I lifted an eyebrow. "How much do you think I'm going to *eat*?"

"As many sandwiches as you can fit in your mouth during the drive," he said. "I will feed you if you have concerns about keeping your hands on the wheel. I would *prefer* to feed you, as *I* have concerns about your keeping your hands on the wheel. But you have lost substantially more blood today than I care for, and as you seem unwilling to take steps to replace it, it seems I must step up and do a husband's duty even before we are wed."

"If you decide you don't want him, I'll take him," said May.

"You don't like men," I said.

"I can make an exception," she insisted. "Jazz will understand."

Tybalt laughed, and somehow that was the best sound the world had ever known. It was good enough to lure me across the kitchen to his side, where I had time to kiss him before he handed me the first sandwich.

"Roast beef and cheese, with blackcurrant jam," he said. "Eat, or I shall stop catering the menu to your idiosyncratic taste in cuisine and start feeding you like a sensible person."

"Yes, sir," I said, and took a bite of sandwich. It tasted better than it had any right to, and my stomach growled in sudden approving hunger. Tybalt was right about one thing: I had done too much bleeding and not enough eating. I swallowed. "Where's Raj?"

"Returned to the Court of Cats to hold sway in my absence." Tybalt's smile faded. "He has been doing an excellent job of late, picking up the things I had allowed to fall away. I do not deserve such a fine heir."

"I think he'd disagree with you." Raj's father had led a

brief-lived rebellion against Tybalt, and he'd died for his crimes. It would have been easy—even understandable—for Tybalt to cast Raj out in the aftermath of Samson's actions. Instead, he had taken the boy even more concretely as his own. They weren't related. They were unquestionably family.

"Perhaps so." He turned to offer a shallow bow to May. "Milady Fetch. The return of my betrothed is appreciated, but we must to Muir Woods if I'm to convince her to sleep any time in the near future."

"That's fine," said May. She snagged two sandwiches from the tray, waving one of them amiably before she added, "You kids have fun out there," and retreated to the hall.

Tybalt picked up the tray.

"You can't be serious," I said.

"Oh, but I am. If I can convince you to eat every one of these, I will go to my grave a happy man."

I blinked. "No."

"Not in the near future, little fish. But someday, when all my lives are spent, I can still count myself a fortunate man, for I will have spent the greatest number of them with you." He kissed my temple as he walked by me to the door.

I sighed. "You have *got* to stop defusing every conversation you don't want to have by talking like something out of a Regency romance."

Tybalt opened his mouth, like he was going to say something. Then he stopped, ducked his head, and said, "I'm sorry. I don't know what else to do. I don't know how else to *be*. I am . . . I'm frightened, October. I'm trying to find my way out of the darkness I've been cast into, and levity seems a safe enough shield. I would not cause you harm if I had any choice."

It should have been funny, him standing there with a tray of sandwiches, apologizing to me. It wasn't. I shook my head as I looked at him. "You're not hurting me, and you're not going to hurt me by needing help, okay? I didn't agree to marry you because I wanted everything to be moonlight and roses forever. I can't even manage that on my own, much less with another person. I love you. I want to help you. The only way you're going to hurt me is by refusing to let me at least try."

He took a deep, shaky breath, holding it for a moment before he let it out and said, "Then let us hurry out, so that we may return home, together, and begin."

"Sounds good to me," I said. We left the kitchen, and I had hope. Maeve help me, I had hope.

TWENTY-FOUR

ARDEN GLARED AT MADDEN as she said, "All right. Call me when you're ready to come home and I'll open a gate for you. Which wouldn't be necessary if I were allowed to go to Portland *with* you."

"And you'd be able to come with me if you weren't the Queen in the Mists, but you are, and that means you can't just pop into neighboring kingdoms without it being a big diplomatic *thing*," said Madden patiently. This conversation had clearly been ongoing since the decision to go to Silences had been finalized. "Stay here, Ardy. Take care of your Court, keep an eye on Nolan, and trust us to act in your best interests. That's why you have us, right? So that you don't have to do everything by yourself."

Arden looked like she was going to argue again. That was my cue. I cleared my throat, pulling everyone's attention onto me.

"Look," I said. "I don't know about the rest of you, but I have things I want to do tonight. Important things, like eating a lot of ice cream and crying. So can we do this? Please?"

"Preferably before the sea witch decides what her demands are regarding the traitor," said Tybalt. We all looked at him. He shook his head. "Time is inconsequential when you've experienced as much of it as she has. Gillian is a Selkie child now, and hence of her protectorate. This false Queen harmed one of the Luidaeg's own. The sea witch is likely to demand recompense, and I would prefer we had all the slices of the story before that occurred."

There was a chilling thought, and one that hadn't previously occurred to me. "We move," I said firmly. "Arden, please. The gate?"

"Wish I'd known becoming queen would involve playing taxi service quite this often," she grumbled, and swept her hand through the air. The portal opened, glittering the purple-black of her hair around the edges as it showed us a view of the royal knowe of Silences. The colors were unusual, showing how much of a strain it was for her to transport us this far.

I offered her an appreciative nod and stepped through, Tybalt and Quentin close beside me. Madden, as the actual representative of Arden's Court, brought up the rear. Given how concerned he was about Arden presenting a diplomatic beartrap through her mere presence, I wondered what he'd think of Quentin's true rank. It was probably best if he never found out, all things considered. It would just hurt the poor man's head.

Unlike Arden's knowe, which had been built in and among the redwoods like a Tolkien calendar painting, the knowe of Silences was a solid, imposing structure of stone, freestanding, constructed to stand up to anything the weather might have to throw at it. Heavy walls surrounded a central courtyard paved in red brick, dominated by a golden fountain of dancing Tylwyth Teg and stags, surrounded by a filigree of yarrow branches.

The formerly featureless walls were a riot of night-blooming flowers and alchemically useful herbs, as if we had stepped into a garden in the process of breaking free of its gardeners. Walking toward us across the brick was Queen Siwan, her arms outspread in welcome. The resemblance to Walther was unmistakable, from her golden hair to the vivid blue of her eyes, and I spared a moment to wish he could have come with us. It would have been nice for him to see his family.

"Lord Madden," she said. "Sir Daye. Your Majesty." She finished with a low curtsy to Tybalt, not acknowledging Quentin at all. He didn't seem to take offense, and neither did I. Some courtesies are basically scripted. "You honor me with your visit. I am so very sorry for its necessity."

"So are we," I said, before she could get much deeper into the formalities. "I'm sure Madden wants to hear you make every apology under the sun, and I bet if he looks real deep in his bag of tricks, he'll find a few apologies he can say we need to make to you. Is Marlis available? She can show us to the place where the false

Queen is supposedly sleeping, and I can verify whether or not
it's her."

Siwan showed no surprise at my bluntness. Instead, she smiled,
and said, "That sounds fine, and as expected. Marlis is waiting for
you inside."

"Excellent," I said, and bowed shallowly before taking my leave,
Tybalt and Quentin making slightly more formal bows before they
hurried to keep up with me. Siwan might dress more like a steam-
punk pinup model than most of the queens I've known—she's a
practicing alchemist, and it turns out leather is better for playing
with fire and caustic chemicals than, say, diaphanous spider-silk
draperies would be—but she's still a queen, and queens like their
formalities. If I wasn't imagining things, Madden had even looked
relieved at the idea that I was going to go do something else. I have
a tendency to mess up formal events.

As promised, Marlis was waiting just inside the entrance, a
smirk on her face. Like Siwan and Walther, she had blonde hair
and blue eyes, although hers were both a few shades darker, and
she was dressed a little more formally than was standard for her
brother or her aunt. "Did you leave or get sent away?" she asked.

"Left," I said.

"I owe Walther a dozen of Aunt Ceres' lavender cookies," she
said, and started walking, leaving the rest of us to catch up. She
glanced at me as I pulled up level with her. "You really think we
lost her?"

"It's that or there are two of her running around," I said. "I'm
not trying to get you in trouble, but I'd really prefer the option that
means we're only dealing with one of her."

"I can see that," she said. "How's Walther?"

"Good. We keep him busy."

"That's good." She nodded thoughtfully. "That's real good."

I didn't say anything.

The Kingdom of Silences—which overlapped with much of the
human state of Oregon—had been one of the false Queen's victims, back when her claim to the throne had been unchallenged.
She hadn't liked the way our neighbors to the north had been questioning her policies, and so she had declared war, crushing their
forces, deposing their royal family, and placing her own puppet
king upon the throne. Walther had been the only member of the

extended royal family to escape from the new regime. He had created a new life for himself, finding his own way in the world, while Marlis had been compelled by loyalty potions brewed by her own hand to serve the man who had destroyed her family.

On some level, I think she'd believed that if they ever got their kingdom back, Walther would come home and stay, the way things had been when they were children. He hadn't. He was never going to. To her credit, she was sad but not angry. Sometimes we have to let our loved ones make their own way in the world.

Tylwyth Teg can fly, using bundles of yarrow twigs as their brooms. As a consequence, the knowe was built something like the staid interior echo of a roller coaster, all high arches and winding stairs. Marlis led us patiently along them all, keeping her feet firmly on the ground until we reached the dungeon.

A single sniff of the air told me what had happened.

"We need to tell Arden to triple the guard on Dugan's cell," I said, walking toward the "Queen" who slept on her cold stone bier. The closer I got to her, the stronger the smell of cinnamon and cardamom became. How had no one seen this but me? It was so *obvious*. "Until we have him locked behind so many wards that the air goes stiff, we can't be sure he's still there."

But no. It was obvious to me because I could smell the framework of the spell, pick the traces of it out of the air, where they should have been safely hidden. Dugan had done his weaving with every expectation that it would pass muster for years. He hadn't been counting on a literal bloodhound.

She looked perfect. She looked peaceful. She looked exactly the way she had the last time I'd been here. Whoever Queen Siwan had on staff assigned to dusting the sleepers was clearly taking their job seriously. I looked at her impassively for a long moment before pulling the knife from my belt, ramming it into her sternum, and slicing her open to the navel.

Marlis gasped. Even Quentin made a small, startled sound of dismay. Only Tybalt was silent as the false Queen's "skin" parted and allowed a cascade of dead leaves and dried flowers to come pouring out. I shoved my hand into the wickerwork of her rib cage, feeling around for her heart. It wasn't there. My fingers brushed against a smooth, hard rind. I grabbed it, ripping out the small pumpkin that had been nestled where her heart should have been.

"Dugan made the change in late October," I said, holding it up for Marlis to see. "Did you have any members of the household staff quit abruptly around Samhain?"

"A kitchen boy quit right after the holiday," she said, sounding horrified.

"He probably spent a month weaving this damn thing, then used blood magic to make it feel like her and flower magic to make it look like her, and we fell for it." I dropped the pumpkin to the bier and turned toward King Rhys. There was no shroud of magic hanging over him. He felt like a sleeping man under an elf-shot enchantment.

Still, better safe than sorry. I picked up his hand and poked him in the thumb with the point of my knife, only slightly disappointed when he started to bleed and I didn't need to do any further testing.

"He's real," I said. "Dugan only freed his Queen."

"But *why*?" asked Marlis.

"Maybe to curry favor with the woman who originally put her on the throne; maybe because he wanted revenge; maybe she had him under some sort of geas; or maybe it was because he's just an asshole," I said. "It's hard to know for sure. We'll find out when he goes to trial, assuming he wants to get out of the pit Arden's going to throw him into."

I almost hoped he refused to tell us. I'd like another excuse to lock him up.

"On behalf of Silences, I wish to extend our genuine regret and horror—" Marlis began.

I cut her off. "You didn't do this. We knew he was a threat, and we didn't verify that he'd been taken care of. All our firebirds are coming home to roost. If you really want to make this up to me, though, while your queen works on making it up to mine, you'll do me one big favor."

Marlis paused. "What?" she asked warily.

Smart girl. "We have business in Portland," I said, indicating myself and my two companions. "It shouldn't take all that long, but it would be a big help if you didn't go running to tell Siwan that we've crossed over into the mortal world. Not just yet."

"Are you plotting insurrection?"

"It's a fair question, given my hobbies, but no. Quentin needs to pick up some donuts for my Fetch, while Tybalt and I need to go catch up with an old friend. We'd just like a little time to ourselves, that's all."

Marlis considered a moment before she nodded. "I won't lie to her, but as long as she doesn't summon me or inquire as to your whereabouts, I can give you what you'd consider 'a little time.' Try not to take more than that."

"We appreciate it," I said, and turned to offer my arm to Tybalt. "Shall we?"

"Indeed," he said solemnly. He looped his arm through mine. Quentin grabbed the back of my belt. Tybalt stepped forward, into the dark and the cold, and the basement was gone, replaced by the endless stretch of the Shadow Roads.

Running from a healthy knowe into the nearest open point of its connecting city is a simple thing, even with Quentin hanging onto me for dear life. We'd been in the shadows for what felt like no time at all before we emerged, stepping into the light of a Portland alley, shielded from the street by the slope of the walls around us. We let go of each other in order to draw human disguises over ourselves, Tybalt and I going for the quick and easy versions, while Quentin detailed his as much as he always did.

"Showoff," I said fondly, ruffling his hair. I had to reach up to do it. I was never going to get used to that. "Meet us here in an hour?"

"If the line at Voodoo is moving at all, sure," he said.

"Okay. How about if you're not here in an hour, we'll come meet you there?"

Quentin nodded. "That sounds good. Um. Good luck with . . . whatever it is you're here to talk about."

I glanced at Tybalt, then looked back to Quentin and smiled encouragingly. "It'll be fine. We'll see you soon."

Tybalt slipped his arm back into mine and tugged me from the alley before Quentin could say anything else. The sidewalk was largely empty at this time of day, and the pavement was slippery with the remains of the latest snowfall. I shivered and stepped closer.

"Remind me never to leave California," I said. "I don't think I could handle the weather."

"My little fainting flower," said Tybalt, and pressed a kiss to my temple as we walked around the corner, two people in love and going for a stroll. We stopped halfway down the block, in front of a small shop with pictures of the X-Men and Avengers displayed in the window. Inside, a bored-looking woman stood behind the counter with her chin propped in her hand, ignoring the world around her as she read a graphic novel.

Tybalt took a deep breath. I squeezed his arm.

"You can do this," I said. "You *need* to do this. Not just for me—I'm not quite that selfish—but for yourself."

"I know," he said. "Knowing makes it no simpler."

"I believe in you."

His smile was enough to warm up the day. "Knowing *that* makes everything simpler," he said, and reached for the door.

The bell above it jingled when we walked through. The woman at the counter—Susie, if I was remembering correctly—didn't so much as lift her head. Customers were apparently a complication for someone else to deal with, while she was paid to stand at the counter and keep up on her comics. I had to respect her single-minded dedication to her craft. I'd never seen her doing anything but reading, and it didn't look like that was going to change today.

We walked past her, heading for the back of the store, where a half-open door marked the entry to the office. Tybalt started to raise his hand, but paused, looking unsure of the gesture.

Screw that. We were here to make things better. I refused to let us be scared off now. Before I could think better of it, I raised my own hand and knocked lightly, calling, "Joe? You here?"

"As I live and breathe—October?" The door swung open, revealing a trim, silver-haired man who appeared to be somewhere in his mid- to late-sixties. That was a lie. His hair was really silver, and his eyes were really blue, but everything else about him, from the wrinkles around his eyes to the rounded tops of his ears, was an illusion.

Well, maybe not everything. The smile was real enough. Joe liked me, with good reason. I was, after all, the reason his daughters were immortal now.

"Hi, Joe," I said.

Tybalt cleared his throat. "You have my sincere apologies for this unplanned visit, but we find ourselves—that is to say, I find myself—in need of aid, and I had hoped you might provide it."

Joe's smile faded, replaced by concern. "Of course," he said. "Whatever either of you needs, forever. My debt to you will never be repaid."

"Can we go someplace where we can speak privately?" I asked.

Joe nodded. "Absolutely." He raised his voice, calling, "Susie, please don't let the store burn down in the next hour."

A grunt from the counter was the only response. He smiled, fond and frustrated.

"Believe it or not, she's my best employee. She just has a sixth sense about who's here as a customer and who's here on personal business. I'm fairly sure she thinks I belong to some sort of naturalist commune. If you don't mind . . . ?" He pushed the door open wider, indicating that we should step inside.

I grasped Tybalt's hand firmly. This time, when Joe shut the door and turned off the light, there was nothing surprising about the transition. I took a deep breath, and then we were falling, moving through the shadows and emerging on the other side in the warmth of what looked like an old carpet warehouse, complete with rolled-up rugs propped against the walls. Cats lounged on every available surface, only a few of them bothering to crack open their eyes and look at us.

Joe's human disguise dissolved, scenting the air with the tang of heavy paper and pine. I took a breath and let my own illusions go. Tybalt did the same. It's not strictly rude to go disguised in the presence of a monarch, but it can be interpreted that way, and we needed him to want to help us.

Not that there was much chance he wouldn't. Joe—Jolgeir, King of the Court of Whispering Cats—looked anxiously between us, and said, "We would have prepared a banquet, had we known you were coming. Something befitting the service you have done for us. Please don't think me rude—"

"I never would," I said hurriedly. "How is Libby? How are the girls?"

This time his smile was all the lovelier for not being hidden behind a false veil of humanity. "Wonderful," he said. "They're absolutely . . . they're wonderful."

"And your Ginevra," said Tybalt. His voice was strained. I wondered whether Joe could hear it as clearly as I could. "Has she shown the strength you hoped for?"

"Hoped for, feared—they're so similar, don't you think?" Joe looked at Tybalt carefully. "My middle daughter is a Princess of Cats, thanks to the efforts of your lady knight. She'll challenge me when the time comes, when her mother grows old enough that I need to step aside to tend her and keep her comfortable. We've already discussed it as a family. You have an heir of your own, don't you? I know I promised you anything my Kingdom had to offer, but my Gin . . . "

I bit my tongue. This was Tybalt's request to make, not mine.

"I do not want to take her," said Tybalt. His voice was surprisingly steady, but his grip on my hand could have shattered bone. "Only to borrow her for a bit. I am . . . I am not well, old friend. I am very far from well. And I wondered if it would be a terrible inconvenience to you if Ginevra were to visit my Court for a time. With her consent, of course, and with the understanding that I am not asking her to follow me to the throne. I have an heir. That he is not ready, now, is no fault of his. I would not have him challenge me before his time. It would be an unkindness to all involved, from both of us down to the very least of my subjects. But I am . . . "

He stopped then, releasing his grip on my hand. Letting go of him was one of the hardest things I've ever done. I did it all the same.

Tybalt raked his hands through his hair, taking a deep breath before he said, "I am not a fit King for my people, for I cannot sleep, and cannot eat, and cannot breathe with the weight of what has been done to me. I am no fit love for my lady, for I cannot bear to be apart from her for fear that we will never come together again, nor can I bear to be with her for fear that what has happened once may come again. My Court suffers. My heart suffers. I desire—no. I *need* time to salve my wounds, and I cannot do it as I am. So I ask you, as has long been allowed by wiser councils than our own, to send your Ginevra to stand regent over Raj while I recover. She will not take the throne, but she will sit before it and hear my Court as they ask for succor. When I am well, she may stand aside and return my place to me, that I might resume my rule."

"Rand . . ." Joe hesitated. "Few are those who appoint a regent and then reclaim what once was theirs. You may no longer be seen a fit King when this is done."

"I never asked to be seen a fit King in the first place," said Tybalt. "I hold my crown in trust for a boy who is not yet ready. He will be, soon enough, and when I retake what is currently mine, it will be only to wipe my fingerprints from the throne and hand it over to one whose heart and house are less divided. It was already my intent to step aside and allow Raj his rule. This merely hastens his ascent. But I say again, he is not ready. Will you allow Ginevra to come to us, to guide him?"

"She is untrained herself," said Joe. "Until recently, none expected her to have the power to hold the position of heir."

Still, I said nothing. Until recently, Ginevra had been a changeling, as had her two sisters. Of the three of them, she was the only one to display the magical strength necessary to be considered a Princess of Cats.

Tybalt looked relieved. "That, old friend, is something I can assist with. No one will challenge a sitting regent who has held the position for less than seven years, who has a kitten in their keeping. It isn't done. Let her hold the throne of Dreaming Cats while Raj continues his education, and let it be her education as well, until I am ready to reclaim my place and boost him toward his birthright. I will send her back to you better prepared to follow you, and perhaps better inclined to listen, after a time spent in my company."

Joe hesitated. "It's her decision," he said finally. "She gets to be the one who says yes or no. I won't trade my daughter, even for a little while, without her full consent."

"I wouldn't ask you to," said Tybalt, and smiled. Openly, honestly, smiled. I felt some of the tightness around my heart give way.

Ginevra would take Tybalt's place while he dealt with the business of getting better. Putting a Queen of Cats in charge of holding the throne wouldn't require him to relocate or the Court to move, not the way putting a new King in that position would, and he would be able to help her without actually being in charge of her. He would be able to recover.

We still had problems to deal with. Gillian needed to adjust to her new life; Janet and I needed to talk about what it meant for her to be my grandmother, and immortal, and *human*. Jocelyn's fury proved that I needed to start finding a way to rebuild Home, or something like it, for the changelings of the Mists. But we were alive. We could have those conversations and make those choices, and that was more than I'd expected at the beginning of all this. We were alive, and we were moving forward. As Tybalt slipped his hand back into mine, that felt less like a good thing and more like everything.

It felt like a miracle. So I held on tight, and I didn't let go. You don't get many miracles in this world. When one comes along, it's up to us to watch over them. It's up to us to watch them unfold.

I stood in the Court of Cats, listening to two Kings discuss how to move forward, and I knew I was witnessing a miracle, and I knew that one way or another, we were going to be okay.

We really were.

Read on for
a brand-new novella
by Seanan McGuire:

SUFFER A SEA-CHANGE

Nothing of him that doth fade,
But doth suffer a sea-change,
Into something rich and strange . . .
　　　　　　　　　—William Shakespeare, *The Tempest*

ONE

December 22, 2013

I COULD HEAR, but I couldn't move, not even enough to open my eyes and see what was happening. Toby—my mother—was screaming, and some terrible beast was roaring, and I was burning up, I was on *fire*; somehow everything I was and everything I knew how to be had been transformed into living flame, eating me up, eating me alive, and I wanted to be screaming, too, and I couldn't, because screaming meant motion, and I was never going to move again.

Someone scooped me into their arms, where I dangled limp and lifeless, a girl made of nothing but the agony of flame. The someone ran, taking great, loping strides that bounced me like a rag doll, ending with a great leap that echoed through my entire body. Then hands were touching my cheeks, my throat, searching for a pulse, and I knew—even with my eyes closed—that they belonged to my mother.

I'm sorry, I thought, and *this is your fault,* I thought, and both those things were true.

"What did you do?" Toby asked, voice low and tight and filled with despair. "What did you *do?*"

"Either you're a liar and you'll restore your child, proving you can do the same for me, or the human brat will die, as she should have done the moment she rejected our world," said the woman who'd been holding me here, that terrible, beautiful nightmare of a woman. "I have done nothing wrong."

I had never wanted to argue with someone so much in my life.

"What about me?" Jocelyn demanded. "You promised me."

Scratch that. I could argue with her *after* I punched Jocelyn in the throat about six or seven times.

"Hush," said the woman. "You'll get your turn."

I think I'm dying, I thought. *Why is everyone standing around talking?* This was the sort of thing that needed to be handled in a hospital, not in a foggy house of horrors.

There was a sharp new pain as Toby pulled the arrow out of my shoulder. Any hope that my paralysis had been the result of a nerve cluster being somehow compressed died as my body continued to burn around me, unresponsive. I was going to die here. There was no other way.

Toby moaned. "Walther," she said. Who the hell was Walther? "The cure."

"She won't make it as far as Berkeley," said a man's voice.

Why Berkeley? I thought. *And who the hell is Walther?*

The man continued: "I could carry her, but not alive, Toby, I'm not fast enough."

I'm right here, I thought, and burned in silence.

There was a pause before Toby whispered, "The Luidaeg, and then Dianda. Save my child and then save my ass. *Go.*"

The man didn't speak again. He ran instead, gathering me closer so that I didn't bounce around as much. Then he jumped for some reason, and suddenly, I couldn't breathe. There was no air. I was choking, I was suffocating—

I was freezing. The cold was intense enough to beat back some of the flames under my skin, and the asphyxia was making my thoughts blurry and slow, almost comforting. He had probably carried me into a hallway or something, and this was just the next step in the progression of the poison that was killing me. I liked it better than the burning.

It almost felt like ice was forming on my face and hair, but that was silly. No poison is strong enough to turn a person into an ice machine. *Tactile hallucinations*, I thought, and it was an almost pleasant idea. None of this was happening. Maybe none of this had ever been happening, and I was home in my bed with food poisoning or something, my body fighting to purge the toxins. Maybe I was going to be okay.

I knew I wasn't going to be okay. But if a girl can't lie to herself when she's dying, when *can* she lie to herself?

I was on the verge of losing consciousness completely when the cold snapped around us, replaced by ordinary air. The fire in my veins surged back to full strength, and I would have screamed if I could have.

"Hold fast, kitten, please hold fast, or I fear your mother will chase you to a place I cannot follow," said the man, voice low and tight and urgent. He walked now, instead of running, and when he moved me enough to free one hand to hammer on an unseen door, it was like driving knives of fire into my flesh.

The door opened, and an unfamiliar voice demanded, "What is it n—is that *Gillian*?" Annoyance became horror in an instant. "Dad's eyes, get her in here. Now!"

There was no arguing with that voice. Even I wanted to obey, and I couldn't so much as open my own eyes. At least I was breathing again. My body still remembered how to do that, although it felt like it wasn't going to remember for much longer. Everything hurt. The worst thing about it was that I couldn't even scream.

The man carrying me stepped up, and a wave of nausea washed over me, distracting even through the burn. A door slammed.

"This way," said the woman.

Another door opened, and I was being placed on a soft, flat surface. A bed, maybe, or a couch. It didn't matter. The cold flash was over, and I was burning alive again, all illusionary ice gone.

"What happened?"

"The false Queen elf-shot her." He sounded like he wanted to rip the woman—the "false Queen," whatever that meant—apart with his bare hands. "She's dying."

"I can see *that*," snapped the woman. "Did she do anything else? Did Gillian drink anything, or eat anything, or make any promises?"

"Not that I saw. Can you save her? Please, can you save her? I'll pay—"

"You'll pay nothing, cat. Don't you have someplace else to be?"

"I—"

"Go. Save her. I'll stay here and try to do the same."

There was a sound like a door slamming, and then a hand was touching my cheek, cool-skinned and rough with calluses. I heard a sigh.

"You're still alive. I don't know whether that's a mercy or not, but I know my sister's work, and I'll wager you can hear me. It hurts more when you can hear yourself dying. What am I going to do with you?"

I didn't answer. I couldn't.

"The cure won't work without fae blood to latch onto, and your mother is good at what she does. Better than she understands. She pulled every drop of her family line out of you; even the prophecies can't claim you now. She was trying to save you."

I was trying to breathe.

The woman sighed and snapped her fingers, and I . . . stopped breathing. The fire in my veins froze solid, becoming nothingness. I couldn't feel my body anymore. I was a mind without a shell, trapped in a dark infinity of my own making, and I knew that if this was eternity, I was screwed. I couldn't see, couldn't move, couldn't do anything but think, and given enough time, even that would fade, replaced by silently screaming until the end of time.

"I can't keep you like this for long," said the woman. "You're too human. My magic will shred you, no matter how well-intentioned it happens to be. But we don't need long. We just need long *enough*."

There was a rustle as she rose and stepped away, and I heard her shout, "Poppy!"

"Coming!" Another woman, this one with a voice like bells that rang and chimed and clattered in every syllable. It should have been impossible for a person to sound like a carillon, but she managed it, somehow.

I wished I knew what she looked like. I wished I knew what either of them looked like, or where I was, or how I could be alive when I wasn't breathing. I wished I knew how any of this was happening. I wanted to believe it was a fever dream, bad sushi burning its way through my system, but that pretty fiction was getting harder and harder to hold onto. *Everything* was getting harder to hold onto. It was like my thoughts were unraveling at the seams, and that was terrifying, because they were all that I had left, and it was an incredible relief, because when they ended, so would I.

"Poppy, this is Gillian."

The second woman gasped. "You mean October's girl? The missing girl? That girl?"

"Yes. She's been elf-shot. I've stopped her clock, but it won't last long. I want you to go to the basement. There are chests there. Find me the chest made of driftwood and pearls. Bring it here as fast as you can."

"I will, but . . . wouldn't you find it faster? Should I wait here with her while you go?"

"No. She could still die. What I've done . . . it's not enough to fight my sister's spellcraft off forever. And I'm not sure that chest has the answer. I just want it here in case I decide to try."

"All right." Footsteps moved away.

The hand with the cool skin touched my cheek again. "You made your choice once. I could respect it. I could let you go, tell your mother that what she wants isn't more important than what you want. But I can't ask you if that's *still* what you want—and I'm sorry, child, I know you ceased to be your mother's property when you popped out of her belly, but I was a mother, too, and I know what it costs to bury your own. I need her good regard, for now at least, and your wishes are none of my concern."

I didn't want to die. I didn't want to *die*! But she'd said she could "let me go," and I couldn't think of anything else that might mean. *Please,* I thought, as loudly and fiercely as I could. *Save me. Whatever that means, do it.*

"There's nothing in your blood to hang conjure or charm upon; we've never spent our arts on saving mortals. Maybe we should have. Maybe it would have been kinder. Maybe . . . " She paused, taking a deep breath. "Maybe there's something I can do. I hope you can still hear me, Gillian. Because this is going to hurt you a great deal more than it's going to hurt me."

The sound of the door opening again, and then the second woman spoke, saying, "I found the chest. Do you have a territory agreement with the spiders down there, or can I go back with a broom and teach them about respecting a lady's personal boundaries?"

"The broom's in the hall closet," said the first woman. "Leave us, Poppy, and don't come back, no matter what you hear."

"Yes, ma'am," said the second woman—Poppy—dubiously. "Call my name if you need me." The door closed again.

Something had shifted in the air of the room, something that grew heavy and oppressive as the first woman began to unbutton my jeans and work them down my hips. I couldn't even tense.

She sighed. The sound was very far away. "I'm going to hurt you, but I'm not going to violate you, not in the way your world has prepared you for. You're safer here than you have ever been in your life—and while you are free to doubt all others, I can't lie to you yet. Never doubt me. If you want to stay alive, I need you naked. I'm sorry I can't ask for your permission."

She went back to undressing me, hands rough and efficient, but never straying into excessive familiarity: true to her word, she just wanted me naked as quickly as possible. When she was finished, she stepped away. There was a creaking sound, like two pieces of stiff wood rubbing against each other. The laundry room door in the apartment where we'd lived when I was little, when I was still waiting for Mom to come home, had made the same sound.

Mom. October. I couldn't decide what to call her even when no one else could hear. She was my mother, but Miranda was the one who'd raised me. She said she loved me, but she was the one who'd left me. And yet, since the first time I'd been kidnapped, since I'd fallen asleep and dreamt of a meadow filled with impossible flowers, I hadn't quite been able to work up the energy to hate her. When I thought about her, it made me sad, not angry, like she was a secret I'd been told once and then forgotten, like—

A bucket of ice water struck me square in the chest, driving the air from my lungs in an involuntary gasp. Every inch of my skin felt suddenly tight, contracting into painful lumps of gooseflesh—but the burning was gone. The fire that had been swallowing me since this started had been doused.

No: not doused. It was flickering back to life, radiating outward from my shoulder, ready to turn back into a bonfire. But it was dimmer, more distant. My thoughts seemed to be getting dimmer, too, fading into a comfortable hum. Maybe death wouldn't be so bad. It felt a lot like going to sleep, now that I wasn't burning, burning, burning . . .

The woman tied something around my soaking shoulders, lifting me up so that it would fall smoothly down my back. She lowered me into my original position, humming under her breath, something sweet and sad, something that sounded strangely like the sea. I could taste saltwater on my lips, trickling between them, running over my tongue. I couldn't swallow, but I could let it move down my throat at its own pace, cooling me, soothing me.

"Her name was Firtha," said the woman, right next to my ear. "She was older than you, but no wiser. She was still a child. She should still be here with me, not gone to dust and whispers in the wind. I cannot bring her back. This will not bring her back. This will end in someone altogether new, and I hope you can forgive me."

She touched my cheek. I opened my eyes.

Seeing the world was a revelation. I stared at everything, unable to move my head, unable to stop *looking*. I had thought I might never see anything but the inside of my own eyelids again. And there, right in front of me, was the woman.

She looked like she was almost my age, like I could have seen her on campus and not looked twice, except for her dress, which was something out of a medieval recreation fair. It was white silk, and it fell around her like a wave crashing on the beach, speckled here and there with darker patches, probably marking where the saltwater she had doused me in had cascaded back onto her. Her hair was thick and black and loose around her shoulders, and her eyes . . .

They were so green, the color of algae growing in shallow water, of kelp, of the vast and living sea. She held up a flask that looked like it had been carved from a single piece of sunset coral.

"This isn't a perfect solution, but you deserve better, and so does your mother, and some debts are too old to ever be paid." She pressed the flask against my lips. I drank despite myself. It tasted like seawater, but sweet at the same time, like she had mixed it with honey, or with the idea of starlight.

My eyes began to flutter closed. I struggled to keep them open. I wasn't tired. I wanted to see the world, to know that I existed outside the confines of my own head.

"Go to sleep," she whispered. She pulled the flask away a beat before her hand slammed into my sternum, her fingernails like claws as they bit into my skin, and I screamed—actually screamed, loud and long and filled with every agony I'd suffered thus far in silence—and then there was nothing.

Nothing at all.

TWO

I was standing on the edge of a cliff overlooking a great and stormy sea. I was naked, or close to it; some sort of fur stole was wrapped around my shoulders, but that was all I had to cover me. I wasn't cold, though. The wind was howling and the waves were crashing and I wasn't cold. Something was wrong with that, something I couldn't fully put my finger on. I should have been cold.

"This is the pause," said an unfamiliar voice. I turned. A girl stood next to me on the cliff's edge. She looked like she could have been one of my classmates, for all that her hair was a deep slate gray that curled around her in the wind like the foam breaking on the rocks below. Her eyes were greener than anything I'd ever seen, so green that they must have been contacts. Human eyes don't come in that color. She was naked, too, without even a shawl to break the line of her body. It was oddly natural, like she had never been meant for clothing.

"The pause?" I asked.

"When a wave forms, when it rises, there's always a moment where it can collapse back into itself, too heavy to sustain the motion it wants to make. A moment when it isn't quite sky and isn't quite sea and isn't quite anything at all. That's where you're standing now." She turned away from the water, looking at me solemnly. "You can't stay here for long."

"I don't even know where 'here' is," I said. "Am I dreaming?"

"Yes. And no. And yes again. It's complicated, being a wave."

She took a step toward me, holding out her hands. "Let me look at you."

I didn't take her hands. I didn't cover myself, either. Under the circumstances, that was about as far as I was willing to go for the weird naked dream lady.

She seemed to understand that she had overstepped. She stopped, hands falling back to her sides, and said, "I suppose this is less a dream and more a haunting. We aren't supposed to leave ghosts. We aren't supposed to leave bodies, either. Well, I left part of one, and so it was only natural that I should leave part of the other."

"What are you . . . ?"

She gestured to the skin tied around my shoulders. "That was mine, when I walked among the living."

I recoiled, hands scrabbling at the knot between my breasts. Fur is always a dead thing, but this suddenly felt heavy, slick with blood instead of water. "Oh, God. Oh, fuck, I'm sorry—"

"Peace, peace!" She put her hands up. "You have to keep it on. Please. It's the only gift I have to give, and if you refuse it now, you'll die."

My hands stilled. "What do you mean?"

"Come sit with me." She started toward the cliff's edge, beckoning for me to follow.

I didn't want to. I wanted to turn around and run away, to find a way out of this strange nightmare wonderland. But I was naked and barefoot, and she hadn't attacked me, at least not yet, and my desire to know what was going on was stronger than the urge to run. Besides, this was a dream. She couldn't hurt me.

I followed.

The woman sat down on the rocky edge of the cliff. I mimicked her, relaxing a little when nothing poked me in the ass. She shot me an amused look.

"Do rocks usually bite where you come from?"

"I have no interest in sitting down on somebody's rusty old fish-hook," I replied.

She snorted. "What a charmingly positive outlook on life."

"You try having your mother disappear when you're a baby and see how positive you are."

"Ah." Her amusement turned sympathetic. "Mother troubles, I understand. I never lived up to mine, however long and hard I tried. She gave me her favor, called me 'precious' and 'pearl,' but

I never *earned* it. What good is adoration that costs nothing, counts nothing? I might as well have been the pearl she called me, valuable only because I was hers, and not because of anything I'd *done*."

It was weird, sitting here with a strange naked lady and talking about moms. Dreams are allowed to be weird, I guess. "My mother . . . I never felt like I had to live up to her. I mean, as long as I didn't *vanish*, I was doing better than she ever did."

"Where did she go?"

"I—" I hesitated. "I don't know. She never said. When she came back, my dad wouldn't let her talk to me."

The woman frowned, politely puzzled. "And you didn't chase after her to ask? I would never have allowed my mother to leave me in ignorance so big as that."

"I didn't want to know." Because there had always been the things that didn't add up, hadn't there? My memories of her were fuzzy. I'd been so young when she disappeared that it wasn't really a surprise—it was more of a surprise that I remembered her at all—but what I did have didn't make *sense*. I remembered the scent of freshly cut grass hanging in the air of our apartment, like someone had dumped a lawnmower out on the carpet. I remembered little dancing lights, and the sound of bells. I remembered her laughing. More than anything, I remembered her laughing.

The woman who'd shown up on our doorstep fourteen years later hadn't been laughing—had looked like she didn't even know what laughter *was*, like she had never smiled in her life. She had been thin and pale and frightened, and when Dad had pushed her away, she had gone almost without protest, like she didn't have the strength to fight. Like I wasn't worth fighting *for*. If she'd really loved me, if I'd been as important to her as a daughter is supposed to be, she would have fought for me. Wouldn't she?

The woman was looking at me with sympathy, so much sympathy that it made me want to scream. I looked away, out at the waves breaking on that vast and midnight sea.

"I guess it didn't seem important," I said. "She left me. Why should it matter if I leave her? She started it."

"Mothers always do." The woman paused before adding, "I'm Firtha, as they call me. Daughter of Antigone."

She stopped there. I waited a few seconds, then glanced back to her, frowning. "Antigone, like the Greek tragedy? What's your father's name?"

"I never knew," she said, and shrugged. "It never mattered enough for her to tell me. My mother is the sea witch, and she might have spun me out of spindrift and seafoam for all I know."

I blinked. "Your mother is *what*?"

"Oh, child, I would tell you so many things if there were time, and I may, if you come to me again: you're a haunted house now, after all. Perhaps we'll have time to become the best of friends and share all our secrets, sisters in every way that matters." Her smile was bright enough to chase the shadows from her words. "Here, though, now, time is short and there's much I have to tell you, because my mother can bring you to the sea, but she cannot make you swim. However much she might wish she could, her power ends at the shore."

"What are you . . . "

"Peace, child, and ask your questions when the time is right. My name is Firtha, youngest daughter of Antigone, and I was born to the sounding sea. The year of my birth does not matter, and in fact, I cannot give it, for the calendar has changed since my beginning. I know the harvest was good, because I was held up as a blessing and a bounty by my brothers and sisters; I know the storms were mild. I grew to my adulthood wrapped in all the love my family had to offer, and I knew nothing of the battles that consumed my kin, either inland or far from shore. I was a creature of cradle and cove, and perhaps if I had been less innocent, I might have lived . . . but so many of us did not that even that bitter medicine lies uneasy on my tongue. I was who I was, and I have no regret of it."

I sat silent, frowning slightly, trying to figure out what she was trying to tell me. My dreams could be weird, but this was a bit much, even for me.

"My mother's eldest sister, more powerful than she when there was land beneath her feet or snow in the air, was a cold woman, and a cruel woman, and she hated that we were happy. She *despised* us for being content with what we had, for refusing to reach for more than we could hold. She called us beasts and burdens, and when that failed to set the hands of our kin against us, she went to the least among the Courts, and she said, 'I have a way you can be uplifted.' And they, fools that they were, listened."

"Wait a second," I said. "What do you mean, 'Courts'? Like King Arthur?"

"I never met him, but I understand he was a gentleman," said Firtha. "Yes, like King Arthur, but more, and more importantly, like Oberon and his Ladies. I speak of the Courts of Faerie, child, to which I once belonged. To which you may yet belong, if you choose to accept this haunting."

I gaped at her. "Fairies aren't real," I said finally. "None of this is real."

"If it's not real, then it can't hurt you to listen a little longer, can it? Peace, little sister. Keep your ears open, and hear me, because your life lies upon the shore. You can't return inland; the cliff walls stand too high, and the climb will kill you. Listen, and choose whether you'll swim or drown."

I swallowed hard and said nothing.

"Merlins they were, with the whispers of Faerie in their blood and bone, but so much of the mortal in them that they could never touch eternity, nor wrap their fingers around most of magic's gifts. Eira—my aunt, my betrayer—pressed knives into their hands and told them where our rookery was lain, told them where we danced and dreamt all unaware of the danger coming from our own kind. They had every chance to put their knives aside. They could have gone to my mother and told her what Eira offered, could perhaps have bargained to acquire what they wanted in a less terrible way. But they were greedy, and they had seen too many doors slammed in their faces to believe that there was any other chance of claiming their place in Faerie."

Firtha's expression grew solemn as she turned her face back toward the waves. "They came at dawn, when magic is at its weakest. They knew we would be off-guard, unable to defend ourselves. They slashed our throats and opened our bellies, and when they had us dead before them, they stripped the skins from our bodies and claimed them for their own. They thought they could become wholly fae through our sacrifice. They thought . . . " She sighed. "Does it matter what they thought? They wanted more than they had, and they destroyed something precious and irreplaceable to fill their empty hands. They killed me. They killed my brothers and sisters and nieces and nephews, and they broke my mother's heart. They speak of her with fear now, when they remember her to speak of her at all, and they did it to themselves. They made her the monster they feared to face."

"You . . . what?" My stomach churned. I pressed a hand against it, trying to calm myself. "You're dead?"

"I told you that you were a haunted house now, lassie. To what did you think I was referring?" She glanced at me, expression caught somewhere between amusement and sorrow. "Our killers went home to their own families, their own children, and said that they would be immortal now, that Eira would reward them, would teach them the way to tease Faerie's secrets from our poor, flayed hides. And those children, who could already see the shadow of my mother's vengeance stretching over them like a sword about to fall, did the only thing they could possibly have done."

"They ran?" Horror had stolen my voice. It came out as a whisper, nearly lost in the wind off the sea.

Firtha laughed. "Running would have done them no good, and could easily have done them ill, for my mother is not the forgiving sort. She would have hounded them to the ends of the Earth, chased them down until every trace of their bloodline had been broken on the coral reefs that were once the bones of her children. She would have had *their* children, and the children of their children, step by step and line by line, so that there was nothing left of them. No. Faerie was closer to the surface in those days. They knew better than to flee before her fury. Instead, that night as their parents lay sleeping, they took the knives still stained with our innocent blood, and they took my mother's vengeance for her."

I shook my head in silent denial. Firtha nodded.

"Oh, yes. They killed their own parents, every one of them: they drenched themselves in family blood, peeled the stolen skins from the backs of their mothers and fathers, and they sought audience with my mother, that they might make apologies for what their parents' hands had done. They hoped she might accept a life for a life as payment and let them go. They forgot that a fae life, which might span centuries if not interrupted, must—of necessity—weigh more heavily in fae hands than a human life."

Firtha turned to fully look at me. Her expression was unreadable.

"She cursed them, or blessed them, depending on which side of the shore you're standing on. She said, 'You bear the stolen skins of my children, who I loved more than any other thing in any other world that time itself has ever known.' She said, 'Your hands are red with the blood of your mothers and fathers, who stole from me that which was most precious.' She said, 'You are not thieves in the night, to be punished as thieves are punished, but neither are you innocent, and I will not forgive you.' And she drew our skins tight around their shoulders, tied them tight, and bound them to Faerie. She gave them what their parents wanted most, and she did not ask them leave, and she did not grant them 'no.' She made them Selkies."

I reached up and touched the knot at my sternum. The fur was slick and wet beneath my fingers.

Firtha smiled. "Yes," she said. "As I told you before, that was mine when I was numbered among the living, and I had joy of it. Oh, how I loved being alive, loved the water around me and the sky above me. There's so much I never had the chance to do—so much that's still yours to experience, if you'll take this gift, knowing now what it cost to make. Lives are wrapped up in that shawl you wear, and at last I can say that mine was given freely, for I know my mother would never have offered it to you if you weren't worthy. You can't be what you were. That shore is closed to you, now and forevermore. But you can live. If you'll consent to a haunting, you can live."

I slowly lowered my hand. "My name is Gillian."

"It's a pleasure to meet you," said Firtha. "Welcome to the family."

That was all the warning I had before she leaned over and unceremoniously pushed me off the cliff's edge. I fell, screaming, to the restless, waiting sea.

THREE

Someone was crying. Not just crying—*sobbing*, big, broken-hearted sobs that sounded like they were going to shake the person apart. I opened my eyes. There was no ceiling above me, just a cascade of diaphanous veils filled with small, glittering points of light, like someone had sliced the sunrise into a thousand individual sheets of gauze. A hand was wrapped around mine. I raised my head.

October was kneeling next to the bed, her forehead against the mattress, crying. I blinked. I had never imagined her crying over me. I had never imagined her *caring* enough to cry over me.

Carefully, I reached out with my other hand and touched the top of her head. She jerked it up, staring at me. Her eyes . . . they were gray, so pale they looked likc they had no color at all, like they were all pupil and sclera and no iris. Her ears, poking through the tangle of her hair, were pointed. But that wasn't possible. None of this was possible. I was dreaming. I had to be.

She was still staring at me, like I was the most incredible thing she had ever seen. It made me uncomfortable.

"M . . . " I began, and caught myself, stopping before I could finish the word. "Toby?"

"Hi," she breathed.

"I . . . your ears. I thought I dreamt it. I thought I dreamt . . ." The meadow. The choice she had offered me the first time I'd been kidnapped. That had been a dream. That had been nothing but a dream. And she had looked exactly like this. "This is a dream. I'm dreaming right now."

"You're not, honey. I'm sorry, but you're awake." She stood up. She didn't *sound* sorry. She sounded like a kid on Christmas morning, like this was her dearest dream coming true. "This is all really happening."

"No, it's not. This *can't* be happening." I clutched the blankets around my chest, sitting up a little straighter. My fingers brushed against something slick and heavy tied around my shoulders. A sealskin. I jerked away from it like I had been burned.

Toby winced. "Gillian . . . " she began and stopped.

"That woman, that *awful* woman, she stabbed me." I looked at my hands. There were webs stretched between my fingers, thin sheets of skin that moved when I moved, like they were a part of me. I closed my eyes. I couldn't handle this right now. "She stabbed me with an arrow and I thought I was going to die, and why can't I remember what she looked like? She nearly killed me. Why can't I remember?"

"She's a pureblood, and humans have trouble looking at the fae. You were too human before. Your head couldn't handle looking at what she really was."

You can live. If you'll consent to a haunting, you can live, whispered Firtha's voice, echoing somewhere in the back of my head.

"What do you mean," I asked, "I was too human before?"

She hesitated. "What did they tell you when they woke you up?"

I opened my eyes. Nothing had changed, and somehow that was the worst thing of all. "The other woman, the one with the green eyes, she made me drink this stuff that tasted like seawater, and then she said, um, 'This isn't a perfect solution, and I'm sorry, but you deserve better, and so does your mother, and some debts are too old to ever be paid.' Then she tied this thing around my shoulders and told me to go to sleep again, and I couldn't keep my eyes open. I wasn't even tired, and I fell asleep."

Something was wrong about that. Something hadn't happened in exactly that order or exactly that way. I just couldn't figure out which part was wrong.

"That was the Luidaeg," said Toby. Her relief was naked in her voice. "You may hear people call her the sea witch. She needed you to sleep so you could get used to the skin."

My mother is the sea witch, and she might have spun me out of spindrift and seafoam for all I know, whispered Firtha. I tried to shut her out. I couldn't think about homicidal ghost women by the sea right now.

"The . . . skin?" I asked, resisting the urge to touch it again. I didn't like Toby talking about it. Something about it made me possessive in a way I couldn't quite explain and didn't want to examine too closely.

Toby looked unsure for the first time. She took a breath, clearly measuring her words. Finally, she said, "Faeries are real."

I didn't say anything.

"Fairy tales get a lot of things wrong, but faeries are real, and when you were born, you were part-faerie, because I was half-faerie. Do you remember a few years ago, when the woman with the red hair snatched you from your bedroom?"

I managed—barely—to resist the urge to snarl at her. It had been the most traumatic thing that had ever happened to me. Of course, I remembered. I would have given anything to forget. "I have nightmares about it," I said curtly.

"Do you remember the dream you had, before the police found you and brought you home?"

"I . . . " I looked at her. "I was in a meadow, and you were there too, only you didn't look the way you looked in pictures. You looked like you were something else. Like you were my fairy god-mother."

She nodded. "Yes. Exactly. What happened in the meadow?"

"There were two more versions of me. One of them who looked like you, and one who looked like Daddy." I hesitated. "You told me I had to choose, because you could only save me if I chose. You looked so sad, and I wanted to be the kind of person who could choose to stay with you, but I couldn't do it. All I wanted was to go home. I wanted my dad and Miranda. I wanted my room and my things, and I guess that's why I'm being punished now, isn't it? Because I chose wrong."

There was a certain brutal satisfaction in watching the color drain out of Toby's face, replaced by a sickly waxen sheen. She looked horrified. I appreciated that. I shouldn't be the only one suffering.

"Oh, baby, no. No, you're not being punished. You're not . . . you did nothing wrong. The choice was yours to make, and you asked for what you needed. No one should ever be angry with you for that. I'm not. I never was." She sounded like she almost meant it. "That meadow, though, that choice . . . I was there with you. It wasn't a dream. It was the magic letting you see what you needed to see in order to understand what I was asking. You had been shot with a sort of poison that only kills mortals, whether human or changeling—um, fae who have some human blood in them—and in order to take it out of you, I needed to change your blood. When you asked me to make you human, I did."

None of this made any sense, except that all of it made sense, because it was answering questions I had lived with for so long that I had almost stopped understanding how to ask them. "That's why my skin stopped breaking out when I helped Dad work on the car, and why I stopped being so tired in the mornings," I said. "Be-cause you took the alien out of me."

The word was intentionally chosen. I wanted to see if her story was consistent. She looked horrified as she responded, "Not alien: fae. And yes. My kind of fae is . . . we're a little odd. We work with blood. We can make it do what we want. But we can only work with what's there. When I took the fae blood out of you, I couldn't ever put it back again."

"And you took it out of me to save my life. Because I asked you to."

"Yes."

I raised my left hand, spreading my fingers until the skin that had formed between them was stretched to its furthest extent. It still felt alien, like something that wasn't meant to be attached to my body. It *was* attached to my body. It was a part of me, as much as my hands or my legs or the sealskin tied around my shoulders.

Anger surged through me, hot and bitter. How dare she? Every time she tumbled in and out of my life, she left me changed in some new, awful way that I hadn't asked for and never wanted. She was my mother. That didn't give her the right to keep doing this.

"So what the fuck is this?" I asked. "Why does everything feel wrong? Why is there fur tied around my shoulders, and why can't I take it off? What did your weird monster friends do to me?"

Toby breathed in sharply. Then, in a carefully measured tone, said, "The woman whose face you can't remember stabbed you with the same stuff you'd been shot with before. The stuff that kills humans. It's called elf-shot. It was tearing you apart, because that's what it does. You were dying, Gillian. So my friend Tybalt brought you here, at my request, to find out whether there was anything that could be done to save you. I was hoping . . . I don't know what I was hoping for. I was hoping for a miracle. What I got was a loophole. That skin you're wearing, it belonged to the youngest daughter of my aunt, the Luidaeg. The woman with the green eyes. When her children . . . died, she put powerful magic into their skins. Anyone who bonds with one of them becomes what's called a Selkie. A kind of fae. Not the kind you were before you asked me to change you, but still fae, and if you're fae, the elf-shot can't kill you."

"You're lying." She wasn't. I could see Firtha when I closed my eyes, could remember her telling me the story of how she'd died— how her entire family had died.

Selkie. I was a Selkie now.

"I'm not."

I was angry and I was scared and I couldn't stop blaming her. This all came back to her. Whether she'd intended it or not. "You— you orchestrated this whole thing! You *wanted* this to happen! You wanted me to have to come and live with you!"

Toby looked at me with sorrow in her eyes, and my heart sank. This was what it meant to be a monster. Now even my own mother was rejecting me. "That's not going to happen," she said. "You may need to take a little time off from school to adjust to the change, and I apologize for that. It's still better than dying. And you're not coming to live with me. You won't even have to see me if you don't want to. Your . . . "

She stopped, looking like she was choking. I frowned.

"What?"

Toby swallowed, and said, "Your mother is here. J—Miranda. She knows about Faerie. She's always known. She'll take you home and tell you how to hide yourself from your father until someone can teach you how to spin illusions, and she can take you wherever you need to go."

I sat up straighter. "Miranda is here? In this weird place?" Hope felt almost as unfamiliar as the webs between my fingers, growing in my chest like a strange flower. "Miranda knows about fairies?"

"She is. When the bad woman took you, she tried to make us think Miranda had done it, that she was the one who'd hurt you. I think she wanted us to fight, to give her more time to get you into hiding." She paused. "Gillian, I'll get Miranda for you, and I won't come around unless you ask me to. You have my word on that. But I need you to think very hard. Apart from the woman you can't remember clearly, was there *anyone* strange around the residence hall in the last few weeks? Anyone at all who didn't feel like they should be there?"

I started to shake my head. Then I stopped, and asked, "Did I really see Jocelyn in that place with all the fog?"

Toby looked genuinely regretful as she said, "I'm sorry honey, but yes, you did."

"That *bitch*." The urge to find a way back there, just so I could rip every goddamn hair out of her head, was incredibly strong. "She was always trying to suck up to me, you know? Always asking questions about you, like you were some kind of hero, and not a deadbeat who ran out on her family when things got hard."

"She said something similar when I came looking for you," said Toby. It was clear that my words had struck home; I had never seen her looking so uncomfortable. "Why do you ask?"

Oddly, I found myself wanting to apologize to her. It wasn't the best feeling. "Because she had a new boyfriend hanging around this past week. I mostly noticed because he was really cute, and I thought he might make a good model for our life drawing class."

Toby sat up a little straighter. "What did he look like?"

"Cute," I repeated. "Um. Tall, skinny, sort of a hipster vibe, like he did all his shopping at vintage stores for 'the aesthetic,' but didn't really know how things went together. He pulled it off, it just didn't look *right*, you know?"

"I do." For a moment, I thought she might say something more. Finally, she gave a little shake of her head and asked, "Was there anything else about him that caught your attention? His hair, maybe?"

"Oh, yeah, his hair!" I would have snapped my fingers, but I wasn't sure they worked that way anymore. I didn't want to test it. "It was this amazing shade of emerald green. I really wish I'd been able to get the number of his stylist. My hair's so dark that I can't ever seem to find anyone who can get it to take color." I plucked at a strand of my hair. At least that was still familiar.

"The man you saw with Jocelyn was tall and pretty and had green hair," Toby pressed. "Are you sure?"

"I notice a good dye job."

"Okay." She rose, taking a step back. "I need to go. I'll ask the Luidaeg to let Miranda come up here and talk to you. Please don't try to take the sealskin off. I'm not sure you could yet, but if you did, I think you'd probably die. Please promise me you won't."

I nodded slowly. "I won't."

"Good." She turned away.

Her shoulders were slumped, and she looked suddenly small, neither the monster of my childhood nor the hero of my infancy. She looked . . . tired. I didn't like seeing her that way. She looked . . .

Human.

"Mom?"

She stopped dead. I wasn't even sure that she was breathing.

"I . . . I'm really angry with you. For leaving, and for being something you never told us about. It impacted my life and I never knew why, and that's not fair. I don't know if I'm ever going to stop being angry with you. But thank you. For coming to save me when I needed you. I don't know what I am now, and I don't know if I'm going to like being it, but I know I didn't want to be dead. So thank you."

She smiled over her shoulder at me, still wan and tired and clearly miserable, but better. Just a little bit.

"You're welcome," she said, and slipped out the door, leaving me alone.

I flopped back into the pillows and raised my hands above my face, spreading my fingers until the light shone through the webs that connected them. I could feel them stretch like any other skin. They were a part of me. This was really happening.

"Well, fuck," I said, and I had never said anything more accurate in my entire life.

FOUR

I would have sworn I wasn't tired, but I must have fallen asleep again, because I woke to the sound of the door swinging shut, with the taste of saltwater in my mouth. I pushed myself upright in the bed, bracing my strange new hands against the mattress. It had more give than I was used to. I thought it might be stuffed with actual feathers, which didn't make sense. No one had done that in centuries.

Then again, no one had believed in fairies—in *faeries*—in centuries, either, and look how that was going.

"Hello?" My voice came out as a dehydrated rasp, which didn't make sense, given how much time I'd spent drenched to the skin recently. I still felt damp. Clearing my throat, I tried again, calling, "Is someone there?"

"Gilly!" Miranda swept the curtains of the bed aside with one hand before she flung herself at me, wrapping her arms around my shoulders and pulling me into a tight embrace. "Oh, sweetheart, you had me so *scared*!"

She pushed me out to arm's length without waiting to hear my reply, eyes raking up and down the length of my body. Her lips tightened when she looked at my hands, and tightened further when she reached my eyes, which she only met for a second before hugging me again.

"Never do that again," she said, voice muffled by my shoulder. "Promise me you'll never, ever do that again."

"I don't think I can lose my humanity more than once," I said. "I'm pretty sure it's like virginity. You've either got it or you don't."

Miranda pushed me back out to arm's length, eyes flashing fury. "Don't you say that. *Never* say that. No one can take your humanity away from you."

"Really, Mom? Because I'm pretty sure I'm not human anymore." I twisted free of her grasp, holding up my hand so that she could see the webs between my fingers. The gesture was horrifyingly similar to the way I had shown those same webs to Toby, and the thought turned my stomach. Was I going to lose *both* my mothers over this?

"You were born human, Gillian. That's what matters."

"Was I? October was just here, and she seemed to think I'd been born half-fae."

"Not half," said Miranda automatically—and froze.

My eyes narrowed. "What was that?"

"Nothing."

"Really? Because it sounded like she was right, and you knew."

Miranda didn't answer.

"*Did* you know, Mom? Did you know Toby wasn't human? That she disappeared because she wasn't human, and not because she ran away from us at all?"

"I couldn't tell you," said Miranda desperately. "It wasn't my place, and the fae, they defend their secrecy fiercely. To the death, even. So I couldn't say anything, and your father didn't know. He thought she'd gotten overwhelmed by her responsibilities and run off. You were both happier thinking you understood what had happened. I didn't lie. I just . . . didn't tell anyone else's secrets. I kept you safe."

"You let me think my mother had run out on me," I said slowly. "You let me think she didn't love me."

"She wouldn't have kept you safe, Gillian. She couldn't. What she is . . . humans aren't meant to live in her world, and you were more human than not. Even then you were more human than not." She tried to grab my hands.

I pulled them back and held them up, showing her the webs again. "Humans aren't meant to live in *our* world, you mean. Are you going to leave me also, since I'm fae now? Like h—like my mother?"

"You're not like her," said Miranda, looking horrified. "You're my little girl. Don't be foolish, Gillian, you know I'll never leave you."

"You knew." I shook my head. "You knew she wasn't human, and you knew she didn't mean to go. When I was kidnapped that first time, when she turned me human to save me, you knew that, too, didn't you? I mean, if you knew everything else, you must have known what she'd done."

"I was aware that she had pulled Oberon's burden from your blood, yes," she said stiffly. An odd accent crept into her words, flavoring them in a way I couldn't quite name. "I thought she had done it as an apology."

"An apology? To who?"

"To you. To your father. To our family. She set you free when she cast you out of Faerie. You could have had a normal life, with none of the trials she'd have set before you. You got so lucky, baby. I thought . . . I thought we were safe."

"She's still my mother, Mom. She's still the woman who gave birth to me, and fae or not, I was—I am—still her daughter. I don't know her." I gestured wildly at the gauzy curtains around me, at the room I hadn't really seen. "But I know that whoever she is, it's the kind of person who makes someone who calls herself *the sea witch* want to do her favors. I know she saved me. Twice, she's saved me. Don't you get it, Mom? You thought you were keeping me safe, but you were putting me in danger, because you made sure I knew *nothing* about the people who might be out there looking to hurt me."

"*I* didn't do that!" Miranda protested, looking shocked. "*She* did that. If she hadn't—" She seemed to realize that she'd made a mistake, because she stopped midsentence, a guilty look flashing over her face.

"If she hadn't what, Mom?" I asked quietly. "If she hadn't come back? If she hadn't tried to make contact? Are you really going to sit there and tell me that you could have stayed away if your positions had been reversed?"

Miranda wouldn't meet my eyes. Which was, in its own way, answer enough.

"How do you know about the fae?"

"I met them a long time ago. They made things difficult for me, so I've spent my life making things difficult for them."

A new thought came to me, accompanied by a wash of tired horror. "You didn't meet Dad by accident, did you?"

"Gillian . . . " She paused and sighed heavily. "You shouldn't ask questions you don't want to know the answers to."

"What if I *do* want to know?"

"Then you shouldn't ask them because you'll break your poor old mother's heart."

I wanted to laugh. I wanted to cry. I wanted to scream and throw things and rip the sealskin off my shoulders and keep it far, far away from her, in case she decided that it was too fae and hence not to be allowed. If I took it off, I'd die. I felt like I was dying anyway. Maybe being poisoned by something magical and impossible triggered a sort of weird repeat puberty, where your emotions went all out of control and weird. It would have been a better answer for the way I was feeling than anything else.

Although I guess simple shock could have had something to do with it.

"Get out."

My voice was low enough that she didn't hear me at first, just continued sitting next to my bed and waiting for—something. I didn't know what, and I wasn't sure I knew how to ask. Finally, she turned back to face me.

"Did you say something, sweetheart?"

"Yes." I made myself keep looking at her. If I turned away, I'd lose, and if I lost now, I lost forever. I could see that, as surely as I didn't know what winning meant anymore. "I said 'get out.' I want you to leave, please."

She couldn't have looked more startled if I had slapped her. "Gilly—"

"You lied to me. My whole life, you've been lying to me, and now I'm . . . I'm not even human anymore. I don't ever get to be human again. And I know you're going to tell me that's Toby's fault, that she's the reason I was in danger, and I guess you're right, but she's also the one who *turned* me human when she could have stolen me away from you forever. She's the one who tried her hardest to let me keep my life the way it was. I guess if you'd bothered to tell me what she was, to tell me how to take care of myself, we might not be sitting here now."

Miranda recoiled, putting one hand over her heart like I had stabbed her. In a way, I guess I had.

"You don't know what you're saying," she whispered.

"Whose fault is that?" The air was too dry. I couldn't breathe. Forcing myself to stay as calm as I could, I pointed to the door. "Go. I need some time."

"I'm your mother."

"You are. No one can ever take that away from you. You raised me. You're the face I picture when I think of the word 'mom.' But . . . I don't know how I feel about that right now. Because maybe no one can take it away from you, but maybe you took it away from someone else. *Please* leave. I don't want to be mad at you, and I think I will be if you stay."

Miranda rose, movements short and jerky. "I'll be right downstairs," she said. "I'm not going anywhere until you're ready to come home with me."

"That's good. Dad probably wouldn't like it if you came home alone. I—" I hesitated. "Does he know? About, um, the fae, and about Toby not being human, and . . . everything?"

"No," said Miranda. "He never did."

Somehow, that didn't make things better. I nodded silently and lay back down, rolling onto my side so that I couldn't see her. I stayed there, perfectly still, until I heard footsteps cross the floor, and the door opening, and the door closing again, and I was alone.

Hot, bitter tears stung my eyes. No matter how much I blinked, they refused to fall. The overwhelming dryness of the air was getting worse, and it was like my body knew it couldn't afford to lose any more liquid. I sat up, shoving the covers aside, and staggered to my feet for the first time since I'd woken up, pushing the gauzy veils surrounding the bed aside.

The room was small and round and like something out of a fairy tale, the sort of place where the witch would keep Rapunzel until it was time for ever after to begin. There were windows. All of them looked big enough for a person to fit through. I started toward the nearest one and paused as I realized that I wasn't naked. Maybe that was a weird thing to be surprised by, but after everything else that had happened since I'd been kidnapped—again—it was just one thing too many. I looked down at myself. I was wearing a plain blue sweater and dark pants, in addition to the sealskin tied around my shoulders.

Wait. It was tied *outside* the sweater. So how could I feel it so clearly? I fingered the knot, trying to make sense of what I felt. There was a layer of wool between my actual skin and the one that had been gifted to me. It should have been a weight, nothing more.

You have to keep it on, whispered Firtha's voice. But it was only a memory. She wasn't here, if she was even real. My dreams weren't usually that literal.

"Here goes nothing," I said, and undid the knot.

Leather knots easily. Leather is made for tying things off and holding things in place. Fur is a different story. Fur is thick and heavy and when I picked the knot at the front of the sealskin apart with my fingers, it separated easily, eagerly even, like it wanted to be free of this stupid situation as much as I did. A small voice that was half mine and half Firtha's whispered panicked warnings in the back of my mind, but I ignored it. I was tired of people acting like they knew what was best for me, like they didn't need to give me clear answers and allow me to make my own choices. I was *done.*

The sealskin came away from my shoulders, falling with a thump. I took a deep breath. See? I hadn't dropped dead or collapsed or anything else ridiculous like that. I was fine. I was—

Every nerve in my body felt like it caught fire at once. I had time for one short, sharp scream before I was falling, and I was unconscious before I hit the floor.

FIVE

"Get up."

A toe dug into my side, prodding me. Whoever it belonged to wasn't being particularly gentle.

My thoughts were fuzzy, forming slowly, and my body was

refusing to respond to my demands, no matter how stridently I made them. I lay motionless, and the toe dug into my side again, harder this time. I wasn't sure it qualified as being kicked—quite— but it was definitely getting close.

"I *told* you. Didn't I tell you? I don't make a lot of demands of the living, I know it's not my place, but Oberon's eyes, child, when a ghost tells you not to do something, you're not supposed to rush right out and give it a try."

Firtha. The toe belonged to Firtha. Which meant I was back in the dream, and my body wasn't really here, and I should be able to do anything I wanted to do.

That, or I had died when the sealskin fell, and I was going to spend my afterlife sprawling naked on the ground at the edge of the sea. Yeah: definitely naked. I could feel every stone and twig digging into the skin of my side. My hip had landed squarely on a big, sharp rock, and it was probably going to leave a bruise.

I could also feel the sealskin, once more lying flat against my back. I opened my eyes.

Firtha withdrew her toe and put her hands on her hips, openly glaring at me. "I can only save you so many times," she said, tone peevish. "Didn't I tell you that if you refused my gift, you'd die? Was that somehow less than clear? Should I have spoken more slowly? Dove into the depths and surfaced with a dead man's bones, used them to perform a little puppet show about how horrible your death would be? Would that, perhaps, have gotten through to you?"

"I'm sorry." I pushed myself into a sitting position. The presence of the sealskin was more comforting than I would have thought possible. I reached up and touched the knot, reassuring myself that it wasn't going to come untied again.

It didn't come *untied,* scolded my own mind. *You untied it, remember?*

I decided to ignore myself.

"Gillian, please. I don't know how many shocks your system can take. This could have been the end of you."

"Wasn't it already?"

Firtha blinked at me, puzzlement in her impossibly green eyes. "What do you mean? You stand, you sit, you walk among the living with my skin across your shoulders. If that's an ending, I don't know what a beginning looks like anymore."

"But I'm not human." I touched the knot again, less gently this time. "If you take this away from me, I die. How is that supposed to feel normal? How am I supposed to go home like this?"

"Ah." She offered me her hands. "Walk with me, child."

Arguing with the ghost of the woman whose flayed hide was keeping me alive seemed like a bad idea. I took her hands, and she pulled me from the stony ground, letting them go before she smiled at me and started walking across the heath.

I followed her, stones and bits of thorny sedge biting into the soles of my feet and making me hop and curse. She didn't seem to notice them. Maybe it had to do with being dead, or maybe she had just been haunting this place for so long that her feet had had the time to get tough as leather.

When we reached the edge of the cliff where we'd met before, I expected her to stop and sit. Instead, she turned, and began making her slow way down a pathway carved into the side of the rock. I hadn't noticed it before. I wasn't sure it had existed.

"Dream logic is the worst," I muttered.

"This isn't a dream," she said, not looking over her shoulder. "It's a memory mixed with an afterlife, and that means it isn't quite the same thing. Close enough, I suppose, but still, the rules are different here. I've never had company before."

"Why not? Hasn't anyone else . . . " I stumbled over my next words and stopped talking. I couldn't think of a polite way to ask whether I was the first person to wear her skin.

"They have, yes; several before you. We never talked like this."

"Why not?"

"Well, the first of them killed me, and the second stole me, and the rest had me passed to them in the manner that's become customary for Selkies. They were told what it would mean to accept me before they tied me around their waists or slipped me over their shoulders, and they had the chance to say 'no, thank you, but no, let this pass to someone else's hands.' " Firtha glanced over her shoulder at me, a wistful smile on her lips. I realized with some surprise that I could see it, despite the dimness of the path around us. My night vision was improving.

"I don't think any of them ever realized I had a name, or that I'd been myself before I was their gateway to the sea. It didn't matter much in their day-to-day, nor will it matter in yours—I won't swim beside you, won't murmur in your ear. But not knowing I was here, they could never invite me closer, and we never knew each other.

Not even as well as I already know you." The smile faded as she turned to face front once more. "Ah, well. Tides go in and tides come out, and none of them needed me as much as you do, little girl who thinks she knows what it means to be human."

"You said they were all asked. No one asked me."

"No one asked me, either. So I suppose we'll be sullen and resentful together, won't we?"

The path had been cut close enough to the cliffside that we were sheltered from the worst of the wind, although not from the foam; it blew upward from the sea, stinging and soothing at the same time, coating us both until—by the time we reached the bottom— we were entirely soaked. I followed Firtha onto the rocky beach, wiping sea spray out of my eyes.

"I could use a towel," I said. "Or a coat. A coat would be awesome."

"Why? Are you cold?"

I hesitated. I wasn't. I was naked and drenched and as comfortable as if it were a summer afternoon. "No," I finally admitted.

"Good. I'd worry the magic was failing if you were, and then all of this would have been for nothing. A tiresome end for a story stretching over centuries." Firtha turned to face me. "Look around. What do you see?"

Arguing with ghosts is the way people die in horror movies. I looked around. "I see the beach," I said.

"Only that?"

"I see . . . I see the sea." It looked deep and wild and strangely inviting, like every wave that struck the shore was trying to beckon me to follow it to someplace I'd never been before.

"And the sea sees you. Or if it doesn't, it'll see you very soon. You belong to the water now, as much as you belong to the land."

I wrenched my eyes away from the waves and back to her face. "Which isn't normal. It isn't *human*."

"Why are you so hung up on being human? Lots of people aren't human. I'm not human. My mother isn't human. I'm pretty sure she'd turn you into a rock and drop you in the Atlantic if you tried to imply that she was. Being human isn't the only way to enjoy the world, and being a Selkie means you'll be able to see and experience things no human ever could."

"But I didn't agree to this."

"Neither of us did, Gillian. You didn't agree to being born, either, and yet here we both are." Firtha held her hands out toward me, palms tilted toward the cloud-swaddled sky. Fine webs ran between her fingers, connecting them all the way to the first knuckle. I reached out, hesitantly, and touched one fingertip to the web between her thumb and forefinger.

"What are these?" I asked. "I'm growing them."

"I wasn't a Selkie," she said. "I was Roane. We didn't have to transform to swim the seas as equals, and when we did change our shapes, no one could steal them from us. We were stronger versions of what you've become—and I'm not trying to shame you by saying that. It's the way of Faerie. Every generation is a little weaker than the one that came before it. Oberon and his Queens begat the Firstborn, and the Firstborn begat their descendant races, and we were as much reduced from our parents as they had been from theirs."

"You didn't answer my question."

"I didn't, and I did. I was Roane, and parts of you will echo me now, because parts of you are mine. I am, in a way, another mother."

"Oh, great," I grumbled. "Three moms. That is *exactly* what I needed."

Firtha laughed, the sound light and lovely and perfectly matched to the sounding of the sea. "You seem stubborn enough to require a more than average amount of mothering, it's true. And my mother will be glad of the adoption, having lost all her grandchildren tides and tides ago. The webs between your fingers are to help you swim. You don't need them the way I did, because you'll rarely be swimming and human at the same time, but that's their purpose."

I squinted at her. "The fuck you say?"

"I'm not the one to teach you how to be what you are now. I don't have those answers." Firtha indicated the lines of her body. "I wore my skin, when it was mine, as everyone else does. Now you have two skins to care for, yours and mine, and each of them will ask different things of you, and neither of them will make you human. I need you to promise that you won't set my skin aside again."

"I—"

"*Promise.* On my grave, on the pearls that were my eyes, swear to me that you'll keep it close until my mother tells you it's safe to set it aside."

"All right." I put my hands up to ward her off. "I won't take it off again. But somebody who *can* explain the things you say you can't had better come along sooner rather than later, because I don't like everything being vague and weird and stupid."

"Welcome to Faerie," said Firtha, and stepped forward, and kissed me on the forehead. I blinked and was suddenly looking at the ceiling of the room where I'd collapsed.

"Okay, I hate this," I announced, and started to sit up before freezing mid-motion. The sealskin wasn't tied around my shoulders. I could feel its absence the way I would have felt a missing tooth, like an aching, unwanted void in the world. And I knew, with an absolute, sickening certainty, that if I broke contact with it again, I would plunge back into the dark.

Would Firtha be waiting there to yell at me again? Or was I running out of chances? I had a nasty feeling that my reserves were almost exhausted. I fumbled on the floor behind me, relaxing only when my fingers struck the soft, pliable leather of my inexplicable lifeline.

Since the sealskin was already untied, I shifted my butt until I could pick the whole thing up and bring it around to where I could see it. It looked like no other piece of fur I had ever seen. It was sleek and shining, almost like it was still alive. The leather was supple. When I turned it over to examine it, there were no scars or seams; the whole thing must have been removed in a single long cut.

I thought of Firtha, naked and alone on the rocky shore, and I shivered.

The fur itself was dark silver, dappled with slate-colored spots. I ran a hand over it, shivering again as a ghostly hand ran along my spine. It felt like I was stroking myself.

Lowering my hand, I swung the sealskin around my shoulders and retied the two long strips of fur at the front into a tight knot. As soon as I took my hands away, it got easier to breathe. I scowled. So this was it: I was stuck. I'd have to spend the rest of my life wandering around with a big chunk of fur hanging around my neck. Bad enough if I'd lived in Alaska or something, but this was California. I was a student at *Berkeley*. The campus vegans were going to eat me for breakfast once they realized I was wearing *fur*, and there wasn't going to be anything I could do about it. Take it off and die. Keep it on and admit that my life had changed forever, and I hadn't been given a single say.

Well. That wasn't quite true. I had a choice: I could decide to keep the skin on and live with what came after, or I could take it off and die.

"That's not a choice," I muttered. "It's an ultimatum."

Anger swept over me, washing the last of my weakness away. This wasn't fair. It wasn't *fair*, and I didn't want it. What the hell made Miranda and Toby think they got to lie to me like this? They both said they were my mother, and they were both right. Toby had given birth to me and Miranda had raised me, and they both said they loved me, but how could they love me if they were going to lie to me like this?

Toby wasn't human. Miranda had known all along, and she had never told me. They'd both treated me like I didn't matter just because I was younger than them, like being a kid meant I didn't get to have an opinion. I was always going to be a kid in their eyes. I was never going to be allowed to grow up and decide things for myself.

I shoved myself fully off the floor, turning in a slow circle as I glared at the room. There was only one door. There were still the windows, though, and I hadn't had the chance to check them properly before. I resumed my trek across the room.

The window wasn't locked. I pushed it open and leaned out, looking down on an impossible, wine-colored sea that wasn't the Pacific. I didn't know what it *was*, but I couldn't imagine any ocean actually coming in that specific shade of purple, like someone had crushed a world's worth of grapes into a single place. I gaped.

"Oh, come *on*," I said, my voice sounding thin and whiny to my own ears. The sky overhead was sunset-bright, colored in bands of red and gold and orange. A few early stars were peeking through the light, and I counted at least five moons overhead, one twice as large as the one I knew, three of them as small as sequins sewn onto the sky.

Looking at the scene was threatening to give me a headache. I stepped back hurriedly, leaving the window open. My heart was beating too hard and too fast. I touched the knot at my sternum, clutching it until my breathing started to return to normal.

Denial seemed like an attractive option. Denial would let me pretend none of this was happening, that I'd been drugged by the woman who had snatched me and this was all an elaborate fantasy that I'd snap out of at any moment. I was probably in a hospital somewhere, with an IV in my arm and a bunch of concerned doctors standing around waiting for me to wake up.

Unfortunately, denial would require me to have been able to make all this up, and I wasn't sure I could have. Too many of the details were things I would never have imagined, like the man who carried me through the cold, and Miranda keeping secrets about a whole other world. And Firtha. I could have imagined a lot of things, but a naked woman who was sort of my third mother now? That was a step too far.

If I couldn't have denial, I could at least have anger. I made a short, sharp sound of unhappiness and rushed the bed, grabbing the gauzy veils surrounding it and pulling them down. They gave way with a satisfying ripping sound, fluttering to the floor. I wasn't done. I started throwing pillows, and when I ran out of those, rushed for the dresser against the opposite wall and wrenched the drawers out, one by one, tipping their contents onto the floor.

The destruction made me feel better, however childish that may have been. I stopped when I ran out of drawers, panting and looking out on the havoc I had wreaked. Then I touched the sealskin at my chest. Nothing had actually changed. Nothing was *going* to change. This was my life now, whether I liked it or not—whether I *understood* it or not. I couldn't go back.

I put my hands over my face and wept.

SIX

Crying is cathartic, but eventually the body runs out of tears, and then it's time to start doing something else. I uncovered my face, wiping my eyes and nose on the sleeve of my sweater, and eyed the door. I hadn't heard a click when Miranda left. Maybe it wasn't locked. Maybe I could get out of here, find a place to clear my head.

Quickly, like I was getting away with something, I crossed to the door and tried the knob. It turned. I said a silent thanks, pulling it open—

—and froze at the sight of the woman with wings who was sitting in an alcove on the other side of the small landing. Wings? Yes. Wings. They were long and thin and the color of maple syrup. When she sat up straighter to look at me, they opened, and I could see right through them. They looked like they belonged on a dragonfly, not on a woman roughly my age. Her hair was electric orange, and her eyes were only a few shades darker, as impossible as the rest of her.

She was wearing jeans and a red Old Navy tank top, and somehow that was the cherry atop the sundae of "nope" that was her existence. She wasn't human. Toby had pointy ears, sure, but she wasn't . . . wasn't *alien* like this woman, this impossible, winged woman. Everything about her was wrong. Her bone structure was too delicate and her skin was too smooth and I didn't know whether she was the most beautiful or the most terrible thing I had ever seen.

"You're awake, then, missy," she said, in a voice that somehow managed to sound like the ringing of distant bells. That, too, was impossible. All of these people were impossible.

"This isn't happening," I said.

She nodded. "Understandable reaction, I'd say. I had a similar one when I woke up and saw myself, all pale and colorless and dim as I am now. How you people can *stand* it, I may never know. How do you feel? I'm supposed to ask as whether you want feeding or drinking or anything of that sort, and then to tell you to go back to your room, please, because it's not time for adventures just yet."

I gaped at her. She hit her forehead with the heel of one hand.

"Oh, that's me, done it again! Introductions come first. I'm Poppy. I'm apprentice to the sea witch, strange as that is to say, and when I've learned enough of her big magic, maybe I'll be able to do enough small magic to go home. Or maybe not. Bigness has its advantages, and I like it here well enough. You're Gillian Daye, daughter of October, fostered to the great betrayer. That's a lineage to live down, eh?"

I blinked. "What are you talking about? And my last name isn't 'Daye,' it's 'Marks.'"

"Oh, like your father, then? That's kind of you. Might change your mind, might not, I suppose. I don't really understand the way you big ones do naming. It's all awfully complicated and doesn't make sense to me." She hopped down from the alcove onto the stairs, her wings fluttering soundlessly to slow her descent. "It's nice to meet you! Awake, I mean. I met you before, but you were passed out at the time, so I don't think it counts. Do you want food?"

"Uh . . . no. I don't think I do."

"Right, right. That's expected, I suppose. You've had quite a shock, and you'll be hungry again soon enough. If you'll go back in your room now, I'll go tell ma'am that you're awake."

I hesitated. "What if I don't want to go back in the room?" I wasn't going to call it mine. That was a step too far.

"Then I'll have to put you back, and we'll both be sorry, no question of that." Poppy looked at me sorrowfully. "I'm still not used to bigness. Please don't make me use it against you."

"None of this makes any sense."

Poppy nodded. "That's a truth if ever I heard one. It didn't make sense to me, either, when I first came here, and sometimes it still doesn't. We'll be good friends as long as you have confusion to clear. Now will you go back in the room?"

She didn't refer to it as mine this time either, and I was almost ashamed to realize that I was grateful.

"I want to know what's going on," I said. "Toby had to go, and Miranda . . . " I trailed off. I wasn't sure how I felt about Miranda. She was my *mom*. She had raised me. I loved her. From the crown of my head to the tips of my toes, I loved her. But she had also lied to me, and the shape of those lies made it look like she had pushed Toby aside to make more room for herself.

I had spent so much of my life hating my biological mother that it was like a physical pain in my gut to realize that she might not be the villain of the piece after all. How many things was I going to need to rethink before this ended?

Poppy nodded enthusiastically. "I can help with that. If you go back in and make it a promise that you'll stay there, I can go and get ma'am for you. She can explain if anyone can."

"And ma'am is . . . ?"

"The sea witch, yes, she is."

Firtha's mother, the one she'd called Antigone. I took a step backward.

"All right," I said. "I'll wait."

Poppy beamed. "Good, good. I'll go let ma'am know." She turned and started hopping down the stairs, neither flying nor walking, but a strange hybrid of the two. Her wings fluttered wildly, never generating quite enough lift to do more than keep her from landing a few steps farther down.

I watched her go, wondering if she realized that I hadn't actually gone back into the room. I couldn't decide whether she was flighty or just distracted by everything around her, possibly including the air. It was like talking to a kitten that had somehow acquired thumbs. In no time at all, she was out of sight. I still counted to ten before I started sprinting down the stairs after her.

She thought I was going to sit up here and wait for a woman people consistently referred to as "the sea witch" to come and get me? Fuck. That. She had at least three names—the one I couldn't pronounce, the one straight out of a Greek tragedy, and the one that belonged to a Disney villain—and she had somehow bound her dead daughter's skin to me to keep me alive, and I was *not* going to hang out to see what she was going to do to me next. I was getting the hell out of here.

Everyone else knew about the fae, and it wasn't hurting any of them. Dad would understand, especially once I showed him the webs between my fingers. He would find a way to fix this. It might mean tracking Toby down and making her undo whatever she'd done, but whatever. He'd tracked her down before. He would do it again, for me.

The stairway was curved, like something out of a castle. I realized, with dull surprise, that the little round room where I'd been sleeping was actually the top of a tower. Maybe getting to my father wasn't going to be so easy after all.

I'd been descending for maybe thirty feet when a woman blocked my passage down the stairs. She was young, around my age, and I wouldn't have given her a second glance if I'd seen her on campus. Everything about her screamed "average," from the faint pocks of old acne on her cheeks to her hair, which was thick and curly and pulled into two fat ponytails tied off with strips of electric tape. The sight was enough to make me wince in involuntary sympathy. She was going to pull half her hair out when she took those down.

She was wearing overalls and nothing else, not even a bra, and when she looked at me I stopped dead in my tracks, some buried predatory instinct warning me that no, this was not a good thing; no, this was not a fight I could win.

She sighed, and said, "Poppy is going to be disappointed in you. She's still pretty new to this whole 'conversing with human-sized people' thing, and she tends to take things at face value. Did you have to start by kicking my puppy? Couldn't you have gone easy on her and just stolen her candy or insulted her hair?"

"I . . . " I stopped. "You're the sea witch, aren't you?" I knew her voice. I had heard it in my dreams, had been hearing it in my dreams since the first time someone had decided to use me as a bargaining chip against my biological mother.

She nodded. "You're quick on the uptake. Good. That's going to be useful. You can call me the Luidaeg."

Sometimes I get fear and bravery confused. Dad says Toby was the same way. I've never been sure whether it was a gift or a burden, but either way, when I opened my mouth, what came out was, "What if I want to call you Antigone?"

The sea witch raised an eyebrow, and for a moment, it seemed as if the unremarkable blue of her eyes was somehow bleeding into green, like Firtha's eyes, like algae on a dead man's bones. "Where did you hear that name?"

"Firtha told me."

Silence fell between us, heavy and immovable. The sea witch's eyes stopped bleeding green. Instead, they bled black, becoming twin voids from which no light escaped.

"Go back to your room," she said.

There was no arguing with that voice. Honestly, I didn't even want to try. I turned and fled back up the stairs, to where the open door beckoned me back to the pretense of safety. I dove through it, slamming it behind myself, and toyed with the idea of locking it. No: bad idea. If she wanted to come in, she would come in, and while she might accept a closed door as being an honest expression of fright, something told me that I wouldn't have time to regret it if I locked the door against her.

Would she kill me after she had gone to so much trouble to save me? She seemed to like Toby, and killing me would definitely upset my mother. Then again, I was the one who had dropped her dead daughter's name—which I couldn't possibly have known, and her reaction to hearing it proved that I hadn't dreamt that ocean, that cliff, that naked woman with the green, green eyes—and if her temper was short enough, that might well have been enough to get me killed.

I didn't want to die. I dove back into the bed, wishing I'd had the sense to leave the curtains alone, and pulled the covers over myself, hiding like a child who believed the monsters couldn't see her if she couldn't see them. It was the only thing I could think of to do.

My heartbeat was like thunder in my ears. I held my breath . . . and hoped.

The door opened. The door closed. Footsteps crossed the floor, stopping just shy of the bed. "I'm not sure whether to be ashamed of you for thinking this was a good way to hide from me or pleased that you didn't go out the damn window. Your mother would do her best to murder me if I let you die that stupid—and honestly, she might succeed. I'm pretty hard to kill, but October is terrifying when she gets upset."

I stayed under the covers. It was a childish response to fear, but a woman's eyes turning black in front of me was something out of a little kid's nightmare. I was comfortable with my choices.

She sighed. "I am the sea witch, daughter of Oberon and Maeve, Firstborn and first among my mother's children. I am unable to lie, no matter how much I want to, and I say to you now that I am not here to do you harm. Because I don't have time for your weird formerly-mortal mood swings, I will make you a promise I have made to few others: I swear, on the rose and the thorn, that when my grace is lifted, I will tell you. If I am to become a danger, I will say so in as many words. Now will you come out from under the damn blankets?"

I poked my head cautiously out of my nest of bedclothes. The sea witch was standing a few feet away, eyes still black, arms folded. She kicked a bit of torn-down drapery.

"I see you didn't like my decorating," she said dryly. "You know, most people, when they don't like something I've given them, suck it up out of fear that I'll turn them into a bushel of sea slugs and scatter them at sea. So this is novel."

"Can you do that?"

She nodded. "If I wanted to. I usually don't want to. There are much better, more endangered things to transform people into. Now do you want to tell me how you know my name?"

"I thought—"

"There's no way you could have heard the name 'Antigone'

unless someone told you. October knows it, but she never uses it, because she's worried I might rip her lungs out."

"Would you?"

"I might." She narrowed her eyes. "You're not answering me."

"I . . . Firtha told me your name."

"Uh-huh. How did my dead daughter tell you my name?"

I sat up, fingering the knot of my sealskin with one hand. The feel of the fur soothed me. "She was there the first time I woke up, in the middle of this big field near the ocean . . . "

Bit by bit, I stumbled through the story of what had happened by the cliff's edge: waking up, meeting Firtha, learning the story of the Selkies. The sea witch listened in silence, not questioning me, not urging me on when I faltered. It was like she wanted to get the story as uninfluenced by her presence as possible, and I was grateful and resentful at the same time. This would have been easier if she'd been willing to help.

But maybe it would have been less honest. And I got the feeling, looking at her face as the blackness bled back out of her eyes, that honesty was something that really mattered to her.

When I was finished, she nodded, and said, "I always wondered if I'd trapped a fragment of them when I enchanted the skins. Our bodies aren't supposed to linger here like that. There are old bargains that come into play. But it's been so long that there was no one left for me to ask."

"Your eyes," I blurted.

She tilted her head to the side. "What about them?"

They were green now, as green as Firtha's eyes, a color that belonged in glass bottles and young leaves, not looking out of a seemingly-human face. I bit my lip, trying to figure out what to say that wouldn't risk offending her. I didn't want to make her angry.

Finally, I said, "They're green. But they were blue before. Why were they blue?"

"Because after my children were slaughtered for the crime of belonging to my bloodline, I tried my best to cut myself off from the ones who remained, to make sure they wouldn't be targeted again for reasons beyond their control. When you ask someone what defines the Roane, they'll always say 'their eyes,' because there's nothing else in all of Faerie with eyes like theirs. You can't tell a Roane by the slope of their ears or the shape of their hands, but you can always tell them by their eyes."

"You're hiding."

"Yes."

"If all your children are . . . if they're gone, why are you still hiding?"

"Habit? Protecting the few Roane who still remain? You've got a lot to learn, kiddo, and you're at a major disadvantage; I don't think I've ever heard of someone joining Faerie as a full citizen this late in their life. Humans, sure, they can get snatched at all stages of their lives, but you? You're one of us. You're more fae than your damn mother is, and don't think that's not going to itch at her. Pureblood girl." There was a sympathetic note to those last two words, like she was sorry but couldn't say it.

I touched the knot again. "Firtha said that all the other . . . the other Selkies had a choice."

"They did," the sea witch agreed. "The first ones chose to protect their families by taking on the burden of their parents' crimes. They left siblings and spouses and children and went to the sea, and in exchange, I didn't slaughter every person who shared their bloodlines. Please don't let the fact that I'm wearing clothes and not drenched in blood fool you: I earned the title of 'monster' fair and square; and those were different times. If they hadn't come to me to seek a way to make things right, I would have pulled the bones from the bodies of every man, woman, and child I could lay my hands on."

"That's horrible."

She shrugged. "That's Faerie, kid. Humanity's past isn't much better. It's just that they've had some personnel changes, while we've kept most of the same players on the board. Go back far enough and everything comes down to blood and fire."

I shivered.

"So yeah, those first Selkies chose, and every time they've passed a skin since then, the new Selkie has had the chance to choose. They hear the story, and they either take the skin and the guilt that comes with it, or they go to the sea, and they don't come back. The deeps near a Selkie rookery are a treasure trove of bones left by the ones who chose innocence over eternity. And skins pass surprisingly often. It's like people think that giving their sins to their children will make them somehow easier to bear." She shook her head. "It's always death or the sea, once a skin is passed along. You just didn't have the opportunity to say that you would rather die."

I swallowed. "I took it off."

Her eyebrows rose. "You're not dead. You must not have taken it off for long."

"I landed on it when I fell."

"That makes sense. The skin is part of you now, until you choose to set it aside. If you were an ordinary Selkie, you'd be fine. You could say 'this was fun, but I want to be human now,' drop the skin on the nearest sucker, and run as far inland as your legs would carry you. But I gave you my daughter's skin for a reason. You'd been poisoned."

"Toby said."

"She's your mother, you know. You could acknowledge that." I turned my face away. She sighed. "Whatever. Your family bullshit is your business, not mine. Elf-shot is tricky. It's magical, alchemical, which means it's brewed like a human drug, but it doesn't always follow the rules. Your *mother* cured you of it once before, by burning it out of your blood when she turned you human. Technically, she shouldn't have been able to do that. Technically, you should have died as soon as the elf-shot realized you weren't fae anymore. Her type of fae, though, they can do almost anything with blood when they've got something to hold onto."

"So why couldn't she cure me this time?" The anger in my words was surprising even to me. It shouldn't have been. Toby kept turning my world upside down, and she never seemed to care, and she never stuck around to pick up the pieces.

You didn't tell her you wanted her to stay, whispered a small voice in the back of my mind. I didn't know if it was mine or Firtha's, and I was ignoring it either way.

"She couldn't cure you because she couldn't change your blood. There was nothing fae left in it for her to grab. I'd say, 'Isn't it nice to know that she has a few limitations after all,' but under the circumstances, I guess it sort of sucks for you." The sea witch shook her head. "I couldn't cure you because the only cure we *have* doesn't work on humans, and elf-shot is my sister's work: I am incapable of picking it apart on my own."

"But I'm not human now," I said. "You keep saying that. Doesn't that mean I'm cured, and I should be able to take off the skin?"

"You'd think, and you'd be right, if we weren't trying to navigate our way through a cascade of loopholes. A Selkie without a skin is a human, plain and simple. They're not even changelings, because the people who started the Selkie lines were the children of merlins, too far removed from the blood of Oberon to have magic of their own."

I stared at her blankly. She sighed.

"It doesn't matter. Look: when I gave you the skin, *my* magic superseded my sister's, because the creation of the Selkies was effectively a blood sacrifice, and you'll be awake if I damn well want you to be. While you're wearing it, the elf-shot can't touch you. Sadly, that also means we can't cure it. If you take the skin *off*, the elf-shot remembers it's supposed to be killing you. You just need to stay a Selkie until the poison works its way out of your system. Then you could go back to being human if you wanted to."

She glanced away from me on the last sentence, creating the distinct impression that there was something she wasn't saying. She'd already told me that she couldn't lie. So what was she trying to hide?

Maybe it wouldn't matter. "How long do I need to stay like this?"

"Not long," she said. I started to relax. "A hundred years should do it, although I'd go a hundred years and a day, just to be safe. Wouldn't want to take the skin off and drop dead within sight of the finish line."

"*What*?!" I was on my feet before I had a chance to think about it, the covers thrust aside, staring at her.

She raised an eyebrow. "Did I stutter?"

"A hundred—that's ridiculous! I'll be dead before I can go back to being *normal*!"

"No, you'll be alive, because this is your new normal. Ever wonder how your mom could vanish for a decade and a half and come back looking exactly the same? Ever ask yourself when it stops being good genes and starts being a little bit ridiculous? You're not immortal. You can be killed. Easier than a lot of us, honestly, because the Selkies are sort of a makeshift solution to a problem I didn't have a lot of time to deal with. But as long as that skin stays on your shoulders, you won't get any older, and you won't die of natural causes." She paused, cocking her head thoughtfully to the side. "Okay, well, you may get a *little* older. Most of us stop aging when we're somewhere around twenty-five, so you have a few years yet of new developments and hormonal changes. All that fun stuff. But when it's done, it's done. We grow up. We never grow old."

I stared at her. "So what, I'm like a vampire now?"

"No. Baobhan Sith are like vampires. You're like a girl who sometimes turns into a seal, who carries the burden of a long-gone crime on her back, and who may, depending on how the world moves us, have to pay the price of what someone else's ancestors did. But you're also alive, and under the circumstances, that's more than any of us had hoped for."

I rubbed my face with one hand. "And Miranda knew."

The sea witch paused. "What?"

"About Faerie. That Toby wasn't human. All of this, she knew. She lied to me." I dropped my hand and looked at her plaintively. "Why did she lie to me?"

For the first time, the sea witch looked genuinely uncomfortable. "Kid, that is not my tale to tell. I won't even try to pretend that she had a good reason. I've known her for a long, long time— longer than seems possible some days—and I've basically never thought she had a good reason for a damn thing she did. But she raised you. It's not my place to get in the middle of your family affairs."

"You're perfectly happy to get in the middle with me and Toby."

"Ah, but Toby is *my* family." She smirked a little at the expression on my face. "Her mother, Amandine, is my youngest sister, and I have accepted October as my niece. So when I intercede on her behalf, I'm doing it for family. When you ask me to intercede on 'Miranda's' behalf, I'm intruding."

There was a sardonic twist to the way she said Miranda's name, like she was calling it into question even as she was speaking. I frowned. "She's human, though. She said she was human."

"Yes," the sea witch agreed. "She's as human as they come, and heir to all the follies of that brief, benighted race."

"So how does she . . . ?"

"Kid, I can spend the whole night trying to explain the many, many ways I am not planning to answer your questions, or we can move on to the part where my daughter has decided that I was right to save you, and that means I need to at least try to help you out. October isn't a Selkie. She can't teach you what it means to be what you are now."

I sat up a little straighter. "But you can?"

"Do I look like a Selkie to you? No. What you are is a watered-down version of a watered-down copy of my glory. I can't teach you jack or shit. I can, however, take you to someone who can. Think of it as a field trip." When she smiled, her teeth were sharp and terrible. "To the bottom of the ocean."

"My mom—"

"If you mean Toby, she's out doing her thing. Getting stabbed, bleeding on everything, taking responsibility for things she frankly has no business taking responsibility for and yet, miraculously, not dying. That's basically the family business at this point. Not dying. She's good at it. Good thing, too. I'm not sure we could make a replacement if someone broke her." The sea witch stopped smiling. "If you mean the other one, she's here. I'm keeping an eye on her. Right now, that means she's sitting in my kitchen, pretending to drink my tea, while Poppy asks her invasive questions and she waits for the other shoe to drop. There is no other shoe. There's just me, having a really shitty day."

Slowly, I nodded. "Can she come with us?"

"You don't want that."

"Don't tell me what I want."

To my surprise, the sea witch smiled again, with fewer teeth this time. "Fair enough, I suppose, but kiddo, your other mother is not what I'd call exactly popular with the fae set. She did some things that aren't mine to disclose to you. Just trust me when I tell you that she got a gold medal in fucking shit up. She's not welcome where we're going, at least not until I explain to them why she's going to have to be."

I crossed my arms. "Why should I go with you if Mom can't come?"

"You know, I'd almost forgotten what it was like to deal with people who aren't afraid of me," she said, half-wistfully. "I should probably find this all spunky and refreshing, but honestly, it's annoying. I have shit to do, and you're interfering with my getting it done. Why should you come with me? Because if you don't, you can't go home to your precious father."

My shock must have shown on my face. She nodded solemnly.

"There: you're finally *listening* to me. Right now, kid, you might be able to pass for human—*might*—and that assumes you're trying to fool someone who doesn't know you. Your father knows you. He'll see the webs between your fingers and the color of your eyes and flip his shit. Worse, maybe he'll start putting a few things together, and realize that your mother was lying to him the whole time they were together. Not good."

My hand flew to the side of my face, like I could somehow feel the color of my eyes in my fingertips. "What about my eyes?"

"Good focus. More and more, I can believe that you are your mother's daughter. Your eyes aren't important."

"Says you."

"Yes, says me, the sea witch, who is very old and very tired and very uninclined to keep putting up with your amateur dramatics." She uncrossed her arms. "You have two choices, Gillian. You can come with me to meet the woman who's going to make you less of a walking disaster, or you can sit up in this room until you're ready to come with me."

"That's not two choices. That's barely even one."

"And yet those are your options. What a trial your life must be." She looked at me with absolutely no sympathy. "You don't like your mother very much. I can't entirely blame you for that. My relationship with my own parents has always been a complicated thing. But believe me when I say that there is no question in my mind that you are absolutely October's child. Stay here or come with me. Choose."

I glared at her. She didn't do me the courtesy of glaring back. It was impossible to shake the feeling that she could stand there, waiting, until the end of the world. Finally, I threw my hands up in disgust.

"Fine. I'll come with you. Happy now?"

"No," she said. Then she smiled, slim and satisfied. "But it's a start."

SEVEN

Going down the stairs was more of an ordeal than I had expected, mostly because they never seemed to *end*. After we had descended what felt like five or six stories, I gave the sea witch a sidelong, narrow-eyed look.

"Where are we?"

She looked back at me, expression almost innocent. "What in the world do you mean?"

"There's no way we're in San Francisco. I mean, apart from the weird ocean outside the window, which you could have done with some sort of fancy projector, or the funky sky, there aren't any *fairy tale towers* this tall in the city. I'd know about it."

"Kid, you have a lot to learn about what you think you know," said the sea witch. "There's a whole world you've never seen before, right next to the one you're used to. We're not in the human city of San Francisco—yet. We will be in a few more steps. Most of my residence exists in a skerry."

"What's a skerry?"

"A reef carved from the great churning ocean of reality, held fast by the will of the one who holds it. Our descendants—people like your mother—try to imitate them, making knowes and shallowings, but a true skerry can contain an entire world." She smiled, wistfully this time. "My little brother, Michael, helped me open this one. He always had a flair for interior decorating. Which was sort of ironic, given that he was completely blind. Sometimes the universe has a sense of humor."

I blinked. "You say things, and I'm sure they make sense in your head, but they don't make much sense outside of it."

"They will." She touched my arm lightly. "Give it time."

I didn't want to. I wanted to find the magic button—there had to be a magic button, there always was in the stories—and make everything go back to the way it was supposed to be. I wanted to be human and go home and not have to wonder how a tower could hide on a reef, or why Miranda had been keeping secrets from me for my entire life.

Miranda. I really didn't know how to feel now that I knew she had been hiding something this big and this *important*. Big pieces of the story were missing, and until I had them, I wouldn't be able to decide one way or the other. It was starting to give me a headache.

The stairs ended at a small landing and a plain wooden door. The sea witch pushed it open, revealing an ordinary hallway with a freshly-vacuumed carpet and a few framed pictures hanging on the walls. Everything smelled like clean sand and sea air. I breathed in deeply, feeling the knots of tension in my back and shoulders loosen.

"Feel better?"

I glanced at the sea witch, startled. She nodded understanding.

"You forgot I was here, didn't you?"

I nodded, too rattled to speak. It seemed impossible for me to have forgotten someone as unsettling as she was, but for a moment . . .

"It's normal, I promise. Selkies are tied to the sea. I'm glad you're already going to Berkeley. Hope you weren't thinking about grad school in Ohio, because that's off the table now." She stepped into the hallway and out of sight, clearly expecting me to follow her.

It wasn't like I had much of a choice. I didn't know where any of the other doors led, and I was pretty sure she'd be able to find me even if I did manage to get out of her sight. I tugged the door closed behind me. There was no click. I looked back at it and blinked.

The door was gone, replaced by a stretch of blank wall. I touched it cautiously. The plaster was smooth beneath my fingers, concealing nothing.

"How in the . . . ?"

"Magic," called the sea witch. "Come on."

The hall ended in a small, almost cozy living room. The orange woman from the top of the stairs was there, leaning against the wall, keeping a wary eye on—

"Mom!"

"Gilly!" Miranda began to stand, then froze when she saw the sea witch looking at her. "Am I not even allowed to hug my own daughter now?"

"I'm not stopping you," the sea witch said. There was a note of hostility in her voice that had been absent before. "Honestly, I'd get my hugs in now if I were you. She may stop wanting them once she knows a little more. You can't stop her from learning her own history."

"That is *not* her history," spat Miranda, glaring at the sea witch.

"It was always her history. You just can't keep it away from her anymore." The sea witch looked at her fingernails, unconcerned. "Gillian and I are going for a little drive, down to Half Moon Bay. You can come with us if you want."

"You think you can make off with my daughter and I won't—" Miranda stopped. "Wait. What did you say?"

"I said you could come with us." The sea witch lowered her hand. "I hate you. I am never *not* going to hate you. But I'm not the child-snatcher here. I have never looked at a mother and thought, 'Gosh, you don't deserve your daughter as much as I do, I'd better do my best to alienate her from you in every way possible, so that even if you come home, you won't be able to convince her that you care.'"

Miranda's cheeks reddened. Squaring her shoulders, she rose, and said, "In that case, I will be accompanying you."

"Dandy," said the sea witch, and snapped her fingers. Miranda stiffened, mouth working soundlessly. "But I can't have you getting into fights with people or saying something that makes them question what a human is doing at the clan-home. So here's the deal. You won't be able to talk about the things you see today with anyone who doesn't belong to the water, and you won't be able to talk at all while we're in the Selkies' home. In exchange, I won't test that whole 'can't be killed' thing you mentioned before."

"What did you do?" I demanded, pushing past her to step in front of Miranda. Angry or not, she was still my mom. "Stop it!"

"I'd say I was sorry, kiddo, but well, there's that whole 'can't lie' thing," said the sea witch. "Some secrets need to be kept, and she—" she pointed to Miranda, "—has a history of running her mouth when she shouldn't."

"You said I belonged to the water now," I objected. "That means she should be able to talk in front of me. Why can't she talk now?"

"Because I'm here," said Poppy, raising one hand in a little wave. "Hello again, October's daughter. I'm no Selkie, no, nor anything that comes from water. I'm all sky and sparkle, I am, and that means her silence applies to me as well. I can go, if you need me to."

"No," said the sea witch firmly. "This is your home, not hers. Stay here. If October calls, let her know that we've gone to Half Moon Bay, and we'll be back when we're back. If she doesn't like that answer, remind her that I could turn her into an apple tree for a couple of decades. That should calm her down."

"I think being an apple tree might be the opposite of calming," said Poppy dubiously.

"Eh." The sea witch shrugged. "What do I care? Come along, traitor and Daye-child. We have work to do."

She walked out of the room. Miranda glared momentarily before following her. I glanced at Poppy, who smiled encouragingly and flashed me a thumbs-up. I didn't know how to deal with that, and so I trailed after them, feeling more confused and out of place than ever.

The door at the end of the hallway was standing open; apparently, they hadn't felt it was necessary to wait for me. The alley outside was dark, and when I stepped outside, I found myself under a dark San Francisco sky, surrounded by trash cans and fire escapes. I stopped dead, blinking in bewilderment at the familiarity of it all.

Suddenly, Miranda was at my elbow. "It feels like it should all be different now," she said, taking hold of my arm and guiding me toward an ugly old car, illegally parked in front of a fire hydrant. "Your whole world has shifted, and still the stars shine, and still the rain falls, and no one around you understands why it shouldn't be that way. They've stayed the same."

"You can talk again," I said.

"There's no one here but us." She made a sour face. "I hope to God that spell doesn't think that talking about your grades or the like is talking about something forbidden, or your father's going to think I'm having a neurological episode. Not my favorite dance to do."

"You're going to tell me everything," I said. "*Everything.*"

"No, I'm not," she said, and stroked my arm gently. "I'll always have my secrets, and you're going to have to live with that. But I'll always love you, and I hope that will be enough."

"This is all very sweet, but could you cut it the fuck out and get in the car?" The sea witch popped out from the driver's seat and leaned against the roof, glaring. "We have a long way to go, and I don't want to spend more time hanging out with a *human* than I absolutely have to." She somehow made the word "human" sound like the direst insult the universe had ever known.

It was a neat trick. I didn't have time to admire it, as Miranda let go of my arm and moved to open the passenger side door. The sea witch raised a hand.

"Uh-uh," she said. "New Selkies ride up front. Human tagalongs ride in the back."

"You can't be serious," said Miranda.

"I can't lie," said the sea witch. "Get in the damn car."

We got in the damn car. There was nothing else to do. I thought briefly about getting in the back with Miranda, to show solidarity, but decided that taunting Firtha's mother wasn't worth it. She was the only person who could make sure I learned the things I needed to know in order to deal with what I was becoming, and also, she was utterly terrifying in ways I wasn't sure I could fully articulate. No. Better to go along with her, at least for now.

I can always run and hide at Toby's place, I thought, and was almost dismayed to realize that the idea wasn't entirely repulsive. She would protect me if I asked her to. Despite our long estrangement, maybe that was what she'd been doing all along.

The sea witch was a surprisingly calm and competent driver. She used her turn signals and allowed other people to merge ahead of us. When she caught me staring at her, she smirked.

"I got my first car three years after they went on sale to the general public," she said. "Had to pay a Gremlin to strip the iron out of it and replace it with enchanted oak and ash and pine carved into the appropriate shapes, but I was on the road inside of a month. New frontiers. That's what the humans are all about, and always have been. Give them something no one's done before, and they'll find a way to start doing it inside of the week. Honestly, changelings were inevitable. As soon as the humans figured out there was something new to fuck, they got right down to business."

"That's vile," said Miranda.

"You're one to talk," said the sea witch.

"What does that mean?" I asked.

The sea witch smirked again, more broadly this time. "Oh, there's a *good* question." She glanced at the rearview mirror, meeting Miranda's stricken gaze. "Should I tell her? Technically it doesn't have anything to do with being a Selkie, so I could refuse without failing in my duty to prepare her. What do you think?"

"Please don't," whispered Miranda. I turned in my seat to stare at her. She refused to meet my eyes.

The sea witch continued implacably. "What will you give me?"

"I'll behave." Miranda slumped in her seat. "I won't try to make trouble while we're dealing with your family."

"An excellent bargain: accepted," said the sea witch. "Gillian, I'm sorry, but I can't tell you about your stepmother's past. It would be inappropriate for me to do so after I've accepted payment not to."

"What if I could offer you something better?" I asked, ignoring Miranda's small sound of protest.

"It wouldn't matter," said the sea witch. "That isn't how my bargains work. I can sell to both sides of a conflict—and have, when they made me—but I can't keep raising the price after something's been agreed upon. Sometimes that's unfortunate. Most of the time it's a good thing. There have to be limits. Things have to stop getting worse, eventually, or they'll all just fall apart. And hell, maybe *that* would be a good thing. It's not for me to say."

I leaned against the car door and looked at her thoughtfully.

"Why do you have to make bargains?" I asked.

"My father, Oberon—your great-grandfather, by the way—had two wives. My mother, Maeve, and her sister, Titania. Well, Titania decided I was too big for my britches, on account of how I didn't actually give a shit about what she wanted, and she cursed me all that way from here to Mag Mell. No lies for me, unless they're told to the blood of my blood, and no refusing a deal. If someone asks me for something within my power to give, I don't have any choice."

I frowned. "What does 'blood of my blood' mean, in this context?"

"It means that when I said I couldn't lie, I wasn't being one hundred percent absolutely accurate," she said. "I can lie to the Selkies. Now that you're one of them, I can lie to you. That skin you wear belonged to my daughter, and that makes you, magically speaking, my child, and a parent has to be able to lie to her children, for the sake of keeping the family from falling apart."

"So when you said I could trust you . . . "

"I meant it. I wasn't lying. I just wasn't being magically compelled to tell you the truth regardless of its possible danger to myself." The sea witch turned her attention to the road. "Some lies are a kindness beyond measure. The Selkies are the only chance I have remaining to be kind."

I didn't say anything. Honestly, I didn't know what to say. I was confused, I was exhausted, and everyone around me seemed to be carrying about thirty layers of secrets on their shoulders, which was at least twenty-nine layers too many.

"You all need therapy," I muttered.

The sea witch laughed and kept on driving.

I've never been much of a beach girl. That would probably sound blasphemous to anyone who's spent their life inland and dreaming of the sea, but it's true. Sand gets in everything, sunburns are worse when you're out on the water, and it's hard to read when a wave could decide to hit your location at any moment. I've always been way more fond of a nice, climate-controlled library or shopping center. Malls may not have been born in California, but the odds are pretty good that they're going to die here.

And yet.

The farther we traveled down the coast, the more the urban sprawl of San Francisco dropped away behind us, replaced first by low, rustic tourist towns and then by nothing but the thin line of eucalyptus and pine, the more the knot in my chest unclenched itself and the easier it became for me to breathe. I hadn't been aware of how tense I'd been until my gut fully unclenched and I was able to sit up straight.

A hand touched my shoulder. I glanced back to find Miranda looking at me sympathetically.

"I've seen this before," she said. "It was with a Hamadryad, not a Selkie, but still. She had been away from the forest for days, traveling on business for her Lord, and when she finally got back within sight of the green, she started to weep. I had never been so glad to be human, and not tied to one specific environment."

I shrank slightly away from her hand, wondering whether she realized she had just implied that I was less than she was now. That my mother was less than she was.

Miranda kept speaking as if I hadn't moved. "She danced with the trees for a day, and then she was right as rain, and we were able to continue on our way."

"What a charming story," said the sea witch, in a flat, emotionless voice. "Oh, look, we're here."

I looked forward.

We were on a small, apparently private road that curved around a grassy hill to reveal a sprawling Victorian house that bristled in all directions, like a starfish. Extensions had been constructed upon extensions that had been constructed upon extensions themselves, until the original foundation was lost behind the veil of new construction. It looked like the kind of place where entire multigenerational families could live in relative harmony, as long as they could all agree whose turn it was to wash the windows. It looked . . .

It looked like home.

The sea witch pulled off to the side of the road and turned off the engine before twisting in her seat to face me and Miranda. "All right," she said. "Gillian, you're with me: you're the whole reason that we're here. Until we leave, or until I say otherwise, my name is Annie. I'm a cousin of this family, and I've accepted the responsibility of bringing you home. Agree with everything I say, and you'll be fine. You have my word that I won't try to trap you in anything you don't want. All right?"

"All right," I said cautiously.

"Good." She looked to Miranda. "You can come with us or you can stay in the car, but remember that you won't be able to speak, and that as long as I'm not talking directly to you, I can lie for the duration of this visit. I will tell lies about the girl you consider to be your daughter. I will also tell truths you may not wish to hear. But I am speaking to you, right now, and I promise you that she will not be harmed if you leave her in my care."

"Miranda didn't come all this way just to sit in the car," I protested.

Miranda looked guiltily away. I blinked.

"Mom?" I didn't mean to sound so young, or so frightened.

"Go with her," said Miranda. She looked back at me, forcing herself to smile. The corners of her mouth trembled with the strain. "She'll keep you safe, and I'll . . . I'll wait here, so I don't make things harder."

"But you *came*."

"Yes. I did, and I'll be here when you come outside. I'll always be here. I love you, Gillian. I do. I'm just . . . " She stopped, taking a deep breath. "I'm not part of Faerie. I didn't want you to be, either. I tried so hard to save you, sweetheart, I swear I did. I couldn't. I'm sorry. Now you need to start learning what you're going to become, and you need to do it without being afraid you're going to hurt me by being happy."

I stared at her. "Mom . . . "

"You heard the lady." The sea witch opened her door and slid out of the car. Somewhere in the middle of that motion, her clothes changed, becoming sturdy canvas pants and a dark gray cable-knit sweater. Her ponytails came undone, the tape disappearing as her hair tumbled down her back in a cascade of tangles and curls. She looked normal. She looked like someone I'd see in one of my classes, half-asleep and clutching a cup of coffee.

She was terrifying, because that was the moment where it all became real. Not just that my body was changing or that a dead woman's skin was wrapped around my shoulders: that I had been riding in a car with someone who belonged in a fairy tale, that all of this was happening and none of it was going away. This was really happening.

The sea witch looked back over her shoulder, one eyebrow raised. "Well?" she said. "Come on."

"Go, baby," said Miranda. "I'll be here when you get back."

Don't leave my mother waiting, whispered Firtha.

I got out of the car. We were finally at the end of the beginning, whatever that was going to mean, and there was no turning back now.

EIGHT

"Remember: while we're here, my name is Annie," repeated the sea witch as we approached the house. "I'm a distant cousin of this family. I'm bringing you to meet their current matriarch, because you're a Selkie without a clan. Do you understand?"

It wasn't far from the truth. I nodded slowly. "I understood you the first time. Why lie? Why not tell them who you are?"

"I have my reasons, and they're not for you to question. Just remember that I can stop your tongue as easily as I stopped hers." She gestured back toward the car.

I frowned. "Why don't you ever use her name?"

The sea witch ignored me and rang the doorbell. The sound of running footsteps drifted through from the other side, and then the door was wrenched open by a girl a few years younger than me. Her hair was brown streaked with silver, like she'd been experimenting with home dye jobs, and her eyes were the same vivid green as Firtha's.

Her ears were pointed. Not as pointed as Toby's but pointed. This was happening.

She looked between me and the sea witch, focusing on the skin tied around my shoulders. "Annie, what have you brought us?"

"This is Gillian." The sea witch's hand landed heavily on my shoulder, keeping me upright. I was obscurely grateful for it. "She's new, and she doesn't have a family to teach her what to do. Is your mother in?"

The girl gasped with theatric delight. "She's wearing one of the Lost Skins? Annie, did you find one of the Lost Skins?"

I could hear the capital letters in her voice. Smiling wearily, the sea witch nodded.

"She's the first to wear it in hundreds of years. Please, I need to see your mother, Diva."

"Of course! Of course! Welcome to the family, cousin!" Then the girl—Diva—was yanking me into a hard hug, as shameless as a child. Her skin smelled like saltwater, and her clothes were faintly damp.

When she let me go, it was to bound deeper into the house, leaving the sea witch and me to follow. I looked at her, mouthing "Diva?"

She shrugged. "It used to mean 'nature spirit.' I think her father named her. I assume her father named her. Liz was never that kind of gooey romantic. I'll be honest. I never asked. There's a chance she'd tell me, and I don't want her to think she's been forgiven."

"What did she do to you?"

"Only what people have been doing to me for centuries," she said. "She disappointed me. Let's go introduce you, shall we?" She stepped through the door, leaving me with little choice but to follow.

A man in an unzipped wetsuit was sleeping on the couch, snoring gently. Two women were sitting at a nearby table, deeply involved in a complicated card game I'd never seen before, and a group of children rushed by, giggling and grabbing at each other. The furniture was old but not shabby, mended and maintained for what looked to have been years. Every wall was at least half-obscured by bookshelves and framed pictures of people who looked nothing alike and everything alike at the same time. It was something in their eyes.

Diva was waiting for us halfway up the stairs. The sea witch smiled at her, and she ran on, leading us to a long hall and a closed door halfway down. She stopped there, an unsure look on her face.

"Mum's having a bad day," she said. "I don't . . . "

"It's okay, hon," said the sea witch, and pulled her into what seemed like a genuinely affectionate one-armed hug. "You run on ahead. I'll deal with your mother."

Diva flashed her a look filled with confused gratitude, hugged her back, and was gone, running back to the stairs. The sea witch watched her go.

"She was her mother's apology to me, in part," she said, once we were alone. "Liz tracked down one of the surviving Roane—there are still a few, living solitary lives as far from the rest of Faerie as possible—and gave him a child. Diva won't ever have to take a Selkie skin for her own. She gets to stay clean. Better than flowers, anyway."

She turned brusquely to the door, not giving me time to answer her. She didn't knock, either, just turned the knob and pushed it open, revealing a small room lined with still more bookshelves and dominated by a mahogany desk. A woman was sitting behind it, head bent, hair a shade of ashy blonde that was sort of gray and sort of golden and sort of both at the same time. She didn't look up, but her hand twitched toward the glass next to her, which was filled with a golden liquid that looked a lot like bourbon.

"Come to try me further, Annie?" she asked, voice tired.

"You know it," said the sea witch. "Gillian, this is Elizabeth Ryan, the head of this clan of Selkies and, hopefully, your new mentor. Lizzy, this is Gillian Daye." Her voice took on a hard edge. "October's daughter."

Now the woman raised her head, gray eyes going wide. "What?"

"It's, um, Daye-Marks, actually," I said. "Hi."

"How is this . . . ?"

"She's wearing one of the Lost Skins," said the sea witch. "It was necessary to save her life. You're the nearest clan, and the only one I trust with her education. Will you teach her what it means to be a Selkie?"

Elizabeth frowned. "Why should I bother, when we've got so little time left?"

"Way to make things all about you, Lizzy," said the sea witch. "You should bother because October has been good to this family, and because Connor loved her. If that's not enough, you should do it because I'm telling you to, and I have it on good authority that I'm fucking terrifying. But most of all, you should do it because if you agree, and if she tells me that you've done right by her, I'll bring the remainder of the Lost Skins to you, to distribute as you see fit. Eighteen more Selkies, Liz. Eighteen more children you don't have to choose between."

Elizabeth put a hand over her mouth. "You'd . . . really?"

"Agree. Swear to me that you'll teach her what she needs to know."

"And that Miranda can be here," I said quickly.

Both of them turned to look at me.

"What's that?" asked Elizabeth.

"Her stepmother," said the sea witch. "She's already bound to silence; she won't hurt anyone here. She knows about Faerie."

"Human?"

"Utterly."

"I see." Elizabeth glanced at me again. "Not your father?"

"He's human, and he, um, doesn't know," I said. "I don't think he'd take it well if I tried to tell him."

"Which you will not do," said the sea witch. "She doesn't know *anything*, Liz, and it's not like Toby can teach her the sea."

"Root and branch, no," said Elizabeth. "Toby can barely stand to look at it. I won't let her harm my family. If she endangers the clan—"

"If Gillian endangers the clan, you call me, and I call Toby, and together we make her understand why that behavior isn't acceptable."

"I'm right here," I said.

"We know," said the sea witch. "Just . . . be quiet a little longer and let me finish my part in this. Liz? Do we have a deal?"

"I shouldn't, but—damn you, Annie. Damn you to hell. Yes, we have a deal."

The sea witch grinned toothily. "Wonderful," she said. "Let's begin."

NINE

I fell asleep on the couch in the living room with a belly full of crab chowder, listening to Miranda and Liz argue about the best way to handle my education. The sea witch—who everyone here called "Annie" without a lick of hesitation, and who almost seemed like another person when she was laughing and easy and not trying to be the scariest thing in the room—had been whisked away to help with the dishes. She hadn't objected. Apparently here, that was normal.

It was safe. People were happy and comfortable and inhuman and that was okay, because it was safe. I was going to have to go home to my father, with a lie about a human kidnapping on my lips and an invisible sealskin tied around my shoulders, but I would be coming here until it felt like my home, too, until I knew how to be what I was now.

They said they could give me the sea. I was starting to think that I might want it.

So I sank down into slumber, until I was standing on a rocky beach, not naked anymore, with the sound of the surf beating itself against the shore. Firtha was already there, and she smiled at the sight of me.

"So?" she asked. "Will this do?"

"I won't pretend I'm happy not to be human anymore," I said slowly. "I wish I'd had a choice. But . . . if this is what I have to be, I guess I could have done worse."

"You could." She stepped forward, offering me her hands. "Now come."

"Where are we going?"

"Where every good daughter of the Roane begins her life in earnest," said Firtha. "Let me take you to the sea."

I slipped my hands into hers, and she backed slowly into the surf, leading me into the ocean of my dreams. One day soon, I'd be going into real waves, into real water, in a very similar way. I was surprised to realize that I wasn't scared. Maybe it was the skin changing me more from what I'd been, but if it was, I didn't mind. I couldn't be scared all the time, and if this was what it took to stay alive, I'd learn to live with it.

In the meanwhile, I was going to the water.

I was going home.